Revenge is not Enough

by

Kayla Danoli

Copyright

Cataloguing-in-publication data

Creator: Danoli, Kayla, author

Cataloguing-in-Publication details are available from the National Library of Australia www.trove.nla.gov.au

ISBN: 978-0-9750287-1-1 (eBook)

ISBN: 978-0-9953533-0-5 (paperback)

Contents

Also by Kayla Danoli

The *Harbour Plaza* series of episodes
Harbour Plaza: Built on dreams
On the Way to Istanbul

Part One

The Nightmare Begins

Chapter 1

"Hey Mister, where would Mr Woodrow be at, please?"

"What would an urchin like you be wanting with our mill manager?"

"Please, Mister, me father sent me to give 'im an important message. It's urgent he says."

"Hmm, like as not, you will find him in his office about now. Go along there and up those stairs," the man said pointing the way. "No mucking about now, mind."

Young William ran off in the direction indicated and pushed open the heavy office door. A young clerk carrying a stack of paper accosted him as he entered the office.

"Here, where do you think you're off to?"

"I've come to see Mr Woodrow. I have a message for 'im. Is this where he's at?"

The clerk headed off down the long office, beckoning William to follow. At the far end, he told William to wait as he knocked on the door. At the response to his knock, the clerk slipped inside and a few moments later held the door open for young William to enter. The clerk closed the door on his way out, leaving William alone in the office with a stern looking man sitting behind a large dark-stained timber desk.

"Ahh, Sir, would you be Mr Woodrow, please?"

"Yes, boy, what is it you want? State your business."

"Please Sir, my father sent me to give you a message…"

"Yes, yes. Well get on with it, boy. I'm a busy man. What is the message?"

"Mr Jennings will be here shortly, Sir. He was quite poorly last night and finds that he will be a little late to work this morning. Mr Jennings says he will be here as soon as possible."

"Blast! Then tell him I'd be pleased if he remembered there is a Board meeting today. Well, off you go lad. You've delivered your message now get on home and deliver mine. Don't hang about now, straight home."

"Thank you, Sir. I'll be off then." Young William's bare feet made little sound as he padded through the office and bounced down the stairs.

Frank Woodrow sighed heavily as the child disappeared from his office. I suppose I'd better get all the paperwork ready for the meeting just in case Jennings doesn't turn up in time, he decided. He was stacking all the bits and pieces on the end of his desk when the industry's Works Engineer, John Dowling, knocked and entered the office.

"What's this then… you trying to do a clerk out of a job now?" Dowling enquired eyeing off the pile of papers Woodrow was stacking.

"There's a confounded board meeting today and Jennings sent a message to say he will be late to work. There's a bit of time before the board members arrive for the meeting, but our Chairman of Directors always makes a point of being here early… very early."

"O-o-h, looks like your day is off to a good start. How is the good Mr McCarthy these days?"

"Cantankerous, bombastic, rude – are there any other words to adequately describe our chairman? He's worse than ever. Ever since his son got himself killed in that horse riding accident over in England, he's been beyond impossible. He'd find fault with God."

Dowling chuckled. "So it's a horse riding accident is it, the story McCarthy is putting about? That's not what I'm hearing about town."

"No doubt the local gossips have their own version. Perhaps you'd care to enlighten me."

"It seems he was shot. More precisely, it seems he got himself shot in a duel over some female, but they covered it up to look like a hunting accident. Oh, they went out horse riding for the day all right. Supposedly, they were hunting deer on one of those large estates at the time."

"You believe there to be truth in the story, or just idle gossip?"

"Young Jack Longman brought an English newspaper back from the home country. It gave the story of the shooting. A couple of the other young lads, who were also holidaying back in the home country at the time, brought the scuttlebutt about it being a duel."

"His only son – his only child – I can see why the facts of the case would not sit comfortably with McCarthy. It might also help explain his worsening demeanour. He would not be happy at his best endeavours to give this situation some dignity ruined by having the truth come out. There are plenty about who would enjoy seeing McCarthy squirm. He has very few friends or supporters, I'm afraid."

"I haven't been summoned to appear at your board meeting today, so I'll leave you to prepare for it. Good luck."

Woodrow spent the next few minutes after Dowling's departure mulling over Dowling's story. If it were true, it certainly went some way to explain the Chairman's worsening behaviour. His thoughts were rudely interrupted when the chairman rushed into his office unannounced.

"Jennings! Where's Jennings? He's not at his desk. Isn't he aware there is a board meeting today?" Patrick McCarthy demanded. "This is 1895, not the dark ages, and we have a large modern company to run. He can't come and go as he pleases. He has a mill cottage on the estate, firewood and water, all free of cost, as well is as a generous salary. In return, we expect efficiency, accuracy and reliability from our Company Secretary. Surely that is not too much to expect." McCarthy ranted, thumping the desk to emphasise each point.

"Jennings' duties require him to leave his desk on occasions to attend to matters in regard to his work. I believe he is fully aware there is a board meeting today," Woodrow replied as he struggled to keep his tone even. It wasn't really a lie; Jennings did have to leave his desk and go into the factory sometimes.

"I shall be in the boardroom if anyone enquires after me," McCarthy stated with a dismissive wave of his hand. His rant over for the moment, he left the office.

Woodrow held his head in his hands for a few moments, silently praying Jennings would appear in time for the board meeting. Nevertheless, he was going to have to speak to Jennings. He had taken a bit of time off lately. Give him his dues though; he always made it up in his own time. Memories of the situation surrounding the demise of Jennings' predecessor came flooding back.

Although now some 18 months ago, accusations levelled at the company at the time still rankled, and Woodrow had no doubt they remained part of the continued unrest between growers and their mill. The thrust of the accusations was that the board paid the then company secretary, Matthew Pettigrew, a pittance and worked him to death. An observation Woodrow secretly believed to be not too far from the truth. Woodrow did not want to think about the likely backlash from growers if they suspected similar circumstances had befallen the current secretary.

An ashen faced Jennings arrived at the office about half an hour before the commencement of the board meeting… and, much to Woodrow's surprise, managed to survive the meeting. As Woodrow later confided to Dowling, "He looked so unwell; I half expected him to topple over at any moment."

The 1895 cane crushing season at Southend Co-operative Sugar Mill continued much as normal. A particularly poor growing season and unseasonal weather had marred operations and delayed the end of the season which was now in its final weeks prior to its end on about 10th November. Board meetings continued according to their fortnightly schedule, but all was not well. Woodrow became increasingly concerned as Jennings visibly deteriorated and his health worsened. There followed more frequent short spells when he was not at his desk, fortunately none when McCarthy was about. On the 22nd October, Jennings asked Woodrow for permission to finish work a couple of hours early that afternoon.

"Dr Boyle will be passing through on his way back to town after visiting patients up the valley and has kindly offered to see me at my home on his way past. I'll make up any time lost, of course."

Woodrow sighed resignedly, "Yes, okay. I suppose it is good of the doctor to see you at home. At least this way, you will lose less time than if you had to travel into town to attend at his rooms."

Jennings was only a few minutes late arriving at the office the next morning, but only just managed to arrive before the chairman of directors marched through the office. The board meeting started early that day as some of the directors wished to attend a function in town later in the day. There was no time for any pre-meeting conversation between Woodrow and Jennings.

Apart from Jennings appearing extremely short of breath, the meeting was largely routine until the chairman opened it to general business. When everything else appeared dealt with, Jennings stunned everyone – including Woodrow – when he asked leave to speak. The chairman glared at him but nodded permission.

"Begging your pardons, Sirs, but I wish to tender a letter from my attending physician, Dr Boyle, for your consideration. If I may, Mr Chairman, here is the letter."

McCarthy read the letter, snorted, then read the letter aloud for the others. "Well, the good doctor states it is absolutely necessary for Jennings to have a few weeks of complete rest to regain his health. How say you to this?" Little discussion followed. They resolved Jennings be granted three weeks leave of absence.

One of the directors then suggested Woodrow should cover the secretary's job during his absence. The crushing season was about to end, surely the mill manager wouldn't be too busy. McCarthy exploded at the suggestion.

"Nonsense man! The next three weeks are the most precarious of the season. If anything goes amiss and delays the end to the season, the start of the wet season likely will be upon us and we will still be endeavouring to harvest and crush the last of our crops under impossible field and financial conditions. We pay Mr Cossington, our auditor, a handsome honorarium. He can keep the books in Jennings' absence." No one spoke against the idea.

At the board meeting on 20th November, a further letter tabled from Dr Boyle recommended Jennings be granted a further three weeks leave. Grudgingly, the board granted the three weeks requested. No one saw or heard from Jennings during the previous three weeks he was absent. The need for a further three weeks leave made Woodrow increasingly uneasy. He could see a distinct resemblance of Pettigrew's final days emerging.

The cane crushing season ended a couple of weeks later than anticipated, delayed by a few rogue showers heralding the imminent onset of the wet season. Time flew by in the usual hurly-burly of post-season clean up and wet season preparations. Nothing more was known of Jennings' situation. Woodrow confided to Dowling his concerns regarding how the chairman might react if Jennings' absence continued to the next board meeting on 11th December. His concerns were well founded.

McCarthy had barely opened the meeting before honing in on Jennings' absence. "It comes to my attention that our Company Secretary has not resumed his duties. Dr Boyle approached me personally this week to advise that Jennings would require yet more time to recover his health. In my opinion, this whole business is thoroughly unsatisfactory. The man should either do the job we employed him to do, or step down. To this end, I move that Mr William Jennings be given notice that, unless he resumes his duties within the next three months, he should send in his resignation."

Some brief discussion followed but none of the directors opposed the motion. Seconded and put to the vote, the motion received unanimous support, albeit reluctantly from a couple of members. However, the chairman had not done with the issue yet.

"My understanding is that, during the secretary's absence, a junior clerk maintained the books and carried out some of Jennings' other duties, with Mr Cossington keeping a watchful eye on proceedings. I believe this to be in keeping with Mr Cossington's role as our company auditor. I am also of the understanding that Mr Woodrow attends to the balance of the secretary's duties. It is my opinion that the arrangements I have just outlined should remain in place and continue until such time as Jennings' situation is resolved."

Cossington objected. He argued that he wasn't paid to oversee a junior clerk. This brought an instant rebuke from the chairman who pointed out that Cossington received a handsome honorarium as company auditor, and that this role fell within the gamut of services an auditor reasonable might be expected to deliver.

The rebuke stung and caused Cossington to lose face in front of the directors; the directors he had worked hard to impress over the previous couple of years. He probably merited appointment to the company secretary's job, but had missed out because of his existing employment as the company's auditor – or so he was told. Now Jennings is incapable of doing the job but the board continues to dismiss me as some lesser individual, Cossington told himself. After a few minutes of such thoughts, Cossington pushed back his chair and marched out of the meeting without as much as a 'by your leave'.

Perhaps it shouldn't have come as a surprise when, ten days later, the chairman called a special meeting of the board to discuss a letter from the auditor regarding anomalies in the firewood vouchers. The chairman outlined the content of the letter before asking Cossington to speak to the matter. Cossington made a great show of clearing his throat, shuffling a few papers on the table in front of him and seemingly considering his response before speaking.

"Over the preceding week, I conducted a random audit of the vouchers covering the delivery of and payment for firewood supplied to the mill. It is with some regret that I felt compelled to bring to the attention of this board several discrepancies uncovered in the vouchers." Cossington went on to provide superficial explanation of his findings.

'…With some regret', my foot, Woodrow thought. Ever astute, Woodrow realised at the outset that, as the mill manager, some 'mud' from this issue was likely to fly in his direction. He had no doubt someone from around the table would raise the question of why he hadn't more closely scrutinised the purchase of firewood for use in the mill's boilers and estate cottages. Woodrow always considered Cossington to be something less than an honourable man and, because of the likely implications for those involved, Woodrow was not about to let Cossington simply gloss over his findings.

"This is indeed a serious issue Mr Cossington brings to our attention, Mr Chairman; no doubt, one requiring an immediate –but careful – response. I suggest the board needs to be acquainted with every minute detail of these discrepancies to avoid a situation where it might be accused of acting without full knowledge of all of the facts." Woodrow cast his eyes around the table as he finished speaking.

"Hear, hear," a number of members responded.

"If there are discrepancies in the accounts, these must be reported in full detail to Treasury. It is a condition of the Government loan used to establish this co-operative venture that Treasury monitor and oversee all financial transactions. So that I may report accurately to Treasury, perhaps Mr Cossington might apprise us in greater detail of the outcome of his investigations?" Mr Harvey, the government appointed director on the board, suggested to the chairman.

The chairman agreed and Cossington was not happy. Adopting an arrogant tone, Cossington made to comply with the request, but it was clear to all around the table that he still provided only part of the story. The directors' questioning was fierce and relentless as they sought to acquire all facts of the matter. At one point, Cossington made the critical mistake of telling one member that the information he asked for was technical and most likely beyond the member's comprehension. That earned Cossington yet another stinging chairman's rebuke.

The meeting dragged on much longer than it should. In its latter stages, Cossington went into a sulk, restricting himself to only desultory response to any questions directed to him. Over the course of the meeting, McCarthy's face developed a glowing red hue as his patience evaporated, eventually reaching his limit. He brought the meeting to a speedy conclusion.

"As it appears our auditor has identified discrepancies in the firewood vouchers, although some of us might remain unclear as to what exactly those discrepancies are, those discrepancies need to be laid before the company secretary." Heads nodded in agreement around the table. "Therefore, it is directed a letter be sent to Mr Jennings seeking an explanation of the matters raised, and that it be made clear that, if his explanation be deemed unsatisfactory, he should consider himself suspended." McCarthy didn't bother to check how the directors felt about the directive before sending Woodrow off to compile Jennings' letter.

They resolved to meet again to assess Jennings' explanation of the issues. Mindful of Mr Harvey's need for time to return after spending Christmas with his family in Brisbane, they scheduled the follow-up meeting for 29th December.

Chapter 2

"Hey, where do you think you're going?" a startled clerk demanded as a dishevelled urchin pushed through the door and rushed down the office towards the closed door at the far end. "You can't just come in here and rush about. What are you doing here?"

"I have an urgent message for Mr Woodrow."

"Well, you can't go bowling into the manager's office unannounced. What is this message about? I'll see if it's worth disturbing him for, and if he will see you."

"No need to bother thanks. Mr Woodrow knows me, and me message is private like and for his ears only." With that, Young William skipped around the clerk and ran to Woodrow's office door. He knocked loudly and waited a second before rushing in – just as the clerk laid a restraining hand on his shoulder. William shook it off before the clerk managed a secure grip, and rushed straight up to Woodrow's desk.

"Begging you pardon, Sir, but I have …"

The breathless clerk came to a halt a couple of paces behind Young William. "I'm so sorry Mr Woodrow, Sir," he panted. "I did try to stop him."

"That's okay, Wingate. You are excused," Woodrow said. The clerk shot Young William a withering look as he left the manager's office. "Now, young Jennings … it is young Jennings, isn't it?"

Young William nodded. "Ay, it is me, Sir."

"Right, so what brings you rushing into my office so early this morning?" Almost a rhetorical question; the lad's presence could only mean bad news about his father, William Jennings senior.

"I bring you sorry news, Sir. Me mother sent me to tell you that your Company Secretary – I means me father, Mr Jennings, that is – died during the night." Young William pulled at his ear as he thought for a moment. "I s'pose that means I'm s'posed to tell you he won't be in for work today… or something like that, I think."

"Good God, lad; thank you for bringing me the news. I am saddened to hear. Please pass on my condolences to your mother and tell her I will call upon her at my first opportunity today to offer whatever assistance I may provide." He barely finished speaking before young William turned on his heel and trotted back out of the office, closing the door gently behind him. Woodrow, while amazed by the lad's stoic delivery of the message, thought he detected the glisten of moisture in the child's eyes as he left the office.

"What a rotten thing for a lad to have to do," Woodrow said aloud as he shook his head in disbelief. "He can't be any more than eight or nine years old." He couldn't help but wonder about fate's timing. Was it a good thing or otherwise, that Jennings had died on the day he was supposed to report to the board? There wasn't time to dwell on the matter. The board meeting was due to start and Woodrow thought it best to apprise the chairman of the situation beforehand.

"Excuse me, Mr McCarthy, could you spare a moment before going into the board meeting, please?" Woodrow asked as he intercepted the chairman of directors on his way into the board meeting called specifically to examine Jennings' response to the allegations of discrepancies in the firewood vouchers.

"Make it quick. I was delayed in town and the meeting is due to start in a couple of minutes."

"Very well; I received word this morning of the death of our company secretary, Mr William Jennings. He passed away sometime during last night." McCarthy nodded, turned and continued on his way to the meeting without commenting on the news.

"Good morning, Gentlemen. As you are all aware, this meeting is called to discuss the company secretary's explanation of the discrepancies in the firewood vouchers as brought to our attention by our auditor, Mr Cossington. However, it now appears this will be a particularly short meeting." Murmurs spread around the table and looks were exchanged but no specific comments were made, so the chairman continued.

"It is my solemn duty to announce the death of our company secretary, Mr William Jennings. Jennings was deceased some time during last evening. I also have to report that, in the ensuing period since our last meeting, we received no explanation from Mr Jennings. This, therefore, changes the purpose of this meeting. We are now required to deal with new business laid before us."

Discussion broke out around the table and increased in volume until, after a minute or so, the chairman called the meeting to order and reinstated silence.

"As a consequence of the death, applications must now be called for the position of company secretary, with applications to close on

8th January. Advertisements are to be placed at the earliest in all the local newspapers. Further, I have a mind to ask the new appointee to pay a bond of good faith of £300. Is there any comment before I put this as a motion?"

One member asked hesitantly, "What about the discrepancies; what are we doing about those?"

"That matter will be left in abeyance for the time being. If there is no discussion or comment, I now put the motion to advertise for a company secretary along the lines already outlined." The motion was carried unanimously. The chairman swiftly moved on to the next item of business.

"This brings us to the matter of the company secretary's cottage. A letter is to be sent to the widow advising she must vacate the cottage within one week of today."

Woodrow was incensed and interjected before the chairman could continue. "Gentlemen, is this not an opportunity for us to exercise some compassion? The widow Jennings has four young children and is due to give birth again in a few weeks. Would it be possible for the board to extend her tenancy by a further week or two to allow her time to make adequate arrangements for her family's future?"

"My God, man, at times I wonder about the state of your faculties. We have a business to run. We are not a benevolent Society." Shaking his head in disbelief, McCarthy paused briefly to draw breath. Woodrow seized the opportunity.

"The company's annual general meeting is only a few weeks away. It has been a difficult year for both growers and the miller. Regardless of the circumstances, growers are likely to blame their plight on the company. Making a show of our compassionate treatment of the widow and family of a senior employee might help ease the way at that meeting, and lessen the chance of a repeat of the Pettigrew debacle."

Some heads were nodding, accompanied by murmured conversations around the table but the chairman prevented any opportunity for open discussion of the suggestion.

"Compassion! She is in receipt of compassion. The man is dead; Jennings is no longer an employee. Therefore, the woman and her brood no longer have a right to occupy the cottage. Given that situation, under normal circumstances she could expect to vacate the cottage by tomorrow. …But no, we will allow her a week to move out. It is not our concern that she has a brood and is about to add to it. It is typical of that class of people. Breed like rabbits! There should be something done about that. It's disgusting." The chairman emphasised this point by slamming his hand down hard on the table causing many around it to jump in surprise.

Woodrow noticed a few angry looks from some of the members but no one voiced an objection. He tried again to temper the situation with reason. "As all of you around this table are growers, you are well aware of the antagonistic relationship which remains between growers and this company. After such a difficult year – in no way due to the company's performance – it is reasonable to expect a hostile reaction from growers at our annual general meeting. Given that situation, it already will be difficult to gain their support for those major issues we will ask them to vote on at that annual general meeting. Anything that further inflames their senses is likely to result in our proposals being rejected out of hand."

A couple of the members aired their support for his thinking, while the rest appeared to be nodding in agreement. They all looked concerned as the reality of the situation began to dawn on them. However, the chairman was having none of it.

"Enough! A letter is to go to the widow advising that she and her brood have one week from today to vacate the cottage. She probably can't read anyway, so someone will need to read it to her. There can be no room for misunderstanding."

"Mrs Jennings can both read and write," Woodrow responded angrily.

"There is little other business to attend to at this meeting, and nothing requiring your input, Mr Woodrow. You should leave the meeting now and prepare the letter to go to the widow under my signature..."

"Under your signature?" Woodrow questioned.

"As I have said: under my signature. I will come by your office to sign it at the close of this meeting."

Woodrow scraped his chair back harshly across the floor and stormed out of the meeting, slamming the door on his way. He marched through the office, slammed his office door behind him and spent a few moments pacing backwards and forwards across his office. He was seething, but there was nothing for it but to write the letter, and write it quickly, for he had no doubt the chairman would waste no time in coming to sign it.

With the letter signed, Woodrow waited until he saw McCarthy leave the estate before he ventured out of his office. He was gone from his office for some time, returning as the last of the employees left work for the day. John Dowling caught up with him as he climbed the stairs of the office building. It had become something of a tradition for Dowling, when he was on site, to drop by Woodrow's office at the close of the day for a tot of rum and a yarn.

Woodrow was not in the best frame of mind; that much was obvious to Dowling. He waited until they were behind closed doors in Woodrow's office before broaching the subject of Woodrow's demeanour. The level of rum Woodrow added to each glass today was further indication that all was not well. Woodrow resisted Dowling's gentle prodding until he downed half the contents of his glass before apprising his friend of the events of the day. This included an almost verbatim report on the board meeting.

Dowling pursed his lips and creased his brow as he thought for a moment. "What was all the fuss about with Jennings' predecessor? I was overseas for much of Pettigrew's time as Company Secretary. What is the story behind the present strained grower relations?"

"Pettigrew was selected from 23 applicants in 1887 when the place was very much a fledgling sugar mill. He became ill towards the end of 1893 and, early in 1894, sought leave to seek medical treatment in Sydney. Shortly afterwards, at the beginning of February I think, we received word to the effect that he had been detained in Sydney due to a further complication with his illness. A few days later, he died while still in Sydney.

"Why would his death cause such a furore?"

"Pettigrew was popular with growers and often acted as mediator in disputes between growers and miller. They saw him as always fair and impartial. His impartiality on such occasion probably led to his falling out of favour with the board."

"Okay, so a good man was lost…"

"It went deeper than that. The company hadn't treated him very well and this appalled some of the former directors who made Pettigrew's treatment known to their fellow growers. When Pettigrew was first hired, we had only a small makeshift office. On instruction, he worked from his cottage on the estate but he received nothing to help facilitate this. His commencement salary was £130 per annum and, in his entire time with the company, he received only one raise of ten shillings per year. Growers accused us of treating him as slave labour."

"Perhaps that wasn't so far from the truth. People with such responsibility and whose honesty and integrity you rely on need to be treated well – especially if they prove to be a wise appointment. I fully appreciate your concerns regarding the outcomes from today's decisions. However, there is nothing to be done, I suppose... except maybe to batten down and prepare for the storm"

"Yes, you're right. Today, I've done as much as I can do for the widow and her family. Over the next couple of days, I will try for individual conversations with the few growers with whom I still have a cordial relationship. Beyond that, I don't have any bright ideas about what else I might do."

"What have you done for the widow? Is there anything I can do to help?"

"Best you're not seen to be involved. I've had a word to a couple of the mill engineers who also live on the estate. They'll see she is all right, help her pack up and all that. Our wagon goes into town for supplies tomorrow. I've arranged for her to ride with the driver."

"I thought she was a local girl. Doesn't she have family around here somewhere to help her?"

"Her father is James Grimsby ..."

"The chap who owns the agency in town?"

"Yes, that's the one. I heard he never approved of the marriage and hasn't had much to do with his daughter since. He hasn't made any move to help at this time. I suppose it is possible he has not heard of his son-in-law's death yet."

With only further brief snatches of general conversation between them, the two men finished their drinks and Dowling took his leave. Woodrow poured himself another large drink. His housekeeper would have prepared dinner before she left this evening and, as there was no Mrs Woodrow waiting for his return, there was no need for him to hurry home. It would take a bit more rum yet to soothe his anger from this morning's encounter with the chairman.

With some degree of grim satisfaction, Woodrow watched the supply wagon leave the estate the next morning with Mrs Jennings perched up front beside the driver. After informing one of the clerks in the front office he would be out of his office for most of the day, Woodrow saddled his horse and rode out to meet up with the first of the growers whom he hope to speak with over the next couple of days.

He arrived at the Rogers' farm in time to join Will Rogers and his wife for a cup of tea and a slab of excellent fruitcake on the verandah of their homestead. Disgusted by Woodrow's news, Will lapsed into deep thought as he finished off the last of his slice of cake. Then, slowly and carefully, he shared the outcome of his deliberations with Woodrow.

"This McCarthy is a bitter and twisted old man. Your presumption is correct; I believe the annual general meeting will be a fiery affair. The only light that is likely to shine out of this whole mess is that McCarthy will no longer control the company after that meeting."

"I know McCarthy is one of the three directors whose turn it is to stand down in rotation at the end of this year, but there is nothing to stop him standing for re-election. If he does, there would need to be at least three good men – no, better men – standing in order for him to miss out on re-election."

Will Rogers chuckled, "Oh, I think that can be arranged. As we both agree, this has been a difficult year. In such cases, the growers' dissatisfaction is invariably directed at the company and, more particularly, at the man in the chair. McCarthy seems to have the doubly bad luck of being the chairman throughout such a difficult year and having to stand for re-election at the end of it. If you're a gambling man, I wouldn't advise you to wager any money on his being back on the board next year." Rogers finished his conversation with a knowing nod and a wink.

Feeling somewhat encouraged by his meeting with Will Rogers, Woodrow rode further up the valley with the intention of meeting up with Tom Kemp… and in the hope of arriving at Kemp's farm in time for an invitation to join them for lunch. His timing was perfect. As Woodrow rode through the gate, Tom Kemp cantered out of a clump of trees along the fence line to meet him. Tom, on his way up to the house for lunch, issued Woodrow the coveted invitation to join them.

Mrs Kemp disappeared off into the house as their 'girl' cleared up after the lunch of cold cuts and salad. The two men adjourned to the verandah to talk and smoke their cigars. Woodrow's conversation with Kemp generally echoed his earlier conversation with Will Rogers. The only real difference this time was the level of vitriol in Tom Kemp's comment about the company, and McCarthy in particular.

Kemp also held the belief that McCarthy would not be re-elected to the board. Woodrow again voiced his concern that, if there were only three or less nominations, McCarthy would be one of the three elected… by default if not by the vote. Kemp laughed loudly at the suggestion.

"My dear Woodrow, we might only be growers, but we are not so naive as to let such a situation arise. Do not trouble yourself about the election. There will be more than ample nominations to ensure no re-election of the retiring directors. I can assure you also that all of those eligible to vote at the meeting will know which nominees are genuinely standing for election and which ones are simply there to ensure the wrong people don't get in."

Woodrow took his leave and headed back towards the mill. It was getting late by the time he arrived back at the office and most of the employees were making ready to leave for the day. Wingate, the junior clerk, halfway to the door, remembered something. Rushing back, he knocked gently on Woodrow's door.

"Begging your pardon, Mr Woodrow; Mr Pearce called in to see you today on his way into town. I advised him you were unlikely to be in for the rest of the day. He said, depending on what time his business in town was completed, he might call at the office to see you on his way home this evening. I took the liberty of letting him know it was your habit to remain in your office until about seven o'clock each evening."

"Pearce, eh… well done, lad. It will serve my purpose well if he does call in this evening. Off you go now and thank you." It would be most convenient if Pearce does call in, Woodrow thought. I will be able to take care of another of the grower visits on my list without having to ride up the valley again.

Jim Pearce arrived not much before seven o'clock. Over a couple of drinks, Woodrow repeated the conversation he already delivered twice that day. His astute guest read the situation swiftly and accurately. At the close of their conversation, Woodrow again received assurances that this grower would do his best to help soothe the likely grower unrest, and that there existed little likelihood of McCarthy's re-election to the board any time soon.

Chapter 3

While Woodrow's day ended on a high note, for Ellen Jennings, the day left her bitter and resentful. It showed the widow the cold reality of the future ahead of her. From the moment the driver helped her down from the wagon in front of her father's store, she felt the impending doom. She wanted to turn away and run from the place, but she had nowhere else to go. She must go inside and talk to her father.

Her mother, Mary Grimsby, was behind the counter when Ellen entered the store. Her father was nowhere in sight. She assumed he was next-door in the agency he recently purchased to expand his business. "Hello, Mother," Ellen said quietly.

"My dear child," Mary exclaimed, "Come here; let me look at you." She hugged her daughter and then held her at arms' length. "We heard about poor William late yesterday. How are you coping, my dear?"

Ellen felt the tears well up again and swallowed hard to control them. She had said only a few words when her father came striding towards them. As he drew nearer, he exclaimed, "Oh, it's you. What's the cause for such a rare visit to my store?" Then, eying off Ellen's swollen stomach, he grunted in disgust, "Can't control yourself again I see."

"James!" Mary exclaimed. "Our daughter is in mourning for her husband who is not yet in his grave. Please show some understanding."

"Hmm, yes, I remember, now that you mention it. When is the funeral?"

"Tomorrow morning," Ellen replied simply.

"I suppose I had better attend for appearances sake. We won't be closing the store, mind. No business can afford to close its doors unnecessarily these days. You may stay here with your mother while the funeral is on."

"Stay here? I expect to be at William's funeral service and then at the cemetery for his interment."

"Nonsense; women do not attend funerals. They are not of the right constitution to withstand such occasions. No, you can stay at your cottage or here with your mother. You will not embarrass me by attending the funeral. There's nothing more to say on the matter. However, you didn't say; what brings you to the store today?"

Ellen twisted her handkerchief tightly in her hands and chose her words carefully. "Now that William is deceased…" she choked back a sob as she said the word, "… now that William is deceased, we must vacate the cottage on the mill's estate. We have nowhere to go and I don't have the funds to be able to rent even a small place. I would be more than willing to get a job and work, but it will be a while before that is possible. My baby is due within the month."

"It's a bit late now to be thinking about the consequences of all this breeding you have indulged in," her father snapped. "But that doesn't answer the question as to why you're here today."

"I've come to ask a favour; for your charity I suppose. As I said, we have nowhere to go. I've come to ask if we might stay here… just till I am back on my feet and am able to make other arrangements, of course."

"What, move in here? Definitely not! I counselled you long and hard that the man you chose to marry was no good; did not have any decent prospects. You chose to ignore me, and he has done nothing except prove me right. Now you want me to take you back… definitely not." Ellen bit her lip hard to stifle the sobs she felt building.

"Ellen, dear," her mother said, "Would you mind going upstairs to make us a cup of tea, please?" Ellen nodded and headed for the stairs.

How many years was it since she last climbed these stairs? She expected nothing much to have changed upstairs. As she started to climb the stairs, she heard her mother's pleading voice: probably trying to intercede on my behalf, she thought. Mother shouldn't put herself through that. He won't change his mind.

Nothing had changed. The kitchen remained unchanged from the last time she was in it. While she busied herself making the tea and setting out the fine china, Ellen was aware of her father's raised voice floating up from below. Although she couldn't make out what he said, she knew what it would be about. Footsteps on the stairs replaced the voices, and her parents joined her in the kitchen.

"There are some biscuits in the tin; perhaps you could set a few out," her mother suggested as she drew out a chair. Ellen arranged biscuits on a plate before joining her parents at the table. After the usual ritual of pouring tea and passing milk and sugar around, Mary prompted her husband.

"James…"

"What?… Oh, confound you woman," he snapped.

"James…" Mary repeated.

"All right, fine." He turned to Ellen. "Your mother and I have discussed your situation. Your mother is not getting any younger and is starting to find managing the store and our home becoming a bit much for her to handle. It might prove beneficial for us all if you were to move back here. You would be required to earn your keep, of course. You would take care of the housework and help in the store. I no longer have any time to spend in the store as the agency next-door occupies all my time these days. Your old room is still empty. You could move back in there… say, on the day after the funeral."

Ellen raised her eyebrows at her mother as she mulled over her father's words. She heard his words, but what was he really saying? Her mother looked uncomfortable and looked away from Ellen. Well, whatever was going on, she wasn't in a position to refuse the offer of a roof over her head.

The only real problem she could see immediately was how they were all going to fit in the small upstairs residence. She and the youngest child – and the new baby of course – would somehow manage to fit into her small room, but where would the older three children sleep? Again, she chose her words carefully as she posed that question to her father.

"You were not listening… once again I find you do not listen to what I say. I said you could move back into your old room. I will not have the children here. How many are there now?"

"Four," Ellen answered sharply, "And one more very soon."

"Good Lord, it would be like being invaded by a plague of rats. No, I will not take the children. I suppose we will have to suffer this new arrival for some time after it arrives … but only until it is six months old, and not a moment longer. Is that understood?"

"What's to become of my children if I can't have them with me?" Ellen was shocked. Although prepared for a hard time of it, she had not imagined imposition of such a condition by her father.

"There's a perfectly good orphanage run by the nuns just outside town. The children can go there. This is where other women who find themselves with no father on hand to support their children, place their offspring into care. It is the same for men who lose their wives. They have to do something with their children until such time as they take another wife who can look after them. The children can stay there for extended periods, such as might elapse before you get back on your feet… or remarry, although I think it highly unlikely any man would want to take on you and your brood." Pushing his chair away from the table, he stood up and looked at both women in turn.

"That's all there is to be said. That is my offer. You may take it or leave it. If you accept my offer, I would expect you to move in the day after the funeral. I will send Alfred with the wagon to collect you and the children. He can drop you here before taking the children on to the orphanage."

Ellen knew when she was beaten. Tears streaming down her face, she nodded at her father. "Send Alfred with the wagon on the day after the funeral," she agreed, "But I will go with the children to hand them over to the orphanage," she added defiantly.

James threw his hands in the air in resignation. "Fine, if you insist; though why you would want to put yourself through that, I do not understand."

"That's probably because you are not a woman," Mary told her retreating husband.

Ellen washed up and put everything away before joining her mother downstairs in the store. The mill's wagon would come past to collect her shortly. The store was quiet. It gave her a chance for quiet conversation with her mother. "You seem to manage the store on your own these days. No wonder you're starting to look so tired."

"Things haven't been easy. You know your father bought the agency next-door with the view to setting your brother up in the business. His intention was to establish an agency to cater for the needs of the pastoralists and farmers in the area."

"Yes, I was aware of the new business. Why did father buy the agency or, more importantly, why did he think Richard would be interested in taking it on? Richard had his heart set on becoming a doctor. He was nearly finished his training. Had he given up on his dream?"

"Your father believed it offered Richard a better future and it also strengthened the existing business. He didn't make the purchase lightly, or spend such a large amount of money without proper consideration."

"…But Richard didn't come home. He went to South Africa and became involved in the troubles there that eventually got him killed."

"Your father tried to stop your brother joining the British soldiers preparing to fight the rising unrest in South Africa. Things became very strained between them but Richard went anyway. Although your father was very angry at Richard for going, he had already spent the money on buying the business so went ahead with setting it up in readiness for Richard's return."

"Only Richard didn't return…"

"No… he was killed not long after he joined the British build-up of troops there." So recently after the event, the memory of receiving news of his death remained sharp and painful. "The whole episode has left your father a bitter and angry man."

"He always was difficult to live with, but I can understand that losing his only son – his pride and heir – would take a heavy toll on him. He never had much time for me before and now, with his only son gone while I survive, it must be hard for him to accept what life has dealt him."

"Perhaps that's true. Anyway, he now spends his days working in the agency, leaving me to run the store. I'm not exactly alone. He employs Alfred, a young lad, to do most of the heavy work out the back and cover the store when we have lunch or whatever. However, you are right I am tired. These days I find coping with the store and the housework and the accounts all a bit much at times. It will be good to have you back again."

"My ride back to the mill has arrived. I must go. I won't take father up on the offer to stay here tomorrow while the funeral is happening. I will take care of my own time tomorrow and be ready to leave the cottage when he sends the wagon for me the following day."

The women hugged before Ellen went to meet the wagon. Again, she was grateful for the driver's helping hand as she awkwardly climbed aboard. The driver dropped her at her door. Immediately, the women from each of the cottages on either side of hers rushed over to be with her. They looked after the Jennings children in her absence and made sure their mother was okay before returning them to her care.

Mr Woodrow called to see her on his way home that evening. She told him of the plans in place for her to vacate the cottage, and asked whether anyone from the mill might be attending her husband's funeral the next day. Woodrow confirmed that he and a few other staff from the estate would be paying their respects. Ellen asked if there might be room for her to travel to the funeral with one of them. Although Woodrow had planned to ride his horse into town, he quickly changed his plans and arranged to collect Ellen and her eldest son, young William, in his carriage.

Her father arrived late for the funeral service and found a seat towards the back of the church. As she followed William's coffin out of the church, the number of people attending the service came as a surprise for Ellen. They included about ten mill staff, quite a number of growers and even four or five directors.

She doubted she would ever forget the look of utter dismay that crossed her father's face at the sight of her, flanked on either side by Mr Woodrow and young William, following the coffin from the church. No doubt, she would hear more about that in the days to come. He made it clear yesterday he considered women were not up to attending funerals.

On her return to the cottage from visiting the store the previous day, Ellen made a start on sorting out the family's meagre possessions. She and William each owned a large steamer trunk. All of the children's belongings would go into one of the trunks. Her own possessions and the few precious household bits and pieces would fit in the other. Then, after returning from the funeral, Ellen made a start on the packing.

The husband of the woman next-door brought a large crate home from the mill for her to use to pack the more bulky household goods. There was little in the way of furniture to worry about. Each of the three older children had a rickety bed with a thin mattress, and the youngest was in a cot. All these were donated to the family by other residents on the state as they became surplus to their requirements.

She thought aloud as she stood surveying the children's bedroom. "I'll leave the beds behind for anyone else on the estate with a use for them after we are gone." Then, as she turned to leave the room, she saw something else. "I will need to keep the old bassinet for the new baby when it arrives," she reminded herself. "The other few sticks of furniture in the living area are not worth keeping, and I will have nowhere to put them anyway... best to leave them behind as well."

That evening, dinner was a sombre affair. Only young William really understood what had happened. The next eldest, Marion, knew something was not right but did not understand her father's death in spite of the effort Ellen put into explaining to the children that their father would not be coming home ever again. Although most of the children didn't comprehend, they sensed it was a time of sadness and remained quiet and withdrawn throughout the evening.

Ellen kissed each one as she tucked them into bed, before returning to the kitchen to finish preparing for their departure tomorrow. She put aside food for the morning. There was little in the pantry. Supplies ran down over the previous couple of weeks when she was preoccupied with caring for her husband. She gathered up what remained and carried it across to the house next-door. They also had a large family, and would appreciate anything that helped feed them.

As she returned home, the pile of firewood outside the back door caught her eye. There was a delivery only a couple of days ago and it remained untouched. The small amount of wood they used over the last week or so young William had split just before Christmas. First thing in the morning, she would get her son to help her divide the firewood into two piles. Her two neighbours' husbands did not get free firewood as part of their salary. Some free firewood would help stretch their budgets.

With everything else taken care of, she spent a few minutes cleaning and tidying the living area of the cottage. Looking around for anything else she might do tonight, Ellen finally had to admit defeat. There was nothing else, no further procrastination possible. All that remained was to go to bed and wait for the morning. Ellen collapsed in the solitary battered comfortable chair and let the tears come.

In a month's time she would have been married for nine years. They had produced four beautiful children – well, almost five. Even without the children, there wasn't too much money to spend but, once the children starting arriving, things became tough – but they had been happy. Up until the last couple of years, William enjoyed his job. That changed when the new chairman of directors took over. William didn't speak of it, but she saw the change; saw her husband's stress level rise rapidly. She held no doubt that somehow that change – the election of that current chairman of directors – had brought on William's early death.

She forced herself to go to bed. She would need all her strength tomorrow. Sleep wouldn't come. Grief consumed her as she lay there. William was only 41 years old, and now he was gone. His children had lost their father. The youngest would never know him, and only the older two would hold any memories of him. Through all those years, she was mistress of her own home, a wife and mother making her own life with her family. Now her beloved husband was gone.

Tomorrow she would no longer be mistress of her own home. Tomorrow she would lose her children... and her independence. Moving back into her parents' home would return her to the rigidly controlled family life imposed by her arrogant father... and from which she so joyfully escaped all those years ago. She gave in to her tears and sobbed as grief and despair possessed her for the rest of the night. She would not find sleep this last night in her own bed.

Chapter 4

Next morning, Ellen woke young William early to help her sort out the firewood and stack it neatly in two similar piles. She dispatched her son on an errand. "Please go and tell both of our neighbours that they should collect one each of the piles of our firewood at their earliest in case the mill decides to reclaim it." While young William went off on that errand, Ellen made breakfast for her family before waking the other children.

Then, she dressed the children for the day, and folded and packed their night attire in their trunk. With the breakfast things washed and packed as well, there was nothing to do but wait for her father's wagon to arrive. It was just after nine o'clock when Alfred arrived with the wagon. One of the neighbours' husbands was home and came over to help Alfred load their few belongings onto the wagon. With the bassinet tied on so it wouldn't tip off and the children perched as safely as possible on board, Alfred helped Ellen climb aboard the wagon. There was one parting look at the cottage and her neighbours waving as they drove off. She struggled to hold back the tears for most of the trip into town.

Alfred told Ellen, "My instructions were to bring the wagon to the rear of the store when we arrive in town so your belongings can be unloaded before the children go on to the orphanage."

Ellen remained on the wagon determined nothing should prevent her going with the children to see them settled at the orphanage. Unloading Ellen's trunk, the bassinet and crate of household bits and pieces took but a few minutes. Then Alfred resumed his seat and they set off on their heart-wrenching journey.

The children and their trunk were unloaded and taken into the main building. There were few formalities to complete. After hurried hugs and kisses all round, the children were taken off to another building. Young William struggled with his tears in an effort 'to be a man' while Marion openly wept. The two younger children looked confused, and the youngest screamed for her mother. Ellen couldn't control herself and wept too.

The nuns were kind but firm. Ellen ensured they understood her situation. "I will be visiting the children as often as possible and I will be doing all I can to establish a new life for them to join me again."

They nodded sympathetically in response to this, but then the nun who appeared to be in charge delivered something of a shock for Ellen. "That's all well and good, but we insist that you do not visit the children for at least another three months." She overrode Ellen's objections and explained. "It will take the children at least that long to settle in and accept their new life. Any visit earlier than three months would only serve to unsettle the children again, making life difficult once more for everyone."

There was nothing more to do or say. The senior nun indicated to Alfred that they should leave. Striving to control his own emotions at the sad tableau played out before him, Alfred gently took Ellen by the arm and led her towards the wagon. The ride back to town was in silence. On arriving back at the store, Ellen hesitated as Alfred made to help her down from the wagon.

There was no point in rushing. She took a few moments – and a few deep breaths – to prepare herself for the next ordeal of the day: having to resume her place as part of someone else's family and again having to live on a daily basis with her father's disapproval of everything she was and did. For the first time in her life, she regretted her pregnancy; wished she had not conceived this child, which would have no future with her after its birth and would have to endure the same fate as its siblings.

Ellen watched as Alfred stored the crate amongst all the other rarely disturbed stuff that languished at the far end in the back section of the store. Then she followed him up the stairs as he carried up her trunk and placed it in her room. Alfred bolted down the stairs, leaving Ellen alone in her room. Nothing had changed; everything was just as it used to be. The only difference being the fresh linen her mother used to make up the bed before Ellen's arrival. Then Alfred was back again, struggling under the weight of the bassinet.

"Where should I put this, Ma'am?"

"Oh, uhmm, it will need to go in here somewhere… perhaps in that corner over there," Ellen replied and pointed to the only bit of space in the small room.

Alfred bounced down the stairs again for the last time as he resumed his duties in the back of the store. Ellen took a moment to compose herself before descending the stairs. Then, with her head held high, she crossed the threshold, entering the store and her new life. Her mother finished serving the only customer in the store at the time and rushed to her side. Hugging her daughter tightly, Mary whispered to Ellen, "It will be alright, you'll see. We can make this work and who knows what the future may hold."

The store became busy and her parents had not yet had lunch although their normal lunch hour had long since passed. Ellen had no interest in food. She suggested her parents have lunch while she minded the store. As her mother turned to make her way towards the stairs, Ellen suggested quietly to her, "Perhaps you might like to take a rest after lunch. I haven't forgotten how to look after the store and, if we get too busy, I will call you." Her mother simply nodded in reply before detouring into the agency to advise her husband that lunch would be ready in ten minutes.

It was as if she had never left; everything came back to her instantly. Everything remained in the same place it occupied before she was married, and the same equipment was still in use. The store became busy again as farmers and pastoralists from outlying areas called in to the store at the last minute to pick up supplies before heading out of town and back to their properties. Ellen didn't call her mother to assist, preferring to manage by herself. She needed to be busy and for her mind to be occupied with things other than her own situation.

As was usually the case, the store became quiet as closing time drew near. Mary Grimsby came bustling back into the store about half an hour before closing. "My dear child, I have left you here alone all afternoon. I don't know what came over me, but I slept for hours."

"You must have needed the rest. I had no problems managing the store alone. However, I'm pleased you've come down now. I need you to show me what you have been doing with the books so that I can complete the end of day accounts. I will go upstairs to prepare dinner now and then come down after dinner to complete the book work."

"This has been a most difficult day for you. Are you sure you feel up to doing all of this?"

"This is my new life, Mother. It needs to begin, as it will continue. I am fine to do as I have said. In any case, I need to keep busy. There is little chance I will sleep much tonight."

About an hour later her parents came upstairs. "Dinner will be on the table in about ten minutes," Ellen announced as they entered the living quarters. James Grimsby poured himself a large rum and took it through to the small sitting room. Mary pulled up a chair and sat while she watched her daughter finish preparing dinner.

"How much longer before your baby is due? We need to be mindful of your condition and your workload as your time draws near."

"Oh, you know how it is; babies come when they're ready. I probablyhave a month or so to go. I am well and I am strong. There is no need for concern about what I am able to do – or not do – in the interim."

In spite of her mother's best attempts to generate conversation, dinner turned out to be an awkward affair. Her father confined his contribution to the occasional grunt or wave of his hand. As soon as dinner was over, James rose from the table and started towards the sitting room. After a few paces, he came back to stand beside his wife. Taking her by the arm, he issued an invitation. "Mary, come through and keep me company in the sitting room." The tone of the invitation and the gentle pull on her arm left her in no doubt that refusal was not an option. Mary shot her daughter a look as she followed her husband into the sitting room.

Ellen cleaned up after dinner before heading down to the small office in a corner of the store. Her mother had not gone over the books with her but she did not think that would be a problem. I doubt it likely anything has changed in that department either since I last took care of the books, she told herself as she descended the stairs. Her assumption was correct. After spending some time going over the books to familiarise herself with the current situation, she completed the day's accounts. Then there was nothing left to do but get ready for bed and what she knew would be a sleepless night.

*****

Life quickly settled into that familiar rhythm remembered from so long ago. The store was doing good business but Ellen wasn't so sure about the agency. From the state of the books, the agency broke even but returned only a very small profit. There were quite a few outstanding accounts. Many belonged to large landholders and had been outstanding for some time, much longer than he would have allowed in previous times. She made a mental note to ask her mother about the accounts at her first opportunity.

Ellen wondered whether her father's frequent absences from the agency somehow were having an adverse impact on the agency's business. Whenever James was away from the agency, Alfred took his place there. Alfred was a good young lad, and perfectly capable of taking care of customers. However, while he was taking care of the agency, his own work in the store's backroom suffered.

Customers dropped their orders into the store first thing on the day they came into town, and they expected their supplies to be ready for loading onto their wagons when they returned to collect them on their way out of town. All too frequently lately customers were forced to wait when they found their order had not been put together ready for collection. Was she imagining it, or were the customer complaints becoming more numerous? Ellen knew she needed to take the matter up with her mother but felt unsure about how to broach the subject. The whole issue hinged on why her father was absent so often and what he got up to when he wasn't there.

Dinner the next night followed much the same routine as the previous evening. However, the third night following her return, Ellen finished the day's accounts a little earlier. When she returned upstairs, she found her parents still in the sitting room. Intending to bid them goodnight, she knocked softly before entering the room. Mary was putting away her needlepoint as Ellen came in. Ellen came to sit beside her.

"May I see?" Ellen asked. "Such fine stitches; you do beautiful work, Mother."

"The eyes are not as sharp as they once were and the hands are not always as compliant as I would like. Nevertheless, it is a relaxing way to occupy time."

James interrupted the women's examination of Mary's handiwork. "I'm pleased you have come up early tonight. It saves me having to go downstairs to talk to you."

"What is it you wanted me for, Father?"

"I think it wise you change your name back to Grimsby." Ellen opened her mouth to protest, but her father held up his hand to silence her. "You are now a widow; no longer married to Jennings. There is nothing to prevent a name change. I have heard the stories of Jennings' misappropriation of company funds – probably the whole town has heard by now."

"Those accusations were not true. William was as honest as the day is long. He would never steal," Ellen retaliated angrily.

"He never gave adequate explanation, so there can only be one conclusion."

"He never gave any explanation. He could not. The letter demanding explanation arrived only a couple of days before his death, at a time when he experienced very few lucid moments each day. How could he reply to those false accusations?"

"Nevertheless, mud sticks, as they say... and some is likely to adhere to you. I run a reputable business. I cannot allow any situation that might result in the integrity and honesty of our dealings with customers to be questioned. No, we must ensure the removal of the Jennings name from any association with this enterprise. It may take a small number of members of the community a short time to forget whom you were married to, but most of the town remains unaware of your connection. There is nothing for it but for you to return to your maiden name of Grimsby."

"So, you won't mind that your Grimsby daughter is seen to be so heavily pregnant when her surname clearly suggests she is unmarried?" Ellen challenged James defiantly.

James turned bright red from his collar up and cursed as he bounded out of his chair. "I will think on this matter further, but only the timing is the issue. The name must change. It is simply a matter of when is the best time. In the meantime, everyone is to refrain from referring to you as Mrs Jennings. Is that clearly understood?" This last question clearly directed at Mary.

"Don't judge him too harshly, my dear. His only interest is to protect the business. After all, all our livelihoods depend on its success. What he has suggested is in all of our best interests," Mary said soothingly.

"The store is doing very well, as you well know from the books. The same is not true for the agency. He should have concerns about that. Perhaps, if he spent more time there, instead of leaving Alfred in charge so often, it might do better," Ellen retorted.

"Your father cannot be in two places at once. He must spend a lot of time out and about encouraging new customers and paying attention to existing ones."

"Strange how that always has him returning smelling strongly of rum. Oh, don't bother defending him to me. I know defending their husbands is what is expected of wives, but don't waste your words on me. His drinking and posturing about at that gentlemen's club have him away from the business too often and for too long. Ask yourself where it will end. Mother, I am a little tired tonight; I'm off to bed. Goodnight."

For a few moments, Mary considered her daughter's outburst. She certainly has developed a feisty disposition over the course of her marriage, Mary thought wryly. She will need to master that quickly if she is to find another husband. Then Mary sighed and thought about Ellen's words. She was right of course, it is a wife's duty to defend her husband regardless of what she considers is the truth of the matter, but it's also a wise woman who knows not to challenge her husband. That woman has a long marriage. Mary knew she must discuss these issues with Ellen, but the time was not right just now. An opportunity might present itself once the birth was over and – hopefully – Ellen returned to her more normal self.

There was more of James and less of Mary in Ellen than either of her parents realised. Of necessity, she accepted everything that happened over the last few days, but she was growing tired of having her life dictated by men who had little respect for her and spared her not a second thought. As Ellen lay on her bed that night willing sleep to come, she made a pledge with herself: I will avenge all that has happened. She wanted revenge for everything that had happened to her and her family, but somehow she wanted more than that. She was unsure what that 'more' was, but she knew without doubt that, alone, revenge was not enough.

Chapter 5

Following the confrontation with her father that night, Ellen felt a little unwell. She couldn't put her finger on what was wrong exactly, but put it down to stress combined with the late stage of her pregnancy. In spite of this, she spent Sunday cleaning the upstairs residence as well as the store. It was the only day of the week they closed and, therefore, the only time to do any significant cleaning without interruption by customers.

As she prepared dinner that evening, Ellen was aware of a couple of twinges of pain in her stomach. Not severe, nothing serious, she told herself. They didn't occur again until the next day. There they were again, just the occasional light spasm during the morning. Still she was convinced they were not serious. After lunch, Mary decided to postpone her afternoon rest, opting instead to come downstairs and restock the cheese cabinet.

The two women chatted briefly to Mrs Sanderson after she completed her purchases. Then, after saying goodbye to her, Mary went back to the cheese cabinet. A few moments later, Mary was startled when, out of the corner of her eye, she saw Ellen clutch at her stomach and double over. She rushed to her daughter's side and steadied Ellen as she straightened up again.

"Has your time come?" Mary demanded.

"No; no it can't be. It is too soon. The baby is not due for another three or four weeks. I'm sure this is nothing serious. My waters have not broken yet."

Mary watched her daughter like a hawk for the rest of the afternoon, choosing not to go upstairs and leave her alone in the store. Things appeared to settled down. As far as Mary could tell, Ellen didn't experience any further pains during the afternoon. The truth was, Ellen did have a couple of weak twinges but they disappeared as the afternoon wore on.

That night at dinner, Mary noted Ellen ate very little. When her daughter returned from doing the books later that evening, Mary took her aside to check on how she was feeling. Ellen admitted she was feeling a little off colour – nothing serious, mind – but hadn't felt much like eating at dinner. Mary was not convinced, and was even less so when Ellen took herself straight off to bed.

Soon after going to bed, the pains returned, gently and spasmodically at first but increasing in frequency and intensity as the night wore on. Mary became anxious when she discovered the next morning that Ellen hadn't prepared breakfast for them. She bustled about and quickly made breakfast for her husband and waited impatiently for him to finish eating and go downstairs before she rushed to her daughter's bedroom. She found Ellen still in bed, looking pale and drawn, and bathed in a lather of sweat.

Mary rush back to the kitchen, collected a cloth and basin of water. She returned to the bedroom and began mopping Ellen's brow.

"Something is wrong. I feel so sick," Ellen whispered and gripped her mother's hand as another intense pain shot through her.

"Hold this damp cloth to your forehead until I return," Mary said before rushing downstairs to where Alfred had just started work in the loading dock area of the store. "Alfred, go and fetch Dr Boyle; quickly now. Tell him it is an emergency with Mrs Jennings. Bring him straight upstairs when he arrives. Hurry; off you go," Mary commanded.

Ellen was out of bed when Mary returned to her bedroom. The nausea had increased and Ellen was now physically sick. The half hour it took for Dr Boyle to arrive seemed like an eternity to Mary as she stood helplessly by holding her daughter's hand and mopping her brow. At last, footsteps came up the stairs.

After examining Ellen, Dr Boyle announced she should be in hospital. They agreed that, between them, he and Mary would get Ellen downstairs and loaded onto the store's wagon. Then Alfred could drive both Mary and her daughter around to the hospital. Dr Boyle wasted no time or words on explaining the gravity of the situation to Mary.

Hospital staff eased Ellen off the wagon and rushed her inside. Before following her daughter inside, Mary had a quick word to Alfred. "When you get back to the store, please let Mr Grimsby know what has happened and where we are. You will need to look after the store – which we haven't opened yet today – until I return. I will make my own way back to the store when I am certain all is well here. Thank you, Alfred. Now please take yourself off back to work."

There was no sign of Ellen when Mary entered the hospital. A stern-faced matron met her and showed her to a small area containing a few chairs. She told Mary quite firmly, "You can't see her daughter yet. Somebody will call you when that is possible." With that, she stalked off, leaving Mary alone with her anxiety and nothing to occupy her. Mary had no idea of the time but felt as though she had been sitting there for hours when a gentleman wandered into the area where she waited.

When no one came to assist him, he spoke to Mary. "Have you seen Dr Boyle around the place this morning? We were supposed to have a meeting but Dr Boyle didn't arrive for it."

She explained as briefly as she could. "Dr Boyle was called early this morning to attend an emergency. I believed it still detains him." Noticing the gold watch chain across his vest, Mary enquired after the time. The man checked his pocket watch. "It's half after eleven," he replied. "Have you been waiting long?" Mary nodded; no point in telling him she had been there nearly all morning.

"Then I'm sure you could do with a cup of tea by now. It looks as though we are both going to be waiting a while yet. Perhaps we should escape for a few minutes and go across the street to the Mrs Smith's teashop for a cup of tea."

Mary hesitated briefly, but he was right, a cup of tea was what she needed right now. Halfway across the street, Mary stopped suddenly. "I'm sorry. I can't join you for tea. I left home in a hurry this morning when my daughter was brought into the hospital and I didn't bring my purse."

"Don't be silly. Come and have a cup of tea. We'll sort that out later if needs be."

As they entered the teashop, Mrs Smith greeted them. "Good morning, Dr Robinson… Mary. I saw you coming from the hospital, Mary my love, is it your lass?" Mary just nodded. "Is she due then? I would have thought it was a bit early for her yet." Mary shook her head sadly. "Oh dear, I do hope everything goes okay. Now, make yourselves comfortable at a table. Your usual, Dr Robinson?" Mary's companion nodded. "And Mary, what about you: a lovely cup of tea and something to eat perhaps?"

"Just tea please, Edith. And I am sorry but I haven't got my purse …"

"Don't you be worrying about that; you can owe me for it. Now make yourselves comfortable. Meg will be out with your tea shortly."

When they were seated, Mary turned to her companion, "Doctor Robinson?"

"Yes, I apologise for not introducing myself earlier. I'm a surgeon from the city. I've been doing a bit of consulting work with some of the hospitals at major towns along the coast. I've only been here once before… just for a preliminary meeting with Dr Boyle. We were supposed to finalise consultancy arrangements today."

"I see. I shouldn't hold you up then… and I really must get back to see if there's any news of my daughter."

"Relax for few minutes and drink your tea. What's happened to your daughter?"

Mary found herself explaining how things had suddenly gone wrong with her widowed daughter's fifth pregnancy, and how she was still so young and had been so well right up until yesterday. Robinson studied a spot on the tablecloth as Mary explained. When she finished speaking, he looked off into the distance for a moment before commenting.

"Hmmm, hopefully all is well and it's just that baby decided to come early." He didn't look or sound convincing to Mary.

Finishing the rest of her tea quickly, Mary stood up. "I really must be getting back. Thank you for your company, Doctor, I…" Whatever else Mary was about to say was lost in the clatter as a young nurse from the hospital burst into the room.

"Oh, thank goodness I've found you." Mary blanched and gripped the back of her chair for support. Then she noticed the nurse wasn't looking at her and she heard the young girl saying, "Matron thought you might be here, Dr Robinson. Dr Boyle has asked for you to come quickly please, he would welcome your assistance."

Robinson was on his feet and fishing in his pocket for change to pay Mrs Smith. "Just go," Mary said. "I'll sort things out here with Edith." The nurse and the doctor were already half way to the door.

Edith came out of her kitchen to investigate the clatter and loud voices. "What's going on out here, Mary?"

Mary outlined for Edith what had happened, and finished by promising to come back tomorrow to pay for their morning teas. Edith shooed her out of the teashop saying, "Like I said before, don't be worrying about that. Now, be off with you back to the hospital to check up on your lass." Mary took her time crossing the street, almost terrified by the thought of what news might await her.

Nobody came to meet her when she entered the hospital, so she made her way back to the same place where she had waited all morning and regained her seat. After some time – she didn't know how long – still nobody had come to see her. Mary decided to take matters into her own hands, and wandered off in search of somebody to ask. She encountered a young nurse – a different one from the one who had come across to the teashop for Dr Robinson – and asked for news of Ellen.

"I'm sorry, Ma'am, only the doctor or matron can give you that information. One of them will come to talk to you when they are free. In the meantime, you should go back to where you have been sitting. That way, they will know where to find you."

Disappointed, and with a growing sense of unease, Mary resumed her seat. She must have nodded off. As if through a thick fog, she became aware of someone calling her name. "Mrs Grimsby, Mrs Grimsby; are you all right, Mrs Grimsby?" Dr Boyle was bending over her.

"Oh, I'm so sorry, Doctor. I must have dozed off. Is there any news of my daughter?" she asked anxiously.

Dr Boyle sat down beside her and patted her hand. Mary gasped. "No, no! Relax, Mary. It has been a long and difficult day for your daughter. To tell the truth, we very nearly lost her and the baby. It was only thanks to good luck that Dr Robinson was in town and we were able to call on his skills that mother and child have survived today."

Mary sobbed, "Is it all over then?"

"Well, it will take your daughter a few weeks to recover from the surgery but she should be okay after that. I am not so sure about her chances of having more children though."

Mary shrugged; that wasn't likely to be an issue any time soon. "What about the baby?" she asked.

"Ah, well, that's not such good news. The baby is very weak. It was nearly dead by the time we got it out. We'll do all we can, of course, but I can't give you any guarantees about the baby's future. I'm sorry."

"I see. Thank you for being so honest. Oh, Doctor, what was it?" Mary asked almost as an afterthought.

"It was a little boy. Look, why don't you go home now? You won't be able to see your daughter for a few hours. Perhaps best to leave it and come back in the morning, I would suggest."

Mary thanked the doctor and made her way back to the store on foot and in a daze. It was late. The sun was already starting to disappear below the horizon when she arrived back. Alfred look up from behind the counter and asked cautiously, "Everything all right then, Missus?"

"Yes, it appears so, thank you. I'm sorry I've been away all day, Alfred. Thank you for taking care of things. I'll take over in here until we close."

Alfred turned to leave, then stopped and turned to Mary. "Begging your pardon, Mrs Grimsby, but just a heads-up, if you know what I mean… Mr Grimsby is in a terrible mood."

"Thank you for the warning, Alfred. Do we know why?" She didn't need to ask. No doubt, it was due to her absence all day.

"Uhmmm, well, ahh … I really don't think it's for me to say."

"That's okay. Thank you again, Alfred."

There remained only an hour or so until closing and few customers came in during that time. Right on time, Mary closed the store, said goodnight to Alfred as he was leaving, and went upstairs to prepare dinner. Now, what could she have ready in the hour before James came looking for his evening meal? As it turned out, she had a bit more time than she thought. James closed the agency at six o'clock, and went to his club for about an hour and a half before returning home. He returned reeking of rum.

James stormed upstairs, slammed back a chair and sat down heavily at the table. "I would expect my dinner to be on the table at this hour."

"And I would have expected you to be home at seven o'clock when dinner was ready to be placed on the table." Not quite true, Mary thought, but he doesn't need to know that.

He had consumed enough rum to render him belligerent. "Alfred hasn't been able to get on with his work today because you've been gallivanting about town all day. I don't pay him to do your job. I'm warning you, there had better not be any further absences tomorrow."

"… or you'll do what? You're drunk, James. I don't think you should say any more."

"I'll say and do what I damn well like… and, right now, I demand a full explanation of where you have been all day."

"Demand as much as you like, James. You know full well where I have been all day – and why. Ellen almost died today. So did the baby and it may yet do so."

"Be a good thing in both cases. If the child goes, it will simplify things; won't have to worry about putting up with it about the place for six months and then having to get rid of it."

That was the final straw for Mary. She was tired, worried about her daughter and grandchild and, more importantly, she had enough of acquiescing with James' every whim and word. "You arrogant, disgusting man. You have gone too far this time. No, don't you dare interrupt me. We had two children but I seem to be the only one of us to be aware of that fact. You appear to think you only had one, just a son. Just so you know, it almost broke my heart when I lost my eldest child – my only son. I would be no less heartbroken if I was to lose my daughter as well."

James spluttered and coughed as he tried to put together some words in retaliation, but Mary cut him off.

"You speak to me of my absence today; let me assure you I will be visiting my daughter in hospital again tomorrow and every other day until she comes home – home to this house. …And, when she does, I will be taking care of her until she is back on her feet. I promise you that is how things will be whether you object or not."

"How dare you speak to me like that? That stupid girl's influence has rubbed off on you already. I'll…"

"You'll do nothing, James, and, while we are on the subject of absences, what about all your absences? It seems to be fine if Alfred can't get his work done because he is covering for you in the agency. Covering your absence while you try to impress those you see as important – the big names – in the community at your so-called gentlemen's club. Do you really think all your posturing and drinking impresses them? As for paying Alfred's wages, you don't pay them. I do, from the store's income. Your precious agency is barely breaking even."

Mary slammed his plate down in front of him, slopping gravy over the edge and onto the tablecloth. "You're drunk, James, and I do not intend to continue this conversation tonight. But, mark my words, I will be continuing this conversation tomorrow and I guarantee you will not enjoy the experience."

With that, Mary turned on her heel, and marched out of the kitchen and off to bed, leaving a stunned and bewildered James sitting at the table. Who was this woman? Mary had never spoken to him like this. He felt as though he'd received a massive blow and she hadn't even raised her voice.

Chapter 6

Still reeling from his wife's tirade, James remained in the sitting room drinking until very late – and the rum bottle was empty – before flopping into bed. Many years ago, he claimed as his bedroom the small room adjacent to the main bedroom, which was once the children's nursery. The sun was quite high next morning by the time he woke sufficiently to haul himself out of bed. He had overslept by at least a couple of hours.

Feeling quite rough after the previous night's rum intake, James made his way to the kitchen. It was deserted. No breakfast anywhere in sight, not even a pot of tea kept warm under a tea cosy. As he went in search of his wife, his head dictated he descend the stairs gently – very gently indeed. The stairs occupied an area of the store's loading dock and ended near the rear entrance to the store proper. As he stepped off the stairs, James looked around for Alfred. He was not out there. Typical, James thought, it's almost as though Alfred knew I wouldn't be around at my usual time this morning, and decided to come to work late thinking I would know about it. Well, he is found out, and will pay the price for his deception, James told himself.

On entering the store, James was surprised to see Alfred behind the counter and just finishing up with a customer. He moved to stand beside Alfred, and leant in close to speak quietly to prevent the retreating customer overhearing. Alfred took a step away. The fumes oozing from James were almost overpowering. James made to step closer again, but Alfred held up his hand. "That's close enough, sir. What were you going to say?"

"Where's my wife. Why are you in here and not out the back taking care of your own duties?"

"Mrs Grimsby said she had to go out. She said she would be gone for an hour or two and asked me to mind the store in her absence."

"What time did she leave?"

"Right after we opened." Alfred checked the clock. "She should be back soon."

"Is the agency open?"

"No. I can't be in both places at once. Mrs Grimsby said to leave the agency closed. You would open it when you came down."

"This is totally unacceptable. Do you know where my wife was going?"

"N-o-o, but I assumed she was going to the hospital."

"The hospital…? Oh, yes, perhaps you're right. I'd better get on with it then."

James moved off in the direction of the agency and Alfred soon heard the scrape of the bolts and squeak of the door as James opened the agency to customers.

When their routine morning teatime rolled around, Mary still had not returned. James' pounding head and lack of breakfast called for desperate measures. He needed at least a cup of tea, but had no idea how to go about making one himself. In desperation, he turned to Alfred. "Would you know how to make a pot of tea, lad?"

"Yes, of course I do."

"You know where the kitchen is upstairs; be a good lad and skip up there and make me a pot of tea if you wouldn't mind. I'll keep an eye on things here while you're about it." Alfred struggled to hide his grin as he exited the store.

Mary returned shortly after James had taken himself off to enjoy his tea. "Has Mr Grimsby appeared yet this morning?" she asked.

"Yes, Ma'am, not so long ago. He asked for a pot of tea, so I made him one and he's gone upstairs to drink it."

"The cheek of him! Thank you, Alfred. Perhaps you could look after the agency until Mr Grimsby comes down again."

"Begging your pardon, Ma'am, but I don't think Mr Grimsby is too well today."

"I'm not surprised. Thank you, Alfred."

James carefully avoided Mary when he came downstairs again, taking a circuitous route through the shelves to reach the agency. It was lunchtime before husband and wife faced each other in the privacy of their kitchen. Mary placed a plate of cold cuts and salad in front of her husband without a word, and then sat down across the table from him to eat her own lunch. She was determined he should speak first. This resulted in lunch being a very silent affair.

When James had finished eating, Mary cleared the table, washed up, and then went downstairs, leaving James still sitting at the table. This was a foreign situation for James. He had never encountered anything like this in his own home before. What was he supposed to do about it? One thing was clear to him though. Like as not, if things didn't improve, there was a fair chance he wouldn't get much for dinner tonight.

There was no contact between the Grimsbys that afternoon. Alfred closed up for Mary and left for the day. As Mary headed for the stairs, James closed the agency for the night. As was his usual routine, James was about to stroll down the street to his club. After a few paces, he stopped. Something suggested this was not a wise move. He retraced his steps and went back inside. Deciding there was nothing for it but to go and face his wife, he wearily climbed the stairs.

"Mary, could you leave off making dinner for a while, please? Come through to the sitting room with me. I suspect we have a conversation to finish."

"Yes, we do," Mary said as she wiped her hands and removed her apron. "I have not yet said all I need you to hear." James' heart sank.

"Look, my dear, perhaps I was a little harsh in some..." James began.

"No, James. Be quiet. You need to listen for a change. I have more to say that is important – very important – as to how we go on from here in the future. At the outset, I think it only fair that I tell you I cannot stand you anymore. I do not like what you have become. There, now that is said and out of the way, let us move on to other important matters." Mary studied her hands for a few moments while James, unsure what he was supposed to do – if anything – studied an area of the floor in silence.

Mary cleared her throat and began again. "It is well past time you acknowledged those who make this business work. It is well past time you showed me some respect. Now there are two women in this family working hard to ensure the business continues to flourish. You will show us due respect and courtesy in future. Mark my word, James, if you do not behave yourself better in the future, then I will have no more of you."

"What are you saying, woman? You dare to stand there and threaten me. What do you imagine you could do about my 'behaviour' if it does not suit you?"

"You do not take me seriously, James, and that is a grave mistake. I might remind you of how we came by this business and of a certain legal agreement drawn up prior to our marriage. I have put up with you as your behaviour and your disrespect have worsened over the years, but your treatment of our daughter – our daughter – over these last few days is disgusting. You have shown no compassion. ... But then, I suppose you're incapable of it from what I have witnessed. Making her give up her children was inhuman."

"You stupid woman! How were we going to fit all that brood in here? …And, if she brought all of those with her, she would need to look after them. We would get no work out of her at all."

"You have not listened to me, James. Calling me stupid is your first mistake. It shows no respect. As for our daughter and her children, we both know the living quarters above the agency need nothing more than a clean to make them liveable. Ellen and her children could well have moved into there. No one in this family is a slave, and you will not treat our daughter that way."

"So you don't like the way things are and you don't like the way I treat you, so what do you imagine for even one moment you might do about it. It is you who should stop and think for a moment; think about what I might do if I become too disenchanted with you and your precious daughter."

"You could do nothing, James. However, I do strongly recommend you make moves to have the living quarters above the agency clean and made suitable to be lived in."

"You will not be moving that woman and her children into that accommodation."

"I have no intention of moving our daughter in there. But, James, if you do not mend your ways as I have pointed out to you, you could find your new home to be the living quarters above the agency."

"You think you could tip me out onto the street? Woman, have you taken leave of your senses? It is I who might tip you out onto the street – along with your so precious daughter."

"Oh dear, James, you are so slow to heed sound advice. I will be going nowhere and nor will my daughter. You will be tipping no one out onto the street. On the other hand, I might consider that necessary. …And, I would remind you again of how we came by this business and of that very important legal agreement my father had you sign. Do not consider for one moment I would be worried about losing face or dignity by tossing you out. However, I cannot say the same for you, if you are to find yourself out on the street. I'm sure all those landholders you try so hard to impress would find your plight a highly amusing situation."

"You dare to threaten me?"

"Oh goodness, no, James; I don't threaten, I promise you. Do you have any questions or need clarification about anything I have said?"

James managed the faint shake of his head. Slumped in his chair, he felt thoroughly intimidated by the stern-faced woman who stood in front of him, hands on hips and jaw set firmly while speaking ever so quietly. Who was this woman, he asked himself yet again. Surely, this could not be the same woman he married all those years ago; the woman who had never once argued or raised her voice to him.

"Good, now that's settled, I'll get on with dinner. It's late. Something quick and light I think; omelettes?"

With that, Mary was gone and he heard her clattering about in the kitchen. A few minutes later, she called through from the kitchen that dinner was about to be placed on the table. James hauled himself out of his chair and slowly moved to take his place at the table. A bowl of salad was already on the table and, as he drew back his chair, Mary placed an omelette in front of him.

Mary wasted no time after cleaning up from dinner before taking herself off to her room. She felt a little weak-kneed, but her resolve was strong. She hadn't made idle threats; she would toss James out if things did not improve. However, right now she had some serious thinking to do. A few thoughts niggled at her all day. Now alone in the quiet of her room, she needed to seriously consider what might be done about those bothersome thoughts.

The next morning, Mary rose early and went directly to the small office in the store. She hadn't attended to the bookwork the night before and wanted to get this done before the store opened for the day. It didn't take very long and, when she had finished, she went upstairs to attend to breakfast. James eventually appeared for breakfast, but remained sullen and uncommunicative.

When she returned downstairs, Alfred was just opening the store. She asked him to complete his own work as quickly as possible as a priority as she would be requiring him to mind the store while she went out to attend to other business this morning. About an hour later, Alfred came through to the store to tell her he had completed all of the orders for the day. Mary quickly grabbed her hat and bag from the office and, on her way out of the store, told Alfred she might not return before lunch.

Her first port of call was the hospital to check up on her daughter. As she made her way down the corridor, she met Dr Boyle coming out of one of the side rooms.

"On your way in to see Ellen?" he asked.

"I'm so glad we've met this morning. How are my daughter and grandson progressing? Please tell me the truth; I want to know exactly what the situation is."

"Ellen is much improved and is progressing very nicely. However, the little fellow is not doing so well. He was very distressed and quite exhausted by the time we got him out and, so far, he has not responded to our treatment. He continues to weaken, and I hold grave concerns that he might not survive until tomorrow."

"Does my daughter know?"

"Yes, like her mother, Ellen insists on knowing the truth of the situation. She has sent a message to the vicar to come to baptise the boy. If you're not in a hurry to leave, you might like to be present. The vicar should be here shortly."

Mary thanked him and went through to see her daughter who definitely looked much stronger than the previous day. Ellen told her mother of the plans to have her new son baptised that morning. "I don't have anyone to be his godfather, but a couple of the nurses have agreed to be his godmothers. I suppose, in reality, it's all just a formality anyway. They don't expect him to survive. I hope you don't mind, but I always intended that, if it were a boy, I would name him Richard in honour of my brother. Despite that name seeming unlucky for our family, he will be christened Richard William Jennings."

Although she hadn't intended to dally too long at the hospital this morning, Mary stayed on until after her grandson was baptised before taking her leave and crossing the street to Mrs Smith's tearoom. After having settled the account for her and Dr Robinson, Mary made her way down to Mr Taylor's office. She did not have an appointment but hoped he might make an exception and see her if she waited.

Mr Taylor's father had been her family's solicitor for a number of years and, when his son took over the practice, he also inherited his father's clients. Both father and son had held a soft spot for Mary. There were very few women in the area who could boast having their own solicitor and Mary was one of them. The Taylor's legal firm did not represent James Grimsby – he used another legal firm in town – but the Taylors did represent Mary… and the Taylors had always considered it a wise move for the Grimsbys to have separate representation.

There was a client waiting to see him, but Taylor asked Mary to wait as he thought the client's business would only take a few minutes. About twenty minutes later, Mr Taylor showed her into his office. Mary quickly explained the reason for her visit and her solicitor advised her of a number of actions he believed she should take. After only a short time, they both emerged from the office. Mr Taylor carried a case containing documents as he escorted Mary to the bank.

They spent about half an hour with the bank manager before Mary and Mr Taylor parted company on the street. He returned to his office. Mary wasn't inclined to go back to the store. It was now well past lunch time so there was no need to rush. She decided to call in to Mrs Smith's teashop instead. After a pot of tea and delicate ham sandwiches, Mary crossed the street to the hospital for another quick visit with her daughter. No one was about as she made her way to Ellen's room.

Mary's heart froze as she entered the room. Her daughter, propped up in bed, nursed a tiny bundle and silently wept. Ellen looked up as Mary came in. "It won't be long now," she said simply.

She rushed to Ellen's side. The tiny bundle barely breathed. Mary drew a chair up beside the bed and sat with her daughter. Suddenly Ellen sobbed loudly. The tiny bundle had stopped breathing. Baby Richard was deceased. For the next few minutes, everything happened in a blur. Dr Boyle was there. He took the baby and gave it to a nurse, and then gave Ellen something to make her sleep. Then Mary was alone with her daughter. She held Ellen's hand until she fell asleep.

After kissing her daughter gently on the forehead, Mary left the hospital and made her way back to the store, calling in at the undertaker's and the church on the way. She spoke to Alfred as she entered the store. "Is Mr Grimsby in the agency?"

"Yes, Ma'am."

"I need to speak to him. Would you mind staying on in here for a few moments longer, please?" Alfred nodded and Mary continued through the store and into the agency.

James was alone, so she said what she had come to tell him. "Your grandson is deceased. Baby Richard died this afternoon. His funeral is tomorrow afternoon. The store will close for the afternoon. You may make your own arrangements about the agency."

Turning on her heel, she went back to the store to relieve Alfred who bolted through to the backroom to put together an order for collection very soon after. The store remained quiet until closing time. Mary closed up and then went into the office to take care of the bookwork. She didn't want to have to come downstairs again after dinner. Alfred loaded the supplies onto the farmer's wagon and then popped his head into the office to tell Mary he was going to work on for a bit to get an order together as a wagon would call for it first thing in the morning.

The day's accounts showed it had been a good day in spite of her absence. With nothing more to do downstairs, Mary wearily plodded upstairs to the kitchen. She had just brought the lamb chops stew to a simmer when James startled her as he came into the kitchen.

"I need to go out for a while. I shouldn't be more than half an hour or so. Will it affect dinner?"

No, not at all. Dinner will take at least that long before it is ready."

After dinner, James took the day's newspaper through to the sitting room while Mary cleaned up the kitchen and then went to her room. She felt physically and emotionally drained as she lay on her bed. Tomorrow will be yet another difficult day, she told herself. Will life ever return to normal, she wondered. Will this family ever experience happiness again?

Chapter 7

As soon as Mary opened the store the next morning, she went in search of Alfred. A wagon parked at the loading ramp to collect supplies and Alfred was busy loading it. She asked him to see her as soon as he finished. A few minutes later, he joined her in the store. Mary briefly explained the events of the last couple of days. "So, the baby's funeral is this afternoon. The store will close for the afternoon. I am not sure what Mr Grimsby plans to do about the agency. If you have orders to fill, you may work out the back or you may go home."

"If it were all right with you, I should quite like to go to the funeral."

"You would be most welcome, Alfred. Now, we had better get on with our duties so that we have everything in hand by the time we close for the afternoon."

Mr Woodrow and Mr Wallace called during the morning to enquire after Ellen. Frank Woodrow, the Southend Mill manager, had called once before to ask Ellen how she was managing. Mr Wallace's farm adjoined the mill estate, with only a fence separating part of his property from Ellen's former backyard. When the Wallaces' grandchildren came to visit, they and the Jennings children often played together. Mr and Mrs Wallace got to know Ellen quite well and were fond of her. Mary apprised them of recent events, adding that the baby's funeral was this afternoon. She was deeply moved when both men attended the funeral. James also was there, although they did not go together. He closed the agency for the time he was at the funeral but re-opened it after returning from the cemetery.

Baby Richard was laid to rest next to his father. Few people attended the funeral. After the burial, those who had made the trip to the cemetery came up and spoke to Mary. As the last one drifted away, Alfred took Mary's arm and led her back to the wagon. There remained a couple of hours of normal trading time left after they arrived back at the store. Mary elected not to reopen the store and, as Alfred had no pending orders, she suggested he take the rest of the afternoon off.

Ellen remained in hospital for another ten days. Mary visited her every day. For some weeks following Ellen's release from hospital, she needed to rest for most of the day, and after that, there was a further period when there was to be no lifting of anything heavy. During her first few weeks at home, Ellen spent most of her time upstairs taking care of the cooking and lighthouse work, and only venturing downstairs in the evening to attend to the bookwork. While time seem to drag for Ellen, her mother was kept busy in the store, as was Alfred, and for them time seemed to fly past.

After Easter, Ellen started to spend more time in the store during the day, allowing her mother to rest for most of the afternoon. Early one morning at the beginning of May, Ellen went to check on something with Alfred and found him loading the store's wagon in readiness for making deliveries. There seemed to be an enormous amount of supplies on the wagon and she asked Alfred where they were all going.

"Those bags at the end there – flour, sugar, potatoes and onions – they are for Ludbrook Farm. The rest of the supplies are for the orphanage."

"You're going to the orphanage this morning? Would I be able to ride along with you?"

"That's not for me to say, but I don't have a problem with it if you want to come along."

"Would you wait just a few moments, please, while I get my hat and tell Mrs Grimsby what I'm doing?"

Ellen ran into the office, grabbed her sun hat and her bag, and paused by the counter on her way out to tell her mother she was taking a ride out to the orphanage on the wagon. Alfred was already sitting on the wagon waiting for her and they set off immediately Ellen settled herself beside him. Neither spoke until they were outside the town area.

"Where is Ludbrook Farm?" Ellen asked.

"It's just a couple of farms before we reach the orphanage. We won't stop there long; just long enough to unload those bags and we'll be on our way again."

Silence settled over the wagon again. Ellen's mind was working overtime: what would the children be like after all this time? Would they remember her? Would they be happy to see her or would they blame her for what their life had become? How hard would this reunion be? She knew the two youngest girls would not understand or remember much, but the older two – young William and Marion

– deserved an explanation, particularly about what had happened to their awaited new sibling.

They pulled up under the trees at the rear of the Homestead on Ludbrook Farm, and Alfred unloaded the bags of supplies and took them inside. Time began to drag on as he and the cook engaged in conversation just outside the kitchen door. Ellen grew impatient to be on their way. Alfred, casually glancing in her direction, caught Ellen's stony glare and quickly wound up his conversation with the cook. Climbing back on board the wagon, he apologised for the delay.

"That's fine, Alfred, but could we move on now please. I don't want to arrive at the orphanage when they're in the middle of their lunch, or something else is happening which does not allow the children to meet with me."

It took little time to cover the distance to the orphanage. Alfred dropped Ellen in front of the main building and waited while she spoke to one of the nuns. The nun disappeared into the complex and was soon on her way back with the children in tow. Ellen sat with her children under one of the big trees adjacent to the main house while Alfred took the wagon around to the back of the building to unload the supplies. He was gone for quite some time, later admitting he accepted an invitation to join the kitchen staff for morning tea. He had lingered as long as he dared in the kitchen to allow Ellen as much time as possible with the children, but eventually found he was beginning to outlive his welcome and returned to collect Ellen.

The children appeared healthy and well cared for. They chatted on about their new friends and life at the orphanage in general. Ellen detected no recriminations directed at her for leaving them at the orphanage. She explained about baby Richard and, while the two older children looked sad and expressed sympathy, she knew the reality was, that what she had told them had little impact, as they didn't fully comprehend. Not surprising I suppose, she told herself. After all, in the end, they had no real connection with the new baby.

Soon it was time to leave. There were hugs and kisses all round – and some tears. A young nun gently herded the children back into the complex while one of the older nuns stood beside Ellen. The older nun put her arm around Ellen's waist, turned her around and gently walked her towards where Alfred waited with the wagon.

She quietly counselled Ellen as they walked. "Don't be fretting about the children. They have settled in well and made new friends. It may seem harsh but, a few minutes after you've gone, they will be back playing with their friends; life will return to normal. It's not that they will forget you. It's just that you're leaving will only upset them for a few minutes. So, don't be distressing yourself about upsetting them. They are fine, and you will find that, if you make future visits, your departure afterwards will not even bring tears."

If the nun was trying to make her feel relieved or reassured, it hadn't worked. Tears still trickled down her face as she climbed aboard the wagon. She sat rigid and silent until they had almost reached the outskirts of the town again. Alfred glanced in her direction several times, but knew to hold his tongue until Ellen spoke. Finally, she spoke very quietly and without looking at him.

"Do you make deliveries to the orphanage often?"

"Usually once a month throughout the year; except for maybe during the wet season, when the road becomes impassable."

"Is there a set arrangement, or how do you know when to go?"

"That priest up at the Catholic Church has something to do with the running of the orphanage. He spends some days out there every week and usually comes back into town on Thursdays. Then, soon after the start of each month, on a Friday, he brings an order into the store for supplies for the orphanage. Friday, Saturday and Monday are usually my busiest days. That's when landowners are in town and collect their supplies to take home with them. So, it is usually Tuesday before it is quiet enough for me to leave the store to deliver to the orphanage – unless a Monday is quiet and I can go then."

"Would it be a problem if I rode out to the orphanage with you whenever you made deliveries to them?"

"Like I said before, it's not for me to say, but it would be no problem for me if you were to ride on the wagon with me."

This was the first bit of good news she had in months. Once the three months settling in period the nuns required had elapsed Ellen had wracked her brain about how to visit the orphanage. She was perfectly capable of hitching up the wagon and driving herself out there, but she knew her father would object and would probably refuse on some pretext or other to let her take the wagon. At least this way – going out with Alfred when he made deliveries – she would get to see the children once a month. After returning to the store that day, she discussed the matter with her mother and received her approval.

Life at the store settled in to a steady rhythm. Ellen spent all day in the store and attended to the bookwork in the evening. Her mother gradually increased the time she spent upstairs. Initially only having a couple of hours rest after lunch, over the next few months, Mary spent less time in the store and more time upstairs. Ellen held growing concerns as, in spite of lightening her mother's load, Mary was becoming more tired and worn out looking. In response to her daughter's concern, in October, Mary finally relented and visited Dr Boyle. If he found anything seriously amiss, he didn't mention it, instead prescribing a tonic and rest as all that was required.

Some sort of détente seemed to have settled between her parents. Cordial to one another when needed, but they lived separate lives. Their only communication appeared to be when they needed to discuss something to do with the business. Nevertheless, the situation improved for Ellen. While most of the time, her father chose to ignore her now, she no longer felt persecuted by him. Ellen tried to discuss the change in him with her mother, but Mary brushed it aside and refused to offer any comment.

Again, Christmas that year was no joyful event. The two women went to church without James. Ellen prepared a traditional Christmas spread for lunch, which her father tucked into with gusto. However, she noticed her mother barely picked at the food. As she cleaned up after lunch she thought about her mother's lack of interest in the lunch and realised that, over the last few weeks, her mother ate very little and appeared to have no appetite. Ellen tried broaching the subject of Mary's poor appetite with her mother before dinner that evening but it was a wasted effort. Her mother insisted Ellen was mistaken and that there was no problem.

Early in the New Year, Alfred was putting together a list of supplies to take to the orphanage. Ellen was excited. She had gone with Alfred every month to visit the children but was disappointed she couldn't see them at Christmas. She had little presents for each of them: ribbons for their hair for the girls and a pretty little lace handkerchief for each of them, and a handkerchief and socks for young William.

She was surprised at the amount of supplies Alfred loaded on the wagon, but assumed some of it might be for delivery to other proper-ties along the way. It wasn't until they were some way down the road that she asked Alfred about the load they were carrying and who it was all for. Alfred's response was a bit disconcerting.

"It's all for the orphanage. I know it looks like a lot this time, but they usually get a big order at the start of each year. Once the wet season starts, the roads become impassable and we won't be able to get supplies through to them. So, they order up big before that happens to ensure they've got enough to see them through."

From Alfred's information, Ellen deduced there might be some period of time when her routine visits to the orphanage couldn't occur. I should explain that to the children, she told herself, so they understand that I might not be able to visit from time to time and they know I haven't just abandoned them again. They spent quite some time at the orphanage that day. Alfred had a lot to unload and, of course, he felt obliged to accept the kitchen staff's hospitality.

The wet season set in the following week and continued for weeks on end. It was the end of February before the levels in the flooded creeks dropped sufficiently to clear water from the roads. It would be the better part of another two weeks before the road to the orphanage dried out sufficiently for a loaded wagon not to bog. At the first opportunity, Alfred announced he would be taking a big order of supplies to the orphanage.

Ellen checked with her mother that Mary would be able to manage the store while she did the run out to the orphanage with Alfred. Mary said she would be all right, but Ellen detected a hint of hesitancy in Mary's response. However, when she questioned her mother about it, Mary told her quite emphatically that she should go with Alfred.

It was Wednesday before they got away, but Alfred was determined to make the delivery as the humid weather suggested more rain was coming. Not having to stop anywhere along the way, they made good time to the orphanage. A nun bought the three girls out to meet their mother. Ellen felt her stomach tightened. Where was young William? She asked the young nun. "Where is my son? I haven't met you before. Perhaps you are new and didn't realise I have a son as well. Young William should come to meet me with his sisters. Please fetch my son as well." The nun looked confused and, after hesitating for a moment, went into the main building. She returned moments later accompanied by the senior nun who dismissed the younger woman as they made their way to where Ellen was waiting.

"Sister Josephine tells me you were asking for your son."

Ellen nodded and said, "Yes, my eldest child, my son, William Jennings."

"I'm sorry Mrs Jennings, but your son is no longer with us. He left us shortly after New Year. Surely you realise he couldn't stay here forever. He was already nine years of age and more than capable of going to work."

Ellen felt the breath knocked out of her. She demanded to know what happened to her son and, more importantly, why nobody had conferred with her before it had happened. The nun seemed impervious to Ellen's distress, and simply pointed out that it was routine procedure.

"We can't afford to keep children here forever. Once they're old enough to go out to work, if someone is looking for a young lad for their business or property, we arrange for one of our wards to take up the position. William has a great opportunity. A Selector was looking for a young lad to work on his property and to train him to take over greater responsibilities as he becomes older. There were two or three boys suitable at the time, but William was the lucky one chosen. You should be pleased for your child instead of standing here creating a fuss."

"You didn't even think it was necessary – or even a courtesy – to let me know what was happening?"

"It wasn't necessary to do so. That is how this orphanage operates and has done since its establishment. If that arrangement was not to your liking, perhaps you should have found some other solution for the problem of what to do with your children."

"What about my daughters? Am I likely to visit at some time in the future and find that one by one they also have disappeared from the orphanage?"

"That is quite possible. Now, if there is nothing else you wish to speak about, I have duties that require my attention. I suggest you take your leave at this point in time so as not to upset the children by your demeanour." With that, the nun gathered the children together and herded them back into the complex, leaving Ellen standing alone and stunned under the tree where she always met with the children.

She knew Alfred would do his best to stretch the visit as long as possible so she could make the most of her time with the children. Because of this, he wasn't likely to return to collect her just yet. Ellen made her way around to the back of the building and, seeing the wagon parked some distance away, walked briskly towards it.

Alfred was surprised when he saw Ellen arrive at the wagon. He was standing in the kitchen, mug of tea in hand, chatting to the kitchen staff when she suddenly appeared outside. He abandoned his mug on the kitchen bench and rushed out to the wagon. There was no need to ask what was going on. It was clear something had gone very wrong. Ellen looked pale and tears gushed down her face to drip onto the bodice of her frock. Without a word, Alfred took her arm and helped her up onto the wagon before quickly running around the wagon and climbing onto the driver's seat. He urged the horses on and left the orphanage at a considerably faster speed than normal.

Ellen wept brokenheartedly all the way back to the store. As there had been no conversation, Alfred didn't know what happened at the orphanage. He brought the wagon to a halt at the back of the store as usual, but Ellen made no move to dismount. He ran around to the other side of the wagon and offered to help her down. It was as if he didn't exist. Ellen just sat there weeping, and not responding in any way to Alfred's encouragement for her to come down from the wagon.

He didn't know what to do. Maybe there wasn't anything he could do. He rushed into the store to find Mary. "Something terrible happened at the orphanage today. I don't know what it was, but your daughter has cried all the way home, and now refuses to come down from the wagon. What's to be done? I have tried talking to her but it was to no avail."

Mary had been dusting some shelves. On hearing Alfred's story, she dropped her duster and ran out to the wagon. Ellen just ignored her mother when Mary tried talking to her, so Mary climbed up onto the wagon and sat beside her daughter. Alfred felt embarrassed. He was trying to work out what he should do when Mary gave him a signal that should go inside and leave the two women alone. He was on his way into the store when he heard Ellen's anguished cry followed by loud sobbing.

Alfred didn't see either of the women again for the rest of the day. Mary finally managed to coax Ellen down from the wagon and took her directly to her bedroom. Alfred was closing up at the end of the day when James walked through the store and queried where the women were. Alfred just shrugged and indicated he thought they were upstairs. He heard James clomping up the stairs and he couldn't help but wonder what would be waiting for James when he arrived upstairs… and, more importantly, how James would cope with the situation.

Chapter 8

Ellen didn't appear in the store the next day but, by the following day, life appeared to return to normal. Then the long established rhythm and routine of the store continued largely uninterrupted for the next few months. The only real change to occur was the increasing absence of Mrs Grimsby from the store. As winter progressed, Mary's time in the store each day decreased. By the beginning of October, the only time she spent in the store was when she took over while Ellen had lunch or when Ellen was absent from the store for any reason.

Alfred had not seen Mary for a few weeks as he had been busy elsewhere whenever she came down to the store. That morning, Ellen left the store early to attend to some personal business somewhere in town. Mary looked after the store while her daughter was away. About mid-morning, she went out back to give Alfred an order to make-up. The sight of Mary shocked him to the core. She was frail and pale, and seemed considerably shrunken. Out of concern, he suggested, "Mrs Grimsby, if you would prefer to go upstairs to rest, I can mind the store. I'm not particularly busy today, and this order you gave me is for collection tomorrow, so I have plenty of time to get it ready before then."

Mary thanked him but insisted she was okay to manage the store until Ellen's return. Alfred got on with getting together the order she gave him, but kept an eye out for Ellen's return. Not too much later, he heard Ellen's voice talking to her mother, followed by the sound of slow, heavy footsteps climbing the stairs. He waited for a few moments after the footsteps ceased before entering the store. Ellen was serving a customer, so Alfred tidied a shelf until the customer left and he could speak with Ellen.

"You might tell me it's none of my business, but is Mrs Grimsby all right?"

"Why do you ask? Did something happen while I was away?"

"No, it's nothing like that, only I got a bit of a shock when I saw her today. I hadn't seen her for quite a while. I couldn't believe she was the same woman. Has Mrs Grimsby been ill or something? She seems to have aged years since I last saw her."

"I do not know, Alfred. The doctor hasn't been able to find what is wrong with her. He says he can't find anything, and thinks she may be suffering from exhaustion after all her years of hard work."

"Do you agree with that?"

"No, I don't think I do any more. Although she has not said anything, last night I saw her wince slightly as if she experienced a pain… at least, I think that's what I saw. It was very quick. I was planning to have a firm talk with her tonight. Thank you for your concern, Alfred."

After she finished everything else that evening, Ellen knocked gently on her mother's door and went in to sit beside Mary's bed. Mary looked worse tonight. Ellen fought back her guilt at having left her mother to run the store that morning.

"Mother, we need to talk. I am very worried about you. Alfred also is concerned for you. He has asked after your health. It's way past time we had an honest talk about your situation. However, before we do, I am telling you now that you will not be working in the store in future. Alfred and I will manage without you. There will be no argument about that. Now, tell me about what is going on with you."

"I don't know what you're on about. Nothing is going on with me. I…"

"That's enough, Mother. I said we would have an honest talk, and I will not leave this room until I believe that has happened. You do not eat, you are fading away and I think you are in some pain – maybe not all the time, but at least some of the time."

Mary raised her chin defiantly as she prepared to dispute her daughter's comments, but Ellen's steely gaze caused her to rethink that approach. With eyes downcast and her bony hands continuing to gather the bedsheet into a tight knot, Mary chose her response carefully.

"It is true that Dr Boyle is uncertain of the nature of my condition. It is worsening and I am experiencing pain more frequently. Most of the time these pains are not severe but, in the last few days, there have been occasions when they have been quite severe. I cannot deny it any longer. I have to accept something is radically wrong with my stomach. I don't eat, not because I don't want to, but because my stomach won't take the food."

"There must be something we can do. If it is beyond Dr Boyle's knowledge, maybe we should be talking to someone else. Perhaps we should go to one of the southern cities where there are more learned physicians."

"My dear daughter, your care and concern lift my spirits, but no. Going elsewhere will not provide an answer – or a cure." Mary held up her hand to stop Ellen interrupting. "No, let me finish. I know my end is coming and I have accepted that this is what has been ordained for me by a power greater than any doctor. I am truly sorry I will not be around to support and help you, but my fate is out of my hands. All I ask is that you stay with me until it is over."

Ellen tried to speak but all that came out was a loud sob. She took a few breaths and swallowed hard before trying again. "Of course I won't leave you, but you must tell me how I can make things more comfortable for you."

They did not talk for much longer. Mary was growing tired and Ellen desperately needed time alone to come to terms with her mother's news. After bidding her mother goodnight, Ellen went directly to her room. She cried herself to sleep that night after questioning long and hard why fate chose to take her mother when Mary should still have many years ahead of her, and why fate kept dealing her the hand it did. Ellen whispered to the empty room, "Haven't I suffered enough? What did I do to deserve what I have been through? Now you choose to make me suffer further by taking my mother. Whatever I might have done, why make my mother suffer because of it?"

…And then she silently prayed – not something she was prone to doing – offering her life in place of her mother's if Mary's life be spared, but she knew that was not how things worked. That's when the tears began and continued until she fell asleep.

The next few months were heartbreaking. Mary's condition deteriorated as her pain became more intense and constant. Alfred had to spend more time than before in the store as Ellen spent more and longer periods during each day caring for her mother.

Christmas 1897 came and went with no break with tradition. Surprisingly, Mary seemed to be holding her own and, by late February, Ellen found herself wondering if Dr Boyle had been wrong. However, such thoughts gradually evaporated as Mary again began spending less time out of bed each day. Her energy level declined and food intake became worryingly low. The household menu changed to include more stews, gravies and soups in an effort to increase Mary's food intake.

More bad news came early in the new year. Once the wet season rains eased a little, some of the roads became accessible but difficult to negotiate. As soon as the road to the orphanage became passable, Alfred received a substantial order for supplies. Ellen was no longer able to accompany Alfred on his delivery runs to the orphanage. Mary and the store now filled her every waking hour. Desperate for her children not to think she had abandoned them, Ellen put together a few bits and pieces in a little parcel for each child. These she entrusted Alfred to deliver to the children.

On his return from his delivery to the orphanage, Alfred reluctantly went to talk to Ellen. He fiddled with items on a shelf near the counter while he waited for her to finish with a customer. Then, after a deep breath, he slowly walked over to the Ellen.

"What is it, Alfred? You have me concerned. By the look of you, something has gone seriously wrong. Was something wrong with the orphanage's order?"

"No, Miss, the order was as required. The problem was with the children…"

"The children … what had happened to them?"

"No, nothing; they are fine, I believe."

"What do you mean by that?"

"They – the nuns – would not let me see the children. I tried everything I could think of to change their minds but they still refused. In the end, I gave them your packages and asked that they make sure the children received them. I'm sorry, Miss. It was the best I could do."

"What nonsense. I do not like that place or the way they run it. …But I have no other options for my children's care at this time. Alfred, would you mind the store for me, please. I need to go out. I might be away for a half hour or so." Alfred nodded; Ellen donned her hat, grabbed her bag, and was out of the store in the space of a few heartbeats. She hurried down the street to the Catholic Church and demanded to see the Priest who seemed to be involved with running the orphanage.

Father Christie seemed none too pleased to see her, but showed Ellen into a small room containing a couple of chairs and a small table. "What brings you here, Mrs Jennings? You appear somewhat upset."

Ellen wasted no time in getting to the point of her visit, including letting it him know how disappointed she was with the way the orphanage was run. When she was finished her tirade, Father Christie spent some time calming her down and endeavouring to find some way forward that met with Ellen's approval.

In the end, they agreed Ellen would write letters to the children and address them to Marion. Alfred would take them with him whenever he made a delivery to the orphanage. Marion, Ellen's eldest daughter who could read and write, could read them to her sisters before penning a reply to her mother. Marion must be allowed to write to Ellen. Father Christie agreed to ensure implementation of the arrangement happened according to their agreement and that Marion was able to write to her mother.

Not entirely happy with the arrangement, Ellen accepted it was the best she could achieve. She spent the time taken to walk back to the store coming to terms with the fact that her situation had not improved any since moving back in with her parents, and that she was no closer to getting her children back than she was all those months ago.

*****

Towards the end of April, Mary embarked on one of her rare trips down the stairs to the store. Her progress was slow with measured steps. Alfred saw her and raced up the stairs to assist her. He met her about half down the stairs.

"Thank you, Alfred. Now I don't have to come all the way down to speak to you." Mary handed an envelope to Alfred. "Please deliver this to Mr Taylor, the solicitor, at your first opportunity. Mind now, I don't want Miss Grimsby aware. So, if you could deliver it sometime soon without her knowledge, I would be most grateful." Alfred slipped the envelope inside his jacket.

"I have to make a delivery to the hotel later today; I will deliver it then."

With difficulty, Mary turned and started back up the stairs. Alfred supported her for the first couple of stairs before Mary stopped.

"No, Alfred. I will be fine. Go back to your work. I don't want my daughter getting curious about what is going on out here."

About mid-morning, Alfred told Ellen he was taking supplies to the hotel, drove off and parked the wagon in the horse yard at the rear of the hotel. After unloading the supplies, he made his way onto the street via the laneway between the hotel and its neighbouring building that housed the solicitor's rooms. He had never been to a solicitor's office before. Straightening his jacket and removing his cap, Alfred tentatively pushed open the door to enter the outer office.

The tiny room held only a few chairs along one wall and a solitary desk occupied by a young-looking clerk. Mr Taylor came out of his office and stood beside the clerk as they discussed some papers on the clerk's desk. Both men looked up. Mr Taylor spoke. "Yes, what is it, lad?"

"Begging your pardon, Sir, would you be Mr Taylor?"

"I am Taylor, and I am busy. Please state your business."

"Please, sir, I have a letter for you from Mrs Grimsby."

Mr Taylor took the offered letter and opened it immediately. He read it quickly and then looked up at Alfred. "Well, lad, was there something else?"

"Will there be a reply, Sir? Mrs Grimsby did not say if I should expect one."

"Ah, well done, boy. If you will wait a few moments, I will pen a reply for you to take back."

With the reply safely in his pocket, Alfred made his way back to the store. He checked the out front. Ellen was busy with a couple of customers. As quietly as he could, he quickly made his way up the stairs and knocked on the door. Mary opened the door and took the letter, and Alfred retraced his steps. He was amazed at how guilty he felt about what he perceived as deceiving Ellen about what he did for her mother, but Mrs Grimsby was the boss, he told himself.

Later that afternoon, Mr Taylor arrived and asked to see Mary. Ellen called Alfred to mind the store and then led Mr Taylor upstairs. She was surprised to find Mary seated at the kitchen table. After welcoming Mr Taylor, she spoke quietly to Ellen. "Perhaps a pot of tea and some biscuits for me and my guest, please, before you return to the store."

As Ellen set the table while she waited for the kettle to boil, she made to set herself a place as well. Mary leaned over and spoke quietly to her daughter as Ellen set the third cup and saucer on the table. "No, my dear; this is a private meeting. You should return to the store when you have poured the tea."

Ellen was about to protest, but her mother's look stopped her and she did as she was asked. Back in the store, Ellen kept an eye on the time. Mr Taylor's visit seemed to be taking an inordinately long time. It was more than two hours later before Mr Taylor bid her good afternoon as he was on his way out of the store.

It was the following week when Mr Taylor again visited the store and asked to see Mary. On this occasion, his visit was shorter and Ellen, busy with a customer at the time, saw him come down the stairs about 15 minutes after she had taken him up to Mary. A couple of days later, Mary again sent Alfred on a covert mission to deliver another note to Mr Taylor. The following day, Mr Taylor again came to see Mary, and this time he brought his clerk with him.

While Mr Taylor and Mary went over the document the solicitor delivered a couple of days earlier, the clerk went downstairs to fetch Alfred. When all four people – Mr Taylor, his clerk, Mary and Alfred – were gathered around the kitchen table, Mr Taylor outlined the reason for their visit: to witness the signing of Mary's new will. He explained to Alfred and the clerk that they were not required to know the contents of the will. They were there simply to witness Mary's signature and sign to that effect. As soon as everyone had signed the will, Alfred slipped quietly back downstairs. Mr Taylor and his clerk left the store about an hour after they arrived.

This rash of visits by the solicitor piqued Ellen's curiosity and, although she asked a few carefully worded questions, Mary quite pointedly refused to tell her anything about what was going on. On the off chance that Alfred might have seen or heard something that might explain the visits, she quizzed him as well. She got no joy from that either. Both Mary and Mr Taylor stressed most strongly about not mentioning as much as one word to anyone about the matter. Nevertheless, Ellen's curiosity persisted. On one occasion, Alfred found himself uncomfortable in Ellen's presence as she wondered aloud about what was going on. He decided to change the subject by raising with Ellen a concern that troubled him for a couple of days.

"I haven't seen Mr Grimsby around for a couple of days. Is everything all right with him?" he asked Ellen. "I'm not prying like, but it's just that after what I've been hearing, I was a bit worried about him."

"What do you mean by 'what you've been hearing'? What have you been hearing, Alfred? Does it have something to do with my father?"

"Well yes, Miss, but it's only rumour mind – pub talk, you know. It's not that I know anything for sure."

"I understand it's probably nothing more than gossip, but you had better tell me anyway."

"Uhm, well, word is that Mr Grimsby has been spending a lot of time with that young Mrs Nielsen – you know, the young widow. Word has it that the affair has been going for a few months, and that Mr Grimsby hinted that they were planning to start a new life."

"That's ridiculous, Alfred. What would she see in him? She's not half his age… and I hear her husband left her well enough off to manage on her own. Although, now you mention it, I did hear some talk that she might be thinking of leaving town. Is there any more to this ridiculous story?"

"Sorry, Miss, I don't mean to upset you. There is a bit more. It's what everyone in the pub was having a giggle about. Turns out Mr Grimsby missed out. Did you ever meet that agricultural machinery salesman that came to town occasionally? You know the one, that smarmy good looking bloke."

"If you mean that debonair salesman that comes to see Mr Grimsby occasionally, yes, I've met him."

"I hear women do call him 'suave' … but that's the one I'm talking about. Anyway, turns out Mrs Nielsen thought he was a better bet and ran off with him last weekend. Seems Mr Grimsby was none too pleased, got drunk and made a bit of a scene over it at his club. I haven't seen Mr Grimsby around since and I was hoping he was okay."

"As I said, Alfred, it is all nonsense spread about by men with nothing better to do than stand around in a pub dreaming up gossip, their imaginations fuelled by alcohol. Let's hear no more about it, shall we?"

With a swish of her skirts, Ellen marched off; her head held high but her mind in turmoil. She hadn't seen her father this week – although that didn't mean much. James had become something of an 'invisible lodger'. She hadn't spoken to him either in weeks. They never seemed to be in the same room at the same time. Even at mealtimes, they ate separately. He ate alone while she was busy feeding and caring for her mother. Later, she ate alone when her father had either gone to his room or gone out again. However, she sensed he was spending very little time at home and assumed he was spending it at his precious club. She was aware he was spending little time in the agency. Alfred struggled to do his own job as he was spending so much time minding the agency in her father's absence. Could it be true that the young widow had occupied his time?

Chapter 9

By early-June, the situation in the store had become impossible. James was notable by his absence; some days not even managing to open the agency. Alfred continued to try to run the agency as well as do his own job. Ellen put in place a new policy. When her father wasn't around, they would close the agency's door and open the connecting door between the store and the agency. All agency customers would have to come in through the store and deal with her – or Alfred if he was covering for her while she attended to her mother.

It only took a couple of weeks to become obvious the arrangement didn't work. Ellen decided she needed help in the store. After obtaining her mother's approval, she asked Alfred if he knew of anyone who might be suitable so she might avoid the process of placing an advertisement in the paper and then dealing with applicants. He recommended Jess Adams who currently worked for Swayne's Store, Grimsby's opposition in town. Ellen was reluctant to consider poaching someone, even from the opposition. Alfred set her mind at ease. After working there for a few years, Jess received notice and was due to finish up at Swayne's at the end of the week.

Ellen almost rejected Alfred's recommendation out of hand. "Why has she been given notice? If she has been there for all that time, why would they suddenly decide to let her go? Is she guilty of some misdemeanour?"

Alfred sprang to Jess' defence. Nothing untoward had happened. "You know about what's going on at Swayne's, don't you?" he asked. Ellen looked confused and shook her head. She decided it was a good time for morning tea. They took tea in the small office from where they could keep an eye on the store while Alfred brought her up to date on the Swayne's Store saga.

Ellen thought for a moment, "I remember old Ned Swayne's store from years ago. I think it was just before I married, he bought the shop next door and turned it into a farmers' agency, and then did some renovations. I think it was to join the two shops together to make one large building. His wife died round about the same time, as I recall. I think there was one son – only the one child. I assume that's who has the shop now that old Ned is gone."

"Yeah; Gilbert is his name. The old man brought him home a short time before he died and, of course he inherited the lot, but didn't know the first thing about running a business," Alfred explained.

"I don't remember much of the son," Ellen said, wrinkling her brow as she trawled through her memories. "I don't think he spent any of his adult life here; was down south somewhere, living off his father's generous allowance, if my memory serves me correctly."

"He was in Sydney for a long time; married a girl down there and lived with her parents. His father-in-law was some big wig in government or something… plenty of money, a big house and all that. When old Ned got sick, he asked Gilbert to come home to start taking over the business, and threatened to cut off his allowance when his son refused. Word has it, the threat worked and that's when Gilbert, with wife and two kids came back to town."

"Well, at least the son had some time with his father to learn about the business. I can't imagine it was an easy transition for him after the lifestyle he'd had for all those years in Sydney."

Alfred laughed, "Nah, he came back all right, but didn't go to work in the store. People around here said he considered it below his dignity to be messing about with bags of potatoes and flour and the like. He spent his time with that Turf Club mob and eventually got a position as secretary of the club. It was only part-time mind, but one of the Turf Club blokes also got him a position as secretary of the local Farmers' Association. The two jobs together still left him with plenty of time to frequent that gentlemen's club on a daily basis."

"Poor old Ned. He was so sick at the end, I believe. He didn't deserve the worry of what might happen to the business after he was gone."

"Everyone says it was a sad state of affairs. Neither Gilbert nor his wife ever worked in their life before, and certainly knew nothing about running the store. For some time after Ned died, Gilbert didn't come into the store. The story was, he was contracted to the other two jobs and had to see the contracts through before he could take over running the store. That's when Jess and the other staff ran the place but, of course, they had no authority to order anything or pay bills, or anything to do with that side of the business, and the place started to run down."

"They are our only competitor in town, and Swayne's always appeared to be very prosperous. It is sad to see old Ned's legacy in such a state. I'm sure he must've worked so hard for so many years to build it up to the successful business it was. So, why would Jess be interested in finding another job? If the staff have been running Swayne's store, surely she must be invaluable to young Mr Swayne – as would be all of those old long-term employees."

"It's not really for me to be saying, Miss, but the word I hear around town is that the Bank is taking a fairly hard line with young Gilbert because of the state of his affairs. Mrs Swayne had a housekeeper and a part-time housemaid, as well as a nanny for the children. The nanny was let go some weeks ago. Mr Swayne said she was no longer required now that the children were both at school. Then, the part-time housemaid was told not to come any more. That left the housekeeper, Mrs Riley, having to do everything, and she is not a young woman any longer."

"I can see that perhaps the domestic help might be considered a luxury by a tough bank manager, but there would only be small savings from their dismissals. If things are as bad as you suggest they might be, surely the bank is looking for more positive measures to right the financial situation."

"Perhaps you are unaware of the staffing arrangements in the store. A couple of men – they have both been there a long time – sort of run the farmers' agency part of the business, while Jess and another young lad who she was training look after the general store side of things. There was also another man worked in the store room. I think his job was a bit like mine – except I don't think he ever worked in the store itself – and I think he also had a young lad as an offsider."

"Hmmm, that is quite a lot of staff. Their wages every week over a period of time would have been a considerable financial drain."

"Yeah, supposedly, that's why Swayne started getting rid of people. One of the blokes from the agency side of things finished up yesterday, the two young lads were finished up last week, and Jess is to finish up when the shop closes on Saturday. Mrs Riley, the housekeeper, told my mother that she couldn't do everything they expected of her and she couldn't stand by and watch the way the staff was treated." Alfred giggled, "She's a crafty old lady, that Mrs Riley. You might recall that two weeks ago there was that big Race Week Carnival. The Swayne's are very involved with all that Turf Club stuff and, during race week, there were all these other functions – balls and dinners and the like – for them to attend. They expected Mrs Riley to stay behind at night to look after the children until the parents came home from whatever function they attended. Mrs Riley gave her notice and walked out the day before Race Week started. She told my mother that Mrs Swayne couldn't even boil an egg or make a pot of tea."

"Oh dear, that could not have gone down well with the Swaynes, but I do see Mrs Riley's point of view. However, I'm not sure I support the way she went about things. If Gilbert is getting rid of all his staff, what's the word on the street about how Mr Swayne plans to run his business?"

"It's no secret, Miss. He told all the staff when he gave them their notice – and he's told all his mates – that he and his wife will run the business in the future. He is keeping Charlie Perkins on in the agency for some time to come. Mr Swayne apparently still has his contracts to complete, but he has told Charlie that, once Mr Swayne has completed those contracts, he will no longer have need for Charlie Perkins's services either. Apparently, Mr Swayne told Jess that Mrs Swayne would be running the store once Jess finished up. Mrs Swayne was supposed to spend this week with Jess learning the ropes, so to speak, but she hasn't come into the store once."

"Well then, it is in our best interest to talk to Jess as soon as possible. Mind you, she will have to measure up to the way we do business here. I need reliability and responsibility in anyone employed here, and we need to think about our customers and the service they're used to getting from this store. If, as you intimate, Miss Jess Adams is an acquaintance of yours, perhaps you could ascertain her interest in obtaining a position with this store. It would be fortuitous if you could speak to her after work today with a view to arranging for her to come for an interview tomorrow evening after work… that is, if she's interested of course."

First thing Thursday morning, Alfred sought out Ellen and announced that Jess Adams was very interested in coming to work at Grimsby's and would present herself for interview after work that evening. While delighted with the news, it threw Ellen into a spin. She needed to devise a couple of tests to ensure Jess met the standard expected of her at Grimsby's. Heaven knows what bad habits she might have picked up at Swayne's without adequate supervision.

The first test was easy: a role-play. Ellen would play the part of a customer whom Jess would need to serve. By late afternoon, Ellen had the second test worked out and was ready for Jess' interview. She, as the store manager, would hand Jess a customer's small order to make up. The scribbled note listed six items. Jess would have to gather the items ready for delivery and enter them on the customer's account.

Jess passed the tests with flying colours. On the first test, Jess demonstrated good service skills, accurately cut and weighed the cheese asked for, and correctly added up the bill and made change. Ellen was a little concerned about the second test. Jess had never been in the store before and might find it difficult to locate the items on the order. It proved not to be a problem. Most stores shelve like products together. Using this knowledge, Jess quickly sourced the items and accurately recorded the order on the account.

"Thank you for coming this evening, Jess, but it is getting late," Ellen said as she shepherded Jess out of the office and through to the back room. "We don't want you out alone at night. Alfred will walk you home, if that's okay with you." Jess nodded. "Okay, well off you go now. We'll see you first thing Monday morning, thanks Jess."

"You mean I've got the job?" Jess stammered.

"If you still want it, the job is yours," Ellen replied.

"Thank you. Yes, I do want it. I will be here on Monday morning."

As Alfred opened the back door to let Jess and himself out, Ellen noticed Alfred was beaming. She detected something more than happiness; pride perhaps. Yes, that was it. There was pride mixed with that happiness. Strange that Alfred should be so thrilled about a new employee starting with us, Ellen thought, but she didn't pay it too much attention. She was just relieved that managing the store and the agency would be easier come next week. Jess was nothing short of a godsend.

Ellen and Alfred weren't the only ones thrilled with what had transpired that evening. The following morning, Jess was at Swayne's early to start work. Mr Swayne didn't appear in the store until nearly ten o'clock. As soon as Jess finished serving the customer she was with, she rushed after Mr Swayne. "Excuse me, Mr Swayne, I want you to know that I will no longer be working for you."

"I am aware. If you recall, it was I that gave you notice to finish up at the close of Saturday trading."

"No, that's not what I meant, Sir. I will be finishing up at lunchtime. I will not be in tomorrow."

"If that's the case, you can go now. I no longer want you hanging around here. Collect your things and go."

"Thank you, Sir. I was hoping that's how you'd see it." With that, Jess snatched up her bag, said goodbye to Charlie Perkins as she marched out, without a backward glance. Later that evening, she recounted the story to Alfred.

"What happened with the store? Who took over when you walked out?"

"I don't know. Mrs Swayne wasn't anywhere about and he – Mr Swayne – wouldn't have a clue what to do. There haven't been many customers of late. I guess Charlie had to deal with any who came in after I left. Poor Charlie; I suspect he is going to be busy now."

"I am pleased you are having the day off tomorrow. You need a break. We are getting busier at Grimsby's, so a rest before you start there will be good."

*****

Jess settled in quickly and was comfortable in both the store and the agency. This was just as well for Ellen who found her mother requiring increased care as the weeks went by. By the end of August, Mary had few lucid moments each day. Early in September, Ellen waited in the kitchen for her father to return for dinner. They had not had any contact for weeks. Tonight, Mary was comfortable and not in need of attention for a while, leaving Ellen free to hand around in the kitchen instead of fussing over her mother.

When James had not come in by ten o'clock, Ellen went to get ready for bed. She was concerned. Perhaps he had found another woman. Ellen had not wanted to believe the pub gossip about her father and the widow Nielsen but some part of her believed it to be true. She pushed such thoughts out of her mind. Her father had come home every other night. His rinsed dinner plate was by the sink every morning. That only heightened her concern. Why was tonight different? The fact that she didn't talk to him tonight meant she would have to stay up late again tomorrow night – or every night – until she managed to catch up with him.

It was a couple of nights later when Ellen finally caught up with her father. She knew he came home the previous nights, but it must have been in the early hours of the morning as she had waited until midnight before giving up and going to bed. He was unapologetic about his behaviour.

"What I choose to do and when I choose to come and go is none of your concern. I am afraid you are developing ideas above your station in this household. You are here under sufferance and nothing more. That does not entitle you to any authority in what goes on in the household. So, what was so important that had you waiting up to speak to me?"

"I thought you should be aware of mother's condition. As I don't believe you have looked in on her of late, I felt it my duty to alert you to the fact that her health is failing fast. Her doctor estimates she has only weeks to live."

"I see. Well, nature – and the illness I suppose – will take its course. Of course, I understand your concern. Once she has gone, your position here will be tenuous at best. I would advise you to start making plans for your future, plans that do not include Grimsby's Store."

"Surely, you will still require someone to help out in the store and keep house for you?" Ellen felt her stomach tighten to the point of almost being physically ill as she watched him consider her question.

"Possibly but, if that is the case, there is nothing to suggest that person should be you. Your mother has fought your case since your husband's death… been your protector, if you will. But, as you have just pointed out, it is likely that, within weeks, all that will disappear."

Tears began to well up. Ellen did not want to give him the satisfaction of seeing her weep. She turned on her heel and, maintaining as much dignity as possible, strode back to her room. There would be no sleep that night. The conversation with her father kept replaying in her mind. He had given her a number of messages she decided, some subtle and others not so much.

It was obvious he still resented her presence and did not intend allowing her to stay after her mother's death. His other comments left her confused. Did he intend replacing her – and her mother – with someone else? If he were already working on such a situation, it would explain his late nights and secrecy about his activities. Her subconscious kept suggesting another scenario was possible. Although she tried to dismiss it, it nagged at her until she finally acknowledged it. That other possibility was that he planned to sell up; to get rid of everything and possibly move away.

In the cold light of day, as she opened the store the next morning, Ellen assessed her situation. It hadn't improved much since her husband's sudden death. True, she was no longer pregnant and, with her children safely in the orphanage, she had a little more freedom to pursue options. However, her financial situation had not improved. She knew that ultimately it would prevent her establishing an independent life. She had not been paid wages since her arrival, only a few shillings here and there and mostly that went on gifts and other things for the children. She resolved not to share her thoughts and concerns with Alfred and Jess. After all, it was only speculation on her part at this time.

Business increased over the next few weeks, requiring all three to deal with customers on occasions. People Ellen had never seen before became regular customers of the store and, in many cases, the agency as well. This made life difficult for Ellen. Her mother now was unresponsive most of the time. Her need for care increased accordingly. While Alfred and Jess understood the situation, Ellen felt guilty about leaving them to manage on their own on many occasions during the day.

At the end of September, Mr Wallace called in to the store. His wife was not with him. It was unusual for the elderly couple to be apart. Ellen enquired after Mrs Wallace – and immediately wished she hadn't.

"She passed away. It was sudden; mercifully she didn't suffer." Wallace wished he could take back his final comment. He was all too aware of Mary's lingering illness and its impact on Ellen. "I've come in to town to finalise the funeral arrangements. My daughter will arrive this evening, so we can hold the funeral tomorrow."

That evening, during their usual chat after closing up, Ellen told Alfred and Jess that she would be attending Mrs Wallace's funeral the following day. As the day was so busy, she hadn't been able to slip out to find out what time the funeral was, but she would do so first thing the next morning. A fit of depression settled over Ellen as she lay in her bed that night. She had very few friends, but Mr and Mrs Wallace were good to her and she thought of them as special friends. She would miss her chats with Mrs Wallace whenever she came into the store.

The funeral was at 11 o'clock. At ten o'clock, Frank Woodrow came in to see Ellen. "I thought you likely to go to Mrs Wallace's funeral." Ellen nodded and he continued. "If it is not too presumptuous of me, I wondered if you would care to accompany me rather than attend on your own. After all, we both have been friends of the couple for a long time."

Ellen gratefully accepted the offer but wondered later whether it might raise the odd eyebrow around town. Who cares, she muttered to herself as she fetched her best hat in readiness for the funeral. Few attended the funeral. Ellen recognised a couple of others who she knew from the mill estate, and a handful of farmers who she recognised as agency customers. Concerned about being away from the store for too long, Ellen chose not to go on to the cemetery after the service. Woodrow walked her back to the store before he headed for the cemetery.

Later that evening, as she attended to her mother, Ellen's mind drifted back over her friendship with Mrs Wallace and her funeral earlier that day. Margaret, the Wallaces' only child, was particularly distressed. Her mother's death was so sudden and, when their only contact for over 12 months was by letter, she was completely unprepared for the loss. As she looked down on Mary's wan and hollowed face, Ellen knew the end of her mother's suffering would not come as a shock to her – just a blessed relief.

*****

That day of Mary's release from her suffering arrived with the start of November. Mary's doctor visited every day over the previous week and, it was during his visit that day, that Mary drew her last shallow breath. When she reflected on it later, Ellen thought it was as though Mary waited until there was someone with her daughter before she finally went. The doctor spent a few minutes with Ellen before leaving. He said he would call at the undertakers on his way past and ask them to come. James was conspicuous by his absence.

"I don't know where my father is," Ellen responded quietly to the doctor's enquiry, "He might have spent the night at his club. It doesn't look as though he came home last night. Otherwise, I don't know where he would be."

Doctor Boyle called at the undertakers as promised. Then responding to a sudden urge, he turned around and headed down the street towards the men's club. Although not a member himself, no one blocked his entry. In response to the doctor's enquiry after James, a staff member indicated a small alcove at the far end of the building. A poker game had just ended and three of the players wandered out of the alcove. Boyle found James, dishevelled and very drunk, alone at a table still strewn with the remnants of the recent card game.

James became abusive when Boyle mentioned Mary. The doctor prevailed until he was confident James understood what had happened this morning. Still Boyle's concern lingered. He expected James to rush back to the store when comprehension finally occurred. Instead, James continued to sit there, apparently deep in thought, nodding and moving cards about on the table. To allow James time alone with his grief, Doctor Boyle quietly took his leave.

Chapter 10

The undertakers came and went. Before leaving, they asked Ellen if Mary left any special requests, particularly in relation to her burial. Ellen didn't know but, the way in which the men asked the question, suggested to her they knew more than she did. The only person who might know about such things was Mary's solicitor, Mr Taylor. She needed to let him know about Mary's death anyway so, immediately after lunch, she called at his office.

Mr Taylor stressed he could not discuss the contents of Mary's will until a formal death certificate was obtained, and that would take some time. However, he understood that, with the funeral scheduled for the next day, any relevant information was required now. He asked Ellen to wait outside, calling her back into his office after he had perused Mary's will.

"Your mother left no instruction relating to her funeral service but was quite specific about her burial. She wishes to be buried next to her parents in what is basically the family plot."

"I didn't know there was a family plot." Ellen was surprised. "I suppose I thought she expected to be buried with the Grimsbys. ... Oh, but they're not a local family, so I don't suppose there is a family plot here."

"I can't answer that. However, she was quite adamant about it – next to her parents, although it seems she never mentioned the family plot to you. The Watt family plot extends across a number of gravesites between two rows of the cemetery. Your Watt grandparents' graves are at one end of the plot, and your husband and baby are at the opposite end. After your mother's burial, there will be a couple of spare gravesites remaining in the middle section of the family plot. She once said her intention was one day to enclose the whole plot with an ornate fence. She saw the fence as somehow keeping the family together."

There wasn't anything else to discuss. Mr Taylor said he would contact her as soon as he received a death certificate. On her way back to the store, Ellen called in at the undertakers' to confirm the burial arrangements. She asked after her father as soon as she arrived back at the store . He still hadn't appeared. A mixture of anger and concern dogged Ellen for the rest of the day: anger that her father hadn't come home so she could tell him about Mary's death and concern about why he hadn't returned.

He should make the funeral arrangements – although she knew he didn't care enough to be bothered. She also knew that despite his lack of interest, he was likely to take offence at anything she did. Well, too bad, she thought. Someone has to do it and I am determined my mother will be seen off with dignity and according to her wishes. It was nearly midnight when she heard James make his way upstairs. Determined to acquaint him with everything before he went to bed, Ellen got out of bed and went to the kitchen where she confronted James.

She was disgusted. James could barely stand unaided. The stench of unwashed body mingled with alcohol fumes met her as she entered the kitchen. He rudely told her to go away and staggered into the sitting room. Anger mounting, Ellen followed him, and reached breaking point when he directed an abusive tirade at her. She had turned to walk away as he spoke, but then she snapped. Ellen whirled around to face James and shoved him roughly down into a lounge chair. Then, totally consumed by anger and pent-up grief, she delivered a scathing verbal attack on his character, his behaviour, and everything else about him.

Stunned, he sat there opening and closing his mouth but no words were forthcoming. Not done yet, Ellen finally got around to Mary's death.

"You wife died today. You weren't even interested enough to be here or to care about it. Her funeral is at two o'clock tomorrow afternoon. If you manage to be sober and can muster enough respect – and any vestige of grief – for my mother, you may attend. If you cannot achieve that, you will not be welcome or missed." While James, still reeling, searched for a response – any response! – Ellen flounced off to bed.

Neither the store nor the agency opened the next day. Ellen discovered James had not spent the night at home. She could not bring herself to think about where he might have spent it. Her disgust increased when he had not made an appearance by lunchtime. Alfred and Jess came in around lunchtime and immediately checked on Ellen. They found her brittle but doggedly controlled. With nothing else to do, the two employees made themselves comfortable in the store's backroom until it was time to go across to the church.

Frank Woodrow tried the front door of the store, but finding it locked, drove his buggy round to the back loading area. Alfred took care of his horses while Jess ran upstairs to tell Ellen she had a visitor. While Jess was gone, Woodrow chatted to Alfred and asked after Mr Grimsby.

"He aint here… and aint been since I don't know when. No use to her at all he be," Alfred snarled and indicated Ellen upstairs with a jerk of his head.

Jess reappeared and took Woodrow up to Ellen. She seemed so much shrunken since he last saw her. They chatted for a few minutes until it was time to leave for the church. Ellen fixed her hat in place before following Woodrow downstairs. The three from the store intended to walk to the church, but Woodrow would not hear of it.

"My buggy is hitched in your loading area. I will drive us all to the church. Everyone climb aboard and we will get going."

Ellen made to argue, saying it would be inappropriate for her to arrive with any man other than her husband or father. Woodrow countered her argument by saying it would not be inappropriate since all of her staff were accompanying them.

Alfred and Jess walked Ellen to the front pew and sat with her. Woodrow sat directly behind Ellen. There was no sign of James Grimsby. He arrived about ten minutes into the service. He had the good grace to sit at the back of the church rather than make a spectacle of his late arrival by marching through to the front pew. James did not continue on to the cemetery after the service. His behaviour on the day did not go unnoticed. One of the men who attended confided to Alfred later that James was 'extremely unsteady on his feet'.

Alfred nodded his acceptance of the news and commented to his informant, "Drunk again."

"Still, more like…," the man replied.

In the weeks following the funeral, James was rarely at home. Ellen managed to catch up with him on one of his fleeting visits for clean clothes. "Do you wish me to take care of mother's things?" she asked stiffly. "I assume you would prefer her belongings were removed and her room cleared out." James gruffly agreed, only adding the comment, the sooner the better.

Before touching anything, Ellen thought it wise to consult Mary's solicitor, Mr Taylor, again, in case Mary left any special instructions. As it was only just over a week after the funeral, Taylor had only received Mary's death certificate the day before but hadn't time to deal with it yet. Again, he would not divulge the contents of her will until he had attended to certain matters relating to it. However, he asked Ellen to gather up her mother's jewellery and a couple of other small items and bring them to the solicitor's office. Ellen was free to dispose of any other of Mary's personal effects as she saw fit.

Ellen delivered the jewellery and other material to Taylor as requested, but it was a few days before she could bring herself to go through everything else. The clothes she bagged up and took to the church for distribution to the needy. Mary's books and other bits and pieces from her room Ellen packed into a couple of boxes, which she then stored under her own bed. James still appeared to be avoiding the place and somehow that suited Ellen. ...But, there remained the matter of finishing off her mother's gave to attend to, including selecting a suitable headstone. Ellen was reluctant to make those arrangements without first consulting her father.

On Sunday morning, she decided the residence didn't need much cleaning. Apart from her, no one had spent any time there. She hitched up the buggy and drove out to the cemetery. Her mother's grave, still needing finishing off, looked uncared for next to its neighbours. When she was there last, they were burying her mother and Ellen hadn't taken much notice of anything around her. Now she wanted to look at the other graves in the family plot. It seemed appropriate to her that the finish on Mary's grave be in keeping with the others in the plot.

They were simple but dignified. Yes, Ellen thought. That's exactly what mother would want. The decision made, she would go ahead tomorrow and arrange it. If her father happened to return in the meantime, she would discuss it with him. If not, she would proceed without his input. He probably had no interest in the matter anyway, she told herself. After spending the rest of the day cleaning and tidying the store, Ellen checked on their finances to reassure herself the cost of any work on Mary's grave could be covered.

There were plenty of funds in the store's bank account. It reflected the increased business they were experiencing. Even the agency account looked healthier than she had known it in the past. Sometime before her illness took a complete hold on her, Mary took Mr Taylor to the bank with her to rearrange the business' financial arrangements. She set up separate accounts for the store and the agency, the opening balance for each according to the records that she and then Ellen so meticulously maintained. Arrangements were also in place for Ellen to have authority to operate on both accounts.

Later, when Mary was too ill to attend to the matter herself, she sent Mr Taylor to make a further arrangement with the bank. Before that, Mary had spoken to Ellen about her daughter paying herself a small weekly wage. It seems Mary wanted to ensure a degree of financial independence for her daughter when Mary was no longer around to support her. Despite Mary's urging, Ellen refused to do so. She felt it improper since the roof over her head and her keep were provided free of charge. In desperation, Mary had Mr Taylor set up a small account in Ellen's name. A transfer from the store account of a few shillings each week went into the new account. While Ellen had authority to operate the account, she remained unaware of its existence. Although a relatively recent initiative, the account already held a few pounds.

As she reviewed the financial situation, Ellen could not help but feel a twinge of sadness. How sadden old Ned Swayne would be if he could see what became of his business empire, and how its demise now so benefitted his business rival. "Will this business go the same way now that mother is no longer around?" Ellen wondered aloud. However, thinking about how the situation at Swaynes' increased Grimsby's trade brought something else to the forefront of her mind. Now she had settled what to do about Mary's grave, another issue that quietly gnawed at the back of Ellen's mind for a few days now fully occupied her thinking.

They couldn't continue to operate with just the three workers. Alfred was spending more of his time helping in the store and the agency than he spent on his own job. It didn't appear her father had any interest in returning to run the agency. It appeared he didn't have any interest in returning to the premises at all. He hadn't been there in weeks.

Alfred relayed pub talk that James was living at his club. Good, Ellen thought. The longer he stays away, the longer I am able to remain here. However, if he does not return, another employee is required to assist. The number of orders received almost overwhelmed the scant time Alfred could spend at the back of the store. Ellen noted he was starting very early and staying late each day to cope with the orders. To her way of thinking, they needed someone to help with the agency, and the agency could pay the wages.

On Monday morning, with still no sign of James, Ellen went down the street and arranged for the completion of her mother's grave. She wanted to talk to Alfred but, the day became so busy, she decided it would wait until after they closed for the day. The Gods of Fate conspired against her. As she was about to close the front door, Frank Woodrow appeared. It was only a social call he assured her as she invited him to join her in a cup of tea. Ellen closed the door without locking it and they sat together in the small office sipping tea and enquiring after each other's wellbeing. Woodrow didn't stay long. He only called to see how she was coping following her mother's death. At some point during their conversation, he mentioned Ted Wallace.

"Have you spoken to Ted Wallace in the last week or so?" Ellen shook her head. "He has decided to sell up and move south to be with his daughter and grandchildren. His farm went on the market soon after Mrs Wallace's death. I spoke to him this morning. It looks like he has a firm buyer lined up. If all goes well, he thinks he will be heading south in a couple of weeks' time."

Ellen felt the wave of sadness sweep over her. Her face apparently betrayed her emotion.

"What's the matter?" Woodrow asked. "Have I said something to upset you?"

"No, not at all; I just felt a little sad. Soon, anyone I ever felt close to will be gone: my husband, my mother, Mrs Wallace and now Mr Wallace as well. I am happy he will be with his family and will have someone to care for him, but I will miss our occasional chats. That leaves only you from my old life to have the occasional chat with."

"Well, I'm not going anywhere – not in the foreseeable future anyway. Although you meet many people here in the store, I don't suppose there is opportunity to develop much in the way of friendships. Never mind, I will continue to call in to see you, if you will allow me that honour."

His kindness, coupled with her melancholia was sufficient to bring tears. Ellen fought them back as she shared with Woodrow how her continued presence at Grimsby's store might not continue too long into the future. She told him of her father's threat to throw her out, and how she wondered whether he might be considering selling out. Woodrow wanted nothing more than to wrap his arms around her and hold her until she felt better. ...But that would be an unforgivable breach of decorum – and their friendship. Ellen quickly regained her composure, apologising profusely as she did so. She assured Woodrow she was okay as she walked him to the door. Ellen did seem all right, Woodrow told himself as he untied his horse but, all the same, he rode home with a heavy heart. By the time Frank Woodrow departed, Alfred also had gone home. Ellen would have to find time tomorrow to talk to him.

Tuesday provided no opportunity for her desired talk with Alfred. However, the hectic pace they all worked at throughout the day, stiffened Ellen's resolve to deal with the lack of assistance situation as soon as possible. Alfred again worked late filling orders. Ellen caught him as he was preparing to leave for the night. Not wanting to delay him any longer than necessary, Ellen launched straight into her discussion of the issue.

"Alfred, I've been meaning to talk to you about our work situation. I don't need to tell you how busy we have become. Your early starts and late finishes are noted. The time has come for us to look at employing another person."

"What about Mr Grimsby? What's going on with him; is he coming back?"

"I can't say. I honestly don't know what his intentions are. Nevertheless, we need to keep the business running and our clients happy. The three of us can't maintain that state of affairs for much longer. I propose employing another – a man preferably – as soon as possible. If you should know of any suitable candidates, please bring their names to my attention."

Alfred couldn't think of anyone immediately but agreed to give the matter some thought. Nothing more was said on the matter at work but, both Jess and Alfred even resorted to asking their family members if they knew of anyone who might be suitable – and available. Thursday morning proved particularly exhausting. Alfred was out making deliveries around town until after lunch. Jess worked in the agency all morning while Ellen coped with store customers. No one took lunch until Alfred returned. It was Ellen's intention that he and Jess would take the first quick lunch break. However, when Alfred returned, lunch seem of little import.

After unhitching the wagon, Alfred rushed through to the front of the store. "Miss Grimsby, Miss Grimsby…" he called excitedly as he ran in. "Oh, excuse me please, Mrs Green. I do apologise for my behaviour." After casting a disapproving look in Alfred's direction, Mrs Green completed her purchase and strode out of the store.

There were no other customers. Alfred began to apologise to Ellen, but she interrupted him. "Don't be worrying yourself about it. Mrs Green will be fine about it. She just enjoyed putting you in your place for that short moment. Now, what had you so excited that you behaved in that way?"

"Swayne's is closed down. The bank foreclosed this morning, closed the doors and threw out young Swayne and his family. They took all the cash from the store. There are still some orders farmers will collect tomorrow. The bank kept Charlie Perkins on to take care of the orders. He will be out of a job at close of business tomorrow. This store and agency now have no opposition trading in town."

"I suppose it is not unexpected. It does seem sudden though. Poor old Ned Swayne must be rolling over in his grave. Charlie Perkins, who worked there for so long and was the last of the staff left there, must find the situation upsetting. However, I am surprised you found Swayne's demise so exciting. Is there something you haven't told me?"

"Well, no, Miss, there isn't more to tell. It wasn't Swayne's demise I was so excited about, it was Charlie Perkins' being unemployed after tomorrow that got me so excited. He will more than likely be at the pub tonight. I could have a word to him, if you wish."

"A word to him about what…?" Ellen was tired and she was still too busy digesting the news about Swayne's to following Alfred's logic.

"…About whether he might be interested in a job here, at Grimsby's."

"Oh dear, of course; now I understand why you are excited. I definitely think it a sound idea for you to speak to Mr Perkins. If he should express an interest, please ask him to suggest a suitable time when he might be available to present for an interview."

'Euphoric' describes the rest of the day for those at Grimsby's store and agency. As Ellen sat doing the accounts that evening, a thought she kept at bay all afternoon insisted on making its presence felt. Should she discuss the issue of another employee with her father before progressing to interview Charlie Perkins? She knew that was the correct thing to do. James' continued absence from and apparent lack of concern for the business suggested he had no interest in what took place. It would all be of no import if, at some time in the near future, James sold the business. Of course, it might mean poor Charlie could find himself without a job again. She decided to press on regardless.

First thing Friday morning, Alfred reported he had spoken to Charlie Perkins the previous evening. Mr Perkins suggested an interview time that afternoon after he finished at Swayne's. The bank said they would close the place for good at five o'clock. Perkins suggested he come to Grimsby's as soon as possible after that. "Most agreeable," Ellen said. "When you are making deliveries during the morning, please call at Swayne's to confirm the time."

The interview went well. Why wouldn't it? Mr Perkins was a personable, well-presented middle-aged man with years of experience in running a farmer's agency. All that was required was to agree hours of work, wages and a commencement date.

"It suits me well to start next Monday. That gives me the weekend off. That's all I need, as it soon will be Christmas and I will have another couple of days off then," Charlie told her. Ellen slept well that night.

With her mother's grave and the workload in the business sorted out, it only left one other issue hanging around to worry her: her own future. James remained invisible, not having ventured near the place since shortly after her mother's death. Alfred brought pub gossip back that confirmed he was staying at his club. In the occasional idle moment, Ellen wondered how he was faring… was he eating well, drinking too much, and taking care of himself properly? …But she usually managed to dismiss such thoughts quickly, counselling herself that he wasn't worth the worry.

*****

November moved onto December. Soon it would be Christmas again. From early in the month, large orders started coming in from outlying properties as they began stocking up for the festive season and the likely onset of the wet season that would follow. Alfred's only time out of the back area these days was to relieve others while they took tea or lunch. An order came in for the orphanage. The size of it perplexed Alfred and he mentioned it to Ellen. There were few items on the order, with only small quantities of everything required.

"Perhaps this order might be only to tide them over until they sent in their large end of year/wet season order," Ellen suggested. "I won't send out the children's Christmas presents with you on this trip. I'll wait until closer to Christmas and send them with you when you delivered the orphanage's big order."

Later that day, one of their new customers came into the store. The McCarthys were Swayne's customers for years and only started to shop at Grimsby's when supplies dropped off at Swayne's. Mrs McCarthy was now a regular weekly shopper for small items, while her husband collected orders of bulk supplies whenever he came to town. Today, it was mid-afternoon when Mrs McCarthy came into the store. Her appearance alarmed Ellen.

Mrs McCarthy looked decidedly grey and was short of breath. "Are you all right, Mrs McCarthy?" Ellen asked.

"I'm a bit exhausted today. Maybe I have to accept I'm an old lady now. Everything seems to tire or exhaust me these days."

Ellen dragged a chair out of the small office located behind the counter area. She placed it beside the counter and helped Mrs McCarthy sit. "Could I get you a glass of water… or, perhaps a cup of tea? It would be no problem."

"You are so kind, my dear. A glass of water would be most welcome." Ellen poured a glass of water from the pitcher she kept there and returned to her customer.

It occurred to Ellen that Mrs McCarthy might feel conspicuous – and a bit embarrassed – to be sitting so prominently. "I think you might find it more comfortable to sit in our office for a few minutes. I was about to make a pot of tea, perhaps you will join me in a cup?"

"Thank you, Miss Grimsby; I should enjoy taking tea with you."

While settling Mrs McCarthy comfortably in the office, Ellen sent Jess to make a pot of tea. Then, the two women settled across the small desk and delicately sipped their tea. "Tell me, Mrs McCarthy, what have you been doing today to so exhaust yourself? At this time of the year, it is too hot to be rushing about."

"Just the usual I suppose: a visit to my dressmaker, lunch with a couple of friends, paying accounts… oh, and sorting out Christmas gifts for our staff."

"You give all you staff a gift at Christmas? That has never been the practice here, but I shall now give some serious thought to following your example. It was a difficult year for our staff and they have worked long and hard. They deserve some mark of appreciation." Ellen felt her spirits lift at the prospect of being able to do that for the other three employees.

In response to Ellen's enquiry, Mrs McCarthy explained the types of gifts they gave to field workers as well as household staff. "As there are so many to buy, I usually spread the shopping over the couple of weeks just before Christmas. However, this year I'm shopping earlier than usual as we leave the week before Christmas to spend a few weeks in the Blue Mountains where the weather was likely to be a bit cooler."

"Do you have a list of the items you came in to buy?" Ellen asked. Mrs McCarthy produced a list from her purse. "You sit and relax – and have another cup of tea, if you like – while I make up this list for you." It didn't take long to gather the items and add them to the customer's account. She was finishing the order when she heard a wagon arrive at the loading dock. She went to the door to see who had arrived.

Alfred had returned with the store's wagon and Mr McCarthy drove in behind him. Both men tied up their horses at the loading dock, and Alfred quickly began loading McCarthy's wagon. Ellen returned to the office. "Mr McCarthy has arrived with the wagon," Ellen told Mrs McCarthy. "I can take you through to the back. It is much easier to board the wagon from the loading dock than having to climb up on top." She guided the woman through the store and helped her onto the wagon.

She noted that Alfred appeared in a hurry to see the McCarthys on their way. She was right. As soon as the wagon was out of sight, Alfred called to Ellen to wait as he had something important to tell her. Ellen already was at the door to the store. She turned and retraced her steps. "What is it Alfred? Since your return from making deliveries, you seem upset."

"Yes, Miss, I am upset. I have bad news and, I am sorry, but I know it will upset you too." Ellen motioned for him to go on. After shuffling his feet a bit and taking a deep breath, Alfred told her his story.

Chapter 11

Alfred's report on his visit to the orphanage to deliver their small order of supplies shocked Ellen.

"You know I couldn't understand why the orphanage ordered so little this time?" Ellen nodded. "They didn't need much because there is no one there… well, there are very few still there. It seems like there are only two nuns and Lizzie, the cook, is the only one left in the kitchen. The children are all gone."

"Gone? What do you mean 'gone'… gone where?" Ellen's stomach tightened and she felt a cold wave spread through her.

"I got the story out of Lizzie, or as much as she knows, that is. There have been big changes lately. That priest who used to sort of run the orphanage has moved on to somewhere else. Soon after he left, they appointed a new bishop to the diocese. The diocese headquarters, or whatever they call it, is in that big city to the south of us. The church runs an orphanage there as well, and the new bishop couldn't see why they needed another one here. He closed this one down. One of the nuns from here has gone to the other orphanage. Two moved into the convent here in town and will work at the convent's school from now on. They got rid of all the domestic staff except Lizzie who will finish up as soon as Christmas is over. That's when the two remaining nuns will go off to somewhere else as well."

"If I understand you correctly, my children – my daughters – are now at that other orphanage?"

"W-e-l-l, no. That might not be true. I managed to speak to that young nun as I was leaving. I asked her for the address of that orphanage and explained that you would want to write to the children. She was careful about what she said, and I don't think the nuns here have all the details of what is happening. However, she said that someone miscalculated. The other orphanage is not large enough to hold all of their own children and those from here as well. They thought there were fewer children here than there were. The bishop's intention is to put all the children together, and then fill their orphanage first. Then, any children they don't have room for will be sent to the church's orphanages in other dioceses."

"When did all this happen? How come the town doesn't seem to have heard about it?"

"They moved the last of the children out at the end of last week, after anyone who was old enough – or nearly old enough – to work was put into employment. An employer has to pay the church for anyone he takes on, so the church seems to see it as a money-making exercise."

"Yes, they are making money. They are selling our children." Ellen snarled. Her immediate concern was for her eldest daughter, Marion, who was now near the age when the orphanage considered a child could be placed in service." There was little else to do today. It was almost time to close up, but she would be paying the church a visit in the morning. She would have plenty to say and many questions requiring answers.

Her visit to the Catholic Church the next morning only added to her anger and frustration. She waited for ages for someone to come to talk to her about what was happening with her children. In the end, she didn't get results until she explained in no uncertain terms to an officious nun that she would remain there until someone came to talk to her – even if she had to sleep there that night. The priest who came to speak with her was pompous initially, but his attitude was no match for Ellen's anger. He soon backed down, becoming quite sympathetic, but admitted there was nothing they could do. "The bishop has decided on this course of action and his word is law as far as we are concerned. However, I agree to try to find out what happened to your daughters but I don't think I will do much good."

About a week after his wife's previous visit to the store, Mr McCarthy came in as Ellen was about to close up for the day. She was surprised. She had never seen him in the store before, although she though he might have been in the agency on occasions. This was the man Ellen blamed for her husband's early death. How could she be civil to him? ...But, this was a business and he was their customer, and a good customer at that. She put on her best smile and summoned up her most polite demeanour.

"I know you are about to close up, Miss Grimsby, but I wonder if I might have a few moments of your time to discuss something in private with you... something personal."

Trepidation threatened to overwhelm her but she fought it down. "Certainly, Mr McCarthy; we can talk here. Most of the staff has left. Alfred is still busy out the back but he will not be able to overhear. What is it you wish to discuss?"

"You were very kind to my wife last week and I know of the wonderful job you did caring for your late mother. As you might have discerned, my wife is getting on in years and now finds even the most routine task too much for her. She needs a… uhmm… a companion; I think that is the right word. She needs someone to help her with personal matters and to take some of the responsibilities of running the place off her shoulders. I know it might seem forward of me, but I have come to offer you such a position. I know my wife thinks highly of you, and I don't think you would find her too disagreeable."

"I'm flattered by your kind words and that you would consider me a suitable companion for Mrs McCarthy, but I have a job and responsibilities here. I am surprised you think I might abandon my responsibilities here."

"You misjudge me, my dear lady. I do not think for one moment that you are capable of abandoning your responsibilities. However, as those responsibilities are likely to disappear in the near future, I assumed my offer would not conflict your conscience."

"I am not sure I understand your reference to my responsibilities disappearing in the near future. Might I ask you to elaborate on that?" Mr McCarthy suddenly looked uncomfortable and avoided eye contact for a moment. Before he could speak, Ellen continued. "Please forgive me, I am forgetting my manners. Perhaps we would be more comfortable continuing this discussion in my office." McCarthy nodded, and they adjourned to the not too comfortable chairs in the office.

"Forgive me, Miss Grimsby, but I fear I have spoken out of turn. It seems common knowledge around town that your father intends to sell this business and move away from here. Of course, I understand that you might consider it your duty to go with him to take care of him, but I don't think that is the case."

"Some time ago, my father did threaten to sell up. That much is true, but I have heard nothing more of it since then. It is not a case of my considering it my duty to care for my father, but rather my father not wanting anything to do with me. I haven't seen him in weeks, and I have no idea where he is or what he is doing. As you thought, your offer might indeed be timely. Perhaps we could discuss your proposal in a little more detail."

After a several minutes, there didn't seem any detail remained undiscussed. Ellen said she would think about the offer but there were other issues to consider as well. "Even if I were interested in taking up the position, I couldn't leave here until after Christmas. This is a busy time of the year. I couldn't leave the others unsupervised and having to carry the load on their own. ...And, it would help if I knew what my father was doing and how he planned to run the business in the future."

"The timing as you outline it is not an issue. Mrs McCarthy and I will leave the week before Christmas for cooler climes. We will not return until at least mid-January. There would be no need for you to give me your answer before then."

That came as something of a relief, as McCarthy's visit had Ellen feeling decidedly unsettled. If only she could talk to her father about what his plans were, she might find it easier to make a decision. However, she did have to consider her future and, if her father's intention was to sell out, she would be left with nothing – not even a roof over her head.

Later that evening, Ellen prepared to indulge in the unexpected luxury that came with being on her own. It had become her habit after her evening meal to settle in the sitting room with one of her mother's books. She hoped losing herself in a good book would provide an escape from the whirlpool of thoughts generated by McCarthy's visit. Conflicted as she was between protecting her future and her responsibility for the store, Ellen knew she faced possibly the most difficult decision of her life. It wasn't until she was settled in a chair and reaching for her book that she realised she finished reading that book the previous evening.

Her mother's books remained packed in boxes in a corner in the back of the store. Ellen opened the nearest box and began picking through its contents. Mary enjoyed poetry and that's what the first few books at the top of the box were. Ellen didn't share her mother's enthusiasm, although she occasionally read a part of one or other of Mary's favourites. Tonight she had no appetite for poetry. She lifted out the poetry books and put them to one side. Then one particular book caught her eye and her hand automatically reached for it. It was Mary's all-time favourite, and it had been for as long as Ellen could remember.

Ellen held the book close, caressing it all over with her hands as if to summon her mother's presence. "If only you were still here…" she addressed the book aloud. "If only you were still around, I could talk to you, I know it would be easier to make this decision – if even there was a decision to make." The book's well-thumbed pages a testimony to its much loved past. Ellen fanned the pages idly as she remembered her mother reading passages from the book to her.

Something fell out from between the pages and fluttered down to land at Ellen's feet. She bent and picked it up: two neatly folded letters. As she unfolded them, the sight of her brother's handwriting stunned Ellen. She carefully flattened them on a nearby bench and confirmed they were two letters Richard wrote to their mother. Their dates suggested Richard wrote them shortly before to his departure to become part of the build-up of forces prior to the outbreak of the Boer War.

While she felt she might be intruding on something between a mother and son, Ellen had to read them. She knew instinctively Mary had not told her the whole story when they discussed what happened to Richard. Ellen began reading and felt her anger mounting with each new sentence. In the first of the two letters, Richard told of how his father pressured him into coming home to run Grimsby's newly established agency.

He claimed James stated he would no longer pay Richard's fees to complete his medical training but, with his fees already paid to the end of the year, the threat was of little immediate consequence. Then, when James realised this manoeuvre would not bring Richard running back home, he ceased payment of Richard's allowance. This effectively left his son penniless to continue his studies to the end of the year, and with no hope of completing the remaining few months next year to finish his training as a doctor.

Ellen shook her head in disgust. If James had ever taken the time to get to know his son, he would know this strategy would never work. Richard was as tough as they come and would not cave in to blackmail. When she reached the end of the letter, Ellen paused to consider what she had read.

It was clear Richard was responding to a letter from his mother and was explaining why he could not continue his training to achieve his lifelong ambition of becoming a doctor. Ellen set that letter aside and turned her attention to the second one. With mounting trepidation, she began reading. By the time she reached the end of the second letter, not only was she consumed with anger, but tears now trickled down her cheeks.

In that second letter, Richard thanked his mother for the money she sent him, but insisted he could not allow her to continue covertly supporting him. He was concerned at the consequences for Mary should James discover that, by sending Richard money, Mary was counteracting his moves to bring his son home. The letter outlined Richard's plans to go to England to join the build-up of British troops being sent to Africa in response the Boers' worsening position in South Africa. Troops received an allowance – a small per diem – that would allow him to build up a cash reserve before returning to Australia to complete his training.

How could her father do this to his son? James knew what becoming a doctor meant to Richard, yet he forced his son to take steps that ultimately got him killed. The family received word of Richard's death from injuries he received in some localised skirmish around the same time as her husband, William, became ill. While it was almost impossible to comprehend that a father would do this to his only son, she knew he would not hesitate to treat her equally harshly or more so.

Had he not already treated her reprehensibly in making her give up her children and treating her with nothing but disrespect? He would have no hesitation in tipping her out onto the street and leaving her destitute… after all, she was only his daughter, as opposed to his adored son. Richard's letters helped crystallise her thinking. She would not wait for James to act against her. She would make the first move and accept Mr McCarthy's offer. The decision made, now all she had to concern herself with was that James wouldn't throw her out before the McCarthys returned home sometime in January.

Chapter 12

With the decision made to accept Mr McCarthy's offer of a position as his wife's companion/help, Ellen thought life would become simple, allowing her to face the store's hectic pre-Christmas period with an untroubled mind. This was not to be the case. Now, the thought of leaving the store and the staff to their own devices in only a few weeks' time bothered her. Also, the memory of the McCarthys' practice of giving each of their staff a small gift at Christmas lingered. Mrs McCarthy's mention of this practice resonated with her at the time, and the idea of doing the same at Grimsby's had gathered strength since then.

Even years later, she would recall the events of that week before Christmas 1899. It began on Saturday 16th December. As had become his practice, Frank Woodrow called at the store just before closing time. He brought John Dowling into town early in the morning to catch the boat for Brisbane where he would spend Christmas with friends.

Woodrow then spent the day taking care of various business matters in town before attending the Turf Club's race meeting. He wasn't a follower of horseracing, but many of his growers were. The social aspect of a race meeting provided the opportunity to catch up with growers for impromptu chats. Over the last couple of years, taking advantage of such opportunities had helped strengthen the relationship between growers and their miller.

Ellen welcomed his visits – in truth, looked forward to them. Frank Woodrow was such a kind and considerate man, and one who had become perhaps her closest friend. She shared with him more than she ever shared with anyone else before, even her mother. He knew about everything that had happened in her life since her husband's death: losing her children, the death of her baby, her ongoing precarious position regarding her father, caring for her mother, and taking on the responsibility of running the business. Woodrow had been in town since early morning and was looking tired by the time he arrived at the store.

After closing the front door, she made tea and they sat in the small office chatting. She asked about his day and he outlined what appeared a hectic schedule. "While I was waiting with Dowling at the wharf, I spotted your father. He was chatting to the mayor while they both waited to board. I managed to get close enough to overhear a snippet of their conversation. The mayor enquired after the reason for your father's trip. He said he was going to Sydney to spend a couple of weeks with friends in that city. They would take-in all the usual Christmas festivities that Sydney offered. After that, he would come back to spend a couple of weeks or more with other friends in Brisbane."

She simply nodded, but Ellen felt a surge of relief. At least he would not be around to create problems at Christmas and, if he were not coming back for several weeks, she could expect to be able to stay at the store at least until the McCarthys returned from their holiday. Then it was Ellen's turn to share her news. "Mr McCarthy has offered me a position that I suppose might be described as a companion for Mrs McCarthy. I would be doing other things of course, like organising the domestic staff and taking care of all of the office work associated with Mr McCarthy's operations."

By the time Ellen finished describing the position, Woodrow looked troubled. "You do know who this man is?" he asked quietly.

"Yes… and I haven't forgotten how badly he treated my husband or me and my children. I still want him to pay for causing William's death… because I do consider him to be responsible."

"Yet you are going to live on his property and work for him… well, work for his wife, but that's the same thing. Why would you do that?"

"It's difficult to explain. I do like Mrs McCarthy and I was surprised at how genuinely fond of her he seems. He was so very different from the opinion I had formed of what the man would be like. That aside, however, my position here is precarious to say the least. Father has made it known around town that he intends to sell up and move away. He also made it clear to me shortly after mother's death, that he intended throwing me out – whether he sold out or not, I suspect. I need to look to my own future. I have managed to put a little money aside in the last few weeks, but I am not sufficiently financially independent to manage on my own if he follows through with any of that."

"…But the McCarthys, is that wise? Surely, something else might come along."

"I have not been rushed with other offers. I will manage this situation, and who knows what opportunities it might present. Opportunities not only for me to become more financially secure, but also to extract some form of revenge for William. I vowed I wanted revenge for what he did to William, but 'revenge' doesn't seem to cover what I want. To me, the word 'revenge' doesn't quite describe it. Revenge – whatever that might entail – is not enough. Oh, I don't know how to explain it. Perhaps, to put it simply, I want some sort of recompense – some sort of compensation – for what has happened to me and my family."

These were not reassuring comments. While his concern for Ellen deepened at hearing them, he accepted that her mind was set and there was no point in attempting to persuade her otherwise. Better to change the subject. "What are your plans for Christmas? With Christmas Day falling on a Monday this year, the store will be closed for three days from Sunday through Tuesday. What might you do with those three days of leisure?"

"There will be nothing festive happening here, even less festivities than for the previous two Christmases, if that's at all possible. This year I can't even send gifts to my children, and neither of my parents will be here, although my father's absence won't be such a bad thing. I'll do my usual cleaning and tidying on Sunday, and then spend the rest of my spare time reading some of mother's books. What are your plans?"

"O-o-h, I have no real plans. I'll probably spend Sunday in my office at the mill tidying up some end of year stuff. My housekeeper will prepare Christmas lunch for me, and Ted Wallace, as he is still in town, will be joining me for lunch and maybe for the rest of the day That's about the extent of my plans at this stage."

"Doesn't your housekeeper have a family of her own to be looking after on Christmas Day? It is very generous of her to leave her family to prepare lunch for you."

"Yes, she does have a family, and I have tried to persuade her to leave some cold cuts on Christmas Eve and not come in on Christmas Day but to spend the day with her family instead. However, apparently she sees looking after me as something of a responsibility and will have none of my suggestions."

"I haven't seen Mr Wallace for some time. I thought he must have already moved south to live with his daughter."

"There has been some delay with the sale of the farm – I think, something to do with bank finance – and that has delayed his departure.

I know he is very disappointed at not spending Christmas with his daughter and her family and that is why I'm particularly keen for him to lunch with me. It's likely the farm sale will be finalised around New Year and he will leave for the south immediately that occurs."

"While we have been talking, it occurred to me there is something better that could be done."

"Better? Better than what, if I may ask?"

"…Better than your housekeeper having to spend time away from her family on Christmas day to look after two of my best friends. I believe a much better proposal to be for you and Mr Wallace – and possibly Charlie Perkins who is also alone – to join me here for Christmas lunch. No, don't protest. I would enjoy the company, and it would be fun again to immerse myself in the preparations that are part of Christmas Day. We could eat downstairs. I could clean off one of those large tables in the back area. With those big back doors above the loading ramp open, we would capture any passing breeze. Yes, I think it could be a very pleasant lunch. Please say you will at least consider it and discuss it with Mr Wallace."

Although concerned about the appropriateness of such a gathering, Woodrow had to admit that Ellen's proposal had more than a little appeal. He felt sure Ted Wallace would have no problems with the change of plan, and he was certain he could talk him round if Ted did have some misgivings. Woodrow tentatively agreed to her invitation with the proviso that Ted Wallace had no objection to the change of venue.

"There is another matter associated with Christmas on which I would welcome your advice," Ellen said. She spent a few moments explaining about the McCarthys' practice of giving staff a small gift at Christmas and how she intended to initiate the same practice for Grimsby's staff. "However, having decided on that course of action, I am at a loss as to what might be appropriate gifts. Have you any suggestions to offer?"

After thinking the matter over for a few moments, Woodrow suggested a number of alternatives involving different price ranges. Ellen clapped her hands together and beamed at him. "Thank you, thank you, for such wonderful suggestions. I must somehow make time this next week to shop for the gifts so I can have them ready to hand out on as they are leaving on Christmas Eve." Woodrow secretly wished he might be a fly on the wall when she handed out the gifts. He imagined the staff would be overwhelmed. He was sure none of their previous employers ever did anything like that.

It was getting late, and Frank Woodrow still had a long ride ahead of him this evening. Somehow, the ride home seemed to be over in a flash, his mind so occupied with the various topics he and Ellen had discussed. …And there was a certain lightness of heart when he thought of spending Christmas Day with her. One way or another, he was determined Ted Wallace would agree to have Christmas lunch at Grimsby's store.

On Tuesday and then again on Wednesday, Ellen managed to slip out to buy the staff's gifts, although it meant sacrificing lunch to do so. She was happy with her purchases – using the store's funds, of course – and was excited about handing them out on Christmas Eve. Wednesday evening, she caught up with Charlie Perkins as he was closing the agency. It might be a bit premature to mention it yet, but somehow she felt confident Woodrow and Wallace would be joining her for Christmas lunch and it was safe to issue the invitation.

"Charlie, I was wondering what you plans were for Christmas Day this year."

"Plans for Christmas; this year's plans are the same as the ones I've had for every Christmas since my wife and child died in that boating disaster all those years ago. I'll spend the three days off over the festive period at my cottage alone, relaxing and doing nothing much at all … maybe pottering about in the garden a bit in the late afternoons when it's a bit cooler."

"How would you like to have Christmas lunch here – in the back of the store?"

Charlie looked troubled by the invitation. "Are you inviting all of us to lunch with you?"

"No, Alfred and Jess have their families to spend Christmas with, and I wouldn't presume to interfere with that. I have asked a couple of friends who are also alone to join me. You don't have to come if you would prefer not to. There is no pressure on you to do so, and I would understand if you said no, but please think about it."

Next morning, Charlie arrived early. He approached Ellen as soon as he arrived. "Good morning, Miss. I just wanted to thank you for your invitation last evening." He's going to turn it down, Ellen thought. After a brief hesitation, Charlie continued. "If you are sure it would be all right, I would be honoured to join you and your friends for Christmas lunch."

"I'm sure it will be all right and, thank you, Charlie. I am delighted you can come. I think it will be a very nice day." As she walked away, Ellen fervently hoped the other two men also would agree to come – especially now that she was committed to having Charlie attend.

As luck would have it, shortly after she threw the bolt on the front door, someone knocked on it. Ellen was almost at the office, but retraced her steps and opened the door a crack. She found Frank Woodrow standing there smiling at her. "I'm sorry it's so late. I won't come in and interrupt your evening. I just called by to confirm that both Ted Wallace and I have accepted your invitation to Christmas lunch."

"That is good news." ...And a relief, she thought, remembering that earlier that day Charlie Perkins also had accepted her invitation. She hummed to herself as she returned to the office to complete the day's accounts. I have a feeling Christmas Day this year will turn out very well, she told herself.

Saturday arrived and brought with it something of a shock for Ellen. The morning was half over when it happened. As she stood studying the calendar hanging on the office wall for no particular reason, Ellen realised she had overlooked something important. "It will have to be this evening," she murmured aloud. So fixated was she on handing the staff their gifts on Christmas Eve, that she completely overlooked the fact that Christmas Eve that year was on Sunday – when the store wasn't open. It wasn't a problem. The gifts were ready. She just felt shocked at how her lack of attention to detail could have wrecked her good intentions.

Jess completed serving a customer as Ellen joined her behind the counter. As soon as the customer was out of earshot, Ellen spoke quietly to Jess. "Could you hang back for a while after we close up tonight, please?" Jess hesitated. "It will only be for a couple of minutes."

The young girl nodded. "As long as it's not too long; I promised to help mum with some cooking in readiness for the relatives who are arriving in the morning. It's our turn to have everybody come to us this year."

Ellen waited until she saw Charlie was free before issuing the same request to him, but she had to wait until Alfred returned at lunchtime after making deliveries all morning before she could ask him to stay back as well. Not surprisingly, the place was busy all day, with Alfred having to help in the store in the afternoon. When closing time finally rolled around, there were still at least half a dozen people in the store. To add to the gathering, Frank Woodrow arrived at what would be their normal closing time.

Ellen suggested he might like to wait in the office until she finished with the customers. When she had walked the last customer out and closed the door behind him, Ellen heaved a sigh of relief. Her feet hurt and she was tired, but it had been a good day for the store. She turned back from the door and faced the curious looks from the three staff members waiting by the counter. She rushed to the office and retrieved a box from under the desk. As she placed the box on the counter, she began her speech.

"I promise not to keep you long. It's already late. I just wanted the opportunity to say thank you for your loyal service to Grimsby's Store and Agency and the assistance you have given me. Please accept this small token of appreciation which comes with best wished for a Merry Christmas." All three looked stunned. Ellen thought she heard a soft chuckle coming from the direction of the office.

Jess found her voice first. "I feel really bad, Miss. I have nothing for you."

"Why would you have anything for me? The gifts are from Grimsby's Store, not from me personally, although they do come with my personal thanks and best wishes."

Alfred cocked an eyebrow at her and chipped in, "…And what has Grimsby's Store given you, Miss?" Ellen's smile was a little brittle when she replied.

"Ah, that's for me to know. I have kept you far too long and I am sure you all have things to be going on with this evening. Off you go now. I hope your festive season is happy and you remain safe, and I look forward to seeing you back here next Wednesday morning. Now, good night to you all." They traipsed out of amidst choruses of 'Merry Christmas' and 'good night'.

Ellen stood and watched them depart until the last one had disappeared out the back door. Then she remembered Woodrow waiting in the office. She turned and found him leaning against the door to the office, and with a wide smile plastered across his face.

"I wouldn't have missed that for anything," he said. "The looks on their faces when you handed them their gifts was priceless, but Alfred was right."

"Right…? What was he right about?"

"What has Grimsby's Store given you?"

"It has given me so much. It provided a roof over my head, food on the table, gave me something to do that helped preserve my sanity through some dark times and, more importantly, it allowed me to regain some self-respect. I think I am a tougher person for these last two years at Grimsby's Store. Now, enough of that; what brings you to my door at this hour of the night?"

"I called to see if there was anything I could help with for the lunch on Christmas Day. I have to tell you Mrs Langton, my housekeeper, is grateful that she may spend the day with her family instead of looking after me. As a token of her appreciation, she is sending me on the day with a plum pudding and a small Christmas cake."

"Oh, that is wonderful. A Christmas cake needs making well in advance so it has time to develop properly before Christmas. I didn't get one made. I was thinking I would need to make a plum pudding tomorrow so we would have a traditional desert for our lunch. Please thank her for me. She has saved me some work, and I am sure her plum pudding will far outshine anything I might produce."

"You have had a long day and you look tired. I'll be off now so you can relax for a while."

A thought occurred to Ellen as she walked Woodrow to the door. "I would be grateful if you could have a word to Ted Wallace before you arrive on Christmas Day. I haven't told the staff yet of McCarthy's offer or my intention to accept it. As Charlie Perkins will be joining us for lunch, I would prefer there was no mention of it in his presence."

"That won't be a problem. I haven't mentioned anything to Ted so, unless you said something, he is unaware of this development. I give you my assurance I won't mention it.

*****

Christmas Eve meant cleaning, tidying and fussing in preparation for lunch the next day. Ellen felt like a new bride preparing for her first major dinner party, and had to admit to herself that she felt a certain degree of nervousness about it. However, when she fell into bed that night, two emotions competed for her attention: satisfaction at her achievement, and excitement at the prospect of what the next day might bring.

A thunderstorm during the night improved the weather. Christmas morning was clear and bright, and some of the humidity had disappeared, making for a slightly cooler day. Charlie arrived early and helped carry everything downstairs while Ellen made a punch. A traditional hot lunch was in the oven. Mouth-watering aromas permeated the whole building. Frank Woodrow and Ted Wallace arrived right on time. Woodrow carried in the plum pudding and the Christmas cake while Ted carried a couple of bottles of 'something to help wash down all that wonderful smelling food'.

Not long after the two men arrived, Alfred and Jess appeared at the back door. They had made their routine Christmas Day visits to friends in the town area and decided to call at the store on their way home. They didn't stay long as it was almost lunchtime and both needed to be home for lunch with their respective families. As soon as they left, Charlie and Ellen disappeared upstairs. Charlie soon reappeared carrying a meat platter adorned by a large roast turkey. Ellen followed him down with containers of the various trimmings. Mrs Langton's plum pudding went down a treat with lashings of freshly made custard.

Her guests lingered chatting well after lunch was over. Ellen was delighted with the way the day turned out. She held some concerns that Charlie might feel uncomfortable and not fit in too well. Her fears disappeared the moment they all came together. The three men spent a good deal of time discussing agriculture and other issues facing men on the land. Charlie could more than hold his own on those topics. All too soon for Ellen, it was time for Woodrow and Wallace to leave. Ted was looking weary. Charlie hung back to help carry everything back upstairs, and then insisted on staying to help with the washing up.

Curled up in a lounge chair with a book she intended reading for the rest of the afternoon, Ellen couldn't help but reflect on the day. She would miss these good friends when she moved out of town to look after Mrs McCarthy.

Chapter 13

New Year 1900 came and went without any fanfare or celebration. Early in the morning a few days later, Ellen took herself down to the wharf. The sale of Ted Wallace's farm finally went through and he was leaving town to make a new life for himself in the south with his daughter and grandchildren. Frank Woodrow drove Ted in to catch the boat, and he and Ellen spent the best part of an hour chatting with Ted while they waited for passengers to board.

They stood waving as the boat departed and long after Ted probably could no longer see them. They both felt melancholy at the prospect of their lives without their good friend. "He was a true gentleman, in every sense of word," Woodrow said, and Ellen thought she detected a touch of huskiness in his voice. "Can I give you a ride back to the store?"

Ellen shook her head and swallowed hard before replying. "No, thank you. I think I'd like to walk." Woodrow nodded his understanding and they went their separate ways: he to collect his buggy, and she at a brisk walk back to the store. Alfred opened up when he arrived and they were all dealing with customers when Ellen arrived back.

Life settled back into its routine. Both the store and the agency were busy and their bank accounts looked particularly healthy. That caused a moment of bitterness for Ellen. All four of them worked hard in the business, particular since Swayne's closed. Her father, whose current whereabouts were unknown, would reap the profit of their labours without having lifted a finger or shown any interest in achieving it.

Around the middle of January, the wet season set in. The rain continued incessantly for days, and a couple of weeks went by without any sight of the sun. Deliveries were impossible except to the immediate town area, and trade slowed as properties became cut off from town by flooded creeks and boggy roads. Alfred and Charlie spent their spare moments carrying out any minor maintenance and adding a splash of fresh paint here and there. It fell to Ellen and Jess to clean and scrub, and rearrange shelves. The women found it almost a hopeless task. Thanks to the wet weather, mould seemed to reappear almost as quickly as they removed it.

Ellen grew restless. It was almost the end of January and there had been no sign of Mr McCarthy – and still no sign of her father. She knew she shouldn't fret. There was nothing she could do about it. Things would sort themselves out in their own good time. However, she found it unsettling not knowing when or if things would happen. She told herself that she should accept the uncertainty as a good thing. It delayed leaving the store and what she knew would be a traumatic experience for all involved.

*****

Mr McCarthy came into the store at the start of February. He sought out Ellen and asked for a few moments for a private conversation. They had delayed returning from down south because the conditions would prevent them returning home once they arrived back in town. Mrs McCarthy had not accompanied him to town, crossing the creeks and the state of the road made their usual route too dangerous. He brought the wagon to town by a circuitous route that had taken most of the previous day.

They finally got around to discussing his earlier offer to Ellen, and he was delighted when she accepted. However, he suggested she wait another week or two before moving to the property. "By then the road should be better. In the meantime, Mrs McCarthy isn't doing much beyond relaxing at home, so there wouldn't be much for you to do right now. I would suggest I come and see you when the time is right for you to move out to the property. We can make the appropriate arrangements to make it happen at that time." Ellen told him that she had not discussed the matter with the staff or her father, and would leave such discussion in abeyance until the time for her departure was clear.

"How is Mrs McCarthy? Did the break over Christmas prove beneficial?" Ellen asked.

"Mrs McCarthy is much revitalised following her stay in the Blue Mountains and the additional enforced rest due to the inclement weather further improves her."

"There is one other matter that concerns me, Mr McCarthy. My role ostensibly will be as companion to Mrs McCarthy. Have you discussed with her? I feel I need to know whether there was consultation and whether she approves of my appointment. It could prove disastrous for me to arrive without her prior knowledge." McCarthy shuffled his feet and hesitated briefly before replying. That was enough for Ellen. "I deduce from your demeanour that your wife is unaware of the discussion we had – or the one we are having now for that matter."

"Er … well no, as you suggest, she is unaware. …But I assure you, she will support your appointment and welcome you…"

"No, Mr McCarthy, that is not good enough. If I am to be her companion, Mrs McCarthy needs to decide whether I am the person whom she wants in that role. I am now firmly of the opinion that my appointment should remain in abeyance until such time as Mrs McCarthy and I have discussed the matter fully. Your wife might have very different ideas from yours about what the position should entail – or whether she even wants a companion! I do not want to give up my life here only to find myself dismissed after a brief period because I am not what Mrs McCarthy wants. I am equally sure that Mrs McCarthy does not wish to find herself lumbered with a companion who she finds incompatible and totally unsuited to her needs."

"Of course, she likes you. She has a soft spot for you and often mentions your kindness and courtesy. I am sure Mrs McCarthy will be happy to have you around to help her."

"Nevertheless, Mr McCarthy, your assurances are not sufficient to persuade me. I need to hear it from Mrs McCarthy. There is little point in discussing the matter any further. I believe I have made my situation clear. You need to consider my position and act according to how you feel about that."

Their conversation had not gone as McCarthy expected and it was clear this did not please him. However, Ellen left little room for him manoeuvre and there was nothing for it, but to end the conversation, and for McCarthy to go away and consider his position. He nodded his understanding of what she said, turned on his heel and left the store. Her stomach tied in a tight knot, Ellen stood unmoving for a few moments after watching him leave.

It was two weeks later when Mrs McCarthy came into the store for the first time since before Christmas. She made her way directly to Ellen. Although Mrs McCarthy's colour had improved considerably, somehow she looked frailer than the last time Ellen had seen her. Ellen noticed she appeared embarrassed, or uncomfortable in some way.

"I know you are busy, Miss Grimsby, but I wonder if I might have a word in private with you."

"The staff can look after things out here. Let's go into the office, Mrs McCarthy."

"I'm not sure how to begin," Mrs McCarthy said, but continued anyway. "My husband is a very kind man…" Hell will freeze over before I believe that, Ellen thought, but smiled sweetly and nodded her agreement. "He is always generous and is very considerate of me. His thought to find me a suitable companion is further evidence of this."

I suspect there is a 'but' coming, Ellen thought, but she elected to say nothing, instead letting Mrs McCarthy get on with her story uninterrupted.

"My husband could not have found a better candidate for the position. He obviously is an astute judge of character, and his description of his last conversation with you only helps to confirm he made the right choice. I was greatly moved by your insistence that I be consulted on this matter before any appointment be made. I understand your concerns for both our sakes. I must say, however, how surprised I am that you would consider leaving all of this to come and live on the property with us."

"That I can walk away from this is a long story and one I would not trouble you with at this time. The staff members are very good and I believe they will make a good show of running the place. However, I wonder if, when on the weekly trips to town, there might be some time available for me to spend at the store to check on how things are running. I appreciate that you might see this as inappropriate, but I believe it to be important for me at least in the first instance."

"There will be quite a bit of time, my dear. There will be things that I now do that you will take over from me, and they will take up some of the time while we are in town. The rest of our day would be very boring for you if you were only going to wait around for me to do the things I do for myself. I would not need you with me when I go to the doctor, my dressmaker, or to lunch with my friends – and occasionally I go to the hairdresser, and other places where I would not require your assistance. During those times I mentioned, you would be free to take care of business for the property and to spend time at the store. I would feel much better for knowing you had something to occupy that time."

"Unless I have misunderstood, I believe our conversation has confirmed you are happy with my acceptance of the position as your companion. If this is correct, then all that remains is to determine when I will commence duties."

"Of course I want you to accept the position, and the sooner the better. I will speak with Mr McCarthy when I return home tonight and ask him to make the appropriate arrangements to collect you and bring you to the property. I must go; I have a couple more things to do before the wagon leaves for home. Do you have any more questions before I go?"

Ellen's mind was in a whirl. There were probably lots she should ask, but nothing occurred to her at the time. It appeared the time had come. The time she had looked forward to and dreaded at the same time. The time when she had to tell the staff she was leaving, and the time when she needed to be sure that they could run the place in her absence.

That night, as she sat in the lounge chair her book unopened in her lap, she cast her mind back over the conversation with Mrs McCarthy and all that it meant. Her courage was starting to evaporate. Was she doing the right thing and, more importantly, was it for the right reasons? How she desperately wished her mother was still around to talk this situation through with her. However, she realised that, if her mother were still around, there would be nothing to discuss because this situation would never have arisen. There was no one else with whom she could discuss it.

Frank Woodrow knew of her plan, and he had made it quite clear he thought she was mad. He would try to dissuade her from doing this, so there was little point in trying to talk to him again. …And what about her father, shouldn't he be told what was about to happen to his business? …But then, she didn't know where he was – and it seemed reasonably clear he wasn't interested anyway. He didn't deserve any consideration; he wasn't worth worrying about. Although she tried hard to convince herself this was the case, her instinct to do the right thing kept getting in the way.

At the start of the following week, Mr McCarthy came to see her. He claimed they were particularly busy on the property at the time and didn't think anyone would be available to bring the wagon into town that week. Perhaps the end of the following week would suit both of them better. Ellen agreed, as that would give her time to finalise things she needed to do at the store and to gather up her few belongings.

She began educating Jess in the intricacies of the store's bookkeeping system. Jess was a quick learner and was very good with figures. Ellen had no doubts about her honesty. The staff knew something was going on. At different times during the week, they had all asked if she was okay or if there were anything she needed help with.

Late on Saturday afternoon, Mr Woodrow dropped into the store. Ellen used the opportunity to tell him she would be leaving town on the Friday of the following week to live at the McCarthy's property. He genuinely looked disappointed at the news and made a half-hearted attempt at talking her out of it. In an effort to lighten the atmosphere, Ellen told him that she would be coming into town with Mrs McCarthy every Thursday, and that she would be spending some time at the store during each of those days. It didn't seem to lighten his mood and he seemed heavy hearted when he departed shortly after.

Again, she found her resolve weakening. She had asked the staff to hang back after they closed on that Saturday evening. That was when she planned to break the news to them but, after Woodrow's reaction, she felt worse than ever at the prospect of the task ahead of her.

The talk with the staff did not go well. At first, her news met with stunned silence. Then the questions flowed, and the accusation that she wasn't telling them the whole story; that there was more going on with the future of the store and she was keeping it from them. It took some time to reassure them that this was not the case; she still had no idea where her father was or what his intentions were concerning the store. She neglected to tell them that he had been quite explicit about her not having any future at Grimsby's Store. She did not think this would help the situation. Alfred was angry and paced back and forth, slamming his fist into the palm of his other hand. Jess burst into tears. Charlie remained stoic but with his jaw clenched firmly.

It had not been an easy conversation, and she appreciated the uncertainties it probably created in the minds of her colleagues. It had to be done, and she believed she had done it as well as she possibly could. Ellen took some consolation from the fact that, although she said nothing to that effect, the staff lay the blame for the situation that lay ahead at the feet of her father, and openly criticised his behaviour since the death of Mrs Grimsby.

There was so little to make ready for the move to McCarthy's property. She would have a small cottage to herself, so would take with her the few household bits and pieces she brought with her when they left the mill's estate. The bassinette she would leave behind. She wouldn't be needing that any time soon – or ever again. Her mother's books would go with her. She didn't know what her evenings would be like, but she hoped there would be time to lose herself in the different worlds of the stories she found in those books.

What to do about the residence above the store? She cleaned out what little food there was. Some weeks ago, she had taken to only bringing up from the store what food she needed as she needed it. The best she could do was to give the place a thorough cleaning and lock it when she left. No matter how much effort she put into it, she was sure her father would find fault with it. It occurred to her that her father probably didn't have a key to the upstairs area. If she locked it when she left and he came back, he wouldn't be able to get in. While there was a certain feeling of satisfaction in that, she decided the best approach was to leave the key in the office downstairs.

Then there was nothing to do but wait for Friday and the arrival of McCarthy's wagon to collect her and her belongings. It had been a tense week; smiles were in short supply and completely non-existent by the time Friday arrived.

All too soon, it was Friday and her transport arrived around mid-afternoon. Alfred loaded their order of supplies onto the wagon and then helped the driver load Ellen's belongings. Unbeknown to her, they had closed the doors of the store and the agency. The three staff gathered on the loading dock to see her off. Tears streamed down Jess' face as she hugged Ellen. Alfred hugged her and then fought back his tears as Charlie shook her hand.

Ellen called, "See you next Thursday," then turned quickly and jumped aboard the wagon. The driver moved off quickly and Ellen waved to those she knew would still be standing at the loading dock… but she did not look back. It was better that only the driver saw her tears.

PART TWO

Changes and Opportunities

Chapter 14

The end of February 1900 saw Ellen end one period in her life and commence a new one. With mixed emotions she boarded the wagon for the trip to *Koreelah,* the McCarthy's property. Her arrival at her new home just on dusk did nothing to quieten her nerves. The driver deposited Ellen and her belongings at a small cottage separated from the main homestead by the kitchen garden.

Ellen let herself in and went on a tour of inspection of her new home. She was touched by the vase of fresh flowers on the small kitchen table. Her inspection took only moments; there wasn't much to the cottage. As she came back into the front room intending to start unpacking, Mrs McCarthy arrived to welcome her and to invite her to dinner at the main house. There was a bit over an hour until dinnertime. She busied herself with unpacking the essentials so she would be ready for the morning. Then, with her face washed and her appearance tidied, she made her way through the kitchen garden to the main house.

Mrs McCarthy introduced her to Maggie, the cook and showed Ellen around the main house while they waited for dinner. The meal was nothing fancy but it was delicious, and it was wonderful to eat something someone else had cooked. At the end of the meal, Mr McCarthy took himself off to his study to smoke and drink a glass or two of port, leaving the two women alone to discuss the schedule for the following day. Time slipped away unnoticed until Maggie came in to say goodnight.

"Oh, Maggie, on your way home, would you mind walking Miss Grimsby to her cottage, please. We will organise a lantern for her tomorrow, but we don't want her getting lost amongst the marrows on her way home in the dark tonight."

Maggie gave a hearty, deep-throated laugh. "Sure, and we can't be having that happen on your first night here. If you're done here, we'll go now." Ellen said goodnight to Mrs McCarthy and followed Maggie out into the night. "You can't be getting lost or nothing if you follow this path through the vegetables, Miss Grimsby," Maggie reassured her.

"Call me Ellen please, Maggie – unless there is some house rule that says you shouldn't."

"There be no rule that I'm aware of, and Ellen is a bit less of a mouthful to say." Maggie stayed with her lantern until Ellen lit a light before leaving for own cottage a short distance away.

Ellen remained too tightly wound up to sleep, and it was still early. She set about unpacking the rest of her belongings and tried arranging them to create something of a homely environment. There was little enough to unpack, so it happened quickly, but she found nowhere to put her mother's books. For want of anything better to do with them, she stacked the boxes in a corner of the room. Although they didn't look great like that, at least she would be able to get at them. With nothing else she could do that night, she got ready for bed. It was surprising that the bed provided as part of the cottage's furnishing was so comfortable –equally surprising was how well Ellen slept that night.

Her days started early and she did not want to oversleep on her first day at her new job. She had nothing to worry about; the sun came up early and streamed in through her bedroom window. As she opened her eyes, the strange surroundings confused her for a few moments. She lay back with her eyes closed for a few seconds listening to the bird song filling the air and she breathed in the distinctive scent of the rosemary bushes disturbed when one of dogs ran through the kitchen garden. In some ways, it was like being back on the mill estate, only this was much quieter and somehow the air smelled sweeter.

Nice as this might be, it was wasting time. Ellen sprang out of bed, dressed, tidied up and was on her way through the kitchen garden to the main house when one of the dogs came to make her acquaintance. "Looks like you've made a friend already," she heard Maggie call to her from the verandah outside the kitchen. "…And you're a bit early. No one be up and about yet."

As Ellen climbed the stairs to join Maggie, she said, "I didn't want to be late on my first day."

"You might as well have a cuppa while you wait for some activity back there." Maggie jerked her thumb in the direction of the far end of the house, which Ellen remembered from last night's tour was where the bedrooms were. "How's this going to work then?" Maggie enquired as she poured the tea. "Are you supposed to wait here until they come through for breakfast or what?"

"I'm not exactly sure, but I think I'm supposed to help Mrs McCarthy dress in the morning, but maybe not today; not until we get a routine worked out perhaps." Ellen thought for a moment. "Maggie, I was thinking about all those steps. Climbing up and down them can't be doing Mrs McCarthy any good. How does she manage?"

"She's not one to complain, mind you, but they do knock her around a bit. She doesn't hardly go downstairs much these days unless she really has to for some reason. It might have seemed like a good idea at the time, lifting the house up the way they did, but it's coming against them now they're getting on a bit in years."

"Oh, so the house hasn't always been up on these high posts?"

"Nah, they built it on short posts. Low, just about knee high; only high enough off the ground so as water wouldn't come inside when it rained heavy. Then the fashion changed and everyone built houses on high posts; supposed to be cooler somehow."

"You sound like you have been on the property for a long time and know its history well."

"Oh ay; I grew up here. I never lived anywhere else. Well, nowhere I can remember anyways. My father was a stockman here and eventually made head stockman. My mother was the cook. In those days, the cook had to feed all the workers as well as the family. …Soon as I was old enough, I came to work here as the housemaid, and then as the cook's offsider. After my father died, my mother stayed on for a bit, before she decided to move to town. My sister was married and living in town. She had a tribe of kids and my mother went to live with her to help with the kids. I took over as the cook."

"Do you still cook for all the workers? I haven't seen any around this morning."

"Yes… and no; I cook for the single ones when they are back here. There are a couple of married ones. They have their own cottages. The property provides all their supplies, but their wives do for them. No workers are around now. They're camping out on the property, rounding up stock and mending fences after the rain. So, it's just him and her for breakfast – and you of course."

Ellen nodded her understanding and was about to ask another question when Maggie started speaking again.

"Better look sharpish; I hear movement down the bedroom end of the world."

"Should I go to see if Mrs McCarthy needs some assistance?"

"Now how would I be knowing that?" Maggie's deep laugh rolled out again. "There ain't never been a lady's companion here before, so how can I be telling you what they do."

"No, of course you wouldn't know. I don't know, and I suspect Mrs McCarthy doesn't know yet either."

"Well, if you want my opinion like, I'm thinking you should go down there and knock on the bedroom door and ask if she would like some help. It's the door on the left."

Mrs McCarthy invited Ellen in to help her dress, and then together the women made their way to breakfast. Mr McCarthy had started breakfast when they arrived and offered only a perfunctory greeting without looking up from the document he was reading at the table, and with only a momentary pause in munching his bacon and eggs. Ellen dished up breakfast for both herself and Mrs McCarthy and then took her place at the table opposite the older woman.

In this house, apparently breakfast is a silent affair. Apart from the initial greeting, no one spoke until Mr McCarthy rose to leave the table. "Well, ladies, what are your plans for today? I hope you haven't included me in any of them. I am riding out to the western paddock to check on work out there, and it will probably be late when I get back. However, if my visit goes too late, I might campout with the men tonight. I shall take my swag in case I choose to do that. Please let cook know that I might not be back for dinner tonight."

"No, our plans for today do not include you in any way," Mrs McCarthy assured her husband. "In fact, we are just about to make those plans, so we will be mindful of the fact that you're not going to be around." She smiled at him as she finished speaking and he chuckled in response.

"Well, I suppose that, if you have no plans, there can be no moaning about them going awry." With that, he nodded to the two women, gathered up his document from the table and left the room.

"Good, now that he's gone, we can get on with planning our day – but we might move to the sitting room to do that. Maggie will be in here shortly rattling about as she cleans up."

"Speaking of cleaning up, perhaps I should go and tidy up your room first, before we sit down to make any plans," Ellen suggested.

"Goodness me; no, don't do that. You will incur the wrath of Elizabeth if you encroach on her territory. Elizabeth is the housekeeper and takes her job very seriously. She would not appreciate what she would see as someone meddling in her responsibilities. She is married to our foreman and lives in that cottage with the rose garden out front. She won't be in for another half hour or so. You can meet her then."

They settled themselves in the sitting room, and Ellen retrieved a small notebook and pencil from the pocket in her voluminous skirt. It was more of a friendly chat than a discussion between a boss and her employee, and the friendship that already existed between the two women was evident as they discussed what Ellen's duties might include. Time slipped by quickly. Their conversation halted when a young woman of about Ellen's age came into the room. She wore an apron and carried a duster, and Mrs McCarthy introduced her as Elizabeth, the housekeeper.

"I'm sorry, Elizabeth, we should move out of your way and not hold you up," Mrs McCarthy said and rose from her chair.

"Why don't we carry on our conversation out on the verandah?" Ellen suggested. Mrs McCarthy seemed a bit taken aback by the suggestion but nodded, and led the way out onto the wide covered verandah. A number of comfortable -looking chairs and side tables were scattered about the length of the verandah. They selected seats shaded from the morning sun.

"You know, we hardly come out here these days. In days gone by, we often used to sit out here; take tea out here even. Mr McCarthy would entertain any man who visited the place out here. They would take tea, or have a drink and smoke to their hearts content without fear of interruption or criticism. When my son was a little fellow, I use to bring him out onto the verandah to play… of course, in those days the house wasn't high like it is now and it was much safer for him to be out here than it would be now."

Sometime during the morning, Maggie brought out tea and crisp little biscuits for morning tea. The women sat together, with Ellen making copious notes, until Maggie announced lunch. It had been an easy morning, with lots of friendly chatter intermixed with the more serious business of what Ellen's duties might include. Amongst other things, Ellen discovered that she could draw supplies from the property's store, although she probably wouldn't need much as there was expectation she would take her meals in the main house.

When lunch was almost over, Elizabeth brought in a lantern and placed it on the sideboard. "This is for you Ellen, so you can see to go home at night. I'll just leave it here for you, but don't forget to take it with you."

Maggie bustled in to clear away the lunch things. "We are just going, Maggie. We'll get out of your way. Come, Ellen, let's leave the lady to get on with her work."

Ellen grabbed her lantern as she followed Mrs McCarthy out of the room. She wasn't sure where Mrs McCarthy was heading in the house but gently laid a hand on her arm to bring her to a halt. "I don't know what your usual practice is after lunch, Mrs McCarthy, but I think it would be beneficial for you to have a rest for at least a couple of hours – unless, of course, there is something else you need to take care of."

"I have nothing pressing I need to attend to. If I'm feeling weary, I do occasionally have a rest after lunch, but I always feel so guilty about doing so."

"There is nothing to feel guilty about, and now that I am here to take care of other things for you, I suggest you make it your regular practice."

Mrs McCarthy gave her warm smile. "You are quite right, my dear. I will do as you say. While I am doing that this afternoon, your time is your own to do as you please. Once we get ourselves organised, it might be an ideal time for you to work on the property's accounts and whatever else needs doing in the office." Ellen took Mrs McCarthy through to her room, made sure she was comfortable, and then wandered out to the kitchen where she found Maggie making bread.

"Was there something you were wanting, Miss… oops, Ellen?"

"No, I suppose I'm at a bit of a loose end. Mrs McCarthy is resting and our planning hasn't progressed far enough for me to have something specific to do while she is lying down."

"Well, there's nothing for you to be doing here in the kitchen. Why don't you take yourself back to the cottage and put your feet up for a while? It might be the only opportunity you'll have once you get this routine of yours sorted out."

Right, Ellen thought, I know when I'm in the way. Maybe I should go back to the cottage. I could read the notes I took this morning and make notes of anything I might need to follow up on or clarify. With her lantern swinging from her hand, she tripped lightly down the stairs and started for the cottage. Humidity was building again. More storms were on the way. She considered what that meant in terms of her daily commute from cottage to main house. If nothing else, it was going to mean trudging through that muddy vegetable garden at least twice a day. She crossed the lawn and was about to start on the path through the vegetable garden when she saw Elizabeth taking washing from the clothes line at the back of the house. Ellen made her way through the well-laid out garden to Elizabeth.

"Elizabeth, I wanted to catch up with you. Have you worked here for a while?"

"More than fifteen years now. I came here just before I got married. I started as what they used to call a housemaid. I took over her position when Maggie stepped up to being the cook."

"So, you would know Mrs McCarthy well. If you have a moment, I'd like to talk to you about something that's bothering me." Elizabeth nodded and suggested Ellen talk while Elizabeth got on with taking the clothes off the line.

"I saw Mrs McCarthy when she came into the store a couple of weeks before Christmas. She wasn't well that day. When I spoke to Mr McCarthy after they returned from their sojourn in the mountains, he said the holiday had revitalised Mrs McCarthy. Then I saw her for the first time since before Christmas when she came into the store a couple of weeks ago. Her colour had improved considerably since I saw her previously, but I saw a degree of frailty in her that I hadn't notice previously. Yesterday, when she came to welcome me to *Koreelah,* I had to stop myself gasping when I saw her. She seems shrunken and the frailty has increased significantly. Are my observations correct, or am I imagining things?"

For a few moments, Elizabeth studied the clothes pegs she held in hand before answering. Without looking at Ellen, she nodded and slowly replied. "Your observations are correct. I notice a marked decline in her condition over the last month or so. She never mentions it, but she must be aware of it. Last week, I plucked up courage to ask her about her health. She said she was fine, but that old age was catching up with her."

"Hmm, I don't know about old age being responsible for her decline, but I am going to have to find some way of asking questions about her health. I don't know how old she is, but she certainly seems to have aged since Christmas."

"Just so you are aware, I think you'll find she is a bit older than her husband. I don't know how much older, mind you, but possibly eight or nine years – maybe even ten years."

"I was not aware of that and I suspect she might be a bit sensitive about that age difference." Elizabeth nodded her agreement. "I have only a rough idea of how old Mr McCarthy is but, if I add that many years onto what I think his age is, it would make Mrs McCarthy in her late sixties – or maybe even in her early seventies. Perhaps her comments about old age are not too far from the truth."

They chatted until Elizabeth finished taking in the clothes and was about to take them into the house. "Before you go, Elizabeth, who looks after the garden and the lawns?"

"That would be Bert. Maggie's husband, Bert, who was employed here as a stockman at one time. He injured his back while out mustering and couldn't ride a horse much anymore, so they kept him on as a gardener. He's a bit of a character, but a good gardener. Again, just so you know and he doesn't come as a shock when you meet Bert, Maggie had the right idea when she chose her husband. Bert is a handful of years younger than our Maggie." Elizabeth tapped the side of her nose knowingly as she delivered the last snippet of information.

Ellen decided it was too much trouble to go back to the cottage. Her only reason for going there at this time was to drop off the lantern. On thinking it over, there was little point in leaving the lantern at the house. She would need it to light her way home from the main house tonight. With that decided, she wandered over to investigate the area under the house. It was a lovely big area with a wooden floor added, probably at the height of the original floor for the house.

It appeared that at some time in the past, they closed in an area towards the rear of the building to create a couple of rooms. This still left a reasonable floored open area, which contained a trestle table and rustic bench seats, as well as a couple of other comfortable chairs. It was like having a downstairs verandah. This downstairs area was shaded by the house above, and a cool breeze blew through the space rendering it much cooler than the upstairs verandah areas. This will do, Ellen thought as she approached one of the comfortable chairs. I'll sit here to read my notes from this morning and not bother going back to the cottage.

She lost track of the time, and was startled when Elizabeth spoke to her. "I'm on my way home for the day, but I thought you should know that it sounds like Mrs McCarthy might be up and about."

"Thanks, I'll go up," Ellen called after the retreating figure. Elizabeth waved over her shoulder and kept walking. As Ellen returned her notebook to her pocket, she wondered when might be a good time to raise the question of Mrs McCarthy's health and how she might go about that. Should she wait a few days before raising the issue, or should she ask now so she could work out what might be required in the future and how to proceed with caring for her boss?

At the top of the stairs, Ellen paused to consider what these stairs meant to Mrs McCarthy. Due to her condition, they virtually kept her confined to this top floor for six days of the week. She only suffered them on Thursdays when she went down to go into town. What a shame, Ellen thought. If they had left the house lower to the ground, Mrs McCarthy would be able to wander through the beautiful gardens, smell the flowers and take in a bit of sunshine. Ellen shook her head as she realised that was how things were; the stairs were there and little could be done about that now.

Mrs McCarthy was sitting on the edge of her bed when Ellen went into her room. "Are you all right, Mrs McCarthy? Can I get you something?" Her concern increased when she notice how pale the woman looked.

"Thank you, my dear, but no. I slept deeply this afternoon and I'm still a bit lightheaded. Perhaps you could help me up. It is afternoon tea time and Maggie will have a tray prepared for us."

"Where do you usually take afternoon tea?"

"Oh, usually alone in the sitting room. Do you have somewhere else in mind?"

"Let's go out onto the verandah this afternoon and enjoy what little cool breeze there is. If Maggie has a tray prepared, I could fetch it and bring it out there." There was no need. As she guided Mrs McCarthy out, she saw Maggie coming down the hallway with the tea tray. With a jerk of her head, Ellen indicated they were heading to the verandah, and Maggie followed them out.

Over tea, Ellen asked about Mrs McCarthy's routine for the rest of the afternoon. "I go to the library to read for a while before taking a bath and getting dressed for dinner, which Maggie has on the table at seven o'clock sharp in summer. Dinner is at 6.30pm in winter because it gets dark earlier and, if the men are in close, they come in from the fields earlier."

"You have a library; how wonderful."

"Oh, I'm sorry, I didn't show you that part of the house last night. It's nothing grand, but I do like to sit in there and read." Later, in the library, Mrs McCarthy explained how the library came about.

"I know it seems strange to find a library tucked away in this part of the house, but this big room wasn't intended as a library. When it became apparent its intended use was no longer relevant, we decided to turn it into a library. By then, books were lying about everywhere you looked in the house. We needed to round them up and keep them all together in one place, so Mr McCarthy had bookshelves built and installed – only on that wall over there initially. When we came to add all the books to the shelves, we found we had insufficient shelves, so he had a similar set of shelving installed on this wall. Do you like reading?"

"I do, but for years, I didn't have time to sit down and read anything. After my mother died, I found I could read for a short while each evening before I went to bed. I started working my way through my mother's books. She had quite a collection – nothing as large as this of course."

"What did she read? Did she have any favourite types of books or authors?"

"There is a wide variety of books by different authors. She had a lot of poetry books, and I think poetry might have been her favourite."

"Do you enjoy poetry books? There are a few in this library, but not many."

"No, I wouldn't say I was fond of it. I do read bits and pieces that catch my attention, but I much prefer books that tell interesting stories."

"Ah well, you will be able to while away many an hour in this library." With that, Mrs McCarthy went to what was obviously her favourite chair and picked up a book from the side table next to it. Ellen lit a lamp for her to read by, and then began examining the hundreds of books lining two walls of the room.

Ellen was still enraptured with the books when Mrs McCarthy announced it was time for her to take a bath. Ellen ran the bath for her and afterwards helped her to dress before they made their way along to the dining room. Maggie placed various dishes in the centre of the table and left them to serve themselves. Mr McCarthy hadn't returned home in time for dinner and it seemed obvious he intended spending the night camped out with his workers.

Mrs McCarthy seemed to tire quickly after dinner. Ellen was relieved to get her into bed and then be able to go home to her own cottage – and her own company – for the night. As she made her way down the stairs with her lantern lighting the way, Ellen saw another lantern coming towards the house. She waited at the bottom of the stairs to see who the visitor might be. It was Maggie. In response to Ellen's enquiry, Maggie explained that her usual practice was to put dinner on the table for the family and then go home to feed her own husband before coming back to clean up after dinner at the main house.

Ellen bade her good night and set off along the path through the vegetable garden. Maggie called after her, "Sleep well, and I'll see you again early in the morning."

Chapter 15

The next day brought the start of what would become her daily routine. Ellen again rose early and sat with Maggie in the kitchen until she heard movement in Mrs McCarthy's bedroom. After breakfast, they went to the office where Mrs McCarthy explained the accounts and the filing system to Ellen. Once morning tea was over, they went through to the library. Ellen learned that any book must appear in the library catalogue before it took its place on the shelves. Those books stacked in piles on a table in the centre of the room still required cataloguing.

Mrs McCarthy worked on setting up the library over a number of years, but now found it required too much effort and concentration. Ellen inherited the task and Mrs McCarthy provided detailed instruction on how to do it. While Mrs McCarthy set herself up to write letters at a table on one side of the room, Ellen made a start on the cataloguing. She had a thick woolly brain by the time Maggie called them to lunch.

Ellen made Mrs McCarthy comfortable for her afternoon rest and then went to the office to attend to the accounts. It was obvious Mrs McCarthy had not kept it up to date over the last couple of weeks but, by the time Ellen needed to get Mrs McCarthy up for afternoon tea, she had sorted out much of the backlog. The rest of the afternoon followed the previous day's routine. The two women spent a couple of hours in the library. The only different today was that Ellen also selected a book and read for that whole time.

She liked the library. It was a large comfortable room, although its single window did not provide much light. It would be uncomfortable to read in there for too long without lighting the lamps. The room held a collection of mismatched chairs and footstools that looked as though, over the years, someone gathered them up and hid them in the library. An assortment of strategically placed side tables and a large rug completed the décor.

There was evidence of clearly defined patterns of behaviour in this room. Mrs McCarthy always sat in the same chair and left her current book on the side table beside it. The lamp on the side table had a feminine look. On the opposite side of the room, was a robust winged armchair, and the bits and pieces on its associated side table indicated where Mr McCarthy usually sat. Over the next few days, Ellen tried reading in various chairs until she found one in a position she liked. She marked her territory by leaving her book on the table beside her chosen chair.

Mr McCarthy returned home sometime late that afternoon, and dinner that night followed what would become the standard pattern. Ellen joined the McCarthys for the evening meal and participated in the polite chat about each other's days. Once dinner was over, Mr McCarthy took himself off to his study for a brandy or port and a cigar. The two women chatted for a while about any plans for the next day before Ellen helped Mrs McCarthy get ready for bed. After that, Ellen's time was her own.

As she lay in bed that night waiting for sleep to come, Ellen reflected on her day. Today was as my days will be from now on, she thought, and wondered how she felt about that. It wasn't an arduous day, but it wasn't particularly exciting either. Her last thought as her eyes grew heavy was that it might not be the greatest job in the world, but she probably could put up with it for quite some time.

A leaden sky greeted her the next morning. The building humidity would soon turn to rain. On her way through the kitchen garden, Ellen reached a decision: today she would ask Mrs McCarthy about the state of her health. Ellen needed to understand what was going on and to find out what treatment – if any – Mrs McCarthy's doctor had prescribed. The only problem now, having made that decision, was when to do it. Ellen was still mulling over that question when she arrived in the kitchen and Maggie thrust a cup of tea at her.

"You might have a problem today, Ellen," Maggie began. That was enough to bring Ellen back to earth with a thump.

"What sort of problem… and what makes you think so?"

"Lamps were still burning after I went home last night, and they were still lit early this morning when I got up. I reckon the light came from Mrs McCarthy's room. Looks to me as though she had a bad night."

"Is that common? Have you noticed this on any other night? I was going to talk to her today about her health. If what you say is correct, I had better do that first thing." Ellen felt her stomach tighten. She didn't know if she could handle any more upsets yet. She was still trying to settle in. She liked Mrs McCarthy and dreaded finding out she was seriously ill. With a fair degree of trepidation, she knocked on Mrs McCarthy's bedroom door.

The woman hadn't attempted to get up and the curtains were still drawn. Ellen moved quickly to open the curtains, commented on the building storm outside, and then caught her breath as she turned to face her boss. "You do not look well enough to be getting up this morning. Would you prefer to stay in bed today?" Ellen asked as she applied her hand to Mrs McCarthy's forehead. There might be a slight temperature, she thought. "I hear you did not have a good night. Is there something I can get you?"

Edith McCarthy flapped her hand dismissively for Ellen to stop fussing. "It's true; I couldn't get comfortable for most of last night. I think a day in bed might be the best thing for me. You have a bit to do in the office and there's cataloguing the library but, if you get that done, I'm sure you could find something to fill in the rest of your day."

"My day is not the concern. It was my intention to ask you first thing this morning about your health. If you feel up to it, I'd like us to discuss that now." A weak protest started but Ellen silenced it by continuing to speak. "The main part of my job is looking after you. I cannot do my job properly if I don't have all the information I need to do that. So, let's take some time now to talk about your health."

Ellen dragged a chair over beside the bed, sat down and looked quite sternly at the frail-looking woman in the bed. "Let's start with the basics: are you seeing a doctor for your condition?"

Edith shook her head. "It's not about having a condition. I am an old woman who grows older by the day. There is nothing unusual about that. As I have said before, I am not as strong as I used to be and I tire easily now."

With a shake of her head to dismiss Edith's words, Ellen asked the question again. "I have heard all that. What I want to know is: are you seeing a doctor?"

There was a deep sigh of resignation before an answer was forthcoming. "Yes, I see my doctor every week when I go to town on Thursdays. I fear it is all a waste of time and money."

"What does he say about your condition..." Ellen though she better rephrase that question to avoid getting a repeat of the 'I'm getting old' story. "What does he say is wrong with you – and what treatment has he prescribed?"

"He is not sure. When I first went to see him, he gave me a tonic. It tasted awful and didn't do anything – nothing more to say about that. He saw the tonic wasn't working, so gave me a different tonic to take."

"For how long have you been taking the new tonic?"

"Only a couple of weeks; he gave it to me the day I came to see you at the store. It tastes vile, but probably hasn't had time to work yet."

"How often and when do you take this tonic?"

"…Four times a day, before meals and at night when I go to bed."

"I haven't seen you taking this tonic. Have you been taking it? Where is it anyway? You should have had a dose of it already this morning before breakfast."

"It's that bottle on the dressing table. I don't feel like breakfast this morning so I don't see why I need to take the tonic. It's so inconvenient. When I'm here with the bottle, I don't have any water to take with it. When I'm somewhere else in the house, the bottle is here and not with me. I get comfortable in bed and glance over and see the bottle, but I couldn't be bothered getting out of bed again to take any."

Ellen was having no more of this nonsense. She fetched the bottle, read the directions and dished out in dose – in spite of Edith's protests. "Of course the tonic isn't having any effect. It is not going to do any good sitting over there in the bottle. It only works when you take it, and from now on, I will be making sure you do take it. Are you going to argue with me on that?" Edith shook her head, but Ellen noticed she looked deflated by what she said. Never mind, Ellen thought, it had to be said and, if I'm to continue in this job and do it well, I can see there will be occasions when straight talking is required. "Now, about breakfast Mrs McCarthy, what message should I give Maggie? Perhaps something light on a tray…"

They finally agreed that Edith might try a lightly boiled egg and Ellen took herself to the kitchen to inform Maggie of the request. It seemed like no time before Maggie arrived with the breakfast tray. Edith insisted she preferred to eat breakfast without an audience and sent Ellen to the dining room to have her own breakfast.

There was no sign of Mr McCarthy at breakfast, so Ellen sought out Maggie to find out why. "He rode out early to set the men on their jobs for today. Said he would be back later for breakfast, and I expected he would come looking for breakfast about now."

"I must talk to him about Mrs McCarthy. Her condition is worsening and I am now quite concerned for her. I don't know whether her husband is aware of how ill I believe she is. If you should see Mr

McCarthy, please tell him I wish to speak with him and that I shall be in the office this morning."

Ellen looked in on Mrs McCarthy a few times during the morning. She told herself that, as the woman was sleeping peacefully, it was probably the best thing for her and that perhaps the tonic had helped her sleep. Mr McCarthy failed to appear during that time, and Ellen queried Maggie about it. He hadn't come back to the Homestead for breakfast. Maggie conceded it was unusual but that they were very busy on the property since the rains. When Maggie left the office, Ellen picked up the morning tea tray and carried it out onto the verandah.

Elizabeth came out through one of the French doors that opened onto the verandah and stood surveying the darkening skies. Ellen, sitting a little further down the verandah, called to Elizabeth to join her. "I'm not sure whether you're supposed to have morning tea or not, but I could do with the company and the tea tray is set for two people anyway." Elizabeth smiled and pulled over a chair. She did take morning tea but it was usually in the kitchen with Maggie.

"I noticed the lady of the house is not up and about today," Elizabeth commented. "How is her condition? It is unusual for her to remain in bed, so I assume it is not good news and that she is deteriorating."

There was much insight into Edith's history from spending a few minutes in conversation with Elisabeth. Although she hadn't been on the property as long as Maggie, Elizabeth was a quietly astute observer of all that went on in the house and had a different perspective. "Edith's condition has existed for a few months now. The woman appears to be shrinking before our eyes. It's my opinion that his wife's deteriorating condition deeply troubles Mr McCarthy and he now throws himself into work on the property as his way of coping with the situation."

They sat in silence for a few moments watching the dense black clouds roll closer. The air hung thick and unmoving, but both women knew that all too soon that would change. It was likely a squall would come through bringing strong winds and heavy rain. That brought back to Ellen her concern about the prospect of traversing a muddy path through the vegetable garden. She mentioned her concern about it to Elizabeth who laughed.

"It's all part of the joy of living on the land," she said. "When the ground is wet, you'd be better off taking the long way round. When you leave the cottage, instead of heading for the vegetable garden, turn right and stick to the grass. It will make it a fair bit longer because you will have to walk around those garden beds down there – and you'll still end up with wet shoes but they won't be muddy." With that, she picked up her duster and stood to leave. "I'd better get a move on and get finished or I'll be walking home in the rain."

As she had finished all there was to do in the office, Ellen headed for the library, looking in on Mrs McCarthy on her way. Edith still slept, and Ellen found herself wondering whether that was a good thing or not. What little light usually entered the library through its single window no longer entered the room, now replaced by the darkness of the gathering clouds. She had just lit several lamps when the squall came.

Ellen stood at the window to take in the spectacle. First the wind came. It attacked the trees mercilessly, bending them to its will and strewing the manicured lawn with leaves. Then the rain came; heavy and in a continuous torrent pounding against the window. Somehow, the dark ferocity of the squall matched her mood today. She would make the most of her time today to get as much of the cataloguing out of the way as possible but she knew her mind would not be on the job completely. Her concern for Edith McCarthy would dominate all day. A sound behind her startled Ellen and she whirled around to discover Mr McCarthy had entered the library.

"You wanted to see me Miss Grimsby?"

"I appreciate how busy you are at the moment but, if you could spare me a few moments, I do need to speak to you."

"No one is busy now that the rain has come again. I hear that Mrs McCarthy remained in her bed this morning."

"Yes, that's what I wanted to speak to you about. I wanted to speak to her about her health but couldn't decide on the right approach. When she was so poorly this morning, it was natural to have that discussion. She divulged a small amount of information about her condition, but I don't believe she told me all there is to know. It's not that I'm prying, but it is difficult for me to know how to help her if I don't know the whole story. Suffice to say, I am concerned for Mrs McCarthy and believe her condition to be grave. I wonder whether, if you have any information about her health, you might consider sharing it with me."

"You correctly have ascertained for yourself that her condition is serious and deteriorates by the day. Her doctor is not encouraging regarding her treatment, but it is the best that can be done for her."

"She has not been taking the tonic the doctor prescribed – there are all sorts of excuses for that. I assured her this morning that I will see to it that she takes it as prescribed future. However, she tells me the doctor has not identified her illness. I find that hard to believe – although, it's possible I suppose – and wonder whether you might know differently."

"I believe what she says is true and that Dr Boyd hasn't told her the nature of her illness. However, I spoke to him myself on this matter only recently. He confirmed Mrs McCarthy suffers from the 'white blood' condition they now call Leukaemia. The arsenic mixture he has given her to take is the only treatment available, although there has been some experimentation in the past with transferring blood from another person to the patient. Such treatment remains experimental and is highly hazardous as the treatment itself has caused the death of many of the patients involved in the trials."

Ellen felt a cold wave spread through her body and could not meet McCarthy's eyes for a few moments. She didn't know what to say but believed a comment necessary, so haltingly began. "This is not good news. Are you saying that, if this arsenic mixture does not work, there is little hope for a recovery?" As she finished the sentence, Ellen felt tears well up in her eyes. She swallowed hard and turned away from McCarthy in the hope that he would not notice.

"That is the understanding I have but struggle to accept. It is better the truth is kept from Mrs McCarthy than have her dwell on the likely outcome of her condition. Mrs McCarthy is a kind and generous woman. She does not deserve what she now must endure for however long remains. I see that you have formed a bond with my wife. While that is a good thing, it will make life hard for you. For my wife's sake, I hope you have the same strength to see it through as you had for your mother. Perhaps you will understand when I say that my only interest is in making whatever life she has left as comfortable and happy as possible."

"I know something of how you must feel. You are right, I am very fond of Mrs McCarthy and will do my best for her but, as you say, I feel we both will suffer difficult times ahead."

McCarthy turned on his heel and left the library, but Ellen noticed the set of his jaw and his need to blink frequently. It was almost lunchtime and Ellen decided to check on her patient before going to the dining room. If Edith were awake, she would need to get her to take another dose of the 'tonic' and try to tempt her to eat something for lunch.

The anticipated battle to get her to take another dose of tonic didn't occur. Edith was dozing when Ellen entered the room, but opened her eyes as Ellen approached the bed. She took the tonic without too much complaint but refused food, and her eyes soon closed again. Ellen checked on Edith again before dinner and found her to be much brighter. After another dose of tonic, Edith agreed to try a little light broth for dinner, and Ellen rushed off to tell Maggie.

Next morning, Edith was much brighter and insisted on coming to the dining room for breakfast. She took her medicine without argument, but Ellen noticed she was still quite weak. After breakfast, Ellen fetched a footstool from the library and made Edith comfortable on the verandah. As there was no work in the office to occupy her morning, Ellen suggested she might read to Edith, but added the proviso that she would only do so if Edith promised to say when she had enough. They spent the morning that way – with periods of chatter interspersed with passages from the book – until Maggie arrived with the morning tea tray.

As they were finishing their tea, Mr McCarthy joined them on the verandah and Maggie rushed out after him with an extra cup and scones. The worst of the storm had passed quickly in the afternoon but the rain persisted as a light drizzle throughout the night. As a result, there was little work going on anywhere on the property again that day. Mr McCarthy didn't stay long once he had taken tea. Perhaps, like Ellen, could see Edith was beginning to wilt. As soon as he had gone, Ellen suggested Edith go back to bed to rest until lunchtime.

While settling Edith in bed, Ellen asked whether, given Edith's weakened state, she thought it wise to cancel Thursday's trip to town. Edith was adamant they should still go. "I have my doctor and dressmaker to see, and one of my friends is having a birthday so we all will be together for lunch.

The rain cleared during the day, and the men planned to resume work around the property the following morning. It occurred to Ellen that, if they were going to town on Thursday, she would be taking Edith in the buggy, as the men once again would be too busy. While she helped Edith bathe and dress for dinner, she broached the subject of the trip to town. "If you are sure you want to go to town on Thursday, I will take us in the buggy. However, before then, I need to look at the buggy to see how it is arranged, and find the tack room to look at the harness, and then establish which horses to use and where they are."

"Is that possible?" Edith said with clear alarm in her voice. "Are you able to handle the buggy? I'm sure Mr McCarthy would find someone to drive us in if I asked him."

"Of course I can handle the buggy. I just need to have a look at it and be familiar with it before we are ready to leave on Thursday. I don't know where to find it, where the tack room is, or anything about what horses to use with the buggy. These are things I need to sort out tomorrow at the latest."

"Perhaps you should have a word to Bert. He will be able to help you with all those things and show you where things are. It would be best to catch up with him straight after breakfast, before he gets too involved in his day's work."

It was obvious some doubt remained in Edith's mind about Ellen's capability with the buggy when she voiced her concerns to her husband at dinner that night. "Ellen claims she is quite capable of handling the buggy and will take us into town on Thursday morning. What are your thoughts on this?" Ellen wished she could disappear under the table. She was not happy that Edith discussed her as if she weren't in the room.

"To my knowledge, Miss Grimsby is more than capable of handling the buggy or the wagon for that matter and, if you insist on going into town on Thursday, that is the only way you will get there." He raised his eyebrows at his wife, encouraging her to elaborate on any other concerns she might have about Ellen's ability. Edith smiled sweetly at her husband and nodded her understanding.

As soon as breakfast was over the next morning, Ellen looked for Bert but couldn't find him. In desperation, she came back to the kitchen and asked Maggie if she knew where he was likely to be. "He be working down the back today I think; working on trimming those hedges that are run amok since all the rain. They've grown so high now, you probably can't see Bert from up on the verandah. You might have to take yourself off down there if you want to talk to him."

Ellen picked her way carefully through the wet grass and patches of mud to the hedge that bordered the back boundary of the yard. An overweight, red-faced man with rolled up shirtsleeves attacked the hedge with some vigour. It was obvious even to Ellen's untrained eye that he would be toiling away down there for some days before the hedge was once more under control. She explained the reason she sought him out and he happily downed tool to show her where to find things.

Bert explained that they usually kept the buggy under the main house, in that area without a wooden floor, but the recent heavy rains made that location too muddy. They put it in one of the large sheds until the place dried out a bit. The tack room, conveniently located in one end of the same shed, held no surprises. So far, so good, Ellen thought. She hadn't come across any problems thus far. Now, what about the horses for the buggy, would they prove a problem?

She followed Bert the short distance from the shed to an area he called the 'home yard', although it looked more like a small paddock to Ellen. "See those two lovely bay ponies over there? They are the ones we use on the buggy. They are quiet and well trained."

"They are fine looking animals," Ellen said.

"Tell you what, Miss, I'll bring the horses in and hitch up the buggy for you in the morning. As I hear it, you will have your hands full with getting Mrs McCarthy ready without having to worry about the buggy… and you won't need to come down here getting all dirty to do it."

"I wouldn't want to get you into trouble for doing something you're not supposed to, but it would be much appreciated if you did that for me."

"No trouble, Miss. I do the same for the boss when he takes the buggy into town. He doesn't much take to getting his clean breeches messed up mucking about with horses and things."

The ride to town on Thursday morning was pleasant. There was a light breeze and the rains had laid the dust. Edith seemed almost her old self and the early start hadn't bothered her in any apparent way. For Ellen, coming back to town caused a certain excitement. If everything went according to plan, she would spend a few hours at the store, and she looked forward to talking to the staff again. As they neared town, a worrying thought occurred to her. What if her father was back; what if he had come back and taken over the store and the agency again? Her visit would not be welcome, and she felt sure her reception would be unpleasant and possibly embarrassing. She tried to put it out of her mind. No good worrying about it, she told herself, whatever happens will happen.

Their first stop was at Mrs Smith's tearooms for a pot of tea before Ellen delivered Edith to Doctor Boyle's rooms across the road and adjacent to the hospital. Edith said her appointment with the doctor usually lasted about an hour. With this in mind, Ellen left the buggy in the horse yard behind the hospital and walked around town paying accounts and attending to other errands for the property.

When Ellen returned to Dr Boyle's rooms, Edith was just emerging from his treatment room. She asked Edith to sit in the waiting room until she returned with the buggy. After helping Edith to board the buggy, they set off for Edith's next port of call: her dressmaker about halfway along the street. Ellen drove her there to save her the exertion of walking the relatively short distance. While Edith endured yet another fitting for her new outfit, Ellen did the banking for the property, and then returned to the dressmaker's to wait for Edith's fitting to finish. Next stop was the hotel. As it was the birthday of one of Edith's friends, they were celebrating with a more lavish lunch today instead of their usual meal at the tearooms.

Edith thought their long lunch could last until two o'clock. After that, she would visit her hairdresser. The hairdresser's salon was across the street and almost directly opposite Grimsby's Store. Ellen insisted that, if Edith felt tired when it came time to leave Miss Bainbridge's salon, Edith should ask the hairdresser to send her junior over to the Store to tell Ellen, who would then bring the buggy around to collect Edith. As she drove away from the hairdresser's, Ellen felt a twinge of panic. She had made those arrangements based on the assumption she would put the horses in the store's horse yard while she spent the afternoon with the staff. What if her father was there and it didn't happen that way? "Well," Ellen said aloud as she drove around to the rear of the store, "I will just have to go back to the hairdresser's and wait there for Edith to be finished."

She brought the buggy to a halt beside the gate to the horse yard. Alfred looked up from what he was doing on the loading dock. He wasn't expecting anyone to collect an order. When he saw who was on the buggy, he jumped down from the loading dock and raced across to open the gate. Ellen drove in, climbed off the buggy and Alfred closed the gate behind her as she exited the yard. He threw his arms around her in a brief hug, before quickly stepping away from her. "Begging your pardon, Miss, I do apologise for my behaviour."

Ellen laughed and returned his hug. "That's perfectly all right, Alfred. I have missed you too." They heard a shriek from the loading dock and looked up in alarm. Jess had come out to the back area to have lunch with Alfred. The sight of Ellen walking back with Alfred brought tears of joy to accompany her shriek of excitement. At the top of the stairs to the loading dock, Ellen stopped suddenly. "Is my father about?" she asked quietly.

"Your father...?" Alfred echoed. "Who is that? There has been no one by the name of James Grimsby around here since you left, not for months, if I remember rightly."

Chapter 16

It did feel good to be back. It was less than a week since Ellen left for Koreelah but it felt much longer than that. While Alfred and Jess ate lunch, they told Ellen how well the store continued to trade. Then it was time for them to return to work and it was Charlie's turn to take lunch. Ellen sat with him to discuss the agency. As the only agency in town now, it was natural for business to increase, but Charlie was a major contributing factor in the business' improvement. He too had not seen nor heard anything of James Grimsby, and somehow doubted the man was still in town.

Ellen pressed him about his belief that her father was not around, but Charlie had nothing specific to offer. It appeared nobody had seen James about the place. Charlie casually asked a few of his drinking mates at the pub about James but nobody knew anything of him. While Ellen found that good news – she could visit the store without worry about encountering her father. Now, she wasn't so much concerned about his whereabouts as what he might doing. Later, when she and Jess were going over the accounts, Ellen voiced those concerns.

"Hmm, I don't know where he might be now," Jess began, "But I can tell you where he has been. Quite a few accounts have arrived from different places." She opened a desk drawer and withdrew a clip holding a number of accounts. "These are all the accounts that have come in for the agency. Will you be paying them while you are here?" Ellen flicked through them.

"I see what you mean about him moving around. There is quite a bit of money involved in these accounts. I will need to check on the agency's bank account before anything else can be done."

"I think you will find it is quite healthy. There has been a lot banked this week."

The arrival of a customer ended their discussions. Jess went to serve, leaving Ellen to catch-up on the financial situation. Her first task was to make up the wages for the staff. Payday was every Friday. She would leave these ready in the safe for Jess to deal with the next day. It occurred to her that it might be worthwhile following the practice employed at Koreelah. There, an extra week's wages were made up in advance and kept in the safe as a precaution against a week when no one came to town to collect the money for the pays. It was reasonable to expect there would be weeks when she was unable to come to town. She did not want the staff to miss payday for that reason. Pays for two weeks were prepared and locked in the safe.

Time passed quickly. Cheques written, envelopes addressed for accounts to be mailed, and the banking prepared, then Ellen heard her stomach rumble and realised she had missed lunch. Almost on cue, Jess appeared with a cup of tea in one hand and a plate resplendent with a thick slice of buttered bread and a goodly wedge of cheese. "I don't think you've eaten, Miss. I thought this might help keep you going."

After thanking her and explaining about the wages, Ellen told Jess she was going to the bank and the post office, picked up her basket and left. She hurried, not sure how long she had before Edith McCarthy would be ready to head back to the property. Ellen need not have worried. It was after three o'clock before the young lass from Miss Bainbridge's salon came to say Edith would be finished at the salon in a few minutes.

After quick goodbyes to everyone, Ellen hitched the horses out front of the salon and went in to walk Edith out to the buggy. The woman looked weary and nodded off soon after they left town. Back at the homestead, Ellen pulled the buggy up to the bottom of the stairs, helped Edith down and sat her under the house. She intended dealing with the buggy and the horses before helping Edith upstairs. However, as she climbed back on board, Bert arrived and insisted on taking care of everything.

By the time Edith was upstairs, she was exhausted. Ellen insisted she go to bed immediately after her bath. After settling Edith in bed, Ellen went to arrange for a tray for Edith in her room. Then she took the wages money through to the office and spent the short time before dinner making up the pays for the next day for property's workers.

Mr McCarthy queried his wife's absence from the dinner table, and grew grave when Ellen explained how exhausting the day was for his wife. "Does she have to go to town every week? I know she has a regular appointment with Dr Boyle, but does it have to be every week? My concern is that these trips to town are doing her more harm than good."

"I don't have any answers for you," Ellen admitted, "But I share your concern. There wasn't opportunity to discuss her day, but I will enquire tomorrow as to how it went. However, I suspect the trips to town are important to her and any attempt to prevent them might bring an adverse reaction."

Alone in her cottage that night, Ellen pondered Mr McCarthy's comments regarding Edith's trips to town. Ellen always believed her father would reappear at the store and that she was lucky to get away before he returned. Now she knew he had not returned and likely was not even in the area, she doubted the wisdom of her move away from home. It effectively left no one minding the business on a day to day basis. She wondered about the long term viability of such an arrangement, and now added the worry of what might happen to the business if the weekly trips to town ceased. There was nothing for it but to tackle Edith on a number of issues, and it should be done tomorrow rather than later.

Friday morning, the men arrived before breakfast to collect their wages. For most of them, it was the first time they saw Ellen and it was the first time she had spoken to any of them other than Bert. After breakfast, she delivered their pays to Maggie and Elizabeth. Edith again had breakfast on a tray in her room – at Ellen insistence – and didn't venture out of her room until about mid-morning. That allowed Ellen time to deal with a few matters in the office before helping Edith dress and then taking her out onto the verandah. Not wasting any time, Ellen got down to the business of finding out about Edith's trip to town, what Dr Boyle had to say, and whether the weekly trips to town should continue.

Edith chose to deal with the questions in the reverse order. "Those trips to town are one of the few pleasures I have left in life. Yes, I agree they have become tiring, but they allow me to maintain contact with my closest friends and to indulge myself. You have made a big difference, my dear. Now that you attend to those tasks I used to take care of for the property, it is a more relaxing day. Yesterday, I indulged in the luxury of a visit to my hairdresser for the first time in a long time. I have no intention of foregoing my trips to town, no matter how much pressure to the contrary might be brought to bear."

Ellen smiled at the determined stance Edith adopted as she spoke. "Good, now about your visit to Dr Boyle, how did that go?"

"Quite well, they are really routine visits. He runs the same tests every week and makes sure I still have an adequate supply of my tonic."

"…But does he comment on your progress. Does he tell you whether he thinks the tonic is working or not, and whether he thinks you are improving?"

"Don't be silly, Ellen, and please don't treat me like a fool. Everyone else does, but I expected different from you. Everyone avoids mentioning my illness. No one will tell me what it is – and that includes Mr McCarthy and Dr Boyle – but I am not so ignorant as to be incapable of working it out for myself. Dr Boyle cannot find improvement in my condition, because none is likely. I know my time is short, and I intend to make the most of what little I have left."

"I do not think you a fool, Mrs McCarthy; far from it. It has not been easy not being able to discuss your condition more openly, but my instruction was not to do so. I do understand your stance on how you are to spend your remaining time, and I will do all I can to help you make the most of it."

"Thank you, my dear… and please call me Edith. I like to think we have become friends and friends call each other by their given names. I understand that Mr McCarthy tries to protect me from the truth – he has always looked after me – and I know he speaks to Dr Boyle independent of me. This cannot be an easy time for him. I am aware that the time will come – quite soon now, I expect – when I will not be able to do the whole trip in one day. After some thought, I decided that, when that time comes, I will continue to go into town on Thursdays, but will overnight there to return home on Fridays. I would stay at the hotel. You could stay in your own room at the hotel or, if you prefer, you could spend the night at home in your own bed above the store."

"It is pleasing that you have given this some thought. Let's wait until that time before making any decision about where I might spend the night. If there is a need for me to be close to you, that's where I will be."

With the more serious topics dealt with, the two women relaxed into general chatter about the rest of Edith's day. Her new dress was coming along nicely and would need only one more fitting. She was looking forward to wearing it at some of the functions she would attend over the Easter weekend. They celebrated her friend's birthday in fine style with an excellent lunch at the hotel. That woman asked Edith to spend the Easter weekend at her home.

Talk of Easter reminded Ellen that the religious holiday celebrated at Easter was less than a month away. Edith's comments provided the opportunity to enquire after her plans for that long weekend. The icons in Edith's room and the odd one in other places about the house suggested to Ellen that Mrs McCarthy might be Catholic, although she had no idea whether that also applied to Mr McCarthy.

"I always attend church on Good Friday and, as I am a Catholic, I try to follow the church's rules regarding Easter. We used to have a priest come out from town to visit the outlying areas about once a month to say Mass, but he hasn't been around since before Christmas. I will go into town as usual on the Thursday before Easter and will remain in town for the weekend. Good Friday will see most of my time at church. The town's major annual turf carnival happens over the Easter weekend. Mr McCarthy will come into town on Saturday to attend the races and other functions. He will return home early on Easter Monday. I will accompany him to the social functions – a ball I think – on the Saturday night and to the dinner on the Sunday night. I will spend most of Saturday and Sunday at my friend's house, although we usually spend some time each day at the races. She will host a get together for a few of us at her house on Easter Monday, and I would look to return home on Tuesday morning."

"It sounds like a very social weekend and one I'm sure you've always enjoyed in the past. My concern is about whether you will be strong enough this year to participate and enjoy all of the events. That is something we will need to think about when it is closer to Easter. Another thing to think about at that time will be whether I should stay close to you at the hotel or whether I should sleep at home."

"My thinking at the moment is that you would be more comfortable in your own bed. The hope is that my condition will not deteriorate too much in the intervening period to prevent that from happening."

Their discussions lasted through morning tea and on to lunchtime. Edith insisted on taking lunch in the dining room with the others but went to rest straight afterwards. Ellen went to the library but, rather than continue with the cataloguing, took up the book she had started reading and settled herself in a comfortable chair. Although she tried reading her book, since her conversation with Edith, her mind was elsewhere and she couldn't concentrate on anything else.

If her father had not shown up by Easter, she would enjoy spending the weekend at home, sleeping in her own bed and checking on both the store and agency's trading. It was unlikely she would see any of the staff over the long weekend, except possibly for a few minutes first thing on the Tuesday morning before she and Edith headed back to Koreelah.

*****

With the first week behind her, Ellen now knew the pattern of her days, and the next three weeks rolled by accordingly. Edith's health seemed to stabilise a little once Ellen began dispensing the tonic. She

130

still tired easily but was somewhat more resilient than when Ellen first arrived.

The week leading up to the Easter break was hectic. It was Mr McCarthy's longstanding practice to give the workers leave for the whole of the Easter period. At some point over the Saturday and Sunday of that weekend, all of the workers spent some time at the turf carnival. Some stayed in town with family or friends to attend the ball on the Saturday night. Ellen made up their pays and distributed them early on the Thursday morning before she and Edith left for town.

That Thursday was much the same as all the others, except that they carried both women's luggage for the weekend and, at the end of the day, Edith settled into her room at the hotel. Ellen completed errands for the property in between ferrying Edith from doctor to dressmaker, to hairdresser and, finally to the tearooms for lunch with her friends – nothing upset the routine of their Thursday visit to town. Then, with what had become her customary trepidation, Ellen took the buggy around to the rear of the store.

No one was in the loading area, so no one welcomed her. Was this an omen? Rather than turning the horses out into the store's horse yard, she hitched them at the loading ramp. Then, with her stomach in a tight knot and her pulse racing, she climbed the stairs to the loading area. Still no one came to meet her. She peered cautiously into the store. The place throbbed with customers. Both Alfred and Jess were serving people and, once she stepped into the store, she could see Charlie busy with a number of customers in the agency.

A quick scan revealed no sign of her father. She walked forward resolutely and took her place behind what then became a very crowded counter. Alfred completed dealing with a customer. Before he could begin serving another, Ellen leant in close and whispered, "I'll help Jess. You go and give Charlie and hand in the agency."

Customer service continued at a frantic pace for about an hour and a half after Ellen arrived but, after that, there were only a couple of customers left in the store. "You should take a lunch break now in case it gets busy again later," Ellen told Jess, "And tell Alfred to go for lunch now too."

Both only took about 15 minutes break. Alfred relieved Charlie so he could have lunch, and Ellen followed Charlie out to chat to him while he ate. "Thanks for sending Alfred to help," Charlie said. "I was beginning to feel like I was drowning in people. Everyone's stocking up today before we close for the long weekend, but it has been busier than usual all week."

"That's good news. I never complain about the place being busy. By the way, has there been any contact by my father?"

"No, not a word, but you might want to talk to Jess. There's something about the agency she wants to talk to you about." She thanked him and they both went back inside.

Alfred loaded the wagon and went off to make deliveries. There was no one else in the store other than the person Jess was serving. Ellen made her way to the office, speaking quietly to Jess on her way past. "Please join me in the office as soon as you finish here."

"Well, that was a busy time. Has it been like that often this week, Jess?" Ellen asked by way of an opening when Jess came into the office.

"It has been busy, but not as bad... or as good if you prefer... as this morning. It was such a relief to see you arrive. There is something urgent I need to talk to you about and, if you don't mind, I'd like to discuss now, in case another customer comes and we get busy again."

Ellen nodded. "It sounds like something serious and it is obvious it worries you."

"Mr Taylor, that solicitor bloke, called here last Friday. He wanted to see you and thought you came to town on Fridays. He seemed concerned when it was Thursdays and we weren't expecting you again until this week – if you came at all. He said the moment I saw you again, I was to tell you he needs to speak to you and I was to ask you to call at his office without delay."

"Any idea what it was about? Did he give you any clues, or has there been anything happen with the business that might cause concern?"

"No, Miss, no clues at all and the business is just a bit busier than usual this week... although... maybe there is one thing... ah, no, I'll not be bothering you about it."

"Perhaps you should bother me about it. Tell me what it is."

"I am concerned about the agency's bank account, Miss. Like I said, we have been busy. It has been good for a while now and I've been banking plenty into the agency's account. When I looked at the account the other day, I got a bit of a shock. There's not much in it... and we have a few bills to pay from that account."

"Are there sufficient funds to cover those outstanding bills?"

Jess shrugged. "Just enough if no more come in."

Ellen thanked her and took out the agency's account file. "I'll look at the situation and then walk down to Mr Taylor's rooms. I have no idea what he might want to see me about, but I need to look at this account before I do anything else."

Jess went to serve a customer. Ellen opened the agency account file and caught her breath. She scanned the transactions that occurred over the last week. Jess was right; the deposits were much higher than usual. The problem was the number of cheques that were processed. Their total far exceeded the deposits for the month. The account was very healthy when Ellen moved to Koreelah but, in spite of the deposits since then, only a few hundred pounds remained in the account. James Grimsby was treating himself well; good hotels in more than one city, eating well at expensive restaurants and hopping on and off boats as he travelled between cities.

Perhaps this was what Mr Taylor wished to speak about, though why he would speak to her about it mystified Ellen. As she made her way out of the store, she decided that, after she finished with Mr Taylor, she would call on the bank manager to discuss the agency's account. Her resolve was to no avail. Neither Mr Taylor nor the bank manager was available. Both took lave for the few days leading up to Easter. The mystery and concern associated with those meetings would have to carry over to the next week.

On her return to the store, Ellen made up the pays for the staff and wrote cheques to pay bills, including those of the agency she told Jess to pay Charlie Perkins from the store account in future. There were plenty of funds in the store account. She also told Jess not to mail off the cheques to the agency's creditors until after making further deposits early the following week. Ellen worked on until closing time. Then, after the staff left for the week, she closed the doors and went across to the hotel to check on Edith.

As she helped Edith dress for dinner, Edith asked Ellen to join her for dinner in the hotel's dining room. Ellen hadn't done anything about dinner and, as she didn't have time for lunch, the invitation was a welcome one. It became apparent the invitation wasn't because Edith wanted company, but because Edith had something to discuss with Ellen.

"A specialist, a close friend of Dr Boyle's, is spending a few days with Dr Boyle next week when on his way back to Sydney from up north somewhere. Dr Boyle wants to do more tests and then have the specialist take a look at me."

"That sounds like a wonderful opportunity that doesn't involve you having to travel anywhere. Do you have any other details?"

"Well, I'm not sure how it suits you, but it seems it might mean spending the week in town instead of going home on Tuesday. Dr Boyle wants to do the tests on Tuesday, and the specialist will be here either Wednesday or Thursday. It seems pointless to go home and then have to come back again a day or so later."

"Staying in town for the week will cause no inconvenience for me. Apart from that, two trips in the same week would be too tiring for you. I think it a wise decision to remain in town until either next Thursday afternoon or Friday morning." Sometime fate smiles on you, Ellen thought. If they were to stay in town, she would be able to call on both the bank manager and Mr Taylor earlier than she thought possible.

"Excellent, my dear," Ellen returned her attention to the conversation when she realised Edith was speaking. "I will have Mr McCarthy confirm extension of our stay in town."

Ellen asked herself, why would you have him confirm it; why not simply tell him that's what you plan to do? The McCarthys' relationship amazed her. Edith was a strong and independent woman, yet she deferred to her husband all the time. On the other hand, her otherwise gruff and bombastic husband would walk to the ends of the earth to accommodate her every wish. This must have been a relationship of great tenderness before she became ill, and now he struggled to cope with the prospect of the inevitable.

It was Ellen's belief that Edith also struggled with the same thought, but in her case, it was the thought of leaving her husband alone and having to cope with the loss of the only other person who mattered to him. This realisation made Ellen reflect on her own life. She was no stranger to the thought that fate had dealt her an unfair hand in taking away from her everyone she loved. Perhaps, instead of looking around at others, she was too quick to focus on herself. The McCarthys also knew grief, firstly with the loss of their son and only child and now Edith's impending demise.

In spite of everything that had happened; in spite of her belief that this man was responsible for her husband's death, she genuinely liked these people and envied their concern for each other. Was it the glass of wine or the dark thoughts? Ellen felt herself spiralling down into the dark abys of depression. "You're very quiet tonight. Is everything all right? You are sure staying in town those extra days is not a problem for you?" Edith asked as Ellen helped her prepare for bed.

"Oh, sorry, I was preoccupied. No, I'm sure that staying in town will not be a problem. My mind was on Koreelah and whether there was anything I hadn't done that might prove a problem for anyone else." It was an easy lie. She did not want Edith to know she was wallowing in selfish emotions, rather than caring for this brave terminally ill woman.

There was little Edith needed Ellen for over the weekend. Ellen took her to church on Good Friday morning, but Edith's friend took her home from church to spend the rest of the day at her home. Ellen's duties seems confined to getting Edith up and dressed in the morning and helping her prepare for bed at night. Her only additional duties were helping Edith dress for the ball on Saturday night – she wore her new gown – and for the Turf Club dinner on Sunday night. She spent the major part of the weekend cleaning, tidying and generally fussing about in the store. However, there is only so much of that one can do, and she was pleased she had slipped into her bag the book from Koreelah's library she was reading.

Late on Saturday afternoon, Ellen went across to the hotel, helped Edith dress for the evening, and then returned to the store to settle down with her book. It seemed like she had read for only a few minutes but it was quite dark outside when banging on the back door of the store interrupted her solitude. Her immediate thought was that a drunken James Grimsby had returned. As she made her way down to the back door, she wiped her sweaty hands on her skirt. With her stomach a tightly wound ball, she cautiously opened the door a crack and peered out into the blackness of the night. "Who is it?" she demanded with all the courage she could muster.

"A friend who heard you might be in town and saw your light in the upstairs window." She stood there speechless and staring at the smiling face of Frank Woodrow.

"Mr Woodrow, how wonderful to see you; please, come in. I presume you are in town for the Turf Carnival."

"Yes, I've been at the races for most of the day. I heard McCarthy telling someone that you and his wife were spending the weekend in town and I hoped you might be staying here rather than in the hotel. Since you are here, I assume your father has not reappeared."

They perched on the nearest suitable object in the loading area and chatted for a while. Woodrow told her of his recent letter from Ted Wallace. He said Ted's letter tended to suggest he was missing the farm but, apart from that, was settling in okay in Brisbane. Time marched on and it occurred to Ellen that, if her friend were intending to go to the ball tonight, he would be late arriving. "Were you intending to go to the ball this evening? While I am enjoying your company, I fear you would be making a late entrance at the ball if you do not leave soon."

"I am not exactly the kind that goes to balls so, in answer to your question, no I am not going to the ball and I have no other plans for this evening either."

"Well, if that is the case, I would ask you to join me for dinner, but I'm not sure how appropriate that might be."

"There is only the two of us who know I'm here. My horse is in the hotel horse yard, so there is no evidence of my visit. I don't see why it would be inappropriate for me to dine with you. In fact, it might be considered rude of me to turn down your invitation."

They both giggled like a pair of teenagers about to embark on some secret escapade as Woodrow followed Ellen up the stairs to the residence. "I'm afraid there are only stewed chops for dinner tonight; I wasn't expecting company. Now let me see, I think there might be a bottle of something in this cupboard. Ah yes, how would you feel about a glass of red wine?"

"Sounds like a perfect accompaniment to stewed chops."

"Good, perhaps you would open the bottle while I look for a couple of glasses."

Their pleasant evening stretched on for quite a while after dinner. Woodrow knew it was getting late but he didn't want the evening to end. However, he spotted Ellen trying to stifle a yawn, and a check of his pocket watch told him it was almost midnight. The pleasant interlude came to an abrupt end. They said their good nights and Ellen let him out the back door and watched him on his way until he disappeared around the corner of the building. As she climbed the stairs again, she couldn't help but feel thankful that Edith had insisted on getting herself to bed after the ball tonight rather than have Ellen come over to the hotel at whatever time to help her.

Ellen slept soundly that night and awoke refreshed, although later than usual. To be in time to help Edith get ready for the day, she had to rush to the hotel without first having breakfast. After breakfast, she spent time in the office on the accounts until it was time for lunch. Then it was time to indulge in her guilty pleasure: losing herself in her book. At about mid-afternoon, there was another interruption to her reading. She didn't mind.

On opening the back door, she once again found Frank Woodrow standing outside. He was on his way back to the mill after the racing carnival had finished and called in to say goodbye and thank her for dinner the previous evening. She invited him in, made a pot of tea, and they chatted about nothing in particular for about half an hour before he left to collect his horse from the hotel's horse yard. Ellen returned to her abandoned book upstairs but couldn't read. Her strange lightness of heart and lack of concentration surprised her.

Soon it was time to go across to the hotel again. She was beginning to think she would wear a track between store and hotel before the weekend was over. Edith had spent much of the day resting and little time at the races. She looked forward to the dinner that evening and was in a chatty mood. The reason for the mood improvement was explained as Ellen was about to go back to the store.

"I think you've met my friend Maria Sainsbury. We – my group of friends and I – were to have lunch at Maria's house tomorrow. She sought me out at the races today to ask me to stay with her while I'm in town. Her husband is off to Sydney on business first thing in the morning and will be gone for the best part of two weeks. She is looking for a bit of company for at least part of that time and was concerned about my staying in this hotel on my own once Mr McCarthy returns home."

"It probably will be more pleasant at the Sainsbury residence than here," Ellen said as she cast her eye around the drab but utilitarian room Edith occupied. "Where is the Sainsbury home? I will need to allow enough time to get there on time when I come to attend to you."

"No, my dear, that's the other good thing about this fortuitous invitation. There will be no need for your assistance. Mrs Sainsbury has a maid who has little to do and will be available to assist me. It will provide a nice break for you and allow you to attend to matters at Grimsby's Store. I'm not sure if I would be speaking out of turn, my dear, but I did hear a whisper that there might be some problem there."

"I don't know what you mean, I'm sure. However, while I'm sure the Sainsbury's maid is more than capable, I am available if you need me. Just ask Mrs Sainsbury to send someone with a message. Now, where is this house where you will be staying?"

As she returned to the store, Ellen didn't know whether to feel relieved or put out about not having to look after Edith for the next few days. However, by the time she reached the store, she decided it wasn't such a bad thing. It would free her to meet with Mr Taylor and the bank manager first thing on Tuesday – who knows how long that will take – and will enable her to spend time with the staff.

First thing Monday morning, Ellen again trekked across to the hotel, intending to assist Edith to prepare for the move to Maria Sainsbury's house. Mr McCarthy met her as she entered the hotel. He was on his way to the horse yard to collect the wagon and head home. "Mrs McCarthy is quite excited about staying with Mrs Sainsbury. I'm not convinced one way or the other whether it is a good thing to do or not. I know she won't be dissuaded from this move but, if you could somehow keep an eye on her, I would be grateful."

"I too am concerned but the prospect of it seems to have done her the world of good. I'm not sure how I can do it, but I do plan to see her as often as possible while she is there." As she spoke to him, Ellen notice McCarthy's colour seemed a little 'off'. She told herself it probably was a result of too much to drink at the dinner the previous night. However, he became unsteady on his feet and reached for a hall table to steady himself, she grew concerned. "Are you all right, Mr McCarthy? Let me help you to a chair."

"No; no, thank you, I'm fine… just the effects of a late night catching up with an old man. I had better get on. I've things to take care of at Koreelah today."

Ellen wasn't convinced he was okay, but he brushed aside the helping hand she offered. He was a man and he was her employer – and she knew her place. She stood aside and he strode past her with head held high as he left the hotel. Perhaps his colour has improved a little, she thought as she continued on to Edith's room.

The Easter weekend ended with a few hours of luxurious relaxation. Relaxation of both mind and body, something Ellen had not truly experienced since her marriage all those years ago.

Chapter 17

Tuesday morning brought a return to a familiar routine: up early, breakfast, then open the store and greet the staff as they arrived. After telling them she would be around for the rest of the week, Ellen put together the few papers she wanted to take with her and, on her way out, told Jess she might be gone for a while. At some point, she decided to visit Mr Taylor first and only go to see the bank manager after she knew what Mr Taylor wanted.

Taylor had not arrived at his office yet his clerk advised her, but invited Ellen to wait, as the solicitor would be along shortly. 'Shortly' amounted to a bit over half an hour. By the time he arrived, Ellen was growing fidgety and frustrated. She followed him into his office and waited while the solicitor fussed about finding the papers he needed. Ellen chose to get things started.

"I received a message that you wished to see me. I am anxious to know what it might be about."

"Yes, thank you for coming. I did not expect you until later in the week, but your early arrival is to our advantage. I am not sure whether you are aware, but Grimsby's Farmers' Agency is in serious financial trouble."

"Yes, it was brought to my attention on Thursday when I arrived. My father appears to have spent money freely. I have put in place measures to cope with the immediate situation but I do not have a long-term solution. My intention was to discuss it with the bank manager when I left here this morning."

"You will get no good news there I'm afraid. The bank is holding quite a few cheques that they can't process due to a shortage of funds in the agency's account..."

"...Other than the cheques already processed?"

"I am afraid so, Miss Grimsby. They add up to quite an amount of money. The bank sent your father a letter requesting he attend to the matter with some urgency, but the letter was undeliverable. Nobody seems to know where to find him. Some of the cheques are for creditors in Brisbane and Sydney. The bank ran a notice in the local newspaper and in the leading newspapers in those other two cities in the hope of getting some response from Mr Grimsby. They – the bank – threatened to foreclose on the business and, as there appears to be no interest in the matter from Mr Grimsby, intend to follow through with that course of action."

"Foreclosure! I'm sorry; I know what foreclosure means – in general terms anyway – but what would it mean for Grimsby's…for the store, I mean? Will the store still be able to continue to trade?"

"Foreclosure would have no impact on the store. Mr James Grimsby owns only the agency. Any foreclosure arising from matters relating to the agency's account, therefore, are restricted only to the agency. Although the agency was bought and paid for – and set up – by the store using store funds, it was bought in Mr Grimsby's name."

"But, as I understand foreclosure, the bank can seek to recoup outstanding monies by seizing any other property my father might own. Doesn't this put the store in jeopardy?"

"Miss Grimsby, your father doesn't own the store."

"Then who does?"

"You do, my dear woman, you do. Did you not read the copy of your mother's Will you were sent?"

"I received a copy of her will?"

"We proceeded with the probate as soon as a death certificate was received, and this was granted without any delay. Your mother left the store to you. It was her property. Perhaps you are unaware of the circumstances surrounding Grimsby's Store." Ellen shook her head, unable to find words at this time. "Very well, let me explain. Your mother was not yet twenty-one years old when James asked her to marry him. Mary Watt, your mother, came from a very well-to-do family."

"I don't know much about my Watt grandparents. They both died while I was quite young. I believe my mother was their only child, or at least their only surviving child. I think, once I got older, I developed the impression of them as having money."

"Your mother's father – your Grandfather – did not think much of James and was concerned about his motivation in asking for Mary's hand in marriage. The store was their wedding present to their daughter. However, before Mr Watt would give his consent for them to marry, he had a legal document drawn up. It spelled out quite clearly that the store belonged to Mary. That it would continue to belong to Mary regardless of her marriage or any other circumstances that might arise, and that James had no claim to the store or its profits then or at any time in the future. Mr Watt would not give his permission for the marriage to occur until James signed the document."

"Nevertheless, I am surprised mother didn't leave the store to my father, out of duty if for no other reason."

"You will recall that in more recent times some changes were made to the way money from the agency was handled. That new bank account was set up to separate the agency's finances from those of the store. Unfortunately, conditions within the marriage at that time had deteriorated to the point where your mother threatened to throw her husband out onto the street. In spite of this, I believe James was of the opinion that he would inherit the store. That is why I made sure both of you were sent a copy of the will, so there could be no misunderstanding about the transmission of ownership."

"He must've intercepted my copy of the will. I never received it; I didn't know any of this."

"It surprised me when you moved out of town. I suppose I should have realised that something was amiss. I could not understand why someone who worked so hard in the business would not pay more attention when they owned the business."

"The explanation is simple. My father told me he would be throwing me out onto the street as soon as probate went through. I had nowhere to go, what was I to do? Mr McCarthy offered me a position that was not too arduous and provided a roof over my head and food on the table. As much as I didn't want to leave the store, particularly once my father disappeared, I had to think about my future, and McCarthy's was the only option available to me."

Quite a bit more time spent discussing the history of the store and Mary's intentions, particularly in the latter stages of her life, helped Ellen understand why her father had suddenly disappeared. The more they talked, the angrier she became. Her grandfather had every right to be concerned about the man his daughter wanted to marry. James was a brute and in no way an honourable man.

"Thank you for taking the time to tell me all of this today. The question remains, what can I do? I don't want to see Grimsby's lose the agency, as it is now a very profitable concern and an important part of the establishment. However, I do not want my father to continue his present ways. I may sound harsh and bitter, but I want him to pay for the life he gave my mother, for the way he treated me and for the loss of my children."

"I advised the bank that I hoped to speak to you sometime this week and that we may be able to negotiate an acceptable outcome for all parties. My recommendation is that the bank should foreclose on James Grimsby's agency at the earliest – this morning if possible…" Ellen gasped but held her tongue so Taylor could continue. "Don't worry, it can all happen at the bank and will be safe. Once they foreclose, the bank will need to sell the property in order to recoup any outstanding debts and honour the cheques already issued. My proposal is that we go to the bank now and set my plan in motion."

"I'm not sure I understand what it is we are going to do when we get to the bank. What you have suggested so far makes me feel very nervous."

"Oh, that's simple. You are going to buy the agency." Ellen stared at him.

"Buy the agency…? How much is that likely to cost and where does the money come from?"

"I believe that, all up, it would amount to not more than £2,000. There are ample funds in the store account to cover this purchase and still leave sufficient money to continue operating comfortably. Apart from that, your mother also had a private account. She received quite a substantial sum of money when her parents died and she quietly added to it over the years – covertly I believe – by siphoning off small amounts from the store's income. You also inherited that money. Therefore, I reiterate, there is more than sufficient cash about for you to purchase the agency from the bank as soon as the bank takes possession of it. So, shall we go to the bank now and buy you an agency?"

They were shown into the bank manager's office as soon as they arrived. Everything happened quickly. The manager gave a clerk some documents and despatched him to the courthouse while those in the manager's office enjoyed a cup of tea. The lad returned. Signatures went onto a number of pieces of paper, and the clerk was off to the courthouse again. In his absence, the manager proceeded to close the existing agency account and set up a new one.

The manager clapped his hands together in satisfaction and said, "There, you'll be able to start operating off that new account now." At that point, the clerk returned and handed a sheaf of paper to the bank manager. "Okay, now these are the bank's copies and these are your copies," the manager said as he indicated the two piles he created from the documents. "Miss Grimsby, do you wish to take yours with you, or would you prefer Mr Taylor to take them for safe keeping?"

Ellen felt as though she was in a daze as it all happening around her. "Safer if Mr Taylor looks after them I think," she answered.

Mr Taylor and the bank manager stood up and shook hands across the desk, signalling the finalisation of the transaction they came for. Ellen remained seated and flicking through the documents Mr Taylor would take with him. Then she looked at the agency's new bank account. It was empty. She waved the statement at the bank manager. "What happened to the few hundred pounds that were in the old account? They don't appear in this new account."

"They were part of the purchase transaction." Ellen was about to protest but the bank manager rushed on. "I know you paid over to the bank the required amount to settle the outstanding debts, cover legal fees and complete the purchase, but the bank needs to make a profit on such deals or it too will go out of business. We have retained the little money that was in the old account to cover contingencies and other costs."

Again, Ellen opened her mouth to protest, but a stern look from Mr Taylor and an almost imperceptible shake of his head silenced her. "Perhaps, before we leave, you could transfer some funds from the store account into the new agency account… just sufficient to carry on with until there are further deposits of the agency's takings," Taylor suggested. What else could she do? There were bills waiting to be paid. With that one final transaction taken care of, they left the bank and went their separate ways.

She didn't remember crossing the street to return to the store, but returned to reality the moment she walked through the door. Her business with the solicitor and the bank took most of the morning she realised, and she came back to a store crammed with customers stocking up again after the long weekend closure. She felt a twinge of guilt, but it was of little consequence when added to the other emotions dogging her at that time. Ellen stepped up to the counter and immediately began serving customers. It was almost an hour later before only a couple of customers remained and Ellen could escape to the solitude of the upstairs residence.

What happened today, she asked herself as she dropped onto a chair at the kitchen table? She needed time alone to try to comprehend all that happened and, more importantly, what it meant for the future. At least she now knew she did not need to fear encountering her father when she came to the store, although how he would react when he found his source of funding gone was a worry. How she wished Frank Woodrow would just happen to stop by today. An intelligent and caring person to discuss all this with was what she needed now. She needed a friend. Over yet another pot of tea, slowly the daze that enveloped her since she first met with Mr Taylor lifted and she began to think clearly. Was that elation she was beginning to feel? Yes, she thought it might be, and she should do something about sharing it with the others.

Downstairs once more, Ellen asked Charlie and Alfred to wait behind for a few minutes after they closed at the end of the day. Her request of Jess was different. Although Ellen wanted Jess to remain behind after they closed up, she also wanted to discuss the changes to the banking arrangements, without spoiling what she hoped would be their later surprise about ownership of the business.

For a short period before closing time, the store became quiet with only a handful of workers likely to dash in on their way home. This was when she called Jess into the office. There wasn't much to tell the lass: there was a new bank account for the agency, she could go back to paying Charlie out of the agency's account, and those bills they were holding could go in the post tomorrow. A couple of last minute customers came in as they were finishing their discussion. Jess went to serve them. Their tardiness delayed the store closing for a few minutes. The agency closed on time and the two men now idled away their time in hushed chatter in the back area of the store.

Then it was time for her announcement. With the staff gathered around her out in the back area, she was hesitant. "Thank you for sparing me some of your own time. I just wanted… uhmm… I have some news to share…" This is not going well, she thought. The downcast eyes and long faces in front of her suggested they expected bad news.

She smartened up her act. "I wanted to share with you some news I learnt today. As you know, I have been concerned about coming back to the store and possibly encountering Mr Grimsby. You don't need to know why that was. All that is important is that he is not likely to appear here again at any time. The other news that I hope you are pleased to receive is that I discovered today that Mrs Grimsby owned this store in her own name and, on her death, it passed to me."

A round of applause from the staff interrupted her flow of words, and she noticed their faces brighten considerably. When the clapping subsided, Ellen continued. "While I know Jess is aware, I'm not sure anyone else knows about this next matter. My father owned the agency and, for some time now, we treated it as a separate business. While I do not want this next piece of information to become public in any way, I believe you have the right to know." Nods all round indicated they understood what she asked. "Good; the agency was in financial difficulties to the extent that the bank foreclosed."

"How can that be?" Charlie Perkins demanded. "How can it be in financial trouble when business is so good and our takings are so high?"

"The situation was no reflection on the business itself. It was my father's lavish lifestyle spending that caused the damage."

"So the bank foreclosed. The agency is gone now. What about my job, do I still have a job here?"

"Oh dear, this is not going as I hoped. Yes, the bank foreclosed and immediately sold it. The reason I was away from the store so long this morning was to attend to important matters. As of late this morning, Grimsby's Farmers' Agency is owned by Grimsby's Store."

Her announcement met with a brief silence before Jess found her voice. "Miss, does that mean… uhmm… If you own Grimsby's Store and Grimsby's Store now owns the agency, does that mean you are now the owner of the store and the agency?"

"That is correct, Jess." Another round of applause and a couple of cheers followed her confirmation. Everyone was grinning and congratulating her. Then Alfred suddenly turned solemn.

"That is great news and we are happy for you, Miss, but what does all of that news you shared with us really mean for us?" Alfred asked.

"I don't suppose it means much at all for you. I was excited about what today brought for me and I wanted to share it with you. There will be no changes made. Everything will go on as it has been. The only difference that it might make is that the business will not be for sale any time soon. …So, dear people, today's events mean your jobs with Grimsby's are safe for as long as you want them – and I hope you will want them for a long time to come."

Although her session with the staff went longer than expected, Ellen thought she detected a lightness of spirit and a renewed spring in their step as they made their way out of the back door to head home. She felt good too. The enormity of the day was beginning to sink in and she was elated at the staff's response to her news. On her way upstairs, she hummed a tune off key while her mind considered what she might have for dinner. Life had returned to normal – whatever that was – and it lifted her spirits to new heights. There remained one other issue to decide: the future. Tonight was not the time to tackle something so complex, she convinced herself, but that issue came to the fore next morning.

Alfred and Jess arrived together the next morning and, as Ellen greeted them, Jess got straight to the point. "Miss, I know you said nothing would change and all that, but that was about our jobs. What about you; will you come back here to live and run the place now?"

"That a good question, Jess, and one for which I have been avoiding finding an answer. Everything happened only yesterday." Charlie came in while she was speaking and Jess explained her question to Ellen. The interruption gave Ellen a moment to consider her reply. "I accepted the job Mr McCarthy offered me and I now have a commitment to care for Mrs McCarthy, for whom I have grown quite fond. For some time in the future, I will continue to honour that commitment. How long that might be I don't know, but I do not expect it will be too long."

There, the decision is made, she told herself as she went through to open the store for the day. That brought Edith to the front of her mind. Today was Wednesday. That was the day Edith was to see Dr Boyle's friend, a specialist doctor of some sort. As soon as things settled down at Grimsby's, she would go across to Dr Boyle's rooms to find out what time Edith would see the specialist. Maria Sainsbury shouldn't have to ferry Edith all over town. Ellen would collect Edith and bring her to the doctor.

Edith's appointment wasn't until after lunch. Ellen left Dr Boyle's rooms and walked to the Sainsbury home at the far end of the main street and overlooking the river. It was large and, reputedly, one of the most well-appointed – if not the most well-appointed – home in town, details that were not lost on Ellen as she approached the house. It was grand and for Edith, it was a world of luxury compared with the homestead on Koreelah.

Although Edith was pleased to see Ellen and chatted brightly, the woman's colour was terrible. After arranging to collect Edith with the buggy and then return her to Sainsbury's after the doctor's appointment, Ellen walked back to the store with her mind weighed down by Edith's appearance. It appeared Edith was attempting a good show of being not so ill. Ellen believed the doctor's report might tell a different story.

As arranged, Ellen took Edith to Dr Boyle's rooms. Today, she elected to remain in the waiting room until Edith was finished and ready to return to Sainsbury's. The wait was long; more than an hour elapsed before sounds suggested the examination might be ending, but it was a further 15 minutes before Edith emerged supported by Dr Boyle.

Ellen caught her breath and rose abruptly from her chair. Edith was pale and looked about to collapse as Dr Boyle helped her into a chair before speaking to Ellen. "Miss Grimsby, thank you for bringing Mrs McCarthy here today. I wonder if you might spare me a few minutes before you leave." Ellen looked towards Edith who responded with a slight nod. Dr Boyle led the way through to his office.

"Dr Thompson ran more tests and has taken samples from Mrs McCarthy. These will be analysed overnight before he sees Mrs McCarthy again in the morning. Is it possible for you to bring her back here at ten o'clock tomorrow morning?" Ellen assured him she would bring Edith at the appointed time. "Thank you. Now, about Dr Thompson's preliminary findings; they are not good. He believes her condition to be much further advanced than initially thought. It is likely the outcome of today's tests will not be good, and I suspect he may be inclined to provide an estimation of how much longer the disease has before it has run its course. As the news is likely to be upsetting for the patient, it is important someone is with her when it is delivered. In fact, Dr Thompson may want Mrs McCarthy to enter hospital for a few days."

Although she knew Boyle was waiting for her to comment in some way, Ellen sat biting her lip for a few moments before responding. "Of course, I could be with Edith tomorrow if needed, but I feel this whole matter is beyond my authority. While I know Mrs McCarthy is able to make her own decisions, I think she needs someone closer than me supporting her at that time."

"That is also the opinion Dr Thompson and I share. Mr McCarthy will be seeing me a little later this afternoon. I will be asking him to accompany his wife to her appointment. However, I would ask that you bring Mrs McCarthy here and be available to stay with her in the event that her husband should feel unable to be present." As much as she dreaded what tomorrow might bring and the prospect of having to be a part of it, Ellen agreed to all the doctor asked.

It was a silent ride back to the Sainsbury home. Whether the tests were painful or if she already had received disturbing news was unclear, but the woman Ellen returned to Sainsbury's was nothing like the one she collected from there earlier that afternoon. After helping Edith into bed, Ellen arranged to take her to Dr Boyle's rooms the next morning and then left

The remainder of the afternoon drifted by with Ellen's mind only half on the job. Jess noticed the boss was preoccupied and enquired if there was something she could do to help. There was nothing anyone could do, Ellen thought; nothing to help alleviate her concern for her friend, and nothing to help Mrs McCarthy. It wasn't until later that night when she was alone upstairs that Dr Boyle's words came rushing back: 'Mr McCarthy will be seeing me later this afternoon', they were the words she remembered. A million questions filled her mind but one dominated: Why?

Why was Mr McCarthy seeing the doctor? There wasn't enough time for him to be summoned and arrive after Edith's appointment. Was the arrangement made beforehand? Did Boyle know the news would not be good and, as a precaution arranged for McCarthy to be there? No, that didn't seem to ring true. Why hadn't Mr McCarthy said he was coming to town? The longer Ellen thought about it, the more convinced she became that McCarthy's presence in town at this precise time was coincidental to Edith's situation rather than planned. Nevertheless, he should have said something to me, Ellen thought. If he is in town tonight, he will stay at either his club or the hotel. She marched downstairs, let herself out the back door, made her way around the building and strode across to the hotel.

The decision to check at the hotel first wasn't because she thought he would be staying there. It was because it was easier for her to enquire after Mr McCarthy there than it was for her to speak to anyone at that toffee-nosed gentlemen's club. As luck would have it, when she reached the hotel, Charlie Perkins came wandering out of the place after spending an hour or so playing cards with some mates. Luck smiled on her tonight. Charlie's surprise at seeing Ellen about to enter the hotel was ill-concealed. After she explained her quest to locate Mr McCarthy, Charlie asked her to wait while he went back inside to enquire. No, McCarthy was not booked in at the hotel.

Together, they walked the short distance along the street to the club. As he wasn't a member, Charlie could not go inside, so he signalled through the open door and a man came out to speak to him. The man disappeared back inside and soon returned. Yes, McCarthy was staying at the club for a couple of nights. Charlie persuaded the man to send someone to McCarthy's room to inform him that a man was asking after him and wished to speak to him.

Ellen stood in the deep shadows off to one side of the doorway as Charlie acted on her behalf. It was unlikely that any of the members would come out to speak to Charlie if they saw a woman with him. Although Charlie had done his best, there was no guarantee that McCarthy would come to the door, perhaps choosing instead to ignore some local bloke who didn't even qualify for membership of the club.

Then from her place in the shadows, Ellen saw Charlie straighten up and stand to attention. He whipped off his cap as a shadow fell across the doorway.

"Begging your pardon, Mr McCarthy, but there is someone who wishes to speak to you."

"What a cheek you have, interrupting my night in this way. I have nothing to say to you…"

"You might not have anything to say to Mr Perkins, Mr McCarthy, but I have plenty to discuss with you," Ellen cut across whatever else McCarthy intended saying and she made no attempt to disguise her disgust at the way he spoke to Charlie.

"Miss Grimsby! What is this about; what brings you here at night… and with this person? McCarthy's tone had softened and he genuinely seemed confused.

"Perhaps it would be better if we discussed the matters I wish to talk about in private. Oh, and this person as you called him, is Mr Charlie Perkins, my employee and a man who served you well for many years at Swayne's Agency and now at Grimsby's Agency."

"My apologies to you both; it was rude of me to speak like that…"

Before he could say more, Ellen turned to Charlie and said, "Thank you for your assistance tonight, Charlie. Perhaps you could leave me to discuss my business with Mr McCarthy. I'll see you in the morning." Charlie turned on his heel, gave McCarthy a filthy look, and strode off for home.

"Now, firstly Mr McCarthy, I was unaware you were coming to town today or that you were to see Dr Boyle. I assume you did see the doctor." McCarthy nodded. "No doubt he told you of Mrs McCarthy's appointment there tomorrow." Again only a nod in reply. "Dr Boyle is quite insistent someone should accompany Mrs McCarthy when she attends tomorrow. I have arranged to collect her and take her to Dr Boyle's rooms, but I need to know if you will be with her when they speak to her."

"I don't think I can do it. I just don't think I can."

"Nonsense; the pair of you clearly care deeply for each other and it should be someone close to her that supports her. She knows what her illness means…"

"Who told her? I expressly ordered that she should not be told."

"Nobody told her. She is an intelligent, well-read woman who worked it out for herself. She knows what her fate is and that she has only a short time left. That's not what her greatest concern is. Although the prospect of what awaits her must prey on her mind, her concern is for how her ultimate fate will affect you. As I said, it is clear to me that you care deeply for each other. This is a time for you to talk together, to support one another. It's not a time for pride or some show of masculine dignity. …And it is not my place to be with Mrs McCarthy tomorrow, but I will not let her face tomorrow alone if you do not step up to do your duty."

"You do not mince your words, Miss Grimsby, and perhaps it is no more than I deserve. I will think on all you have said, but please collect my wife and take her to Dr Boyle's rooms tomorrow as arranged."

They said goodnight and parted. 'My wife', he actually said 'my wife', Ellen thought as she crossed the street to the store. That is a first; perhaps things are changing. Nevertheless, McCarthy's attitude and behaviour when he first appeared in the hotel's doorway continued to bother her, even later as she lay in her bed begging sleep to come that night. Sleep eventually did come, but it produced a troubled and restless night. The next morning found her depressed and ill prepared to face what the day promised to bring.

The day went much as expected; Ellen took Edith to Dr Boyle's. Mr McCarthy was waiting when they arrived. Edith was both surprised and concerned by his presence. The lady looked so frail this morning and moved only with great difficulty. Overnight, her skin seemed to have sprouted red blotches; red marks of some kind. Ellen remained in the waiting room while the McCarthys disappeared into the labyrinth that comprised Boyle's surgery. The wait was long and Ellen's foreboding increased with each passing moment. When they emerged, the news was not good. Although not unexpected, some degree of hope lingers until the final verdict comes and all hope is gone. Then, follows the struggle for acceptance of the inevitable. This was the situation the McCarthys and Ellen faced that day.

McCarthy asked Ellen to take Edith back to the Sainsbury home and help her to pack her belongings. He would expect them both back at Koreelah by the end of the day. Edith made no comment and went quietly as they helped her out of the surgery and into the buggy. There was no conversation between the two women until they reached their destination.

"You look worn out," Ellen told Edith. "Would you prefer to rest for a few hours before heading back home? I could come back later to pack and collect you, and we could still be home in time for dinner."

"Thank you, my dear. I do feel a little weak. Perhaps if you could come back at around three o'clock, it still would allow us to be home before dark."

The concern that nagged Ellen all the way back to the store was whether Edith would last the trip back to Koreelah without her condition worsening. It was more than a two-hour drive and, although better sprung than the wagon, the buggy was not a comfortable ride.

There was any number of things to take care of at the store now that she was leaving earlier than anticipated. Three o'clock came round quickly, and they were soon on their way out of town, with Edith propped up as comfortably as possible in one corner of the buggy.

Chapter 18

Ellen felt a wave of relief sweep over her as she took the buggy through the gates and started on the long driveway to the homestead. Edith's colour, poor at the start of the trip, had worsened and become grey. There was some activity happening at the homestead. Mr McCarthy was waving his arms about and directing a couple of men from the property in something they were doing under the house. Ellen brought the buggy to a halt as close as possible to the bottom of the stairs. She glanced over at Edith and wondered how the woman was going to get down from the buggy. Mr McCarthy rushed over as soon as the buggy came to a halt.

He climbed aboard. Between them, he and Ellen managed to get Edith down and helped her across to a chair under the house. "The time has come for Mrs McCarthy to abandon those stairs," McCarthy announced. I have arranged for some changes to allow her to stay down here in these rooms under the house. There is more to do but, until we can complete the job, at least Mrs McCarthy will be reasonably comfortable tonight."

After inspecting the room and fetching Edith's personal effects required for the night, Ellen helped Edith inside and into bed. It was the first time Ellen had seen inside these rooms, and she was surprised to find what she thought was one large area, actually contained two separate rooms: a good-sized sitting room and a smaller bedroom. The sitting room area contained a few comfortable chairs and a daybed. After he arrived home, Mr McCarthy had the workers bring Mrs McCarthy's bed down from upstairs and set it up – with Elisabeth's help – in the bedroom.

Edith said she wasn't interested in eating anything for dinner, and fell asleep soon after Ellen tucked her in. After checking out the daybed, Ellen went in search of Mr McCarthy. "I have put Mrs McCarthy to bed. She doesn't wish anything for dinner. I will come back to dine with you but, in the meantime, I will go across to my cottage to collect a few things. I feel I need to stay close to Mrs McCarthy. I will sleep in that sitting room to be near her. Perhaps, after dinner, you might share with me the outcome of your meeting with the doctors this morning."

Dinner was a sombre affair that evening. Maggie placed the plates in front of the diners without a word, her face testimony to the concern and sadness consuming her. After placing a plate in front of Ellen, she turned to leave the room, but Ellen reached up to lightly catch her arm and give it a gentle squeeze. "It's not fair; it's just not fair," Maggie exclaimed, choking back a sob. "It's not fair what such a lovely woman as Mrs McCarthy be going through. She never did nobody any harm! Always so kind and gentle, and this is what that bloke who is supposed to be all loving and wonderful dishes up for her." Tears welled up in her eyes as she spoke.

"I'm sorry, Maggie, but I don't understand; what bloke would that be?" Ellen asked gently.

"That bloke Mrs McCarthy has in those pictures in her room. That bloke the Priest used to yabber on about all the time – telling us about how loving that bloke was of all his creatures. Well, Mrs McCarthy – and the boss here – they're his 'creatures' too, and look what he is putting them through. …Doesn't seem to me that he be showing them too much love."

Ellen, not knowing how to respond to Maggie, glanced at Mr McCarthy for assistance. No help there; he was giving his cutlery close examination and didn't look up. She swallowed hard and patted Maggie's arm. "We must all be strong and support the McCarthys at such a difficult time. They have been given a heavy load to bear and it is up to us to do what we can to help them deal with it."

Maggie nodded and turned on her heel, making sure she turned away from Mr McCarthy so he could not see the tears starting to trickle down her plump cheeks. She left the dining room with somewhat less reserved decorum than usual. A heavy silence filled the room follow-ing her departure, and the meal was consumed with little enthusiasm and in silence. "Would you join me in a brandy?" McCarthy asked when they finished eating. "I suggest we take them through to the sitting room where we can talk in comfort and privacy while Maggie clears away in here." Ellen noted he picked up the brandy bottle as they left the room and took it with him.

McCarthy knew there was no putting off telling Ellen of the doctors' prognosis. "There is no good news. There had been the suggestion that Mrs McCarthy might consider travelling to Brisbane to undergo some new experimental treatment for leukaemia. They explained it was dangerous and involved transferring blood from one person to another. Sometimes it worked, but often it proved fatal. They didn't know why this happened. After they explained everything, she dismissed the suggestion at once, and the doctors appeared relieved. They admitted they considered her hardly strong enough to make the journey."

Ellen simply nodded and avoided eye contact with McCarthy lest she lose control of the tears she struggled to hold back.

"My wife is an amazingly strong woman," McCarthy stated. "She didn't want to waste time on useless conversation and asked them directly to tell her honestly what lay ahead. She has only weeks left at best and, towards the end, they will not be pleasant. Dr Boyle will prepare an elixir for her to take closer to the end when it becomes unbearable. It will make her sleep through the worst of it."

"Can they not admit her to hospital to do something to make her time more comfortable?" Ellen pleaded.

"It was suggested she could go into hospital – and now rather than later – but Mrs McCarthy refused. She said Koreelah was her home and had been for many years now. This is where she insists on ending her days." He heard Ellen stifle a sob, and swallowed hard before continuing. "I know that it will be hard for everyone, especially you, my dear woman, as we live through those weeks." There was no need for further conversation. They sipped their brandies in silence.

McCarthy gestured towards her with the brandy bottle. She declined a refill. "No, thank you. I must see to Mrs McCarthy. I have left her alone for too long as it is." With that she left, and went downstairs to what would become her living quarters for the next few weeks. Edith was a pale withered shape amongst the snowy white sheets, but she appeared to sleep peacefully.

The next day, Ellen's insistence that Edith remain in bed met with no argument, and the day revolved around sips of water, doses of her regular 'tonic', and sponging to keep her comfortable. Saturday found Edith much stronger. Elizabeth came to enquire after Edith, although it wasn't one of her regular days, and Ellen enlisted her aid to move Edith out into one of the comfortable chairs outside the rooms. Elizabeth promised to return before lunch to help get Edith back to bed, and then left. Ellen drew a chair close to Edith. "Would you like me to read to you this morning?" she asked.

"No, I think not. Perhaps we could just talk for a while."

"Of course; I would enjoy that. What shall we talk about?"

"Humour an old woman if you will please, and explain something that has me curious. It might be none of my business and you should feel free to say so. However, I have a vague recollection from quite a few years ago of your marriage to someone– not a local lad as I recall – yet you go by your maiden name: Miss Grimsby."

Ellen hesitated briefly as she pondered how to reply, and if she wanted to. Then she shrugged and launched into her story. "Your memory serves you well. I did marry – nigh on thirteen years ago now – a man a few years my senior and fresh out from England. I have been widowed a few years now."

"What about children, were there none? If there are, you could have them live here with you in the cottage you know."

"I had four beautiful children and a fifth was born about three weeks after my husband's death. The baby survived only a day before joining his father. The others are no longer with me." Edith encouraged her to go on. Like Pandora's Box, once the lid lifted, the story of Ellen's struggle after her husband's death rushed out. She told of turning to her parents to take her and her children in when they had nowhere else to go. Somehow, something suggested it was best not to mention their connection with the mill whose board of directors of which her husband was chairman at the time.

"Thanks to my mother's intercession on my behalf, my father agreed I could return to live with them again, but he would not take the children. They were to stay in the orphanage until I was on my feet again, found somewhere for us to live and could support them myself. That time never came." Ellen told of visiting the children until her mother's illness made it impossible for her to leave the store. "…And then when Alfred delivered an order before Christmas, he was told the orphanage had closed and the children moved to other orphanages run by the church. I knew nothing of it and went to see the Priest who was involved in running the place. The new bishop transferred him to somewhere else. Perhaps he was the priest who visited here."

The women discussed details of Ellen's story for a few minutes before Edith returned to her original question: why had Ellen reverted to her maiden name.

"Shortly before my husband's death, someone who sought to benefit from scurrilous slander made false accusation against my husband. He put it about that my husband had used his position to extract funds from his employer's clients in order to line his own pocket. It was not true, but my husband was on his deathbed at the time and could not fight the accusation. When I moved back to live with my parents, my father was concerned that the accusation against my late husband should not reflect on Grimsby's Store. He thought it might generate caution about dealing with Grimsby's and insisted I revert to my maiden name in a bid to prevent any obvious connection between the accusation, myself and the store."

"That is an incredibly sad story, but you seem comfortable enough being called Miss Grimsby again."

"Yes, I suppose it is who I was and who I still am. Without the children, it doesn't make a lot of difference. It might be different if I still had the children."

"As I said before, they could live here with you if you want to bring them home from the orphanage." Ellen explained how she didn't know where the children ended up and how she had no way of finding them. Edith took a moment to think on that before speaking again. "Well, my dear, we need to start asking the church some questions."

"I don't know much about the Catholic Church or how it is organised. I wouldn't know who to contact."

"Quite understandable; however, I am Catholic, and I am very familiar with the Church and who's who in the local diocese. Better than that, there is a good friend who may be able to help. Our families were close for most of our lives. They had two daughters and four sons. The girls were the youngest in the tribe and the youngest girl was my best friend. She became a nun – joined the Sisters of Mercy. She is in Ralston and has something to do with the orphanage there. I owe her a letter, but I haven't felt up to writing lately. Now would be a good time to correct that situation. I will tell you what to say and I'll sign it, but I would be pleased if you would write it for me."

Ellen fetched the necessary writing materials and sat at a small table next to Edith's chair to write the letter as Edith dictated it. After all the usual greetings and catching up that usually happens in a letter, Edith sought her friend's assistance in finding out what happened to Ellen's children. She gave Ellen's name to Sister Justina and asked that she communicate directly with Ellen on the matter. The letter would go to the Post Office with the next person from the property to go into town.

A month slipped by without a response for Sister Justina. At first, Edith had asked every few days if there had been a reply but, as the month ended, she no longer enquired. Ellen continued to travel into town once a week, but now she mostly made the journey alone and on occasion rode in on the wagon with one of the men. Dr Boyle now made weekly visits to the property to check on Edith, but Ellen noticed that on each visit he spent some time with Mr McCarthy behind closed doors. When she saw McCarthy surreptitiously taking some form of medication, she formed her own opinion about what went on behind those doors when the doctor visited.

*****

By early June, Edith was rarely out of bed. Winter arrived blustery and wet. Even on the nicest days, Edith was no too weak to be out of bed. Around the middle of the month, Boyle started her on the special medication that kept her so doped up that her lucid moments were rare. Ellen nursed her twenty-four hours a day. On one of the few occasions when Edith was lucid for a while, she spoke with Ellen.

"I hope you can find it in your heart to stay on here at Koreelah after I am gone. No, don't protest. My time is close. Afterwards Mr McCarthy will be at a loss. I beg you to consider staying on to continue to run the house and the office and to look after him. It will not be easy, I know. He can be a difficult man but, underneath it all, he is a caring person. It troubles me that I think he is ill also. If my suspicions are correct, he will need someone just as I do."

What am I supposed to say, Ellen thought. I do not want to upset this woman at this time. Of course, I could stay on for a while after she is gone – until the place settles down again at least – but I'm not sure about the caring for him bit. However, she resolved it with her conscience that it was okay to agree with the wishes of a dying woman, even if you were only intending to follow through on some of what you agreed to do.

The end, when it came, came quickly. On a particularly cold wet day at the end of June, Edith passed away in the early hours of the morning. As previously arranged, Ellen went out onto the verandah and rang the dinner bell: six slow strokes. Within minutes, Elizabeth and Maggie arrived and insisted on taking care of Edith. They suggested that the sitting room so recently Ellen's bedroom, might be where the undertaker would wish to lay out the body. Ellen gathered up her belongings and returned them to her cottage before making her way to the office. She wrote a quick letter to Sister Justina advising her of Edith's death. Mr McCarthy came looking for her and announced that, as soon as it was first light, they should go into town to make the necessary arrangements.

It was early when they arrived in town so they went to the undertaker's home. By the time McCarthy and Ellen were on their way to the church, he was loading up his wagon to leave for Koreelah. Ellen remained in the buggy while Mr McCarthy made the necessary arrangements with the priest on duty. With everything arranged, they headed back to the property calling at the post office on the way out of

157

town. Ellen posted the letter to Sister Justina and collected the bundle of mail for the property.

The place looked deserted when they returned, with the exception of the undertaker who was busily plying his skills in the downstairs sitting room. McCarthy promptly locked himself in his study. Elizabeth had gone home, and the kitchen was silent as Maggie also went home as a mark of respect. Ellen collected the book she was reading from the library and was on her way back to her cottage when she decided to check the mail in case there was something urgent amongst it. Nothing needed urgent attention, but she was surprised to find an envelope addressed to her.

Although little interested in what its contents might be, she tore open the envelope. Apprehension engulfed her the moment she saw Sister Justina's signature. It came as something of a relief to find that the letter contained nothing of any import and only provided an update. The nun had been at the Ralston orphanage only for a couple of months, and she knew nothing of Ellen's children. The records for that orphanage contained no registration information for them. Justina advised that she would endeavour to check other records, including those from when the children first went into care, to see if she could discover where they went and might be now. However, Ellen detected an inference in the nun's words that she wasn't hopeful of achieving anything quickly due to the state of the various records.

Somehow, given the present upheaval in her life once more, Sister Justina's letter had little impact. Later, when she re-read the letter, the fact that the children never appeared to arrive at the Ralston orphanage would cause concern. For the moment, there were other things weighing her down. She pushed the letter into her pocket, descended the stairs and slowly made her way back to her cottage. An abnormal heavy silence hung over the place. Even the birds were silent, and only the occasional bellow from a calf intruded. She ran her hand through the rosemary bushes as she passed through the kitchen garden and paused briefly to inhale their scent.

Everyone was up early the next day. Although the ground remained muddy from the recent rain, it was a bright sunny day for the funeral, with a gentle warm breeze prevailing. News travels fast even in the bush. A surprisingly large crowd gathered for the funeral the next day. Despite the priest's protest, the service was short and simple, as Edith had wanted. She had made her preferences clear, stressing that she did not wish it to become a drawn-out ordeal for those who chose to attend. The scarcity of women at the service was in keeping with the tradition of the day: only Ellen, Elizabeth and Maggie.

As soon as the service finished, the three women headed upstairs while the rest of the men stood around Mr McCarthy shaking his hand and offering their condolences. The women brought trays of sandwiches and cake and enormous pots of tea downstairs and set them out on the table under the house. Off to one side of the area, Elizabeth's husband and a couple of the workers set up another table. It catered for those who needed something stronger to fortify them after the event. Maggie was concerned about how many there might be for lunch, but she needn't have worried. When lunchtime rolled around, the last of the guests were leaving. The rest of the day saw the place once more plunged into silence. Tomorrow would see work on the property as usual.

*****

About midway through August, Ellen noted that life on the property seem to have settled down again. The domestic staff now went about their duties without the solemn long faces that prevailed after Edith death. She felt it was fast approaching the time when she would be able to take her leave of Koreelah and move back to the store. The problem seemed to be finding the right time to discuss the situation with Mr McCarthy, and identifying who would do what after she left. In her own mind, she decided the end of August would be a good time to bid farewell to Koreelah. However, at the start of the last week in August, there still hadn't been opportunity to discuss the matter with McCarthy.

As she took morning tea on the verandah, she idly watched Mr McCarthy bringing the buggy back after his usual morning check on the workers. She suddenly realised she had not seen him on a horse, at least not since Edith's death. Was she game enough to ask him about this, she wondered. Some inbuilt instinct told her it had something to do with the state of his health, and that it wasn't because he'd suddenly become too old to travel on horseback. There was nothing for it she convinced herself, other than to broach the subject with him that evening over dinner.

The opportunity did not present itself at dinner, as McCarthy headed into town on the buggy straight after lunch, having advised Maggie he might be gone for a couple of days. In the event, he returned late the following day but took a light supper on a tray in his study rather than joining Ellen in the dining room for dinner. His behaviour was so unusual, Ellen became concerned, and she determined she would tackle him first thing the next morning.

Straight after breakfast, Ellen took up a position on the verandah where she waited for McCarthy to finish breakfast. As he left the dining room, she asked him to sit with her as she had some important issues to discuss. Their conversation didn't go as she had hoped. He chose to be obtuse, claimed his health was fine and she should stop fussing about things that didn't concern her. If she had upset him, she apologised but she was concerned for him. Brushing aside her apology, and still angry about what he saw as an intrusion on his privacy, McCarthy sprung up out of his chair and started down the stairs.

When he was about halfway down the stairs, Ellen saw him stop. His knees buckled and he grabbed for the banister. He dragged himself over and half draped himself over the handrail. Ellen rushed to the top of the stairs and caught a terrified look from her employer. She rushed down the stairs screaming for Maggie as she went. Between them, the two women managed to lift McCarthy away from the handrail and sit him down on a step.

Maggie was yelling for Bert who rushed from their cottage in response. Elizabeth and her husband, Jim, curious about all the yelling, abandoned their breakfast and came outside to investigate the commotion. The sight of the huddle on the stairs and Bert thundering across the yard had them running as well. It became quite crowded on the stairs. Ellen feared one of them would fall down and be injured. She made the other two women retreat a few steps up the stairs while Jim and Bert each got under an arm, and carried McCarthy down and laid him on the ground.

Ellen knelt beside him. In a hoarse whisper, he told Ellen to fetch some medication from the desk drawer in his study. He was grey and obviously in great pain. The medication didn't seem to make any immediate improvement. Jim brought the wagon around and together they managed to load the patient on to it. Jim took the reins and urged the horses into a gallop. Ellen sat beside Mr McCarthy and shaded his face from the sun with a parasol. As the wagon swayed and lurched at speed along the unmade track, she found it almost impossible to remain upright and was sure she was collecting quite a few bruises as they made their way to town.

In a shower of gravel and dust, Jim brought the wagon to a stop in front of the hospital. Dr Boyle, on his way to start his morning rounds and startled by their arrival, rushed to investigate. He ran back into the hospital and soon the wagon was swarming with people. McCarthy was loaded onto a gurney and quickly wheeled inside. Ellen followed them and started a long vigil in a waiting room while Jim took the wagon around to the horse yard behind the hospital. It was some time before he joined Ellen.

While Jim dealt with the wagon, Dr Boyle came to speak with Ellen. I have to tell you that Mr McCarthy is gravely ill. He has suffered a stroke. It is not unexpected. I have been treating him for some time now for his condition, and it was inevitable that this should happen. I would not discuss a patient's condition with anyone other than family but, as you appear to be what now passes for family for Mr McCarthy, I feel obliged to discuss his condition with you. This is especially so as you appear to be staying on to care for him since Mrs McCarthy's passing."

"I don't know that I'm caring for Mr McCarthy. I organise the house and the office and take care of some matters, but there isn't much caring involved."

"There will be a need for that in the near future. He will remain in hospital for several days now, until we get things settled down and he regains some strength. Then we will assess the extent of the damage from the stroke. After that, he may return home but only on the understanding that he changes his lifestyle to manage his condition better. That might help in the first instance, but over the next few months, his condition will deteriorate. I will be suggesting he visits specialists in Brisbane at his earliest opportunity. They might recommend some further period in hospital while there."

"Dr Boyle, you haven't stated the nature of Mr McCarthy's illness. Am I right in assuming it is a heart condition?"

"I do apologise; yes. He has a heart condition and the stroke resulted from associated problems. It is difficult to tell how serious the stroke was. He suffered some major disabilities initially, but only time will tell what the long-term effect will be. I could not give you any indication of what that might be at this stage. He has had a problem for a while, but he chose to ignore it – and me – while his wife was so ill. His heart condition is now affecting other parts of his body and will continue to cause increased problems as time goes by. My belief is that, probably by several months from now, he will require full-time care. I can only speculate on how soon that might occur. It is as well you know what lies ahead. I doubt it will be an easy time for him – or for you if you continue to care for him."

"I don't know how he will cope if he is left disabled in some way. He can be a difficult person now but, if he were to find himself severely disabled, I don't dare think about how he would be or what he might do." Dr Boyle understood and quietly agreed with her concerns.

When Jim returned from seeing to the horses and the wagon, Ellen suggested they go across to the tearooms where they might discuss McCarthy's situation over a pot of tea. The news didn't come as a surprise to Jim. In a similar way to that of Ellen, Jim noticed a change in the boss, but he assumed from the outset that the change was due to failing health. After collecting some bits and pieces for the property from Grimsby's Store, they checked on Mr McCarthy again before heading back to the property. In view of Dr Boyle's advice that he intended keeping McCarthy in hospital for several days, Ellen decided she would come into town and stay at the store until McCarthy's release from hospital.

On returning to Koreelah, Ellen attended to a few things to make sure the place would continue to run smoothly in her absence, and then spent some time packing personal items to take to the hospital for Mr McCarthy. Sleep didn't come easily that night. Dr Boyle's prognosis of Mr McCarthy's condition occupied her thinking. The suggestion that she might soon find herself having to nurse the man as his condition worsened was not a suggestion she welcomed. She had now nursed three terminally ill people whom she was close to: her husband, mother, and her friend Mrs McCarthy. Those people she cared for in varying ways, and that, in her mind, made Mr McCarthy's situation a very different one.

Early the next morning, while the dew still clung to everything, Bert brought the buggy around for her and she headed into town. She arrived at the store chilled through and with her hair wet from her early morning ride in the damp air, her arrival coinciding with that of Alfred and Jess to start work for the day. Alfred took care of the horses while Ellen opened up the store and told the staff that she could be in town for a few days. A few minutes later, she was on her way to the hospital to check on Mr McCarthy's progress. Dr Boyle was doing his rounds of the wards when she arrived, so she waited patiently for him to finish before speaking to him.

"Mr McCarthy has not improved much overnight and I now consider he should remain in hospital for a least a week and possibly two," he told Ellen. "The medication I prescribed will make him sleep for most of the time he is here, at least for the first few days until there is noticeable improvement in his condition." As McCarthy was sleeping when they spoke, Ellen said she wouldn't go in to see him then, but would continue to look in on him once or twice a day. There was a spring in her step as she walked back to the store. The prospect of a few days back at the store – at home – lifted her spirits.

It was almost three weeks later before Dr Boyle pronounced Mr McCarthy fit to go home. Although still exhibiting some paralysis down one side, the man was as pompous as ever. Ellen thought he would want to leave for Koreelah at once, but McCarthy had other ideas. He chose to spend an extra day in town and checked into the local hotel for the night. No assistance was required from Ellen, he assured her. He had a couple of personal matters to attend to and his tone was sufficiently brusque as to leave her in no doubt that she should mind her own business. It was around lunchtime the following day when McCarthy sent a lad from the hotel to tell her he would be ready to return home immediately after breakfast the next day.

Ellen was ready to go early the next morning as requested. She opened the store, said goodbye to the staff and went across to the hotel. McCarthy was waiting, and climbed up onto the buggy. Ellen thought he would want to take the reins, but he drew the rug across his knees and sat with his hands in his lap. "Is there something delaying our departure?" he growled.

"Not at all; if you're sure you are comfortable, we will be off." Without waiting for his response, she flicked the reins and they headed out of town. The trip passed in silence. Ellen found her mind wandering across a myriad of topics as they trotted along in the early morning air. Spring had arrived; and so it should. It was now September. Many of the trees already sprouted new green growth. Soon the days would lengthen. Ellen found herself wondering how many more times would she make this trip before she finally said goodbye to Koreelah. Already she was wishing to be back at the store.

It was a couple of days later before Mr McCarthy announced over dinner that he had asked Dr Boyle to arrange for him to spend some time with the specialists in Brisbane. "I asked for it to be around mid-October. I expect or at least, Dr Boyle thinks I will need to spend some weeks there and that possibly some of that time may be in hospital. Do you have any problems with that?"

"No problems at all; I'm glad you have taken the doctor's advice." Then a shocking thought occurred to Ellen. "You're not expecting me to accompany you to Brisbane are you?"

"Would it bother you if I were?"

"It most definitely would. I can tell you now I will not be going with you, whatever the consequences of that might be."

"What if I need your assistance?"

"Then perhaps you had better arrange for one of the men to accompany you. I do not wish to go and it would be highly improper of me to do so."

"Are you so … so … straight laced as to refuse a critically ill man's request for assistance?" …But Ellen glimpsed the hint of a smile, which he quickly hid.

Ah, so that's the way he wants to play it, she thought. "It's not about being straight laced, Sir. It's about common decency and about adhering to what is proper and acceptable in polite society. I will not be going with you… and that will not change. It is up to you what you choose to do about it." He could control himself no longer and laughed aloud.

It was the first time Ellen had heard him laugh. She couldn't remember even seeing him smile before, but here he was thoroughly enjoying teasing her. …At least, she thought he was teasing. She made a mental note to reinforce her refusal to accompany him at every opportunity, just in case he wasn't teasing.

There could be no doubt that McCarthy found his new restricted lifestyle frustrating. After breakfast each day, he descended the stairs to sit in a large wicker butterfly chair under the house. Jim came every morning to determine what work the boss wanted done that day. Following about a week of doing nothing all day except sitting under the house, McCarthy decided he needed to go about and look at the property. Soon after he went downstairs, Ellen heard him call Bert over to where he sat. A short while later Bert drove the buggy up to the house and helped Mr McCarthy climb on board.

Ellen watched the buggy until it disappeared from view. Bert was taking the boss on a tour of inspection. She decided it probably was good for him get out. It might revive his interest in what was happening on the property… but she would keep a careful eye on him for any sign such trips were too tiring. This routine continued for a few days. Then, one morning, Bert was nowhere in sight. Ellen heard McCarthy call his name, but there was no response. She went to the library and looked out the window, which overlook the back yard and all the way down to the hedge that marked the boundary of the homestead area. She couldn't see Bert, but could see enough activity happening on the other side of the hedge to tell her Bert was busy pruning. McCarthy called Bert again, and Ellen detected a certain note creeping into his voice. Best she deal with the matter before McCarthy worked himself up too much.

Ellen rushed down the stairs and explained that Bert was working too far away to hear his name called. "How am I supposed to know what is happening on the place if I can't get around. The man knows I want to inspect the place every morning."

"That's not Bert's job."

"That's well and good, but I haven't seen the men this morning to allocate their jobs for the day. I told Jim not to hang around waiting for me to come down of a morning, as I would see him and the others out in the paddocks. I don't know what they are doing today – could be nothing for all I know. Why are you standing there? You could take me around in the buggy."

"Excuse me, did you just ask me to drive you around the property in the buggy?"

"Well, somebody has to, and you can handle the buggy."

"True, but I have to make up the wages for the men for them to collect tomorrow. That is my job... not being your chauffeur."

"Make up the pays this afternoon, or some time later today. Go and get the buggy." Ellen turned on her heel and started walked away, but she was heading for the stairs. "Where are you going, Woman? I said to get the buggy."

"…And, if you had been in the least way polite about it, I might have considered it. However, since you couldn't even manage to say please, I'm not very interested in what you are asking for." With that, McCarthy watched her flounce up the stairs, and heard a door slam a moment later.

"Damn and blast the woman. Who does she think she is? She would dare to treat me like that?" he fumed aloud.

"She knows exactly who she is and what her job here is," Dr Boyle said sternly as he came around the corner of the house. "…And it would serve you well to remember how much you need her. So, be nice to her. She will not stand for your nonsense, and definitely won't put up with any rudeness."

"I'm a sick man. Surely, I deserve more consideration than that. If she is to care for me, I expect her to be somewhat more obliging."

"Perhaps you are confusing 'obliging' with 'subservient"... and I'm here to tell you Miss Grimsby is not about to be subservient to anyone who disrespects her."

"Humph, so what did you want, Boyle? What brings you here and how come I didn't see you drive up?"

"My horse is where I usually leave it. I employed no stealth in my arrival. Perhaps your hearing is failing along with some of your other parts. As to why I am here, I came to tell you of the arrangements for your trip to Brisbane."

McCarthy realised the doctor also wasn't about to stand for any nonsense from him and amended his demeanour. He motioned for the doctor to sit and continue. "Your first appointment is in mid-October. All the details of what has been arranged are in this document," Boyle said as he handed McCarthy an envelope he withdrew from the inside pocket of his jacket. "Well, I'll be off then; patients to see and all that. I assume I will see you at my rooms again next week…" Boyle said over his shoulder as he went to get his horse.

A couple of days later, Ellen took a morning tea tray downstairs to Mr McCarthy. He invited her to join him, as he wanted to discuss his Brisbane trip with her. One of the workers – not Jim – would accompany him and stay with him in Brisbane for as long as necessary. "You look surprised. Is there some problem with that arrangement?"

"No, I was expecting it to be Jim who would go with you."

"I can't take Jim away. With both of us gone, who would run the place? It is too close to the end of the crushing season to take away the most experienced man on the place." He picked up his cup, then immediately put it down heavily. "I hadn't noticed until this very minute, but this yard looks unkempt. Everything is overgrown, the weeds have come through and the grass needs cutting. I understood managing the gardener was part of your job. How do you explain this state of affairs?"

"Very easily; you keep taking the gardener away from his duties. If Bert cannot get on with his job, the garden will get away from him – and it has. He is supposed to be the gardener, not your personal servant."

He glared at Ellen for a few moments but remained silent. He could recognise the truth when he heard it. "What am I going to do?" he asked as he dropped his head in his hands. "Oh, I don't mean right now. I mean as things become worse. I struggle to do for myself now, and I accept that soon even the little I manage now will be beyond me. Will you still be here… will you still be here to care for me as you cared for Mrs McCarthy?"

"I will continue to do what I can to assist in any way I am able, and will keep the house running as smoothly as possible. However, I will not be able to care for you in the same way I cared for my mother and Mrs McCarthy. They were women, and that made it possible for me to do what they required. Much of that care, particular towards the end of their suffering, was of an extremely personal nature. It is not possible for me to do that for you?"

"I don't see why not."

"Only a wife could provide such personal care for a man – or a mother if the man were young enough. In the absence of both of those, a professional nurse might be a substitute… but not a single female employee." McCarthy grunted but let the conversation lapse.

As they finished what had been a silent meal that evening, McCarthy stunned Ellen with a question she never imagined possible. "So, Miss Grimsby, will you marry me?" Dumbstruck for a few moments, Ellen silently questioned the effectiveness of her hearing.

"Marry you…? Why would I do that? What makes you think I would even consider such a thing? Was that some sort of proposal… if so, where did it come from?"

"It came from me. That is where it came from. You spoke of the personal nature of the care I would need in the future and only a wife or a professional nurse might provide such care. I don't have a nurse. I have you. If it is marriage that you require in order to care for me, then I will damn well marry you. Is that what you were angling for anyway?"

"How dare you! I was not angling for anything, just acquainting you with the facts of your situation. No, I will not even consider marrying you. I give you my undertaking that I will look after you to the best of my ability and as decency permits, but that is as far as it goes. …And…" McCarthy made to interrupt. Ellen held up her hand to silence him. "…And that undertaking only holds true if you start showing me some respect. If that is too much to ask of you, I will leave you to your own devices, and for you to work out for yourself who you might get to look after you. Do I need to clarify any of that?" Ellen scraped her chair back and flounced out of the room without a backward glance, almost barrelling into Maggie on her way in to clear the table.

For the next couple of days, the relationship between Ellen and her employer was cordial enough but somewhat stiff. Maggie shot them both wary glances whenever she was around them, and Elizabeth seemed to be giving Ellen a wide berth. However, as usual, these things settle down eventually, but the best description of their relationship after was 'formal'.

Chapter 19

Mid-October rolled around and Ellen took Mr McCarthy into town to catch the boat for Brisbane. Jim followed them with the wagon and the worker who was to accompany McCarthy. Ellen intended staying at the store during McCarthy's absence and advised the staff at Koreelah accordingly.

The store and agency were doing well and, as she drove McCarthy into town, she was aware of how much she looked forward to spending time there. During a quiet period after lunch on that first day back, the staff asked to discuss something with her. Their news overshadowed her happiness at being home again. "Sorry to be bothering you with this when you've only just come back," Alfred began, "But we are concerned about something that happened last Saturday."

Ellen noted they all looked uncomfortable and she felt her stomach tighten with apprehension. "That's fine, Alfred, if it concerned you, I need to know about it."

Alfred shifted his weight from foot to foot a couple of times before continuing. "Last Saturday, as we were closing up for the weekend, Mr Grimsby came into the store…"

"He was drunk," Jess interrupted, "Very drunk." Ellen nodded and motioned Alfred to continue.

"He marched straight into the office and scratched around in there for a few minutes before coming out and shouting at Jess. He wanted the key to the safe…"

"I changed the place where we hide it. It just seemed like the right thing to do after you told us how Mr Grimsby was no longer involved with this place."

"A very wise decision as it turns out, Jess. Thank you for thinking to do that. I assume my father was angry when he couldn't find the key. What happened then?"

"Well, Jess played dumb like, and said she didn't know about the safe as you looked after that. He didn't believe her. He pushed Jess and she fell up against the counter. Charlie and I heard all the shouting and Jess scream and we ran into see what was going on."

"He lost his balance when he shoved me against the counter," Jess said, "He grabbed at the bag of pumpkins over there to stop himself falling over. I was a bit groggy from hitting my head on the counter, so it took a few moments to find my feet again. That's when these two arrived."

Alfred took up the story again. "As Jess was peeling herself off the counter, he came at her with one of those weights for the scales that are there beside the bags of potatoes and pumpkins. We got there just in time," Alfred grinned wickedly. "Charlie's got a deadly right hook, Miss. You should have seen it! Oh, begging your pardon, Miss. No, perhaps it was best you did not see your father knocked out cold."

"Has he been back since that ruckus on Saturday?" Ellen asked.

"No…," Alfred began.

"Well, yes, I think he has," Jess cut in. Alfred spun around to face her, concern etched across his face. "It's all right; nothing happened. After these two threw him out onto the street and we locked up, I tidied up the office and put everything back the way it should be. When we came back this morning, I went into the office and found everything strewn about again."

"Did he find the key to the safe this time?"

"No, Miss. It wasn't here to find. I took it and the key to the upstairs area home with me on Saturday… just in case, if you know what I mean." Ellen laughed and the two men clapped and cheered.

"Well done! Well done and thanks to all of you. I now have a couple of things I must do immediately, but I would like us to talk again after we close up this afternoon."

Ellen grabbed her hat and bag and left the store, heading for the hardware store, and a long conversation with it owner, Col McLean. After telling him Grimsby's suffered a break-in over the weekend, she asked about having all the locks changed. Col liked a chat and, not wanting to give him any real details of their 'break-in', Ellen had to choose every word carefully. With his curiosity dealt with as much as it was going to be, Col said he and a lad would come over to the store later in the day to fit new locks.

Mr Taylor's office was next on her list of visits to make that morning. There was a short wait before she could tell him of her father's visits and her concern at his behaviour. Ellen's intention was to take the matter to the Police. Taylor agreed and said he would accompany her, and they walked around the corner to the Police Station together. The Sergeant on duty showed unexpected interest in her story. When Ellen finished recounting details of her father's visits, she expressed her concern for the safety of herself and the staff if James Grimsby came to the store again.

"Now that is interesting," Sergeant Hinkson said, speaking directly to Mr Taylor. "Do you happen to know where we might find Mr Grimsby now?" Both shook their heads and Hinkson continued. "See here," he said, brandishing a sheet of paper. He directed it towards Mr Taylor, making it impossible for Ellen to read what it said. "This here warrant for the arrest of Mr James Grimsby for several counts of fraud was received late last week. We knew he hadn't been in town for a while and didn't expect he would come back here. So, tell me Mr Taylor, what is the situation with Grimsby's Store and Agency? Who owns what now? There's little to interest us if the man is breaking into his own property."

Taylor started to respond, carefully picking his words. "Mr James Grimsby has no…" Ellen cut in before he could say more.

"I own Grimsby's Store and Agency, and have done since probate was granted on my mother's estate some months ago. Mr Grimsby, my father, continued to own the farmers' agency side of the business until more recently when the bank foreclosed on it. I bought the agency from the bank and added it to the store's operation. …So, in answer to your question, Sergeant, I own the business in question and James Grimsby has no claim to it or any right to be there. Apart from that, his assault on a female employee in itself is probably grounds for arrest. Is there anything else you need to know about my business?" This arrogant Irish twit needs to accept that women are real people who do exist in the community, Ellen thought as she tried to calm her temper.

"Quite," Hinkson replied, looking a tad uncomfortable. "…But you don't know where your father might be staying while he is in town?"

"He hasn't access to cash to stay at the hotel or his club, but he did have a mate, Bill Jackson, who I think has a shack near one of those beaches just outside town. He is a hopeless drunk but my father might find a free bed at his place. I don't think any other of his so called 'friends' would take him in."

"Thank you, Miss. We will look into it," and tapping the side of his nose and winking at Mr Taylor, he added, "Be quite a feather in our cap I would think, if we were to apprehend someone owing so many people so much money."

They left the Police Station together. Taylor left her when they reached his office and Ellen continued alone to the store. As she crossed the street, she saw Col McLean and his offsider enter the store. Ellen stepped up her pace and joined the small group beside the counter as Col finished explaining to a confused Jess why they had come. Ellen took control. "Come with me, Mr McLean. I will show you the locks that need changing."

It took Col McLean and his lad longer than expected to complete the job but, late in the afternoon, Col appeared in the office doorway and announced they were finished and were heading off. Ellen felt a sense of relief sweep over her. Regardless of what happen with the Police, at least the place was now safe from after hours' visits. Then it occurred to her that it really did matter what happened with the Police. If James Grimsby were still in town, there remained the chance of another violent incident.

At the end of the day, Ellen met with the staff to explain the measures to deal with her father she put in place earlier that day. "Col McLean changed all the locks, so we should have no more unauthorised after hours visits. The new keys are in the new hiding places you created for them. Here Alfred, this is your key to the back door so you can let everyone in first thing in the morning when I am not here. I spoke with the Police. There is a warrant out for James Grimsby's arrest for fraud and they were interested to learn he was in town, and are now searching for him. While this might be effective in some ways, it won't prevent him turning up during opening hours. We all need to be alert and look out for each other."

"Do we know where Mr Grimsby is at now, or if he is still in town?" Alfred asked.

Ellen shook her head. "No, but the Police are looking for him and there aren't too many places he could be if he is still here. I am sorry I have kept you back again but I did want to bring up to date on what I have put in place. Off you go to your homes and mind how you go." They turned away and Charlie called 'goodnight' as he headed for the door.

Alfred and Jess started to walk away but stopped abruptly. Alfred turned back to Ellen. "Excuse me, Miss, if you have a moment, there is something I would like to say."

"Of course, what is it, Alfred?" Charlie returned to stand behind Alfred and Jess.

"Well, Miss... uhmm ... Jess and me ... well, we've been sort of keeping company for a while now. We didn't say anything before because... well, you know, it was sort of a private thing." Jess appeared to have developed a keen interest in her boots, and kept her head lowered as she looked at them.

"Now I see how you knew so much about what was happening at Swayne's Store, and about Jess' job and everything."

"We're hoping you don't mind, Miss, but Jess and I are getting married at Christmas."

"Congratulations! It comes as a surprise, but I am happy for the both of you." Jess lost interest in her boots. With her face a delicate shade of pink, she beamed at Ellen.

"We thought about it last Christmas but there were too many things going on, so we decided to wait. We both come from big families but most of our brothers and sister have moved away from here. Christmas is a time when at least those living not too far away can come home. That's why we decided on Christmas. We know you have other things you have to do but, if you could get away, we would love you to be there with us."

"I wouldn't miss it for the world. What day is it?"

"Boxing Day, Miss. Well, Jess," Alfred said, and slid a sideways glance at his partner, "That leaves only one problem still to deal with."

"One big problem…" Jess agreed. Ellen asked what was so worrying for them.

"We still haven't found anywhere to live. We can' afford horses or a wagon of any sort, so we need a place in town so we can walk to work. Oh, I meant to ask, will it be all right if Jess continues to work here after we are married?"

"I certainly hope she will. There must be places in town available for rent."

"There are two or three, but they are big houses and the rent is far too expensive. We just need somewhere small that we can afford." Ellen rather lamely commented that they keep looking and with luck, something would become available before the wedding.

With nothing more to discuss, there was a chorus of 'goodnights' and people once more moved towards the door. Ellen followed them to lock the door behind them. They were at the bottom of the steps when an idea occurred to her. "Hold on, can you come back for a moment please?" They rushed back up, and there was a note of alarm in their voices as they asked in unison what was wrong.

"No, nothing is wrong. I had an idea; that is all. Alfred, why don't you and Jess think about living here?"

"This is your home and we hope one day you will move back here permanently."

"No, not above the store; I was thinking about the area above the agency. Alfred, do you know if it is a dwelling similar to the one above the store?"

"Yes, I went up there once just after Mr Grimsby bought the place. It is smaller than upstairs here, but it is meant to be lived in."

"Good; well how do you feel about living above your workplace? I don't know what it is like, but it is empty and, if you were living here, you could keep an eye on the place when I am away." Jess was almost bouncing up and down with excitement.

"If you are sure Miss, that would be perfect, wouldn't it Jess?" Jess couldn't find words. She just clapped her hands together and nodded excitedly.

"How about we take a look at what it's like before you all go home? Is anyone in a hurry to go?" Shaking of heads all round. "Right, does anyone know how you get up there? I don't think I have ever noticed a set of stairs."

"There is a set of stairs—a bit like this place – but Mr Grimsby put a wall up across that end of the loading area when he was doing the place up a bit just after he bought it… to stop people going up there uninvited when the back door is open I suppose. The door in the wall opens directly to the bottom of the stairs." Alfred recalled.

"That door is locked," Charlie said. "When I rearranged all the bags and bales we stack out there, I tried the door to see if there was more stuff stored behind the wall. I couldn't get in because it was locked."

"Can you show me this wall with the door, please?"

They went through to the area at the back of the agency. While Ellen and Jess stood back out of the way, Charlie and Alfred moved the bales of feed stacked in front of the wall. When they reached the last of the bales, Charlie stood back and looked at what remained. "That's strange," he said. "This stuff is not stacked hard up against the wall the way it used to be. There's a gap between the bales and the wall up that end where the door is."

They left the last of the bales in place and went to stand with the women. On his way past the bales at the door end of the wall, Charlie ducked in behind the bales and gave the doorknob a half-hearted turn. He stopped, his hand still on the doorknob, and looked questioningly at Alfred, who rushed over to try the door. They turned to Ellen, and Alfred said quietly, "It's open; it's not locked."

"Come away quickly!" Ellen commanded. Her voice barely above a whisper, she said, "Come back to the store with me." She continued through to the back of the store and down the steps at the loading dock, locking the door behind them. "Alfred, run to the Police Station please. Ask them to come immediately and bring them here to the back door. Tell them Mr Grimsby may be here. Now go quickly; run! We will wait here outside."

It seemed like an eternity, but it was only a few minutes later when they heard the pounding of heavy boots on the hard ground heading in their direction. Alfred appeared first, with Sergeant Hinkson and a couple of Constables close on his heels. "Now then, Miss Grimsby, what's this drama all about?" the Sergeant, red-faced and out of breath, demanded between gasps.

As quickly and succinctly as she could, Ellen explained about the wall and the unlocked door, and her suspicion that James Grimsby might be using the upstairs area of the agency as his hideout. After considering her comments for a couple of heartbeats, the Sergeant agreed it was worth a look.

Alfred led the Police through to the door. The Sergeant motioned Alfred to go back to the others whom he had told to stay outside the building. With Hinkson in the lead, the Police slowly and quietly climbed the stairs. Alfred didn't do as instructed. He only went back as far as the store, before moving back to stand in the back area of the agency. There was no way the others were going to wait outside either. They snuck back into the agency. Charlie went to join Alfred in the back area, while the two women waited near the agency's counter.

A few moments later, the sound of crashing and thumping reverberated through the building. Charlie and Alfred scampered back to guard the women. The commotion was over in seconds, replaced by grunting and swearing and the sound of boots on the stairs. Sergeant Hinkson emerged first. The two Constables with a handcuffed James Grimsby between them followed, struggling to descend the narrow stairs three abreast. Grimsby tripped on the last step and his guards hauled him roughly back to his feet. The Sergeant was beaming. Grimsby scowled. Ellen ran ahead to open the front door for them. They marched Grimsby back to the Police cells. Then the drama was over and everyone congregated at the back door again. It was summer and its long days stayed light until late, but night had descended by the time the staff headed home. The darkness shrouded them and they became invisible long before they turned the corner of the building.

First thing next morning, when Ellen greeted the staff as they arrived for work, she suggested they do what they were about to do last night: go up and have a look at the dwelling above the agency.

They traipsed up the stairs in single file behind Ellen. At the top of the stairs, she stepped aside and motioned to Alfred to open the door and lead the way in. The place was gloomy and not particularly inviting, with many years of disuse visible in the dust and cobwebs that abounded. Evidence of James Grimsby's brief stay didn't help improve the look of the place.

"I'm sorry, I didn't know the place would look so depressing," Ellen said. "Nevertheless, since we're here, let's have a look around to see whether we think there is any hope of making it habitable again."

Jess was way ahead of her and had already disappeared off into one of the rooms leaving the other three standing in the kitchen area. "Oh, I think it will be just wonderful. There's a fair bit of cleaning to do but it would suit us perfectly. What do you think, Alfred?"

"You are right about the cleaning, but it is just what we need. Those bits of furniture that are still here, will they stay? They look a bit the worse for wear but with a clean-up and maybe a bit of paint they should come up okay, and they are certainly more than we've got now." There wasn't much: a table, couple of chairs, a kitchen dresser and another couple of small cupboards.

"Of course they can stay," Ellen confirmed. "Besides, leaving them here will be easier than having to carry them downstairs … and then what would I do with them?" Everyone laughed, and Ellen and Charlie made their exit, leaving Alfred and Jess alone to inspect the place further.

It was just on closing time a couple of days after the arrest of James Grimsby when a gentle tap on the office door made Ellen look up from the paperwork she worked on. Her heart seemed to skip a beat as she looked up into the smiling face of Frank Woodrow. "I heard you were back in town for a while – and about your recent excitement. May I…"

Ellen smiled broadly as she motioned him to a seat opposite her. "It is so good to see you and, as you say, we did have a few moments of excitement."

"…And I hear your employer is poorly and has gone off down south for some period of time. Will you remain in town while he is away?"

Ellen explained the situation with Mr McCarthy's health and the specialist treatment in Brisbane, concluding with the information that she planned to stay in town for the duration but would visit Koreelah once a week to take care of matters there. "I am pleased to hear you will be back in town for a while," Woodrow said, nodding sagely.

"Now, tell me all about the excitement with your father. There are some very interesting versions of the story roaming the town."

Time slipped away as Ellen updated Woodrow on all of the happenings of the last few days. Jess interrupted their chat when she poked her head around the door to say she had locked up and that she and Alfred were off home for dinner but might return later to start cleaning upstairs. Woodrow looked surprised and queried whether Ellen now employed two of her staff to clean her place above the store.

"Goodness, no; as I mentioned earlier, we were on our way up to inspect the area above the agency when we realised something was amiss. That led to the arrest of my father," Ellen told him, and then went on to explain about the young couple's impending nuptials. "I offered to rent them the space above the agency because they were having trouble finding somewhere affordable in town. It is filthy but, once it is cleaned up, it should be quite comfortable for them." Woodrow approved of the move as it provided for some security both when Ellen was in town and, more importantly, when she was away.

"You may tell me it's none of my business, but how much longer do you intend to stay at Koreelah?" Woodrow asked tentatively. Ellen shrugged and, with no rebuff received, he continued. "Your task of caring for Mrs McCarthy ended some time ago. What keeps you there still?" Ellen found explaining her current situation difficult: how Mr McCarthy already was ill when his wife died, how he needed her to keep the place running until he recovered from his wife's death, and then the stroke he suffered.

"I had thought to leave at the end of August, but everything conspired against me. After the stroke left him with some complications, I felt compelled to stay on to help where I could. I suppose what happens next will depend on the outcome of the specialist's treatment in Brisbane."

"You can't stay out there forever. Who is going to keep an eye on the store and agency if your father is incarcerated for any period of time?"

"I don't believe Mr McCarthy will be around forever and, as for the store, I am concerned about it… but that's another story." In response to his questioning look, Ellen explained about the episode with her mother's will and ownership of the store passing to Ellen. "My father owned the agency but, after the bank foreclosed because of his debts, I purchased the agency from the bank. After all that, the situation now is that I own the whole business. The staff does a great job of running the place in my absence. I am lucky to have them, but I can't expect them to carry on doing that. I know I should be here, but the right time for me to leave Koreelah just hasn't presented."

"From what you say, I am beginning to think the 'right time' might not come along until he has gone to be with his wife. What if he is much improved after his time in Brisbane, will you feel able to leave then?" Ellen, taken aback by the degree of terseness – the accusation even – in his voice, found herself unsure how to respond – but only for a moment.

Her ire raised, she tilted her chin upwards and replied, "That remains unclear. Mr McCarthy has asked me to marry him."

"What! The bloody cheek of the man... Please excuse me, I do apologise for my language." Ellen smiled and waved away his apology with a dismissive flap of her hand. "Whatever possessed him to think you would accept? You did turn him down, of course?"

"Hmm, well, not so much turned him down as explained how the type of very personal nursing he was likely to require in the future could only—properly – be provided by a professional nurse or a wife – neither of which I am. He asked me to marry him so I would stay on to care for him. ...So, you see, unintentionally I invited the proposal. I didn't say no, but asked for time to consider his proposal."

"You would consider marrying that man...? That man whom you believe – and rightly so – drove your husband to his early grave and ultimately led to the loss of your children? You said that, for what he did to your husband, you wanted more than revenge. Now, you say you are considering marrying him. I do not understand you, and I must say I am disappointed by all of this."

He looked both furious and disgusted at the same time. Ellen regretted sharing the information in the way she did, and looked for a way to end the tension now existing between them. "I have not forgotten my quest for revenge. Marrying McCarthy might provide more revenge than I ever thought possible."

"You have some feelings for the man that you would even consider marrying him?"

"No, of course not, but there are a number of things to consider in making my decision."

"I do not understand your logic in what you say."

"Let me explain. A marriage to McCarthy would not be a marriage in the fullest sense, if you understand what I suggest. His health would prevent that, in spite of whatever treatment he might receive. I believe he will not be around for too much longer – again, in spite of his treatment. As his wife, in the event of his death, I would be entitled to something – quite a bit I should think – as he has no other family. That could prove useful in the event that the process I have started to locate my children is successful."

"I still can't believe you would consider marrying such a man, a man I have no respect for at all."

"I admit I was confused at first. He seemed such a genuine person and devoted to his wife. Since then, I have seen the other side of the man on a couple of occasions. It is ugly and I now think that might be the real nature of the person. There is no respect for him; more a case of duty and possible revenge that drive me to consider his proposal. I will make no decision until I am able to assess his condition after this period of treatment."

Woodrow's countenance hadn't changed; his disapproving glare remained in place. Her attempt to defuse the situation hadn't worked, but she needed to do something before the atmosphere between them deteriorated further. With a glance at the clock, Ellen exclaimed, "Oh dear, it is getting late. I have kept you chatting for too long. It will be dark soon and you still have a long ride ahead of you."

With a curt nod, he picked up his hat and stood up. "Not so long… and it is cooler for both me and my mount to go home after dark." A few more moments, then stilted goodbyes and he left.

She let him out the front door and watched him cross the street to retrieve his horse. As she relocked the door, she realised she would not sleep well tonight. Her emotions were in turmoil. Even she had not truly faced her motivation for considering McCarthy's proposal until she had to explain it to Woodrow. It saddened her that it caused such a chasm between them. In her heart, she knew she had come to think of Frank Woodrow as more than a friend. She did not want to lose whatever it was they had.

Chapter 20

Ellen's weekly routine reversed for the next few weeks. Whereas she had come into town every Thursday with Mrs McCarthy, she now went out to Koreelah once a week. After lunch every Thursday, she took the buggy out to the property, made up the workers' wages, stayed in her cottage overnight and returned to town on Friday morning after paying the workers. Her overnight stay allowed her to deal with the mail, bookkeeping and any other issues requiring attention. This arrangement saw her back in the store by early Friday afternoon.

She gave no further thought to McCarthy's proposal for the next couple of weeks. In fact, it was not until the day she saw Frank Woodrow going into the hotel across the street. It was Saturday and he probably came into town to attend the races. Would he take the time to visit the store, she wondered as she straightened a display of clothes pegs. As the day wore on, and Woodrow failed to appear, her despondency increased. After closing for the day, she sat in the office, her head in her hands, rueing her handling of their last meeting. It was clear he was angry, even disgusted, at what she shared with him… and, she told herself, he had every right to be. There was a time when she would not have been so forthright… but at that time, Frank Woodrow was no more than a mere acquaintance.

A brisk knock on the store's front door abruptly ended her self-re-crimination. She hesitated. Should she answer the door or not? It could not be her father. No, they would not have let him out of gaol this soon. It might be important. She wearily heaved herself out of her chair and made her way to the door. As she opened her mouth to ask the caller to identify them self, they knocked again, louder this time. There appeared to be some urgency in the knocking. Employing extreme caution – it could be her father, she counselled herself – Ellen opened the door a fraction, and gasped in surprise. Frank Woodrow stood there, hat in hand and looking quite uncertain about being there.

"Mr Woodrow, please come in. It is good to see you again." She stood aside and closed the door behind him. "Come upstairs and I will make us a pot of tea." Awkwardness stretched between them and their exchanges were noncommittal and stilted.

No real conversation began until they both were at the kitchen table with their cups of tea. Then Woodrow began. "I came to apologise for my behaviour the last time we met. I had no right to speak to you the way I did, or to question decisions you make regarding your life. Please forgive my rudeness, my presumption and intrusion."

"There is nothing to forgive. I realise your comments were out of concern for my best interests, and I thank you for caring. In hindsight, I regret the manner in which I acquainted you with what transpired in recent weeks. In fact, I don't think I had admitted to myself the underpinning motive for my considering McCarthy's proposal. Hearing it put into words both horrified me and shocked you. However, I would be less than honest if I tried to explain my motivation in any other way. If that makes me a lesser person in your eyes, I regret it but must accept it."

"…And it would be less than honest of me to say your reasoning doesn't concern me. It does but, thanks to the passage of time, I now see how this might provide opportunity for the revenge you so richly deserve." Silence prevailed briefly after Woodrow finished speaking. After a few sips of tea, Woodrow moved the conversation to a new topic.

"You mentioned something about trying to locate your children. How is that happening, and is it progressing?"

"Slowly…" Ellen answered with a shrug. For the next few minutes, Ellen explained how Mrs McCarthy enlisted her lifelong friend and nun, Sister Justina, to help track down the children's whereabouts. Her labours produced nothing to date other than the information that the children did not go to the Ralston orphanage. Ellen learnt that the relevant records were either non-existent or were difficult to locate, but she remained confident the nun would find out something for her.

"Is there anything I might do to help with the search," Woodrow asked, without having any idea of how he might contribute.

Ellen shook her head. "No, it's up to Sister Justina. Without the information from the records, we couldn't begin to look for them. I know it is slow going, but I knew that from the start. She has to be careful about how she goes about looking for the information we need. It could have serious consequences for her if she attracts too much attention to what she is doing."

"What will you do if you find them?"

"Bring them home to me, of course. Although I don't know about young William, I understand a farmer took him – bought him – to work on his farm. If he has good employment, it might be better to leave him to continue with it."

"What do you mean: 'a farmer bought him'? Only slaves are bought and sold... and slavery is illegal in this country, I believe."

"Oh, they would not have anyone consider it in that way. As they explained it to me, a farmer – or anyone else – chooses a child of about nine years of age to employ in some capacity and, in return makes a donation to the orphanage. To my mind, that amounts only to another way of saying they buy a child to work for them."

Their time together lasted for an hour or more before decorum demanded Woodrow should leave. Ellen expressed her concern about him riding home again in the dark, but he allayed her fears by explaining he was staying at the hotel for the night and would ride home early in the morning. They said goodnight, their relationship restored once more. Sleep remained elusive for some time that night as Ellen lay in her bed reliving Mr Woodrow's visit. Happiness won out over the need for sleep.

✱✱✱✱✱

Five weeks slipped by with incredible speed. It wasn't until she saw Jim, the foreman, in the agency that she realised how long it had been since McCarthy went to Brisbane. She went across to him and invited him to take tea with her in the office. Jim explained his presence in town. "There was a letter from young Cecil Glover, the worker who accompanied McCarthy to Brisbane, in that mail you took to Koreelah last week. The lad wrote that he would be returning on today's boat. I came to collect him." They caught up on other matters relating to the property until it was time for Jim to meet the boat.

About an hour later, in response to Ellen's request, Jim returned to the store with Cecil in tow. Ellen only recognised the lad as one of the workers who collected their pay on Friday mornings. After enquiring after his trip, Ellen sought information on Mr McCarthy's current situation. "...And how is Mr McCarthy's treatment progressing? I assume it must be going well if he has seen fit for you to return to the property and for him to manage on his own."

"He is a little stronger, that much is true. He says he is much improved and that he looks forward to returning to the property – maybe in a week or two. He intends writing you details of his likely return when he knows more."

"I am pleased to hear you think he is a little stronger, but I believe I hear some doubt in your comments about whether he is truly improved."

"If truth to be told, Miss, I don't see much improvement in him at all. He is a bit stronger, right enough, and no longer needs my help to dress or to assist with other personal matters. In spite of that, I don't believe his overall health has improved. His colour is still very grey and he has no breath to speak of even for the short walk to the doctor's rooms. It seems to me that his stay in hospital only rested him and helped restore some strength to the point where he no longer believes my assistance to be necessary."

Jim appeared concerned by the lad's assessment, but simply shrugged and said nothing when Ellen looked to him for comment. "Thank you, Cecil," Ellen said. "I must let you and Jim be on your way. I'm sure there will be plenty for you both to do on your return to the property."

The lad's news put something of a damper on Ellen's spirits for the rest of the day, but the day became busy. She had little time to dwell on Cecil's information until later that evening when, alone in the sitting room and with her book abandoned in her lap, she mulled over that earlier conversation. It came as something of a shock when she realised that the despondency she felt following Cecil's news was not because of the perceived lack of improvement in Mr McCarthy's health, but resulted from the news that he soon might return.

Doubts crowded her mind: what was the real status of his health? … How much care would he require on his return? … Would his first priority on his return be to pursue an answer to that marriage proposal? Her doubts and concerns made for a restless night that, next morning, left her feeling below par and struggling with a bout of deep melancholia. By the time she went down to open the store, she had put it behind her, and determined her response should McCarthy again raise the question of marriage. It was time to stop thinking of herself and focus on her quest for revenge and to providing something of a life for her children when − not if − she got them back. There would be a marriage, no matter how much the idea repulsed her.

It was another two weeks before the letter arrived, rekindling all the doubts and dread. McCarthy would be returning the following week. He would arrive on Wednesday and spend the night at the hotel before travelling out to the property with her on Thursday. Ellen shared the news with her staff that evening after closing time, ensuring all of them endured a glum evening. How depressed she felt was reflected in the dismal cheese on toast that served as Ellen's evening meal that night.

Ellen met the boat at the appointed time and her concern at the appearance of Mr McCarthy made her suggest that instead of going to the hotel first, they should detour to Dr Boyle's rooms as a priority. McCarthy would have none of it, but the voyage from Brisbane had taken its toll. He was so weak as to need assistance to climb onto the buggy. It proved too much for Ellen to manage alone, and she was grateful when a male bystander rushed to lend his strength to helping McCarthy up.

After seeing McCarthy to his room at the hotel, Ellen took the buggy back to the store, but then crossed the street again to Dr Boyle's surgery. She was sure that McCarthy would not appreciate what she was about to do, but her common sense outweighed any concern she might have for his reaction. There was a few minutes wait before Dr Boyle came out to see her. "I'm sorry to bother you, Dr Boyle, when I know you are so busy but I feel I must speak to you about Mr McCarthy."

"How is the old rascal, have you heard from him?"

"He returned from Brisbane on this morning's boat. I have serious concerns for him. The voyage home, I think was almost too much for him and he disembarked from the boat in a poor state. He refused to come to see you. He is spending the night in the hotel. The reason I am here, is to ask if you could – somehow surreptitiously – visit the hotel and look in on him."

"It would seem he hasn't become anymore intelligent about the state of his health during his sojourn in Brisbane. I will make a point of dropping by the hotel after surgery today and will be suitably surprised to find he has returned… and, of course, I will want to know all about how his treatment went." Relieved by Dr Boyle's understanding of the situation, Ellen returned to the store to prepare for her relocation to Koreelah again the next day. A gloomy staff made their way home that evening after Ellen advised them of her departure the next day.

At about 10 o'clock the next morning, Ellen collected McCarthy from the hotel and they set off for the property. It was obvious after only a short distance, that they needed the horses to travel at no faster than a walk if McCarthy was to enjoy any degree of comfort on the ride home.

There was no fanfare; no one rushed out to meet them when they arrive at the homestead. After all, over the last few weeks, this was the time she would normally appear at Koreelah on Thursdays. However, as she climbed down from the buggy, Bert rounded the corner of the house. His surprise at seeing the boss in the buggy was evident, and he ran to help McCarthy down. It took both Bert and Ellen to half carry him up the stairs and into his bedroom where, between them, they managed to make him comfortable and get him into bed.

Maggie, having heard Bert's voice upstairs where it shouldn't be, rushed around to see what was going on. "Oh, my Lord, why did nobody think to let me know? Now I ain't got nothing prepared for the man's lunch and it's already late. I'm thinking the best I can do quickly is cold cuts and salad. He is not likely to be impressed with that but, might he settle for that just this once—seeing as how I didn't know he was coming and all that?

"I'm sorry you were caught unawares, Maggie. It was all very short notice. Don't fret yourself about lunch. Mr McCarthy is already dropping off to sleep and won't be looking for anything to eat any time soon. I'll join you in the kitchen shortly to make a sandwich or something, if that's all right with you."

When the men collected their pays the next morning, Jim came to stand beside Ellen but waited until all the others went before speaking. "I hear from Bert that the boss wasn't too good by the time he got back yesterday. What's his situation this morning? Is he going to want to talk to me first, or perhaps go on a tour of inspection? I'm wondering if I should hang around, or whether I should just go and get on the job."

"Mr McCarthy is not up yet this morning. I doubt he would want a tour of inspection and I would counsel him against it anyway. If you could tell Bert where to find you, should Mr McCarthy want to speak to you later, I might ask Bert to fetch you."

McCarthy had no interest in the property at all that morning, and was poorly all day. The next morning found him a little more interested in what was going on around him and, with Bert's help, Ellen managed to have him installed in one of the squatter's chairs on the verandah for most of the day. Just before lunch, Jim dropped by to see if the boss was up to a chat, but the chat only lasted about ten minutes before McCarthy became exhausted and he sent Jim on his way.

There had been little opportunity for Ellen and Mr McCarthy to discuss anything very much. Over the next few days, he spent most of his time either in bed or on the verandah dosing and generally not showing much interest in anything. With every passing day, so little improvement occurred that it was almost a week later before, with

Bert's help, they moved McCarthy downstairs to one of the wicker butterfly chairs under the house.

It became apparent to Ellen that McCarthy was unlikely to become fit enough to negotiate the stairs in future. He now needed to move into the rooms under the house. With Elisabeth's help, Ellen moved as many of his belongings as she thought necessary into the downstairs bedroom. It would mean she would spend a lot of her time each day running up and down the stairs, but that became part of what she agreed to by returning to Koreelah to care for him.

Dr Boyle visited any time he was in the area and, after a couple of weeks, felt compelled to share his concerns for the lack of an acceptable degree of improvement in McCarthy's health. Bert took him around the property only once since his return, and they were gone for less than half an hour before McCarthy asked to return to the homestead.

With only a few more days to Christmas, Ellen felt compelled to enquire about Mr McCarthy's intentions for the festive season. It was not a lengthy conversation. He still had little appetite and wanted none of the usual Christmas fare prepared. In short, he was not interested in any form of festivities, or fuss and bother, and suggested Ellen should spend the Christmas weekend in town with her friends. McCarthy had already discussed the matter with Bert, and there was agreement that Bert and Maggie would look after him if Ellen went to town over Christmas.

"I will only go if you are quite sure you can manage without me. I know Bert and Maggie are quite capable, but I am also aware that it is not part of their duties to be taking care of you. I will not leave the property, except maybe to attend a wedding on Boxing Day, unless you give me your solemn assurance that you will be okay if I'm not here."

"Damn it, woman, you are not indispensable... and I am not totally incapacitated. What little attention I will need, Bert and Maggie are quite capable of providing. I would much prefer you were not hanging around here fussing over me."

Ellen pulled herself up to her full height and peered down at McCarthy. "Sir, we both know that is not the case. You are not capable of looking after yourself without quite considerable attention. However, if as you say, you would prefer me not hanging around to fuss over you, as you put it, I am quite happy to leave. As you intimated, Bert and Maggie might well be able to care for you well enough." McCarthy growled but made no comment. "Furthermore, if you speak to me that way again, regardless of what your preferences might be, I will be gone and you may make your own best arrangements for your future."

"You are impossible! Of course, I need you here... but I thought you might wish to be with your own people for Christmas and we could manage here without you for those few days. I didn't ask you to marry me to have you flounce off and abandon me. ...And on that subject, have you given the matter any thought? I don't suppose you're in a position to give me your answer yet by any chance."

"I thought on it long and hard. I have said nothing because I didn't want others to see me as taking advantage of you when you are so ill. Yes, I will marry you... but ... I can't lie to you. I do not love you or hold for you any of that deep affection that usually is part of marriage. However, I consider it important that, until such a date arrives, each of us has the right to withdraw from this agreement without penalty. If you cannot agree to that, then there is no agreement."

"Thank you. Now, perhaps you could leave me. I need to think on this matter and what arrangements are required."

When Ellen looked in on him the following Monday morning, she found McCarthy struggling to finish dressing and Bert, with great patience, trying to assist him. It was early. She expected to find him still in bed. "Would somebody mind telling me what this is all about," she demanded.

"Wait outside the pair of you," McCarthy shouted. "I'll be out to join you when I'm ready." By the time McCarthy finished speaking, Bert had already opened the door and was on his way out. Tempted to argue, Ellen thought better of it and followed Bert out.

"Come on, Bert, what is this about and why are you here at this hour of the day?"

"I'm sorry, Miss, I thought you knew about it. The boss is going into town today. He called me over as I was going home last evening and told me what time to be here this morning to help him get ready. You don't need to worry though. He's asked me to drive him. I've got the buggy harnessed up already, so I'll go and bring it over while I'm hanging about waiting for him."

McCarthy emerged from his room before Bert returned and Ellen made the most of their time alone. She expressed her concerns about his determination to go into town and its likely impact on his already fragile state. As she expected, her words went unheeded. He had set his mind on a trip to town and God himself would not have been able to dissuade him.

She stood with fists clenched and her anger mounting as Bert helped McCarthy onto the buggy. Bert climbed into the driver's seat, gave Ellen an uncertain look and a shrug, and the buggy was off on its way down the track. Ellen stood and watched them go for a while before marching upstairs to tell Maggie that Mr McCarthy would not require breakfast this morning.

The day dragged on and still the buggy hadn't returned. It was just on dusk before it appeared on the track – with only one person on board. Ellen rushed down to meet Bert as he harnessed the buggy. "What has happened? Where is Mr McCarthy? He didn't take any clothes with him, so he wasn't planning on staying in town."

"No, Miss, he didn't plan to stay in town, but that's what's happened. He had a bit he wanted to do in town – you know, going from place to place and all that. I drove him everywhere so he wouldn't have to walk, but it was all too much for him." Ellen caught her breath and felt a wave of cold dread sweep over her. Bert held up his hand to silence her as she was about to speak. "Is not too bad though, Miss. He is in good hands. In the end I took him to Dr Boyle – not that he wanted to go of course. The doctor put him straight into hospital."

"Did Dr Boyle say anything about his condition or how long he might be in hospital?"

"No, Miss, not really but the matron said he would most likely be there for a few days. The doctor said he would call in the next time he was up this way again to let you know what was happening."

It was the end of the week before Dr Boyle called. He explained that McCarthy had simply exhausted himself rushing around town taking care of whatever was so important, and that the doctor had put him into hospital to let him rest up before making the trip back to the property. Boyle paused and thought for a while before responding to Ellen's query regarding when Mr McCarthy might be ready to be collected from the hospital. His answer was not reassuring. "I believe you still come into town on Thursdays. If this is the case, it would not hurt Mr McCarthy to stay in hospital until your next trip to town. Yes, I think either next Thursday afternoon or Friday morning would be a good time for him to be released."

With nothing to keep her at Koreelah, after Dr Boyle left, Ellen hitched up the buggy and went into town. She would stay at the store in the interim and plan on returning to Koreelah on Thursday evening. All the way into town, she debated with herself whether she should visit McCarthy on a daily basis during his stay in hospital, or if it were better for him to remain ignorant of her presence in town. By the end of her journey, she had decided the latter was the best approach as, if he knew she was in town, he would demand to be released and taken home the moment he knew.

After lunch on Thursday, with the help of the nursing staff, McCarthy boarded the buggy and they headed back to Koreelah. The sight of the old, pathetic figure huddled in the corner, the rug drawn up to his chest, gave a gentle tug to Ellen's heartstrings. Stop it; she chastised herself. This is no time to go soft. He is still the same man he always was – still the same man who treated your husband so badly and is responsible for everything else that followed. By the time they reached home, her resolve had returned. She would pursue her revenge, and she found herself hoping the man lasted long enough for her to achieve it.

Once she had taken care of Mr McCarthy the next morning, she went in search of the gardener. "Bert, please tell me the places that Mr McCarthy visited when you took him into town."

"Well now, Miss, let me think. First up, he went to see a solicitor, and then he went to the church – that seemed to take a while. When he left there, he went to the courthouse – that also took a while – and then he wanted to go to the bank. Oh, after he finished at the church, we went to the hotel for lunch. Oh, I almost forgot; straight after lunch, he went to his club for a few minutes. I don't know what that was about but it didn't take long. He was almost in and out again. He just kept getting worse as the day went on. By the time he finished at the bank, he was hardly able to breathe. I rushed him straight to Dr Boyle's rooms, but I tell you truly, I didn't think he was going to make it. Gave me a right fright he did."

"Thank you, Bert. I'm sure it must've been a worrying experience for you. He should never have gone to town in the first place. Don't upset yourself; it's not your fault. He's the boss and we all have to do as he asks."

It took a few days before Ellen decided Mr McCarthy was strong enough for some pointed discussion about what he had been up to in town and the consequences of all his running around.

"Blast it, woman, there were things to organise. We neither of us knows for how much longer I'm going to be around. If we're going to have this marriage, it needs to happen soon. The arrangements now are now in place. I arranged the minister and organised the license. I suppose the next thing is to let people know it's happening so they can turn up on the day."

"That's something I can organise, but it would be useful for a number of reasons if I knew when all of this was going to occur."

"… All of what is going to occur?"

"Is it some form of restricted information, or am I allowed to know the date of my impending marriage? So far, it appears only you know when you are getting married. I am beginning to wonder whether I am to be involved or not."

"What? Oh, I see. Did I not tell you? Our marriage is on 18th January. I assume you have no problems with that."

"So soon! I anticipated waiting until after the wet season to ensure good weather for the day, and that people would be able to get here. It seems I was mistaken."

"We will have to take our chances. There's no point in waiting until after the wet season. Who knows how long that might last? It might outlast me. I suppose the first thing you should do is start letting our staff know what's happening. Maggie and Elizabeth will need a bit of warning so they can buy in whatever they need to prepare the wedding breakfast."

"What time of the day is this marriage supposed to take place? I imagine the two ladies in question might be interested in what sort of food they need to prepare."

"I imagine the food is much the same whatever time of day it occurs. However, ours is set for 11 o'clock, so the food they prepare will provide lunch for our guests."

"Speaking of guests, how many do you envisage turning up on the day? Do you expect just a handful, or half the town?"

"Obviously, that is something we still need to discuss. If you are to start inviting people to the wedding, we need to have decided who we want to come. Could we leave that discussion for another time? This conversation is beginning to exhaust me."

Ellen was pleased to end the conversation. Her mind was a whirl and she needed time alone to digests the information she received. She felt her resolve weakening, but after a couple of deep breaths, Ellen marched off to the kitchen to break the news to Maggie and Elizabeth who were currently enjoying their usual morning cup of tea.

Chapter 21

Time seemed to speed up, as if all the clocks had gone mad. Christmas came and went. After spending the morning at Koreelah, Ellen took the buggy into town. She spent the rest of the Christmas break at the store, attended Alfred and Jess's wedding, only returning to the property at the end of the Christmas break.

The first two weeks of January went by in a blur. It was the height of summer. Thunderstorms were common and, for the rest of the time, the humidity was stifling. The wet season was building, and Ellen wondered how soon it would be before the heavens opened and the unrelenting monsoonal rain set in. The track through the property to the homestead alternated between being a quagmire and a hard deeply rutted track that now meandered way out of its normal alignment in many places as buggies and wagons endeavoured to avoid the worst of the wheel ruts.

Maggie moaned daily about the weather. She insisted there had to be a wedding cake. Although she had made the cakes for some monstrous final arrangement, she didn't dare ice them in the current climate. The dampness would make the cake colouring bleed through the immaculate white icing with which she intended to adorn it.

One morning shortly after they found out about the impending wedding, Elizabeth slipped into the office and stood in front of Ellen as she worked on the accounts. "You may tell me it's none of my business, but you don't seem to be doing much about preparing for this wedding. I know you sent out the invitations, but what about getting yourself ready. What are you going to wear? Surely, the occasion warrants are new gown of some sort."

Stunned, Ellen looked at Elizabeth for a few moments while she contemplated what she said. "I don't know what to say. I hadn't given it any thought, but I suppose you are right. I need to think about what I'm going to wear on the day, and it probably is appropriate to acquire a new gown for the occasion. Thank you for reminding me. I will visit the dressmaker when I am in town this week." I must start showing some interest in this forthcoming event, Ellen told herself. People are not fools; they may well already have noticed my lack of enthusiasm.

Housework almost became ignored as Elizabeth and Maggie spent the two or three days in the lead up to the wedding firmly ensconced in the kitchen. Various menus for the wedding breakfast appeared before Ellen for approval, but she couldn't get excited about any of them. As a last resort, she explained her mind was so preoccupied with the forthcoming event, that she was unable to make a decision, and would they please help out by deciding between them what would be best for the guests.

Mr McCarthy took to complying with instructions to 'rest' in order for him to be strong enough to make a good showing on the day. With some misgivings, and in consultation with Maggie and Elizabeth and their husbands, Ellen decided that Mr McCarthy should spend the couple of days prior to the wedding in town at the hotel. Bert would stay with him and bring him back to Koreelah in time for the wedding. She sold the idea to McCarthy on the basis that there was so much to do – all the cooking and setting up downstairs for the breakfast – and he would only be in the way. Besides, it would be improper for him to be here the night before the wedding and bad luck should he see her on the day of the wedding. While not entirely happy with the arrangement, he offered little resistance.

*****

As with all things, the day finally arrived, as did the extra staff hired to set up and deal with the guests. Their arrival, a bit before eight o'clock, caused Ellen something of a reality check. This was it. In a few hours, she would no longer be Miss Grimsby – or Mrs Jennings for that matter – but Mrs McCarthy. She thought of her predecessor and wondered what she would make of today. …And, in amongst the turmoil, was the big question: how long would she have to endure being Mrs McCarthy?

The day dawned breathless and heavy. Not a leaf moved in the still air and the debilitating humidity hung over the place like a treacle curtain. Ellen busied herself in the kitchen along with the other two women. Bert came in for his morning cuppa, only to be shooed out of the kitchen. "We're too busy today to be worrying about cups of tea for the likes of you and anybody else who should be helping those people set up downstairs," Maggie told him.

"I don't know why they are so busy setting up in the garden. By the looks of that sky, there's a squall coming sometime today. Like as not, it will arrive when it is least wanted," Bert retorted.

"You pay no attention to the old fool," Maggie advised Ellen. "It always rains first thing in the morning if it is going to rain at all that day. It hasn't rained today, and it had better not. I do not want my cake to start sweating." Elizabeth told Ellen she would come over later to help her dress and get ready for the wedding, and then the two women chased her out of the kitchen and back to what previously was Mrs McCarthy's bedroom.

In the week leading up to the wedding, the women stripped the bedroom of every reminder of Edith McCarthy to ensure it invoked no unpleasant thoughts or memories while serving as a dressing room for Ellen on her wedding day. Fresh flowers picked by Elizabeth on her way through the garden that morning sat in a vase on the washstand. Ellen knew there was another arrangement somewhere that was to be her bouquet. It now lay in a spare meat safe hanging on the verandah, a wet bag draped over the safe in a bid to keep the bouquet cool and fresh.

With nothing else to do, Ellen stood at the window and watched the activity below. People scurried everywhere. Some staff carried chairs out to the garden, others hung strings of cheap decorations from the trees, and a couple of young women were fussing with a small table and a stark white tablecloth which refused to stay flat in the slight breeze that arrived. The tableau below unable to hold her attention for long, Ellen paced the room a while before perching on the side of bed, with the latest book she had started reading. She couldn't concentrate but persisted with the book, although she had no idea what she read.

After some indeterminate time, she found herself squinting at the pages. Realising the light had faded considerably, she returned to the window to check the sky. Yes, it was going to rain, and she suspected it was going to rain very soon. Would it hold off until after the ceremony and until they all were sheltered underneath the house for the breakfast? For everyone's sake, she fervently hoped so. It was almost time for her to start getting ready. She paced the room to fill in a bit more time before returning to the window once more.

The leaden sky provided a stark backdrop for the crimson-canopied avenue of Poinciana trees still heavy with blooms. She rested her head against the greyed window frame and watched the first big drops create dark splodges on the dry timber. Along the rough driveway, two carriages picked their way slowly through the puddles and ruts towards the homestead, the first of a long line that soon would follow.

The groom had arrived along with Bert, while the minister and another man whom Ellen didn't recognise were in the second carriage.

Rain, now heavier, continued to fall. It pooled in the chairs set out in the garden. Those with padded seats became sodden. Catering staff scurried to move them to shelter as the drops turned into a downpour. Then the wind came and Bert's forecast squall arrived. Flimsy decorations strung around the garden and the front verandah flapped violently as the squall came through. Some strings broke free at one end to trail out wildly in the gale before finally freeing themselves from their tethers and disappearing across the countryside. The next wave of carriages making their way down the track collected a shower of crimson blooms as the Poincianas gave up their blossoms to the wind.

Ellen cast an eye at the wedding dress hanging on the front of the cupboard. She should have climbed into this already. Under other circumstances, she would be purring with delight at the prospect of wearing such an elegant but understated gown. Today it held no appeal. Elizabeth would come in shortly to do her hair and 'finish her off' as she liked to call it. A sound telling-off was in store if Ellen were not dressed when she arrived.

With her head still against the window frame, she watched the trees flailing about in the wind as the rain came down in sheets that slammed against the windowpane. Was this an omen; a sign of ill portend for the future of today's marriage? Was this weather a warning of the foolhardiness of what she was about to embark upon? She watched as the first of the invited guests arrived, and were ushered to relative safety under the house by umbrella-bearing staff. She shook her head to dispel the thoughts that plagued her. There could be no backing out now, time to dress.

As Ellen stepped into her gown, Elizabeth knocked gently and entered. There followed a fine episode of tut-tutting at the bride's tardiness in her preparations. It didn't matter; it took Elizabeth but a few minutes to work her magic. She stepped back and eyed Ellen up and down. "You look stunning; just the bouquet needed now to complete the picture." Elizabeth struggled to open the door. Although the squall had passed, a stiff breeze remained in its wake. With her skirt lifted high off the wet verandah, she collected the bouquet from the meat safe. The squall had claimed the bag from the meat safe, allowing the wind and rain to reach the blooms in the bouquet. After gently shaking the rain from the flowers, Elizabeth carefully carried the somewhat ruffled-looking bouquet to the bedroom.

"The rain has eased to a light drizzle," Elizabeth announced as she returned to the bedroom. "With that breeze still blowing, the last of the rain should be gone soon."

"That would be a good thing. At least I wouldn't have to hold an umbrella over my head at the same time as I hold up my skirts to prevent them dragging on the wet stairs. Although, if I did get drenched, I probably wouldn't look any worse than those guests that were soaked as they arrived."

"You will not be drenched. Both your hands will be free to hold up your skirts. I will be holding an umbrella over you and carrying your bouquet. Now, smarten yourself up, please. I know brides reputedly get cold feet at the last moment, but this is ridiculous. You agreed to marry this man and the big moment has arrived. Try being at least a little excited about the new life you are about to embark on."

Elizabeth was right of course, Ellen realised. It was unfortunate that Elizabeth recognised the situation for what it was. It would be unforgivable if others also witnessed her lack of enthusiasm. "You're right, Elizabeth. It's just last minute nerves… and concern for how stressful today might be for the groom." The lie came effortlessly, and she smiled widely at her friend.

Jim's arrival on the verandah halted any further conversation. He called through from outside. "Everyone downstairs is waiting for the bride to arrive."

"We're ready," Elizabeth replied. "We'll meet you at the bottom of the stairs."

The sky remained leaden and the stiff breeze continued when the two women descended the stairs, but the rain had stopped. At the foot of the stairs, Ellen took Jim's arm and he escorted her to the small table, which they moved hurriedly undercover when the squall came through. All of the female guests and some of the men crammed into the remaining space under house, but quite a few of the men remained standing outside on the soggy grass. The table and an appropriate surrounding space where the ceremony would take place took up a fair slice of the room where guests would stand around to eat.

Patrick McCarthy sat in a wicker butterfly chair off to one side of the small table. Bert stood by his chair and helped him up as Jim escorted Ellen up to the table. The minister was in position behind the table and the ceremony began immediately. It was short and simple… and required all of Patrick McCarthy's strength to remain standing throughout.

Then it was over. She was now Mrs Ellen McCarthy.

Everyone flocked around hugging Ellen and shaking McCarthy's hand. Several of the women, including Maggie, their lace handkerchiefs to the fore, gave their eyes a few final dabs. A second chair was drawn up beside the one Patrick again occupied, and Ellen sat beside him as the eating and drinking – and delivery of dreadful toasts – got under way.

By mid-afternoon, the last of those who were going home that day had left. A number of the unaccompanied men were staying on for a 'men's weekend'. They set themselves up in one of the unused workers' bunkhouses for the weekend. With the wedding out of the way on Friday, it gave them the whole weekend to indulge in their favourite pursuits. Jim had organised a program comprising shooting on Saturday, fishing on Sunday, swimming in the creek whenever so inclined, and demolishing the two hogsheads of rum that arrived from town earlier in the week.

Dr Boyle was among those staying on. He arranged a locum from Ralston to cover the hospital for a few days while he was at Koreelah. While the others would return home by Sunday evening, Boyle intended staying until Monday morning when he would ride up the valley from Koreelah to attend his various outlying patients before returning to town on Tuesday. During their stay, the men ate under the house along with the property's single men. Maggie took great delight in showing off her culinary skills.

The wedding left Patrick McCarthy exhausted and, although he rested for the rest of the day after the guests left and again all day Saturday, Sunday saw little improvement in his condition. Ellen's concerns deepened as the weekend progressed. When he came up to the house with the other men for Sunday lunch, Ellen asked Dr Boyle if he would look in on her husband before he set off on Monday morning. Boyle offered to check him then, but McCarthy was sleeping at the time, and they agreed Monday morning would be soon enough.

Ellen took Sunday lunch upstairs with Maggie and Bert and then took her book to the sitting room downstairs to read for a while and be near her husband. She dosed off, the book falling to the floor with a loud thump. It woke her and, as she stooped to recover the book, she became aware of noises coming from McCarthy's bedroom.

McCarthy, in great pain, was thumping the bedhead with one hand while grasping his chest with the other. Hoping Maggie was still upstairs, Ellen raced to the bottom of the stairs and screamed for Maggie. There was no response from upstairs. However, as she repeatedly called Maggie's name, a carriage rolled up on its way back to town. It was the local magistrate calling in to say goodbye and to thank McCarthy for the great weekend. Alarmed by what he saw, he began to climb down from the carriage but Ellen rushed over and stopped him. "Get Dr Boyle; quickly please. It's Mr McCarthy…"

Jim and Elizabeth, aware something was amiss at the homestead, ran to be with Ellen. They waited anxiously with Ellen as Dr Boyle tended to Patrick. After a couple of minutes, Boyle appeared and ordered Jim to bring the wagon around to the house. Patrick had suffered a heart attack and his condition was serious. They loaded Patrick onto the wagon. Jim drove while Bert sat beside Patrick and held a large umbrella to shield him from the sun. Jim ignored the track, preferring to stick to level ground off to one side of it as he whipped the horses into a gallop. Dr Boyle followed along behind as they rushed the patient to the hospital.

Ellen grabbed a few things she would need and ran to get the buggy. The magistrate, who continued to stand around bewildered by all that was happening, intercepted her. He offered to drive her to town. She rejected his offer, as she needed the buggy in town with her. Once she explained, he harnessed a horse and helped her hitch the buggy, and then followed her into town to make sure she arrived safely.

By the time they arrived, Patrick was undergoing treatment by both Dr Boyle and the locum. The magistrate left Ellen with Jim in the hospital's waiting room. A young nurse gave them a hard look as she walked by, and then returned a few minutes later with a tea tray for them. Neither wanted tea but thought they should be polite and drink some. Somehow, before its contents went cold, they managed to drain the pot.

It had been dark for quite some time when Dr Boyle emerged from wherever they had taken Patrick. He looked grim as he drew a chair over to join Ellen and Jim. Ellen felt her larynx spasm and caught her breath. "Is he… is he …?" she stammered.

"He is still alive, Mrs McCarthy." Mrs McCarthy; I suppose I have to get used to that now, she thought. She realised Dr Boyle continued speaking. "…Condition is serious. I would even say it is grave. We have done all that can be done for him. One of us will stay with him at all times during the night. I assume you both will stay in town tonight. Jim hesitated and looked at Ellen. "Yes," she replied. "I will stay at the store and Jim will stay at the hotel." Then, to Jim she added, "They must charge your stay to Koreelah. I will see the property pays for it."

"Good," Boyle continued, "We will know where to find you if, at any time, we should need to call you to be with Mr McCarthy. Now, I suggest you go and settle yourselves for what I know will be a long night ahead for all of us. There is nothing for you to do here."

Jim went to the hotel and Ellen took the buggy around to the store's horse yard. As she was about to start up the stairs to the loading area, the back door flew open revealing Alfred with a large stick in hand framed in the doorway. "What the hell is going on out here?" he bellowed.

"I'm sorry, Alfred, I didn't mean to alarm you. I will be staying here tonight and maybe for a while after. Go back upstairs. I'll talk to you all in the morning." Ellen climbed the loading dock stairs as she spoke. Alfred only needed one brief glimpse of her face to know he wasn't going back upstairs just then.

He took her bag, locked the door behind her and, with his arm supporting her, guided her up to her own kitchen and sat her down. "What has happened, Miss? You look terrible worried. What disaster has occurred? Oh, begging your pardon; I suppose I should say 'Mrs McCarthy' now."

"You may continue to call me Miss. I might be widowed again soon anyway, so it won't matter one way or the other." Ellen dropped her head into her hands. Alfred stood shuffling his feet for a few moments, unsure what to do, before deciding to fetch Jess. A couple of minutes later, all three were seated at the kitchen table as Ellen recounted details of the day's drama.

"Would you like me to stay with you tonight, Miss?"

"Thank you, but no, Jess. I need to be alone. Now, you pair must get back to bed. You have a store to open in the morning." She remained seated at the kitchen table as they left.

It seemed like a long week. One in which time dragged on slowly. Ellen's daily routine included an hour or so at the hospital in the morning and again in the afternoon. Jim called at the hospital on the Monday morning. After looking in on Mr McCarthy, he told Ellen he was heading back to Koreelah. She told him that, if things remained as they were, she would return to the property on Thursday afternoon and stay overnight to ensure the workers received their pay as usual on Friday morning

For the first few days, there was no sign of any improvement in Patrick's condition. Dr Boyle assured her that was as expected and that, if there were to be any improvement, it would be slow and might take quite a while to happen. Ellen found herself wondering what 'quite a while' might mean. Could he be like this for months, or even years? Was he even aware of what was going on around him? She had not factored such a situation into her thinking when she agreed to marry him.

The only glimmer of light that week came on Wednesday afternoon. Ellen sat beside the bed looking across at the unresponsive form between the stark white sheets. I wonder how the funny practice began, she wondered as she thought on Edith and Patrick's practice of only referring to themselves and addressing each other as Mr and Mrs. Given names were never used. She heaved a sigh. It was time to be getting back to the store. She scraped her chair back and, as she stood beside the bed looking down on her husband, she idly wondered how he would address her. Would he address her now as Mrs McCarthy, would he continue to call her Miss Grimsby? Would he expect her to call him Mr McCarthy at all times? She acknowledged that would not be difficult for her as, for the past so many months that is how she had addressed him.

As she stood pondering the matter, his eyelids fluttered and his eyes open for the briefest of moments. In that brief instant, Ellen thought she detected a hint of a smile and his right hand moved slightly towards her. She gripped his hand and squeezed it gently, but there was no response. The eyes closed once more. Ellen looked down at her hand still gently holding Patrick's pale veined one. Sadness swept over her. She had grasped his hand instinctively, not out of love or devotion, but as a response to someone who had reached for her.

As she stood there still holding his hand, she wondered about how long this might go on. What if it went on for years, or that he only partially recovered and remained a semi-invalid for decades? How would she cope? That was not part of her plan.

Her reverie came to an abrupt end when matron and a young nurse barged into the room. Ellen fully expected to receive her marching orders from the crusty matron, but the woman surprised her. Matron Ogilvie displayed a soft side, a side Ellen was sure most of the town had never seen. "He opened his eyes," Ellen blurted out, "only for the briefest of moments, but they did open."

"That's a good sign, my dear. It shows he's still with us; he's in there somewhere. In some cases, there are moments like that, but it is wise not to place too much hope on such a fleeting moment. Now, we have work to do in here. I'm afraid I have to ask you to leave."

Ellen nodded and walked towards the door. As she passed matron, the woman patted her on the shoulder and told her to stay strong.

While crossing the street back to the store, Ellen tortured herself with the question of whether Patrick's opening his eyes today was a good sign or a bad one. With her mind so preoccupied, as she reached the door, she barrelled unseeingly into Frank Woodrow exiting the store.

Concerned by the distracted look on her face, Woodrow took her by the arm and led her back into the office. "Is everything all right? You look like you've seen a ghost. McCarthy hasn't taken a turn for the worse as he?"

"No, nothing like that. I was preoccupied with the number of thoughts, that's all. It's nice to see you again."

"I heard this morning that McCarthy was in hospital in a bad way. I wanted to make sure you're okay and to ask if there's anything I can do to help." Ellen shook her head. No one could help, but as she and Woodrow spoke, she felt herself relaxing. They chatted on until Jess poked her head around the door to say she was locking up for the day. "I should be on my way." He stood, picked up his hat and gave her a long look. "You look drained. I know it's a trying time for you, but try to get some rest." Then Jess let him out and he was gone.

Heavy black skies greeted Ellen on Thursday morning as she crossed the street to the hospital. As expected, there was no change in McCarthy's condition but, as she sat beside his bed, something hilarious occurred to her. It hadn't hurt her reputation having matron barge in while she was holding Patrick's hand. She was sure she carried the stigma of being a gold digger who only married an old infirm man for what she could get... and why not, it was the truth.

The fine upstanding women of this town would be quick to brand her as such. It might create some doubt in some of their minds when news of the sight that greeted matron leaked out into the community. ...And leak out it surely would. Matron would never breach a patient's confidentiality by discussing them outside the hospital, but the same did not apply to discussing patients with nurses and domestic staff as they shared the staff dining area. Domestic staff appeared to have no compunction about sharing their knowledge with the wider community. Gossip about a 'tender moment' shared between husband and new wife might go some way to restoring her reputation.

As arranged, Ellen drove the buggy back to Koreelah that afternoon, arriving just before dark. She was back in town by mid-morning the next day and went directly to the hospital. The twice-daily visits resumed. Were the visits a waste of time, Ellen wondered, or were they simply for appearances sake? She was convinced McCarthy didn't know what went on around him, or whether she was there or not. Regardless of whether they were a waste of time or not, they must continue, she resolved.

The weekend was uneventful except for a brief visit from Mr Woodrow on his way home after the Turf Club meeting on Saturday. She had survived the first week of the new marriage and there was no change in McCarthy's condition. That was what she recorded in her diary on Sunday evening and, as she read over the entry, she wondered what the coming week might bring.

A young nurse met her on the doorstep as Ellen opened the store on Monday morning. "Can you come now please, Mrs McCarthy; Dr Boyle says it's urgent," the nurse gasped, out of breath after her dash from the hospital. Without thanking her, Ellen ran past the nurse, across the street and into the hospital. Dr Boyle met her as she ran down the corridor towards Patrick's room.

"Whoa, steady on; take a breath and calm down a bit," he said as he guided her to a small alcove containing a couple of chairs. "Your husband suffered another heart attack this morning. It was mild, but is of concern…"

"Can I see him?"

"No, not at the moment; as I said, this attack was mild, and we haven't yet been able to determine the extent of any damage it caused. However, you should prepare yourself for the worst. A major heart attack likely is imminent – some time in the near future. That is the usual pattern of things. I can't give you any idea of when it might occur, but it will most probably come soon after the one he had this morning."

"I see," Ellen whispered. "When will I be able to see him? Is he likely to regain consciousness at all?"

"Hmm, leave it until tomorrow before you try to see him again. It is highly unlikely now that he will ever regain consciousness. Perhaps it would be better to pray for a swift end than to hang on to false hope. I will send someone for you if there is any change at all in his condition."

In a daze, Ellen wandered across the street to the store and dropped down onto a chair in the office. Guilt enveloped her. Yes, she had not wanted this marriage to last too long, but she did not expect it to end so soon. Dr Boyle seemed insistent that she prepare herself for Patrick's death. About that, and that it would be soon, he seemed quite definite. What could she do – should she do – to prepare for it?

Of course, he would want a burial at Koreelah next to Edith and with a similar service… or would he? Doubts began to creep in, and

Ellen realised she knew nothing about the man or what he might want. She resolved to speak to his solicitor in the off chance Patrick had discussed the matter with him. Given that the man was not yet dead, was it appropriate to broach the matter with the solicitor at this time?

The heavens had opened and the rain deluged the town. Ellen stood on the doorstep still pondering Patrick's imminent demise as she watched the rain turn the street into a muddy stream. A figure cloaked in an oilskin sloshed out of the mud and onto the narrow footpath in front of her. "Mr Woodrow; your boots are ruined!" she said. He shed his oilskin and hung it on one of the pegs set in the front wall, then stamped his feet and wiped the mud off his boots on the coir mat that lay on the footpath – and repeated the performance on a similar mat just inside the door – before following her into the office.

Mrs Langton, his housekeeper, had asked him to pick up a couple of items from the store, but it presented a good excuse to check on Ellen and see how she was coping. After only basic pleasantries, their conversation focused on Patrick McCarthy. While Ellen shared with Woodrow Dr Boyle's words regarding a likely major heart attack, it occurred to her to seek Woodrow's advice on whether or not to talk to Patrick's solicitor at this time. He listened to Ellen put forward every possible argument for and against such a move before advising her to approach the solicitor as soon as possible. If her approach were right, the solicitor would understand her motivation in approaching him.

By the time Ellen saw Woodrow to the door, the rain had eased into a steady drizzle. The street was still awash, but she was determined to visit McCarthy's solicitor before the end of the day – and before her courage evaporated. It was mid-afternoon when it occurred to her to drive to the solicitor's office to avoid tramping through the mud. Alfred hitched up the buggy, and she felt foolish as she drove the short distance and hitched her horse out front of the solicitor's office.

Ellen did not know Mr Bronson, Patrick's solicitor, and was unsure what to expect. There were a couple of people already waiting to see him when she arrived. As the solicitor appeared busy that afternoon, Ellen suggested to the clerk it might be better if she came back another time. He assured her Mr Bronson would be free in a few minutes. The others in the waiting room were there only to sign documents and Mr Bronson's articled clerk was in charge of that. As predicted, about ten minutes later, Bronson showed a client out of his office and invited Ellen in.

Bronson, a short round man with a thick thatch of snow-white hair and a matching bushy moustache, sat – more like perched – behind an enormous dark stained timber desk. As was the case with most of the town she suspected, Bronson was aware of McCarthy's situation. Ellen explained the reason for her visit and waited to see how Bronson reacted. He laid his hands on the desk with fingers steepled upwards and stared at them in silence for a few moments. "As I'm sure you are aware, Mrs McCarthy, I can't discuss your husband's will with you at this time…."

"No, of course not, that's not why I'm here. I just wondered – hoped – he might have mentioned to you what his wishes were in the event of his death."

He wasn't surprised that Ellen didn't know about such things. Nobody would expect such a new bride to know what her husband's wishes regarding his funeral might be, or that he would die so soon. "Well, as it happens, he did mention what he wanted: a simple service, burial at Koreelah beside Edith and no fuss. He was quite adamant about the 'no fuss' bit; only a few words before he was dispatched and with very few people in attendance."

"How few people did he have in mind… and who were they?"

"His wife – that is, yourself – the workers on the property and a very limited number of people from the town." He saw Ellen open her mouth but continued before she could pose the question he knew would be hanging on her tongue. "There were only three townspeople on his invitation list: his doctor, the magistrate and myself… oh, there would be four of us, if you count the minister."

Light misty rain began to fall as Ellen drove the buggy back to the store. Alfred, busy preparing orders at the back of the store, rushed down to deal with the buggy. It was late, and by the time she helped Jess with the last of the customers, it was time to close up. She anticipated sleep would be elusive that night and that was the case. After reading until quite late, she took herself to bed but sleep wouldn't come. Around midnight, she gave up, got dressed and went down to the office.

There were thank you letters to write to those who sent gifts and good wishes for their marriage. Somehow, there wasn't time to deal with these until now. Just a few short polite notes, that's all that were required but it felt like a monumental task that took her ages to complete. She was putting the last of the notes into an envelope when a loud banging on the front door made her jump. She hesitated; who could be calling at this hour of the night? Then someone was calling her name; a female voice. At the door, she hesitated again, still unsure about whether it was safe to open the door or not. A movement beside her made her spin around. The racket outside had woken Alfred and he had come down to investigate.

"Who is it and what you want?" Alfred shouted through the door at whoever was banging on the other side.

"It's Nurse Callahan. I need to speak to Mrs McCarthy. Is she there?"

Ellen felt a cold wave sweep over her. "Quickly, Alfred, open the door." The door was barely open a crack before she was asking the nurse what had happened. Jess had now joined them at the front door

"Dr Boyle sent me. He asks that you come quickly."

Ellen remained glued to the spot, unable to move. Alfred grabbed her by the arm and dragged her out through the door as he shouted to Jess to lock the door behind them. Then, with Alfred still hanging onto her arm, they ran in tandem across the road to the hospital. Dr Boyle met them as they ran in through the front door of the hospital.

"I'm sorry to call you in at this hour, Mrs McCarthy, but Mr McCarthy has had another heart attack. I'm afraid it was a major attack this time…"

"Is he… Is he…?"

"No, he is still alive, but his condition is grave. In my opinion, it is unlikely he will see the night through. I will take you through to him, but I must tell you how he looks might shock you. Do you wish to see him now?"

"Yes, I must see him." Ellen looked from Dr Boyle to Alfred. "Alfred…"

"I'll wait here for you, Miss."

The doctor was right about his appearance coming as a shock. She found it hard to believe he was still alive. Dr Boyle dragged over a chair for her to sit beside the bed but she preferred to stand. As she stood, looking down at him and stroking his hand, he seemed stricken by some terrible pain. He uttered a loud gasp or roar of some kind, and the upper part of his body seemed to bounce up off the bed. Dr Boyle had just checked his pulse before the spasm occurred and was entering it on his chart when the attack happened.

Boyle dropped the chart onto the bed and immediately checked for a pulse. He checked Patrick's pupils for a response. There was none. He looked up at Ellen and gently shook his head. Ellen clapped her hand across her mouth in a bid to stifle the scream that escaped. "I'm sorry, Mrs McCarthy, he's gone."

Gently shepherding her from the room, Boyle escorted her back to where Alfred waited. When Alfred saw them come out of the room, he bounced up out of the chair. It was obvious things were not good. Just one look at Ellen told him that. He searched Dr Boyle's face for answers. Boyle gave an almost imperceptible shake of his head. Alfred nodded to indicate he understood, and then stepped up and put an arm around Ellen's shoulders. "If there is nothing you need her for right now, I'll take her home," Alfred said.

Jess had locked the door behind them as instructed but kept a vigil for any sign of their return. She ran and opened the door as she spotted them crossing the road. There was no need to ask what happened. It was clear to her, long before Alfred and Ellen reached the store, that Ellen was a widow once more. Together they took Ellen upstairs and sat her in one of the lounge chairs in her sitting room. It was almost breakfast time but nobody felt like eating. Jess sat beside Ellen and held her hand. Alfred, feeling at a loss, elected to make a pot of tea for everyone. A rummage in a cupboard produced a last part of a loaf of bread, so he made toast and took a tray loaded with tea and toast through to the sitting room.

Tea and toast despatched, Ellen then sent the others away. "You have a store to run today. I'm afraid I won't be much help. I will make all the necessary arrangements today, so I will be away from the store for much of the day." Jess and Alfred went to get ready for work. Ellen stayed upstairs until she deemed it an appropriate hour to call on the undertaker and the minister.

She went to the undertaker's first to ask him to collect the body. Next stop was the church to organise the minister to come to Koreelah. Ten o'clock on Friday suited him, so she doubled back to the undertaker's with the burial details. With the arrangements in place, she headed off to advise Mr Bronson of her husband's passing and of the funeral arrangements. As she passed the hospital, she decided to call in and enquire after Dr Boyd. He was not at the hospital but should be at his rooms she was told. Ellen called at the surgery and left the funeral details with Dr Boyd's receptionist. Then, it was on to what she hoped was her last call: the solicitor's office.

Bronson took her into his office as soon as she arrived and proceeded to make all the usual sympathetic noises. He assured her he would attend the funeral, and he agreed to inform the magistrate of the arrangements. That was it; everything was in place for Friday. Ellen went back to the store. In need of something to keep her mind occupied, she spent the afternoon working on the accounts.

Alfred's first delivery that morning was to a farm adjacent to the Southend Co-operative Sugar Mill. On his way back to town, Alfred detoured through the mill estate. Woodrow looked up in surprise as a clerk showed Alfred into his office. "Alfred; what brings you out here?" Woodrow almost bit his tongue the moment he said it. A visit from Alfred could only mean one thing… and Alfred confirmed it.

"Apologies for intruding, Mr Woodrow, but I thought you might want to know Mr McCarthy passed away early this morning."

Woodrow wiped a hand across his face. "How is Mrs McCarthy?"

"Our boss is an amazing woman; so strong," Alfred replied with no attempt to conceal his pride. "Her husband died, she lost her children, her mother died, and then the woman she cared for died as well… and now this new husband is gone. As you might expect, she was upset this morning. She was with him when it happened. She is making all the arrangements today and I expect she will go back to the property tomorrow."

"Thank you, Alfred, it was considerate of you to let me know."

Ellen closed the back door behind Charlie Perkins as he left for the day and started up the stairs. She had only gone about half way when she heard loud knocking on the back door. She retraced her steps to answer it. Frank Woodrow stood there, hat in hand. "I've come to offer my condolences, but I will go away if you prefer not to talk to anyone right now."

"Mr Woodrow; how kind of you to call. Do come up with me, I could do with someone to talk to. I hope you didn't ride all the way into town tonight just to see me."

"Not exactly; there was a meeting in town this afternoon that I was in two minds about attending. When I heard of McCarthy's passing, I decided I would come into town and try to see you after the meeting. How are you holding up?"

"I don't know. I'm so confused. I don't know whether I feel sad or relieved, but definitely guilty… and, if this is revenge, so far I don't find it so sweet."

They spoke at length for more than an hour, mainly with Ellen unburdening her emotions. It came as something of a surprise, but she felt hungry. She realised she hadn't eaten all day. "Are you hungry?" she asked. "Perhaps you have dinner plans." Woodrow shook his head. "Good; I need something to eat. How do you feel about an omelette?"

It was a light but enjoyable meal, and they talked on afterwards until nearly midnight. Woodrow noticed Ellen yawn and, feeling confident she would now sleep reasonably well that night, he made moves to take his leave. Ellen made a fuss about his riding back to the mill at that hour of the night. "I'm not going back to the mill tonight. I'll spend the night at the hotel and ride back in the morning." Relieved, she followed him downstairs to let him out the back door.

He paused in the doorway and turned back to her. "I'll see you on Friday at the funeral…"

"Oh, it's meant to be a private service with just the workers and a couple of others. It's not being advertised and associates are not being invited."

"Be that as it may, the company has tradition that requires the incumbent chairman of directors and the mill manager to attend the funeral of any former company directors or managing directors. I'm sure Mr Barrington Finchley, the current chairman of directors, will have heard of McCarthy's demise and full well intends attending the funeral. I think he might consider it an affront should anyone try to dissuade him from attending."

"Far be it from me to dictate who may or may not attend, and I would not wish to offend Mr Finchley or stand in the way of tradition. If the decision be made to follow tradition, I will see you and Mr Finchley at Koreelah on Friday." Woodrow smiled at her, said good night and was gone.

She was up early the next morning and so was Alfred. "I need to tell those at Koreelah what had happened and have them prepare for the funeral tomorrow," she told him. He hitched up the buggy for her and she drove out of town before most of the townsfolk began to stir for the day.

Chapter 22

A light drizzle set in as Ellen made her way along the track to the homestead. Jim, busy in the shed, saw her arrive and rushed to meet her. He helped her down from the buggy as Bert appeared from around the other side of the house. "I thought I heard someone arrive," he said as he rushed over. "I'll take care of the buggy for you, Miss." Ellen smiled to herself. It looks like I'm going to remain 'Miss' for a while yet, she noted.

"Thank you, Bert, but I would like a word with you both while you are here." Jim's jaw tightened and he began inspecting the toes of his boots. She took a deep breath and continued. "It is with sadness that I have to tell you that Mr McCarthy passed away early yesterday morning. I spent much of yesterday dealing with his funeral arrangements. His wish was for burial here on Koreelah beside the previous Mrs McCarthy. The funeral will be at ten o'clock. It will be a small intimate service in accordance with Mr McCarthy's wishes."

"I'm so sorry, Miss. I knew when I saw him at the hospital before I returned here that he could not recover this time."

"Yes, I think we both knew it. Jim, put some men to preparing the grave for tomorrow please, and let them know there is an invitation to them all to attend the funeral. Tomorrow will be a day of mourning. There will be no work at all that day. Another concern I have is that I don't feel it is appropriate somehow to be handing out pays on the day of the funeral. Instead, I would prefer staff collect their pay last thing this afternoon. Would you be able to let everyone know?" Jim nodded. "Good; the only other thing to do is to make sure everyone knows what has happened so, if you come across any of our people during the day, please make sure they know."

"What will happen now, Miss? I am mean what will happen to this place now he is gone… and, I suppose, what will happen about us?" Bert asked.

"Mr Bronson assured me that, if this were to happen, the place could carry on as normal. There was provision for that to happen in some way until such time as probate was granted and the terms of his will took over."

"What does that mean exactly – when you say carry on as normal? Will we still have our jobs? … Will the place be sold out from under us?"

"I don't know, Bert. I don't know what is to happen to Koreelah. I don't even know what is to become of me or what my future connection with the place might be. In fact, I feel I don't know anything. I am as much in the dark as you are and can tell you nothing more than I already have said. When I spoke to Mr Bronson, Mr McCarthy was still alive. There wasn't too much he could share with me at that time, and I suppose I didn't want to pre-empt anything by discussing what might happen." In spite of her best endeavours, Ellen's voice began to break as she spoke, and she fought back tears.

"There, there, Miss, don't you be fretting yourself about these things we don't know about. Let's get him in the ground first, before we start worrying about other matters. We can worry about finding out what we need to know some other day after the funeral."

"Wise words, Bert; thank you. Now, you both have things to do and I must go and find Maggie."

"Excuse me, Miss, but I was wondering if you would like Elizabeth to come to stay with you for a while. I know she would if you need some company."

"Thanks, Jim, but no. I need time to myself to come to terms with what has happened and there hasn't been much opportunity for that so far. I'll see you both later this afternoon when I hand out the pays."

Maggie and Elizabeth had just settled with the morning cup of tea when Ellen came into the kitchen. "Oh, look who is back," Maggie said, clapping her hand together and beaming at Ellen. "You have been missed at our gossip sessions. I'll get another cup."

"What's happened, Ellen? You look less than happy about being back." Elizabeth asked.

The whole story of the two weeks since the wedding came tumbling out for them, with both Elizabeth and Maggie needing to delve into their pockets for handkerchiefs as the story unfolded.

"You poor dear," Maggie said, and blew her nose loudly. "Your time at Koreelah hasn't been a happy one; nothing but one tragedy after the other. …But don't you go troubling yourself now. We will be looking after you and everything else for tomorrow. That's what friends do. They stick together and help each other out when things get tough."

"I hope you do consider us friends and not just your employees…" Elizabeth added.

"Of course you are. Why would I be sitting here blubbering in the kitchen with you if I considered you merely employees? Maggie, would you mind very much if I ate here in the kitchen with you and Bert while I'm here, rather than sitting alone in the dining room? I don't want to intrude or make things awkward for you…"

"You're more than welcome to join us – might even brighten up the conversation, which is pretty dull on occasions. There is only so much I need to know about pruning roses!"

The drizzle that dampened the last part of her journey to the homestead disappeared, and Ellen found herself hoping the rain would stay away while the men were preparing the gravesite. She couldn't think of anything worse than, at the time of the burial, finding the grave half full of water. With the weather the way it was for the last few weeks, there was no guarantee the rain would stay away today or, more importantly, for the service tomorrow.

She busied herself in the office with the pays and the accounts until five o'clock and she heard the men coming back in readiness to collect their wages. Maggie poked her head round the office door, "There is quite a few of the men already downstairs. Are you ready to go down?" Ellen stood up and hefted the box containing the pays onto her hip. Then, after a couple of deep breaths, she started towards the door where Maggie waited. "Here, give me that box. I'll carry it and we'll go down together."

There was an unusual quietness about the gathering. When the men came together like this, there was usually plenty of banter and laughter – but not today. The mood was sombre. Each of the workers mumbled their condolences as Ellen handed them their pays. When all the others had left and only Jim remained, Ellen approached him about preparations for the funeral. "We've been lucky so far, Jim. The rain has stayed away. It might be wise to cover the grave in case it does rain between now and ten o'clock tomorrow."

"We put some sheets of iron over the grave and a bit of an area around it. Hopefully, it will keep the important bits dry."

Dinner was a sombre affair that night and Ellen retired to her room early for a restless night. No rain fell during the night but a heavy cloud cover greeted them the next morning. Maggie and Elizabeth rushed about preparing food and drink, and setting up tables under the house. Ellen stood on the verandah watching the workers making their way towards the homestead. They came in dribs and drabs, a bit like Brown's cows, and congregated in the front garden. Ellen had to smile at the strange scene below. Dressed in their 'Sunday best', they would pass for strangers except for their familiar faces.

Dr Boyle was the first of the guests to arrive, and followed the undertaker's hearse down the track. A few moments later, came the Minister, followed by the solicitor and magistrate who travelled together. It was about ten minutes before the service was due to begin that Barrington Finchley's shiny new carriage drew up in front of the homestead, and Finchley and Woodrow rushed over to join those gathered around the grave.

The service was short and to the point, with no long readings or fancy eulogies, just as he wanted. A watery sun made an appearance for the duration of the service, but the black clouds rolled in again shortly afterwards bringing with them the prospect of more heavy rain that night. After one polite drink, the minister, solicitor and magistrate headed back to town. Before he left, Bronson came over to speak to Ellen. "We seem to have seen a bit of each other lately," Ellen quipped.

"Yes, and I suspect will be seeing quite a bit more of each other in the near future. When you feel up to it, I'd be pleased if you could come to see me. It is not urgent, but sometime in the next week would be good." Ellen agreed to see him early the following week.

Frank Woodrow drew Ellen off to one side of the gaggle of Koreelah workers who looked set to do justice to the food and drink before going back to their own accommodation. "Are you staying on here or going back to town?" Woodrow asked.

"I'm going back to town. I'll wait until this lot go, and then I'll head back to the store. I don't think I'm ready to stay here again just yet."

"Let me drive you back into town. You look drained and I am concerned about you taking the buggy back on your own. Finchley can meet me in town and take me back out to the mill on his way home." Ellen hesitated for a moment, but the offer was too good to turn down. She agreed on the proviso that Mr Finchley was comfortable with the arrangement.

Finchley and Jim settled in chairs short distance away from the rest of the group and appeared engrossed in a heavy discussion on the shortcomings of milling performance the previous season. Woodrow confirmed that Finchley was perfectly happy to drive back by himself and collect Woodrow afterwards somewhere in town. In fact, the arrangement suited him well as he was enjoying chatting to Jim and was in no hurry to leave.

Lunchtime rolled around. The married men wandered back to their cottages for lunch leaving only the single men for Maggie to feed. Jim invited Finchley back to the cottage to dine with him and Elizabeth, while Ellen and Woodrow joined Maggie and Bert for lunch in the kitchen. When the single men drifted back to their barracks, Bert and Woodrow fetched the buggy around to the house. A few minutes later Woodrow and Ellen were on their way back to town.

The first few miles of the journey passed in silence before Woodrow decided it might be better for Ellen to chat rather than sit and think. "What are your plans for the next week or so, how long do you think you will be in town?"

"I don't really know. I need to see Bronson to find out what happens now with the property – and what my situation is in relation to Koreelah. I told them there that I'd be in town for a few days, but I will go back out to the property next Thursday to pay the workers on Friday morning as usual if, as Bronson suggested, that's how things should proceed for the immediate future."

First thing Monday, with some trepidation, Ellen took herself off to Mr Bronson's office in a bid to determine the future of Koreelah and all those involved with it. Bronson confirmed at the outset that Patrick McCarthy had left a will and that he made it in the last few weeks before his death. "You and I will be working closely together for some time, Mrs McCarthy, as Patrick appointed us joint executors of his will. Of course, the usual formalities require completion before anything can be sent for probate and, before that can happen, you and I have plenty to do."

It took Ellen a moment or two to comprehend the enormity of the task that lay ahead. She knew nothing of her husband's private affairs other than she believed he owned Koreelah. "I appreciate what you're saying, Mr Bronson. My intention in coming here this morning was not to question the content of Mr McCarthy's will, but to establish whether Koreelah may continue to operate as it does now and how that might occur. I would be grateful if you could explain those things to me, as they are a concern not only to me but also to everyone involved with the property."

"Very well; I have advised my clerk that we will be in conference for some time and should not be disturbed. I will go through with you what is required for the continued operation of Koreelah until probate is through but, as one of the executors of Patrick McCarthy's will, you do need to know what it contains. There is no reason why we can't go through that today. However, it does remain confidential until the granting of probate."

Time slipped away. Someone brought tea sometime during the morning. Then, in a daze, Ellen made her way back to the store. It was almost lunchtime. After Jess returned from an early lunch, Ellen took herself upstairs, telling Jess that she would be there for the afternoon and would prefer not to be disturbed. Armed with a cheese sandwich and a pot of tea, she settled herself in one of the sitting room chairs and willed her mind to focus calmly and logically on all she learned at Bronson's office that morning.

There would be no sale of Koreelah. Everyone's job was safe. Everything would continue as it had in the past. The only difference being that Mr Bronson would co-sign cheques and have a say in the hiring and firing of workers until Patrick's will went for probate. The piece of information that presented the greatest shock and remained almost impossible to comprehend was that Patrick had left everything to Ellen: Koreelah, money and various other investments.

McCarthy also set up a separate bank account in Ellen's name into which he deposited a considerable sum of money prior to his death. Bronson explained that Patrick intended Ellen to use the money in the account to pay death duties and any other costs associated with probate. She discovered that, prior to his death he also transferred several other small investments to her name. No doubt, Bronson's shrewd advice was behind that, she thought.

It had grown quite dark outside by the time Ellen hauled herself out of her chair and ventured into the kitchen in search of something for dinner. With nothing in the cupboard, she went down to the store for something quick and easy to prepare. The place was in darkness and closed for the day. She peered out through the front window. The rain had started again. It came down in a heavy sheet, obscuring the hotel on the other side of the street. Someone smiled down on us, she thought, keeping the rain away until after the funeral and my visit to Bronson today.

Ellen settled back into the routine she employed when McCarthy was receiving treatment in Brisbane: staying in town during the week with only an overnight stay at Koreelah on Thursday nights. Although they experienced considerable wet weather, the proper monsoon hadn't arrived yet. So far, the creeks had not risen so high as to block the roads. However, Ellen knew that would happen once the wet season set in properly. What to do if the roads became impassable constantly occupied her mind.

The workers were still entitled to their pay every week. She kept an extra week's wages in the safe at the property in case of the unexpected occurring but, if the creeks came up, the roads could remain impassable for weeks at a time. …And there was now the added complication of Bronson having to co-sign for any cash withdrawals from the bank. Well, she thought, if Bronson is co-executor, he can share the problem of how to deal with such a potential situation. She took the problem to his office the next morning.

Some weeks, Ellen would only overnight at Koreelah, other weeks she might spend a few days there if her presence was required. Life was busy, but good – very good. Frank Woodrow continued to drop in whenever he was in town and Ellen found herself relishing their conversations. She had so much to learn about owning and running a property. Jim was a capable manager but he looked to her for guidance and approval. The final decision on major issues rested with her.

Conversations with Woodrow included 'agricultural' topics such as the intricacies of sugar cane growing and milling, and buying and selling of cattle. She now understood why farmers were concerned about the late arrival of the monsoons. There had been plenty of rain; what could the problem be? Now, she understood that, if the monsoons arrived too late in the first half of the year, it would have heavy impact on the forthcoming cane crushing season and the quality of cane supplied to the mill – which in turn meant lower payments to growers. There was no point in owning a large property like Koreelah if you didn't understand the issues that affected its continued viability. The livelihood of its every worker depended on her maintaining profitability.

Easter came and went, and the occasional storms and showers continued with temperatures showing no sign of moving towards autumn. The countryside looked lush and green. Just about everything in the house and stables sprouted furry mould on every surface. However, Easter marked something of a milestone for Ellen and she shared it with Frank Woodrow on his next visit.

"You look more relaxed today, as though a load has lifted from you," he commented when he arrived. "Have you had good news of some sort… the children, perhaps?"

She laughed. "How discerning of you, but not good news exactly. All of the administrative matters relating to Patrick McCarthy's death are complete now with the granting of probate and settlement of Bronson's account this morning. It does feel like a load lifted from my shoulders. Life will be simpler now I no longer need to consult with Mr Bronson on every little matter to do with the property or its accounts."

"…So how do you intend to go forward from here? Are there changes planned for the property, or your involvement with it?"

"No, I see no reason to change anything at this time, although that may change in the future. I will continue to spend most of my time in town, here at the store, while spending time as necessary at Koreelah. My priority now is to see how I might help Sister Justina with the search for my children. Now, I can focus on bringing them home and offering them a very good life." …But, as she would soon discover, locating the children might not bring the happiness she anticipated.

*****

It wasn't until early in June that Ellen received a reply from Sister Justina in response to her offer to help search for the children. Not particularly enlightening, the letter thanked Ellen for her offer but made it clear there was little anyone from 'outside' the organisation could do. However, she reported she had found where the last couple of groups of children from the orphanage were sent, and hoped to have further information on those children soon. 'Soon' was almost a month later.

Another brief letter from the nun cast a dark cloud over Ellen for days. The children were part of a group sent north to another church run orphanage. That orphanage, having agreed to take the group, by the time the children arrived, found itself overcrowded and with nowhere to house the new arrivals. A benevolent church member made available a disused warehouse for conversion to accommodation for the overflow of children. So far so good, Ellen thought. At least I now know where my two youngest daughters are. However, the rising excitement she felt evaporated when she turned the page.

The two girls were dead. They died only a couple of weeks apart during September-October the previous year from some mysterious fever. It was unclear whether the source of the illness was rats or something else. The warehouse, on the banks of Ross Creek, was part of an import business until shortly before its owner, an import agent, handed it over to the church. It had its own wharf in the creek, allowing ships to tie up and unload directly into the building. Rats were a problem, particularly anywhere around places where ships docked, and what they termed a 'plague epidemic' had hit the city.

There was no doubting Ellen's anger and disappointment when she related the contents of the nun's letter to Woodrow. He was at a loss for what to say that didn't sound trite, but he didn't get a chance to comment anyway. Ellen began a long and determined speech about what she intended to do.

"I've still got two other children out there somewhere. I won't stop looking for them and I won't let Sister Justina stop either. Unless I am mistaken, the prospect of a few hefty donations to the Ralston orphanage – anonymously received via Justina – should keep her interested. All this … the store, the agency, Koreelah… everything is for nothing if I can't find them."

Her resolved wasn't without result. However, it resulted in little extra information over the next couple of months. The only information forthcoming was that young William had found employment 'out west somewhere' on the other side of the range. In spite of her persistent digging, the nun found no further details of his leaving the orphanage or of his employer.

Ellen's relentless obsession with finding the remaining children seemed to drain the life from her. Every day, Frank Woodrow's concern for her increased. It wasn't affecting her businesses. Everything was doing well and she kept everything up to date, but to Woodrow, her spirit seemed to be gradually slipping away. He spoke of the matter of the children with anyone he thought might offer some clue he could follow up.

In desperation, finally he wrote seeking the help of a long-time friend. They started at school together and remained friends throughout life. That friend was now the magistrate with jurisdiction over a large area of country on the western side of the range that divided the western pastoral country from the coastal agricultural strip. It was a long shot, he knew, and the delay in receiving a response suggested his enquiry had drawn a blank. …But, there was always hope. Well, at least until something to the contrary turned up.

PART THREE

A New Life

Chapter 23

It was early-November before Tyson Dangerfield's response to Frank Woodrow's letter arrived. He apologised profusely for the delay in writing, citing as the culprit a long and involved case that occupied him for many weeks. The rest of the letter created a glimmer of hope.

Dangerfield mentioned a grazier in the area who he thought took on a young lad about 18 months previously. He stressed that it might have no connection to the boy Woodrow enquired about, but this was the only situation he could think of that might fit with the events Woodrow described. At the time he arrived at the property, Dangerfield remembered the lad certainly appeared young enough to be the boy in question. That news only served to pose another problem: how to get Ellen to see the boy Dangerfield mentioned without building up her hopes only to have her experience another crashing disappointment if it weren't young William.

A possible solution arrived a couple of weeks later. With the mill's cane crushing season finished for the year, Woodrow planned taking a few days off to travel out west to inspect some stock for the small property he owned. He purchased the property, at the foot of the range and not far from the western boundary of Koreelah, a few years back with the intention of retiring there one day. While he ran a small herd of his own, he supplemented the property's income by agisting other cattle from the drier country on the western side of the range. Arrangements were in place with a western agent to look at stock there in early-December.

His next trip to town provided a chance meeting that set in motion a plan to have Ellen see the boy Dangerfield mentioned. When he visited the store, he found Jim, now Koreelah's manager, in the office with Ellen. In town to pick up something for the property, Jim called on Ellen to discuss a few things about Koreelah. Over cups of tea, Woodrow mentioned his impending western stock-buying trip.

Jim became excited. "We should be introducing some new blood into our herd as well. Our old bull will soon be past his prime. We run the risk of losing quality through inbreeding if we don't get a new young bull soon. What do you think, Boss."

"I remember we discussed this a few weeks ago," Ellen replied. "A trip over the range to see what might be available to buy would make sense now that the crushing season is over and things are a bit quieter on the property."

"You're more than welcome to come with me. I'll be taking the carriage, so there will be plenty of room, and I'm sure the agent will be happy to find a couple of bulls for you to look at. My plan was to spend about three nights at the Wayfarers' Hotel."

"Sounds good to me… What about you, Miss, would you come with us?"

"I hadn't thought about it. Although now you ask, if we saw a suitable beast, I would need to purchase it at the time. Yes, I think I should accompany you. Let's work out the trip's details."

Details of the trip took no more than a couple of minutes to finalise and included Woodrow agreeing to write to his stock agent asking him to include a couple of good young bulls for them to inspect. Ellen offered him writing materials and Woodrow scratched out a short note and posted it before leaving town. What am I missing, he asked himself as he rode out of town. That was all too easy. However, he didn't question it for too long. The first part of his plan for Ellen to see the lad Dangerfield mentioned was in place. Now, all that remained was to ensure that somehow they would get to visit the 'right' property.

Ellen was excited about the trip, although she knew it would be something of an endurance test. She had never been across the range and looked forward to seeing the country on the other side… and, if she were honest, she would admit the prospect of travelling with Frank Woodrow added a certain appeal.

On the Sunday night about a week after they first discussed the trip, Jim came into town on the wagon. He spent the night at the hotel before collecting Ellen the next morning and travelling to Woodrow's house on the Southend Mill Estate. There, they abandoned the wagon and climbed aboard Woodrow's carriage. Then, as the local roosters began their early morning chorus, they set off for the range.

They reached the top of the range around lunchtime. Once they were through the gap and heading down the other side, Ellen broke out the parcel of sandwiches she made earlier that morning. They ate lunch in silence on the way down the western side of the range and washed it down with water. Ellen noted the change once they crossed the crest. The dry burning heat of the west replaced the humidity of the coast, and arid country featuring stunted scrub and spinifex-like grasses replaced the lush green country of the east.

As evening approached, the trip – long, hot, dusty, and rough despite the carriage's fine springs – was fast losing its appeal. Ellen almost heaved a sigh of relief when they turned into a street and she saw the Wayfarers' Hotel on the left about halfway along. Stiff after the long ride, she climbed awkwardly from the carriage. Jim continued to the hotel's horse yard to deal with the horses and carriage while Woodrow and Ellen registered.

Later, they regrouped in the lounge for a drink before dinner, and Woodrow's stock agent soon joined them. He had arranged three properties for them to visit the next day. Two had stock of various ages to inspect, and the third has a few yearlings and a young bull available. After arranging to collect them in the morning, the agent left. Woodrow could hardly control himself when the agent listed the properties they would visit the next day. His plan had come together beautifully with little effort on his part.

The next morning dawned hot and remained that way for the day. As arranged, the agent arrived soon after breakfast, collected them, and they were soon bumping along in his less than comfortable open carriage to the first property. That property had a few nice beasts for sale, as did the second property, but Woodrow would not commit to buying any until he had seen all that were on offer.

With their visits to two of the properties complete, on their way to the last property, they pulled up beside a creek. Under the trees on the creek bank, they ate a picnic lunch of cold cuts, salad and freshly baked bread packed by the hotel. The trees provided a welcome shade after the open carriage. With their energy sapped after the long morning in the sun, there was little conversation as they lunched. The creek, now reduced to a long narrow waterhole along the centre of its bed, attracted a wealth of birdlife and a few wallabies to quench their thirsts.

Ellen sat idly watching the animals and listening to the birds in the trees around them. Jolted back to reality by a sudden gust of wind, she heard Jim say, "Looks like we are in for a storm. Perhaps we best make a move so we can get done and be back at the hotel before it comes." The other men agreed. There followed a flurry of activity. With everything packed away, they climbed back into the carriage and set off again for the final property on their list, Robson Tremaine's place.

They passed through a gate surmounted by an impressive metal sign confirming it to be Tremaine's property, and found the owner hanging about the homestead waiting for them. After only a brief conversation, he left them on the verandah with afternoon tea provided by Mrs Tremaine, a mousey woman who looked haggard long before her time. A few minutes later, Tremaine returned and took them to a nearby yard to look at a handful of heifers. As the men inspected the animals, Ellen noticed a lad leading a beast by a halter towards an adjoining round yard. Tremaine saw him too and suggested they move to the round yard to look at the young bull the lad brought.

Tremaine led the group through a gate into the adjoining yard before going to open a gate in the opposite side of the yard to let in the boy and his charge. The lad came towards them with his head lowered and almost completely hidden under a battered felt hat. He stopped a few yards away from the group, and stood holding the beast as if showing him off at some agricultural show. Tremaine launched into his sales pitch including how quiet the animal was and details of its pedigree. The men cut him short, preferring to make their own assessment of the beast.

Jim and Woodrow walked over to and around the bull, running their hands all over it. Thinking she should make some pretence of knowing about such matters, Ellen went to join the two men. As she approached, she noticed the lad never once lifted his head, never once acknowledged their presence in any way. Their close inspection complete, the two men returned to stand with the owner and the agent. Ellen, having decided to mimic their inspection, walked up to the animal and placed her hand on its flank.

As she slid her hand down along its hide, she quietly commented to the lad. "He's a fine looking animal; in good condition and quiet. You seem to have him well trained." She caught her breath in shock as the lad lifted his gaze to her. "William, is it really you? Don't say or do anything. Just stand there while I look at this animal."

The lad lowered his eyes again but Ellen sensed a new energy in him. She continued speaking softly to him as she moved around to the other side. "Are you happy here? Are you well cared for?

"No!" was the whispered venomous response.

Ellen took a step back from the bull and, with her back to the watching group, continued softly to William. "Say nothing about knowing me. If you are asked, I didn't speak to you simply commented to myself about the animal. I promise I will be back for you." Then, with an approving nod of her head, she took a step back while adding, "Quietly have your things packed ready."

It took Ellen all her self-control to compose herself as she returned to join the men. She smiled in turn at Tremaine and the agent and said, "A fine looking animal in my opinion."

Woodrow detected something had changed and quickly cut in. "Thank you, Mr Tremaine. We will have further talks with our agent tomorrow. However, I think it is time we headed back to our hotel before that storm arrives."

Back at the carriage, Woodrow and Ellen lagged behind as the others climbed aboard. Woodrow silently raised his eyebrows in question at Ellen. She replied with an almost imperceptible nod and a fleeting smile. You old fox, she thought. You set that up for me… and her heart gave a little flip. The ride back to the hotel was not nearly as tedious as the trip out had been.

The stock agent dropped his clients at the Wayfarers' Hotel, and departed after extracting a promise that they would be in touch should they decide to purchase any of the stock they inspected. The arrangement was that, after freshening up, the three visitors would meet in the ladies' lounge for a drink before dinner. About 20 minutes later, Woodrow knocked gently on Ellen's door. He escorted her down to the lounge and took advantage of their few minutes alone to speak about events at the Tremaine property. "Was that your son we saw today? I gathered by your reaction that it was." That was enough to open the floodgate for Ellen and her emotions tumbled out.

"Yes! Yes, that was young William. I don't know how you did it, but thank you for setting up that meeting. I must get him away from there. I can't go home without him. I don't know how it can happen, but I must take him back with me."

"I didn't have much to do with it. A whole lot of coincidences happened today. I couldn't say anything beforehand in case the lad working there wasn't your son… and I didn't know until this morning that we were to visit that particular property. Have you considered that he might not want to leave… might be settled and happy with the Tremaines?"

"He's not. I asked whether he was happy and well cared for, and he said no. He looked so different… so… so… oh, I don't know; so sullen and sad somehow."

"He certainly isn't the same chirpy young kid who bounced into my office on a couple of occasions. I have asked an old friend to dine with us tonight. He might have some ideas about how to go about getting your son back. He should be along shortly. …And it probably wouldn't hurt for Jim to know what's going on, seeing as how he will be involved if we do take William back with us. We should...." Woodrow stopped speaking abruptly and stood up. A tall, slim well-dressed man was striding to meet him. Jim entered the lounge at about the same time and followed the stranger to the table occupied by Woodrow and Ellen.

After shaking hands with the stranger, Woodrow made the introduction. "Ah, Jim, good you're here. Now I'll only have to do this once. This is Tyson Dangerfield. We go back a long way, all the way back to school days. Tyson is the magistrate in this part of the country and had something to do with my deciding to come here to inspect stock."

"If this is going to be a long story, we could all die of thirst along the way. I'll get us all drinks. Don't go on without me," Jim said. With Jim gone, Woodrow told Tyson about their visit to the Tremaine property. "The lad in question led a bull out for us to inspect. He is the missing lad I mentioned to you. Your guess was right on the money. Jim is unaware of the story so, if you don't mind, we'll take a few moments to explain before talking about today's episode." It was a few minutes before Jim returned. To Ellen, it felt like forever.

They gave Jim an abbreviated version of the story of Ellen's children going into the orphanage and young William being taken by Tremaine after payment of a large 'donation' to the orphanage. "Damned illegal that," Tyson exclaimed. "Amounts to buying a person, that does – and a child at that in this instance. We've heard whispers of it going on in the region but haven't been able to prove anything. However, it looks like we might be on to something this time."

"Mr Dangerfield, I want to get my son out of there. He looks so miserable and downtrodden. It almost broke my heart to see him like that. Now I think on it, Mrs Tremaine looked nearly as bad. What can we do... how can we get him out of there?"

"...Preferably without finding ourselves on the wrong side of the law," Woodrow added.

"The word around the place is that mostly the boys aren't treated all that well, and not paid proper wages. The boss gives them only a couple of pennies each week and keeps the rest of what the boy should get for himself. They do it under the pretext of recouping what the boy cost in the first place. They never tell anybody how much that was – or that they actually bought the boy – and the boy isn't game to say anything. That practice allows them to keep 'recouping' the payment indefinitely if they so choose. Many of the boys turn to crime to get some extra cash. Some run away and resort to crime to survive, while others turn to crime to raise some cash in the hope of buying their way out of their situation."

"What happens to those boys… the ones who turn to crime, I mean?" Ellen asked.

"Most of the time, no good comes of it. They end up before the courts or worse, but there is never any evidence to be able to bring charges against the bloke who triggered the problem in the first place."

"So, what can we do legally about this lad we want to rescue?" Woodrow asked again

"Ah, I see just the man we need to talk to standing near the bar. Excuse me for a moment while I fetch him." They watched Tyson walk over to a tall swarthy man who waited to buy a drink. Tyson held his hand high in the air, clicked his fingers loudly and pointed to the man standing next to him. Within moments, the new arrival had a rum thrust into his hand and Tyson and his companion were on their way back to the table. "Good trick that…" Woodrow commented with a grin at Tyson who shrugged in response.

"Madam and gentlemen, let me introduce our local copper – well, officer in charge out this way really – Sergeant Tom Frankston. He's the man we need involved in this exercise to get your son back." The next few minutes involved bringing Frankston up to date on the story of young William and his discovery at Tremaine's place.

"Perhaps we should relocate to the dining room," Ellen suggested. "According to that clock above the bar, they expected us to arrive for dinner about five minutes ago."

"You're right of course, and now there will be an extra one… if Sergeant Frankston would care to join us." Frankston accepted Woodrow's invitation and the group moved to the dining room.

They were the only diners that evening so, after much fussing around by a waitress to set another place, discussion of young William's situation continued uninhibited. Woodrow led the discussion. "My thinking is that we should go back to Tremaine's tomorrow and Ellen should offer to buy the bull. That would give us a legitimate reason to be there, and we could use the excuse that we were saving both parties money by cutting out the middleman, the agent."

"…But how does that help me get young William away from there? All that will do is maybe let me see him again." Ellen seemed agitated that Woodrow's suggestion was the best available. Tyson intervened.

While looking directly at Frankston, Tyson suggested an extended version of Woodrow's plan. "I think your plan has merit, my friend, but it needs a bit of fine tuning. My thinking is that you should do as Woodrow suggests, but take Sergeant Frankston with you. Perhaps you could drop him off somewhere before you reach the Homestead so that Tremaine is unaware of his arrival. Once you've done a deal on the price for the bull, and shaken on it, perhaps you could offer him some money for the lad."

Frankston nodded and, after a moment's thought added, "It sounds like a solid plan to me. The only thing I would suggest is that, when you offer him money for the lad, you start low – say, initially offer him £10 – but be prepared to negotiate up to maybe as much as £25. I don't think Tremaine would have paid that much for your son, but I hear tell that about £20 is sort of the going rate."

"Surely Tremaine isn't going to go for that plan. It would amount to having to admit that he'd bought the boy in the first place, wouldn't it?" Jim asked.

"Oh, I'm sure he's going to protest and put on a show," Tyson suggested, "But he'll take the money eventually. You will just have to be tough and determined – keep hammering him and don't let him back away. Once you've agreed a price – and I'm sure that will happen – give Frankston here some sort of sign to come and do his job. Likewise, if Tremaine looks like he might finally balk at a deal to sell your son back to you, call Frankston over to join you and he can help persuade Tremaine to part with the boy – and possibly even without any money changing hands, because it would be illegal to sell a boy like that, wouldn't it?"

Well after they had finished eating, the group remained in the dining room discussing the following day's plan of attack. By the time they all said good night, a plan was in place from when they finish breakfast until they all arrived back at the hotel at the end of the day. Ellen was both excited and nervous. So much could go wrong in spite of all the planning. However, somehow she knew she would be taking young William back across the range with her. Nevertheless, she didn't sleep well and rose early afterwards.

Next morning, they collected Tom Frankston from the Police Station and set off for Tremaine's property. A short distance before the homestead, Tremaine's track passed through a dense patch of bush. They deposited Frankston in the bush to make the last of his journey on foot to the rear of a barn that hid him from the house. While he patiently waited, Woodrow's carriage continued around to the front of the house where he hitched the horses to a railing.

Tremaine came out of the shed only a short distance away from the house, his surprise at seeing them again evident. He rushed over to where the group dismounted from the carriage and demanded not too hospitably, "What brings you back here today, and where is that agent fellow? Shouldn't he be with you?" Jim took the initiative of replying.

"Well, it's like this you see, we liked the young bull you showed as yesterday but can't see any sense in letting money go to a third party when we could do a good deal between ourselves. If you have a price in mind for the beast, perhaps we could do a deal now and take him off your hands when we leave."

"I'm not sure that would be aboveboard," Tremaine suggested.

They all snickered, and Jim continued. "There's nothing wrong with that idea. You can sell to anyone you like. The sale doesn't have to go through an agent so he can rake off his fee. Much better that the money stays with the people involved in the deal. That's why we've come directly to you. Now, do you have a price in mind and do you want to do a deal here and now while we're here?"

Tremaine hesitated briefly but eventually named a price, and the usual thrust and parry of the negotiation process ensued. At the end of the process, Ellen had a very good deal and Tremaine would receive ample rewarded for his animal. Ellen produced a chequebook and made to write a cheque for Tremaine, then hesitated. "Before I write this out, how about I include a sum for the lad as well… say, an extra £10?" Tremaine spluttered and feigned indignation at the offer, but Jim and Ellen persisted.

At one stage, Ellen cast a nervous glance at Woodrow. She was certain Tremaine was going to refuse any deal for the lad, and wondered whether this might be a good time for Sergeant Frankston to arrive. Woodrow gave a slight shake of his head and encouraged her with his eyes to keep the negotiations going.

It took longer than expected, but Tremaine caved in and settled for £20 for the boy. They shook on the deal and Ellen wrote out the cheque in a flash. Woodrow gave the signal and, while Ellen signed the cheque, Frankston magically appeared beside Tremaine. Ellen and Jim ran off to find young William, leaving Woodrow behind to explain to Frankston that Tremaine sold a lad to Ellen for the princely sum of £20. Frankston wasted no time and had Tremaine cuffed and marching back to the house by the time Ellen located William in the feed store.

The question of how Frankston planned to take Tremaine back to town idly crossed Woodrow's mind. There might just about be enough room in his carriage but, surely, Frankston wouldn't expect them to ride back with Tremaine a passenger. He needn't have worried. A few moments later, a police wagon came out of the clump of bush behind the house and drove up to collect Frankston and his prisoner. While Frankston secured his prisoner on the wagon, Jim and Ellen, with Young William in tow, came around the corner of the house to join Woodrow at his wagon. There was no problem finding room for William's pitifully small bundle of belongings rolled up in what looked like an old sheet.

William dumped the bundle in the carriage before going to fetch the bull. With the bull's halter securely tied to the rear of the carriage, they all climbed aboard and Woodrow turned the horses for town. Jim sat up front with Woodrow, leaving the rest of the carriage to Ellen and young William. There was little conversation on the way back to town. There was no need for words; Ellen simply sat with her arm firmly around her son's shoulders.

Back in town, they called briefly at the courthouse to tell Tyson Dangerfield of the outcome of their trip. The police wagon arrived back in town much earlier and Frankston kept a watch for Woodrow's carriage to arrive. It had a slow trip back to town to avoid injury to the bull tied on behind. Frankston came over to meet them while they talked to Dangerfield. "I wonder if I might get a few statements from you lot before you leave town," he asked. "You can leave the bull in the police yard if you like. Bob Murchison is driving a small herd to the coast on Friday. He is happy for anything you buy to be included with the mob he is taking over the range."

Jim took the bull across to the police yard, and Ellen and young William accompanied Frankston back to the police station to make their statements, leaving Woodrow alone with Dangerfield to catch up on each other's stories. Ellen gave her statement and then sat with William while he told his story starting from when Tremaine visited the orphanage to select a lad. She felt her eyes brim with tears but, deciding it was not good for William to see her cry, Ellen used having to speak to Jim urgently as an excuse to leave.

As she hurried out of the Police Station, Jim closed the gate on the police yard. She stood beside Jim and they leant on the rail and watched the bull explore his new home for the next few days. "Jim, I need to talk to you about young William," Ellen began. "I hate to ask this of you, but is it possible you might find a position for him at Koreelah?"

"Of course there is work for him on the property. In fact, we will be one man down shortly. He wanted to tell you himself the next time you were at Koreelah, but Cecil Glover is leaving."

"Cecil Glover…? Why, what has happened to make him want to leave? He will be missed."

"Yes, he will be missed. I don't know if you are aware that his father is a big landholder in New South Wales – owns thousands of acres I believe. It seems he decided his only son would get better training elsewhere rather than at home where he might receive 'special' treatment. Cecil worked on a couple of properties before he arrived here. I think he would have stayed but his father wrote asking him to return home. It appears his father is getting on in years and has been ill for a while. I'd say that, in a short time, Cecil is most likely to take over running the place for his father. Anyway, he will finish up at Koreelah in time to arrive home for Christmas."

"Getting back to William; I might keep him in town with me for a few days while we get reacquainted before I bring him out to Koreelah. Then, I will stay a while to make sure he settles into the bunkhouse okay. I'm sure the older lads will look after him, but I don't want him to feel I'm abandoning him again so soon."

"Nonsense! He won't be staying in the bunkhouse. He will live with Elizabeth and me. Elizabeth needs someone to fuss over. Our only son got himself swept away and drowned in a flooded creek a few years ago. It will do the boy good to be in a stable environment and be well cared for again. He can stay at the big house when you are at Koreelah and, when he is a bit older he can decided whether he wants to stay in that small cottage you used when you first arrived at the property, or whether he wants to move in with the others in the bunkhouse."

It did make sense for him to live with Jim and Elizabeth, Ellen told herself, but she still felt as though she was abandoning him again. She decided she would wait for an appropriate moment to discuss the matter of his future with young William. That might not be for a few days yet she suspected.

Ellen started back towards the Police Station. She had gone only a few steps when Jim asked a question that stopped her. "Have you asked William if he wants to work on the property? What happens if he decides he would rather work at the store and learn how to run that?" Jim asked. Ellen turned to look at him when he spoke and now stood staring at Jim.

"I don't... no, I haven't asked him, but surely he wouldn't want to stay at the store. I don't know what he wants to do because I never thought to ask him. Some mother I am." With that, she picked up her skirt and climbed the Police Station stairs.

While Jim and Woodrow purchased the heifers they wanted from the agent, Ellen took William to the hotel and booked him into a room. Later, they were both in Ellen's room when Woodrow tapped on the door. "Would you like to join us for a drink before dinner?" he asked. Ellen shook her head and glanced in William's direction. "Okay, then we will meet up again in the dining room at seven o'clock. Jim and I will be in the bar if you should want us in the meantime."

She led William out through the French doors onto the wide verandah that circled the pub's upper floor, and they dragged over a couple of chairs from further along. "We have so much to catch up on, Son. I'm not sure where to begin. I suppose the first thing I need to ask is, how was today for you? Are you happy with what has happened; happy to be away from Tremaine's place?"

"I don't have no problems with it. That man, that Mr Woodrow bloke, did he used to be the mill manager when we lived there?"

"Yes, and he still is the manager there. He helped when your father died and he has become a good friend over the years since then. It's thanks to him that we found you, but that's a long story. What about Jim, what do you think of him?"

"I like him. He's kind and treats Reggie gently."

"Reggie...? Who is Reggie?"

"The young bull..."

"Oh, I'm sorry. I didn't know he had a name."

"He had no name – no proper name like – so I named him Reggie. Everyone needs a name, don't they?"

"Yes, it is probably easier if everyone has a name, but why 'Reggie'? What made you pick that name?"

"Reggie was my best mate at the orphanage. He was older than me and looked out for me when I first went there. Then they took him away. That was a while before Tremaine took me."

"Do you know what happened to Reggie or where he ended up?"

"Yeah, I ran into him at an agricultural show not long after I was at Tremaine's. We had a good old yap while we leant on the fence around the ring watching the stock paraded. Then Tremaine came along and caught us talking. He got upset and carried on about me not being able to be trusted when I was off the property. He said I wasn't supposed to talk to anyone other than him or his wife but, seeing as I couldn't be trusted to behave I wasn't allowed to leave the property again."

Ellen fought down her anger and tried to sound normal. "While you were chatting to Reggie, did you manage to find out where he was living?"

"That's the funny thing; he lives only a couple of properties away from Tremaine's. They treat him pretty badly; knock him about a fair bit I think. They even changed his name. Now everyone has to call him 'John'. What's wrong with 'Reggie' for a name?"

"Nothing, it's a fine name for a lad… and for a bull. Do you know the name of the people he lives with?"

"Yeah, the bloke's name is Sawyer; Jack Sawyer. I think, from what Reggie said, he must be a nasty piece of work."

"Did Tremaine knock you about too, or treat you badly somehow?"

"Nah, nothing too bad… slapped me around a few times, but that was when the grog had him. I learned to stay out of his way after he had been on the grog. That left him with only Mrs Tremaine to swear at."

"…Sounds like he is a nasty piece of work as well."

"Not as bad as Sawyer, I don't think. I can't remember Tremaine ever hitting his wife, but old man Sawyer used to take it out on Mrs Sawyer; hit her badly and often I think."

At a loss for further comment and needing time to collect her thoughts, Ellen resorted to commenting on the weather. "That breeze that's come up is a welcome relief after today. It's so cool after the heat of the day."

"It's coming off rain… probably get a storm tonight," William replied. Ellen marvelled at how much her son had matured since she last saw him. I doubt this is a lad who would be happy working in a store, she thought, but I still have to ask that question. A knock on Ellen's door curtailed any further opportunity for conversation. It was Jim.

"I'm going over to the police yard to check on the bull. I thought William might like to come along," Jim said. William was standing beside him by the time Jim finished speaking.

"Off you both go then," Ellen said. "I'll see you down in the dining room later. Don't be late for dinner, please," she added with a meaningful look at William. Ellen remained on the verandah enjoying the cool breeze until a couple of minutes before seven o'clock. As she was about to enter the dining room, she saw Woodrow standing at the bar with Sergeant Frankston and Tyson Dangerfield. She waved to catch Woodrow's eye. When he came over, she asked if she could speak privately to Sergeant Frankston.

The dining room was deserted. They went in and Ellen related the conversation she had with William about his mate Reggie who also 'disappeared' from the orphanage. "From what William says, Frank Sawyer physically assaults Reggie and he thinks the man also assaults Mrs Sawyer. I suppose it's none of my business, but I hate to think of another child being in the same situation as my William and having no one to care about what happens to him. If you should happen to rescue Reggie – who they have renamed John – he has a good home waiting for him with me and William."

Frankston and Dangerfield dined with them again that night. It proved a pleasant evening with interesting light conversation. Ellen excused herself early and went to bed, leaving the men to their port and cigars. They planned an early start for the long trip back over the range the next day. Young William was correct, a heavy downpour occurred just after midnight.

The trip home that Wednesday somehow didn't seem as long or as draining as the trip out. A light breeze accompanied the slight drop in temperature, and the storm the previous night meant there was little dust to bother them. At Woodrow's house, Ellen, Jim and young William transferred from Woodrow's carriage to Koreelah's wagon to complete the trip into town.

Chapter 24

Those travelling back over the range weren't the only ones up early that Wednesday morning. Sergeant Frankston roused his Constable before dawn and they set off for the Sawyer's property with Frankston on horseback and the Constable driving the police wagon – 'just in case they had need of it' Frankston told his subordinate. As the passed through the gate onto Sawyer's property, Frankston rode on ahead leaving the constable to drop back a bit.

When Frankston arrived, there was no one about. The place looked deserted until a young lad appeared from inside one of the barns. In response to a wild guess, Frankston called out to the lad. "Reggie?" The boy halted on his way across to the new arrival, and stood and stared for a moment. Then the front door of the house creaked and the boy turned on his heel and bolted back into the barn.

With more creaking and scraping, the door finally opened wide enough for someone to come outside. A man, bleary-eyed, staggered out onto the narrow verandah and leaned against the wall. He bellowed, "What the hell do you want? Who the hell do you think you are, coming in here yelling out like that?"

"I would be Police Sergeant Frankston, and I want to talk to you about that young lad who just disappeared into yon barn."

Sawyer lurched across the verandah to Frankston and stood unsteadily with his face only a few inches from Frankston's nose. The rum fumes were almost overpowering. "No young lad here that's any of your business. Now, get back on your horse and bugger off my property."

"No, I don't think I can do that, Sir, not until we've had a chat about that lad I saw."

"Like I said, none of your business… nothing to do with you, so get off my property, before I run you off."

"Are you threatening me, Mr Sawyer? It sounded to me like a threat. That would be a serious mistake on your part."

"You take it any way you like, but you are leaving now." With that, Sawyer turned away unsteadily, stopped after a couple of steps, and then turned again to face Frankston. He hesitated for a moment and then came at Frankston swinging. The punch missed its mark, but the attempt swung Sawyer off his feet.

It took him over the edge of the verandah and landed him on his face in the dirt. Frankston dived onto Sawyer, planting his knee in the belligerent drunk's back to hold him down while he snapped the handcuffs around scrawny wrists. Then, in response to s shrill whistle from Frankston, the constable brought the wagon round to where the action happened. They bundled Sawyer on board and secured him to the railings before the constable headed back to town with the wagon and the prisoner.

Out of the corner of his eye, while he was busy with Sawyer, Frankston noted a movement on the verandah. Now free to investigate, he turned to the verandah as the wagon drove off. Mrs Sawyer remained partially hidden behind the front door, but she had witnessed the melee outside and her husband's arrest. Frankston considered his options briefly before mounting the single step to the verandah.

"Good morning, Mrs Sawyer; my apologies for all the fuss so early in the day. I've arrested your husband for threatening a Police Officer and attempted assault. He might be missing for a day or two."

"What will happen to him?"

"…Not for me to say, Ma'am, that's up to the court to decide."

"Lock him up and throw away the key for all I care… and it would be a good riddance if they did," she said, her venom coming as no surprise to Frankston. The woman's black eye and busted lip clear testimony to the state of the couple's relationship.

"Perhaps you should have that eye looked at…" Frankston suggested. Mrs Sawyer shook her head and put her hand up as if to hide the damage done. Frankston shrugged and continued, "I came here to talk to your husband about the young lad working on this property. I think when I asked him about the boy, it's what got him all fired up. Perhaps I could ask you a few questions about him, and then I could be on my way." Mrs Sawyer stepped aside and motioned Frankston in.

"I didn't think this day would ever come," she murmured, as they got comfortable in a couple of threadbare ancient lounge chairs. "I heard you call out to him when you arrived… 'Reggie! That's his name, of course, but my husband insisted we call him 'John'. Are you going to take him away with you?"

"Maybe… that depends on what you tell me about him. You see, we believe something illegal – a criminal act – happened to enable your husband to bring Reggie here. What can you tell me about how he came to be here?"

"I can do more that tell you; I can show you." She got up and went into what Frankston assumed to be a small bedroom off the side of the sitting room. He heard her rummaging about for a few moments before she returned carrying a parcel, which she handed to Frankston. "I've been saving that," she said gesturing to the parcel with her head. "Call it insurance if you like, but I knew it would be important one day. Today is that day, I think."

Frankston removed the old newspaper and string from the parcel to reveal an old cheque book and a diary from three years previous. Frankston frowned and looked up at Mrs Sawyer who remained standing a short distance in front of him. "What's this?"

"Bring it to the table and I'll show you... should answer all your questions, I reckon." With no great show, she opened to cheque book to where a small torn sliver of paper marked a cheque stub, and then she flicked through the diary until she reached the date she wanted.

The cheque stub indicated the cheque was a donation of £15 to the orphanage. Frankston noted the date on the stub before turning his attention to the diary. Mrs Sawyer opened the diary at the same date as that on the cheque stub. He quickly scanned down the page until a brief entry almost jumped off the page at him: *Paid £15 for the boy Reggie. More than I wanted to pay but he seems fit enough for farm work. At that price, he will be working for pennies for a long time to pay it off, so the price will probably work out all right.*

After reading the entry a couple of times, Frankston looked up at the woman who stood with her arms folded tightly about her and her jaw set hard. "You realise this could be very damning for your husband?" he asked quietly.

She nodded. "Reggie is not the first one. He had another one before... nearly beat him to death one night. It took me weeks to get him patched up again, and then he ran off. I gave him a bit of bread and a small piece of salt beef when he left, but I don't know what happened to him. My husband's a cruel man, Sergeant, always has been. When the grog has him, he knocks both the boy and me around. I'd be better off without the bastard and the boy will be better somewhere else."

"I'm not sure Reggie will want to leave, although there is a good home waiting for him if he chooses to go there."

"If he is reluctant to leave, you will have to persuade him to go. It's no good for the lad to stay here where he's been treated so badly."

"How will you manage if the boy goes – particularly if your husband is locked up for a long stretch?"

"I'll be okay. The carter boys from nextdoor are always offering to help. I'll employ a couple of them – and pay them properly. That will help their father out too. No need to worry about me, Sergeant, I'll be fine. I'm not sure how his fancy woman in town will manage without him though. Shall I call Reggie for you?" Frankston nodded. "R e g g ie! Come up to the house. It's safe; he's gone," she yelled.

When the boy tentatively joined them in the sitting room, she spoke to him quietly and reassuringly. "The Sergeant here wants you to go with him…"

"Why am I going to jail? I ain't done nothing wrong."

"No, Reggie, he wants to get you away from here; says there's a good home waiting for you on the coast." The boy looked unconvinced, so Frankston opted to explain a few things.

"We got your mate, William, away from Tremaine's yesterday. He's on his way back home today. He told us about you. He was worried about what was happening to his mate. …But, like Mrs Sawyer said, there is a good home waiting for you over the range if you want to come with me and maybe start a new life."

The woman nodded to him encouragingly. "Go and get your things together and saddle up your pony."

"Socks isn't my horse. He belongs here, to the property."

"He's yours now. I just gave him to you along with his saddle and bridle. It makes up for some of the wages you never got paid." The lad, torn between staying and leaving, hesitated.

"Come on, lad, hop to it," Frankston said. "We need to get going soon." The boy ran out of the house and soon had his horse tied up beside Frankston's. They were about to mount up when the boy turned and ran back onto the verandah. He threw his arms around the forlorn woman standing there and hugged her tight.

After a moment, she gently prised him away. "Off you go now, and make a good life for yourself. If you think of it, perhaps you might write me a note now and then – just to let me know how things are for you."

Reggie trotted back to his horse and climbed into the saddle. Frankston wasn't sure, but he thought he saw the glisten of tears on the boy's cheeks as they turned and headed off up the track. No one spoke until they passed under the sign above the gate and were on the road to town.

"She was good to me. Although I told her not to, she stuck up for me, and always copped a hiding for her trouble. It just meant we both ended up getting a hiding." He went quiet for a couple of minutes before speaking again. "So, what happens to me when we get to town?"

"Bob Murchison is walking a mob over the range. He's leaving early Friday morning. I'm sure he would appreciate an extra drover along on the trip. In the meantime, you can stay at our house with Mrs Frankston and me."

It was still dark on Friday morning when Frankston took Reggie over to where Bob Murchison was busy herding his mob together for the trek over the range. Bob explained to Reggie that it would take two days. They would go through the gap and make camp tonight at a place just over the summit, before the long drive to the port the next day. Reggie found it all so new and exciting that they were some way along the road before he realised he didn't know where he was supposed to end up or with whom. How would he know where to go? Bob wasn't much help; said he didn't know anything about it other than Reggie would be leaving him when they reached the coast.

They camped under the stars that night – the rain seemingly having taken the night off – and awoke to a glorious morning for the run down the eastern side of the range. They made good time but, at the foot of the range, Bob halted the herd. While the stock took advantage of a nearby creek to slake their thirst, the men boiled the billy and indulged in tea and damper spread thickly with syrup.

Reggie was curious about why they waited there instead of pushing on into town, but he didn't question it. It was cool under the paperbark trees and he dozed off. The sound of horses approaching woke him with a start.

<h1 align="center">Chapter 25</h1>

Once they reached Woodrow's house after their trip over the range, Ellen and young William joined Jim on Koreelah's wagon for the trip into town. William, using his bundle of possessions as a pillow, fell asleep in the back of the wagon soon after they set off for town. Ellen checked over her shoulder to make sure he was asleep before speaking quietly to Jim. "I'll bring William out to Koreelah with me tomorrow and then we'll hang around there until the bull arrives on Saturday. I need William to spend a few days in town with me after that before he goes back to Koreelah – if that's what he wants to do."

"You haven't asked him about that yet?" Jim asked.

"Somehow the right opportunity hasn't arisen. My thinking now is that it might be better to wait until he has a look at the property before he makes that decision." Jim raised an eyebrow questioningly at her but said nothing.

Jim dropped his passengers at the store's rear loading area. Alfred, hearing the wagon draw up and not expecting anyone to collect an order, came out to investigate. William was off the wagon and up the stairs to shake Alfred's hand. "I thought I would never see you again," he told Alfred, who threw an arm around the lad's shoulders and wrapped William in a bear hug.

"Welcome back. I thought you were gone for good as well. Go down and hand your mother's stuff up to me," Alfred said. Ellen watched the reunion with her heart bursting with happiness and pride. Sometimes life can be sweet.

A few moments later, they were in the store, and Ellen was introducing William to Jess and explaining how Jess was married to Alfred and they lived above the agency. Then they swept through to the agency and William met Charlie Perkins. With the introductions complete, it was time to take William upstairs and get him settled in – for a few days at least. William's eyes darted everywhere as they made their way back through the store to the stairs. About halfway up the stairs, William stopped and went down on his haunches. When Ellen turned to see what was going on, William was sitting on a step surveying all the lay below. The realisation that William had not visited the store, or the dwelling upstairs, since he was a baby came as a shock.

After her father's arrest and Ellen realised he would not be coming back, she had moved into the large bedroom. That left her previous bedroom free for William. It took only a few minutes to show him around, get him settled in, and to freshen up. "I'm sorry, William, I have work to do in the office. What would you like to do while I am busy?"

"Aw, don't worry about me; I'll find something to do. Is it all right if I go and give Alfred a hand?"

"You may ask Alfred if you can be of help to him, but he is busy and might not have time to spend showing you what to do." Ellen looked out from the office a while later and smiled at the sight of William carrying various boxes from the agency out to the loading area. It was good he was getting a feel for what the store was like. It would help him make the decision about whether he wanted to stay at the store or go to Koreelah.

As was her usual practice, after lunch on Thursday, she and William set off for Koreelah in the buggy. William spent the trip alternating between bouts of chatter and bouts of silence. The place looked wonderful. The recent rains made everything green again. Even the cane paddocks, now bare after the harvest, had a good show of green shoots coming through. Bert met them and, after meeting William, took care of the buggy while Ellen took William upstairs and introduced him to Maggie. "We will be here for a couple of nights this time – maybe three nights. Can you put up with another one dining with you and Bert? It seems too formal for just William and me to eat in that large dining room."

"Of course you should still eat with us. It'll give us a chance to get to know the young bloke, and we will be able to tell him a bit about the place and its history."

Jim called in just before dinner and they arranged for him to take William on a tour of the property after everyone collected their pay the next morning. Conversation over the dinner table that evening was rowdy as Bert and William established a lively repartee and swapped banter throughout the meal.

After the workers collected their pays, Jim caught up with Ellen for a chat. "I'll take William for a ride around the place as arranged and we should be back by lunchtime. Lunchtime came and went without any sign of William. It was after one o'clock when they returned.

Jim came straight over to apologise for their late return. "I'm sorry we're so late. I didn't think it was going to take nearly that long, but your son had questions about everything, and explaining things takes time." Lunch took a long time that day. William was so excited about what he'd seen and been told, he babbled on, barely taking time to draw breath – or to put food in his mouth.

By the time they finished lunch, most of the afternoon had disappeared. They took advantage of the opportunity to catch up on what had happened in each other's life over the last few years. Seated in the big wicker chairs under the house, they chatted on until it was time to freshen up for dinner.

Somehow– and with Bert and Maggie's help – William managed to persuade Ellen to allow him to breakfast with the single workers. Maggie explained she provided meals on the trestle table under the house for them whenever they were anywhere near the homestead at mealtime. The arrangement always included breakfast and the evening meal. Lunch they often ate out in the paddocks or wherever they were working. Later, Ellen admitted to Maggie that she didn't know why she was reluctant to let William eat with the men. "Maybe I'm concerned that he is growing up too soon, growing up before he's had a chance to be a child."

"…And maybe it's because you don't want to let him go – don't want to share him – now he is back with you," Maggie suggested. "The lad has grown up while you were apart. He's now somewhere between being a boy and a young man. It's only natural for him to want to be around other young men, and you will have to learn to accept this new situation if you don't want to lose him again… and I suspect you won't find that easy."

That night, as she waited for sleep to come, the wisdom of Maggie's words became obvious. Next morning, William woke early and rushed downstairs to join the other young men. By the time Ellen went for breakfast, Bert had eaten and gone, leaving Maggie and Ellen alone in the kitchen. "Thank you for speaking such wisdom last night. I believe what you said is right."

"Oh, I am right, you mark my words. You have to let them go if you want them to come back. Try hanging on to them too tightly and, like as not, they will rebel, run off and you might never see them again." Ellen nodded her understanding but didn't feel uplifted in any way by Maggie's words. William bounded up the stairs and into the kitchen, interrupting any further conversation.

"Some of the men are going to check the fences down by the creek. They might have a swim afterwards. I said I'd go with them." Ellen opened her mouth to protest but caught Maggie's steely eye and reconsidered her response.

"Sounds like a fine way to spend the morning but take care. We will expect you back here for lunch."

William raced off to join the others, and Maggie couldn't resist a comment. "I see you're a fast learner. Well done, my dear."

At a loss about what to do for the morning, Ellen wandered into the office and started idly flicking through paperwork lying on the desk. A few minutes later, Jim poked his head and asked if he could interrupt. Ellen nodded and motioned him to a chair. "I saw William ride off with the blokes this morning. Good to see he is settling in like that. I don't think there will be any question about what he wants to do – once you get around to asking him that question," Jim said.

Ellen nodded and admitted, "It is obvious, even to me, that he is happy here."

"Anyway, I didn't come to talk about William's future," Jim continued. "I really came to tell you what the plan was for today. Just before lunch, Cecil Glover and one of the other young men will ride across to the foot of the range to meet Bob Murchison with his mob. They'll cut out the stock needed and walk them across to Koreelah, dropping off Woodrow's stock at his place on their way past. It's better to collect the stock there than have Bob walk them all the way into town, and then for us to have to walk them all the way back here. They should arrive back here with the stock around mid-afternoon. We'll put the stock into the second yard until they get used to the place and we're sure they are okay. I imagine young William will want to come down to check on his bull."

"There would be no stopping him. I want to have another look at the new stock as well, so I'll bring him down to the yard with me."

"Straight after lunch, I'll head out to the boundary to wait for the boys and their charges. Once they are safely on the property, I'll ride back here to open up the yard for them."

She filled in some of the morning by writing a note to Sister Justina to share the good news of having found and rescued young William. Another 'anonymous' donation went into the envelope as an incentive for Sister Justina to keep looking for Marion, Ellen's other remaining child. Lunchtime arrived, but William didn't return until quite a bit later than expected. He arrived looking bedraggled after his swim, and bursting to tell Ellen about his morning.

Again, lunch was a protracted affair. By the time Ellen had cleaned up afterwards, it was time to head down to the yard to look at the new stock. Although Ellen assured him she was capable, William insisted on hitching up the buggy. When he went to take the reins, Ellen told him firmly, "This is my buggy and I drive it. Only in exceptional circumstances does anyone else drive me around in my buggy." William sulked all the way to the second yard, but he soon got over it when they arrived at the yard.

The stock had arrived. William jumped down from the buggy, ran over to the yard and climbed up onto the middle rail. "R e g gie," he bellowed, and the young bull came trotting over to him. ...But the bull wasn't the only one to react.

Over near the gate, a young lad on horseback twisted around in his saddle and yelled, "What?"

"Eh... who's that?" William asked as he stopped scratching the bull's nose and craned his neck to see who had answered. Then the bedlam broke out. William was over the top rail and running towards the lad on horseback. "Reggie, is it really you?"

The lad vaulted from his saddle and ran towards William. "Wills...!" he yelled. They ploughed into each other, wrapping their arms about each other, and tumbled to the ground together to lie in a scrambled heap laughing uncontrollably.

Through the racket they were making, they heard Jim. "Are you two all right? How about you get up and shake yourselves off a bit."

"Come on," William said, tugging at Reggie. They ran towards Ellen who stood on the bottom rail to watch the boys' reunion take place in the yard. The boys pulled up in front of Ellen. William, out of breath and over-excited, was unable to speak. Reggie was in better condition and spoke for the pair of them.

"Good afternoon, Ma'am. Apologies for our behaviour just now, we don't always carry on like that."

"She's not a 'Ma'am'," young William cackled. "She's mi mother."

"Oh, pleased to me you, Missus...uhmm...?"

"Everyone here calls me 'Miss'. You have a choice. You may call me 'Miss' too, or 'Mum' if you prefer."

"Mum...? I don't understand," Reggie said, his brow furrowing in confusion. "The copper said something about a new home, but..."

"I promised Sergeant Frankston that, if he rescued you from Sawyer, you could have a good home with me and William... if you wanted it. It is your choice whether you live with us or move on to somewhere else, but both of us would be happy if you chose to stay with us."

There was a fleeting moment of eye contact between the boys before Reggie responded. "Thanks, Miss, living with you pair sounds pretty good to me."

"Hey, Mis…" William started, but Ellen held up a finger to stop him.

"William, you also have a choice about what you call me: mum or mother… nothing else."

With a cheeky grin, he started again. "Yes, Mum, but I was going to ask if we could stay here again tonight instead of going back to town."

"I think that's an excellent idea. It's a bit late to be going back now, anyway."

"Good… and can we go back after lunch tomorrow so I can show Reggie around the place in the morning?"

Ellen was laughing as she replied. "I don't suppose it will hurt if we don't go back until tomorrow afternoon. Now, come on, let's get back to the house and clean up before dinner."

On their way home, Reggie walked his horse alongside the buggy. When they reached the homestead, Ellen left the boys to deal with the horses and the buggy while she walked up to the house. As she reached the bottom of the stairs, Elizabeth came out from under the house to meet her. "We've made up two beds for the boys in the bedroom down here under the house."

"I thought they would sleep upstairs," Ellen replied.

"We made up an extra bed upstairs as well but, if you want to get any sleep tonight, it is better that they sleep downstairs. They will be awake half the night giggling and yapping, and generally making a racket."

"Thank you; I hadn't thought about it. You are right; of course, those two won't do much sleeping tonight. I had better go and see Maggie about dinner, seeing as how there will be an extra one tonight, although you and she seem to have worked that out already."

"Jim called in on his way back from the boundary and told us about Reggie."

They ate in the dining room that evening and the boys, in raptures about sleeping in their own room under the house, retired early. After they left, Ellen realised she probably wouldn't see them again until lunchtime the following day. They would breakfast with the single men, and then William had his heart set on showing Reggie around Koreelah.

The next morning, when Ellen saw the single men leaving the house after breakfast, she went down to see how the boys fared on their own the previous night. Everyone else had gone, but the boys remained at the table chatting. Ellen pulled up a seat and joined them. Their time together didn't last long as William was keen to set off with Reggie. After reminding William that he must return in time for lunch today, Ellen rose to leave. She turned back to the boys and, with a serious look on her face, said gravely, "Well, William, you now have a serious problem to deal with." William blinked at her and opened his mouth but nothing came out. Ellen continued. "You are going to have to find a new name for your bull. You can't go on calling him 'Reggie'. It would be too confusing with two Reggies about the place."

"…But he knows his name and comes to it when I call him. He wouldn't understand if we changed it. I know what we'll do. We'll change Reggie's name… maybe we should call him 'John'."

Reggie's look of horror quickly disappeared as he realised William was teasing him. They both dissolved into gales of laughter. Ellen gave up and continued on her way. As she reached the bottom of the stairs, she heard Reggie quietly speak to William. "What's your mother doing here? Did she make a special trip so you could check on the bull?"

"…A special trip? No, she came to see her bull."

"What do you mean… her bull?"

William chuckled, "She owns the place; she owns Koreelah. Now, get up and come on so I can show you what she owns."

The boys chattered about Koreelah all the way back to town, leaving Ellen alone with her thoughts. Her most pressing problem was working out how she might fit another bed into the small bedroom she had allocated to young William. As soon as they arrived at the store and the boys dealt with the buggy, Ellen walked them through the store to the small storeroom at the end of the loading dock at the rear of the agency. She remembered they stored two small beds there when they cleaned out upstairs for Jess and Alfred to move in. The beds and their mattresses were still there.

Alfred, curious about the noise downstairs came down to investigate. "I didn't mean to disturb you, Alfred," Ellen apologised, and explained about needing the extra bed for Reggie. "Oh, I'm sorry, I haven't introduced you. Alfred, this is William's mate, Reggie. He was at the orphanage and suffered the same fate as William until they rescued him too. The two boys will stay here with me and will help in the store in the busy lead up to Christmas. After Christmas, they will move out to Koreelah."

"We can use the extra help. Do you want to move this bed now?"

"Perhaps we should wait until Charlie is here to help tomorrow. Besides, this is your day off and I don't want to intrude on it."

"We don't need Charlie. With these two strapping lads helping, we'll have this bed upstairs in no time. Come on, you pair; get on the other end of this bed."

While the others manoeuvred the bed out of the storeroom, Ellen rushed ahead to prepare the room for the extra bed. On her way up the stairs, a better idea occurred to her. She rushed through the living quarters to the bedroom previously occupied by her father. Yes, this was a bigger room and better suited to containing two beds. She pushed the existing bed to one side of the room and, when the bed arrived, had it placed on the other side of the room. Another trip and the mattress arrived as well. While the boys followed Alfred back downstairs chatting to him, Ellen made up the extra bed. Good, she told herself, this is where the boys will stay whenever they happen to be in town.

Over dinner that evening, Ellen acquainted the boys with her plans. "Tomorrow, we will go to buy you both new clothes – and boots – and then you will both get haircuts. After that, until Christmas, you will help in the store. There will be plenty to do: helping Alfred put orders together ready for collection or delivery, helping Charlie in the agency, and restocking the shelves. Much of Alfred's time will be taken up with deliveries, so he will need all the assistance he can get here at the store."

Her plans didn't meet with any horror, although the boys did exchange glances at the mention of haircuts. However, Reggie seemed troubled. "As I see it, there's only one problem with all that, Miss. I don't know anything about working in a store. I don't think I'll be much use."

"It's easy, Mate," William assured Reggie. "I did it for a couple of days before we went out to Koreelah. Alfred tells us what to do and I'll show you how."

The following day went according to Ellen's plan. She bought the boys clothes and boots and then left them at the barber's for their haircuts. On her way back to the store, Ellen called in to the Post Office to post her letter to Sister Justina. It was lunchtime before the boys returned to the store. Ellen suspected they spent the rest of the morning exploring the town, but now it was time for them to start helping in the store.

Alfred gave them a couple of orders to get ready for farmers to collect later that afternoon and, halfway through the afternoon, Jess asked them to bring in another bag of potatoes. Everyone was busy until closing time. The day didn't produce any problems and the boys chatted until bedtime about their day. It came as something of a relief that they seemed to have enjoyed themselves.

As she lay in bed that night, Ellen decided she would not take the boys with her on Thursday when she went to Koreelah. They would be more useful at the store, and she didn't want them getting any fancy ideas of moving to Koreelah until after Christmas. It wasn't just because they needed help in the store. Their brief time together until Christmas, would allow them to get to know each other better before they separated again.

Chapter 26

As fate would have it, Ellen's letter to Sister Justina crossed with one from the nun. The boat taking Ellen's letter south to Sister Justina had brought the one for Ellen. However, the contents of Justina's letter left Ellen in a quandary: what should she do about the possible clues the nun provided.

First thing the next morning, she took Sister Justina's letter to Mr Taylor's office. She would accept whatever the solicitor suggested as a course of action. Taylor arrived at his rooms at the same time as Ellen. He showed her straight into his office.

After explaining about rescuing young William from Tremaine, she got onto the information in the nun's letter. "Sister Justina managed to locate a couple of entries in the orphanage records that could be important. In the last couple of days before they closed the orphanage here, there was an entry made in the register: 'MJ into service'. Justina cross-referenced that entry and found a suspicious looking record of a donation: 'Donation by Mrs Braddock £15'. I can't help wondering whether the two entries refer to my daughter, Marion, whose initials are MJ."

"It sounds compelling," Taylor admitted, "But do we know anything about this Mrs Braddock – like where she comes from or anything else that would help locate her?"

"I'm not sure, but I asked Alfred if he knew of anyone by that name. He said there is a Braddock family on a big property on the north side of the river. Is there some way we can find out if this is where the girl went and whether it was my Marion?"

After promising to talk to her again within the next day or two, Taylor asked her to leave him to give the matter some thought. Ellen was disappointed when Taylor didn't contact her the next day, but Taylor had not wasted time after she left his office. He arranged to lunch with two good friends, the local magistrate and Sergeant of Police. Intrigued by the story, by the end of lunch, they had agreed a plan.

While Ellen waited, her frustration increasing, on Wednesday morning, Mr Taylor and the police sergeant rode out to the Braddock property. They agreed the police officer would do all the talking. At *Colevale,* *t*he Braddocks' property, a woman in her early twenties answered the door and showed them through to the sitting room to Mrs Braddock.

"Apologies for taking a few moments of your time, Madam, but we are investigating the disappearance of a young girl," the police officer began. "We have reason to believe she might have had help to disappear. I wonder if you wouldn't mind telling me, if all your household staff is present and accounted for."

"I can't believe you would dare to imagine any of my staff is involved. I assure you I carefully vet everyone I employ, and I would not consider employing anyone thought capable of such a thing."

"No, of course not, Madam, but we are carrying out routine enquiries at all the properties around the area. How many domestic staff do you have? Perhaps, if we might see them – to verify they are all here – we could be on our way again." Mrs Braddock rang a small bell, and the young woman who showed them in, appeared almost immediately.

"Crossley, please assemble all the domestic staff in the kitchen. We will be along there directly." The woman rushed off to comply with her mistress' request. After a moment, Mrs Braddock stood up and moved towards the door. "Gentleman, if you would follow me, we will go through to the kitchen…" There, she introduced her staff: Mrs Gordon, the cook, Crossley, the housekeeper, and Rosie, the housemaid. The two men exchange a questioning look at Rosie introduction.

"…And there is no one else?" the police officer asked.

"There is only the outside help, Winston. He does the garden and is my driver."

"Perhaps, if we could just see Mr Winston, we could be on our way and leave you in peace."

Mrs Gordon started to move towards the door that opened into the back garden, but stopped abruptly when someone knocked loudly on the door. The woman partially opened the door to the caller. "Good day to you, Mrs Gordon. I've brought your potatoes. Where do you want them?"

"Uhmm, would you wait outside for a few minutes please. It's not convenient just now. There are visitors in here, but they are just leaving."

"Right you are; I'll wait out at the wagon until you call me."

Mrs Gordon quickly closed the door and apologised. "Sorry about that, it's just the man making deliveries. He can wait until we're done here."

"Thank you, Mrs Braddock – ladies – we'll leave you to get on," the police officer said.

"I'll let you out this way," Mrs Gordon volunteered, so eager to have them vacate her kitchen.

The two men rounded the corner of the building and encountered an agitated Alfred pacing up and down beside his wagon. Alfred rushed up to the men, "Excuse me, Mr Taylor, were you just in the kitchen?" Taylor nodded and Alfred rushed on. "There was a young girl in there. I saw her when Mrs Gordon opened the door a bit."

"Calm down, Alfred. What has you so agitated?"

"That young girl that was in there, that's Marion Jennings, Miss Grimsby's missing daughter. Miss Grimsby has been looking for her everywhere, even had a nun helping her search the records for clues."

"Are you sure about this Alfred?" Sergeant O'Malley asked. "How can you be so sure? Do you know this Marion Jennings?"

"I took the children out to the orphanage with Miss Grimsby when they first came back to town. Then, when Miss Grimsby couldn't visit the orphanage anymore because her mother was too ill, she gave me letters and gifts to deliver to the children. I'd recognise Marion anywhere, and that was her in that kitchen just now."

O'Malley thought for a moment before giving Alfred directions. "Here's what you're going to do, lad. The cook can come out of that kitchen any minute now and tell you to bring her potatoes. You deliver the potatoes, act normal and, most importantly, you say nothing about this. Do you understand? You must not let on that you saw Marion. After you've delivered the potatoes, take your wagon down to that clump of trees over there at the start of the track and wait there until I give you a signal to come back to the house." Alfred agreed to the arrangement without hesitation. "Right then," O'Malley continued, "Look lively Mr Taylor. I believe we have more to be talking to Mrs Braddock about. Looks like we'll have to go around and knock on that front door again."

Crossley opened the door to them again. "I thought you were gone. Did you forget something?"

"Well, yes we did forget something… something else we need to ask Mrs Braddock about."

"I'm sorry; Mrs Braddock is not available right now. You will have to come back at another time, or perhaps I could give her a message for you when she is free." O'Malley was having none of that nonsense, and roughly pushed the young woman aside.

"No, I don't think that suits at all. I presume I'll find her in the sitting room," O'Malley said as he marched off in the direction of the room where they met Mrs Braddock earlier. Taylor, looking extremely uncomfortable, followed him, and Crossley fell in behind.

As O'Malley entered the sitting room, Crossley ran to the head of the queue. "I'm so sorry, Madam. I... I couldn't stop them," she blurted out.

"Thank you, Crossley. I'm sure you tried." Mrs Braddock added a sniff as she eyed O'Malley up and down.

O'Malley took charge. "Thank you, Crossley; we have things to discuss with Mrs Braddock in private. You're free to go about your duties. Please close the door behind you."

Mrs Braddock stood up, her face flushed with anger. "How dare you come in here ordering my staff about? Who do you think you are, and what right have you to come in here like this? You mark my words, O'Malley; I will be reporting your ruffian tactics to your superiors."

"Will that be before or after your appearance in court, Mrs Braddock?" O'Malley queried as he opened his notebook at a fresh page.

Mrs Braddock blanched and her hand flew up to twist the heavy necklace she wore. "What... What do you mean? What court case?"

"Oh, didn't I say? The court case that will follow after I charge you for people trafficking – because that's what buying a child from an orphanage amounts to, and it is illegal."

"I have no idea what you're talking about," the woman said with a toss of her hair and a false show of bravado.

"Ah, but I think you know very well what I'm talking about, Mrs Braddock. We have evidence of the transaction." With that, O'Malley opened the door and spoke to Crossley who was lurking in the hallway. "Crossley, would you ask the young girl, Rosie, to join us in the sitting room now, please." While they waited for Rosie to appear, O'Malley continued with Mrs Braddock. "As I was saying, we have evidence that you purchased a child from the local orphanage shortly before it closed down. In the face of that evidence, it seems pointless for you to deny it." ...But, deny it most strenuously she did.

O'Malley was losing patience. "Perhaps it's just as well the orphanage is gone. You won't be purchasing any more children from there."

"They were a waste of money, all of them. None ever stayed long and they were becoming more expensive," she muttered venomously, more to herself than anyone else.

"Unless I misunderstand you, you just then admitted that it was common practice for you to engage in such transactions."

Although in a hopeless position, again the woman strenuously denied any illegal activity. However, her denial, which turned into a tirade of criticism of O'Malley's character, ended abruptly after a gentle tap on the sitting room door. With obvious trepidation, the young housemaid took a couple of paces into the room and then stopped and twisted her apron into a ball. "You wanted to see me, Madam?" Before the woman could reply, O'Malley interjected.

"No, Miss; I asked for you to join us. I have a question for you: is your name Marion Jennings?"

The girl shuffled her feet nervously and, keeping her eyes downcast, avoiding eye contact with her boss. "I... Uhmm... I am called Rosie, Sir," she stammered.

"Well now, I'm sure you know how serious it is to lie to a police officer, so I'm going to give you another chance to answer truthfully before I consider what I need to do about the offence you just committed. So, the question is: are -you – Marion Jennings?" O'Malley spoke slowly and enunciated clearly while maintaining a hard gaze on the young girl.

"I didn't mean no offence, Sir, but the truth is, I used to be Marion Jennings but now I'm called Rosie."

"Thank you, Rosie. I think we might overlook that first little fib you told me. Now, you need to go quickly and pack up all of your belongings. We will be leaving here in a few minutes and you will be going with us."

"... But, please, you said you would overlook that I didn't tell you the truth the first time. Are you taking me to jail? Mrs Braddock, I don't want to go to jail. Is there nothing you can do to help?"

"No, I'm sorry Marion, Mrs Braddock can't help you. She has a few problems of her own to deal with right now. Anyway, we aren't taking you to jail. You haven't done anything wrong. No, my dear girl, were taking you to your mother who has been going out of her mind trying to find you. Now, off you go, and get packed up quickly so we can be off."

Rosie ran off, slamming the door behind her. A couple of moments later, a man burst into the room, demanding to know what was going on. "Ah, I assume you would be Mr Braddock."

"I am and Winston came to tell me there was some problem at the homestead. I have no idea why you are here, but you are way out of your league if you think you can come into my home throwing your weight around. I demand to know what is going on."

As he finished speaking, Rosie rushed into the room and, unaware of Braddock's presence, started speaking as she came through the door. "I'm packed and ready to go, Sir."

"Those uniforms are my property. You had better not think you're taking them with you," Mrs Braddock snarled at the young girl.

"No, she hasn't packed them, Mrs Braddock. I asked Crossley to wrap them up separately. I'll be taking them with me. They are now part of our portfolio of evidence."

Mrs Braddock bit her lip and, without raising her eyes to meet O'Malley's gaze, she asked quietly, "So, what happens to me now?"

"Well, that's not really for me to say. I'll put together all the evidence and give it to the magistrate along with my report on the investigation. The magistrate will study the case and decide whether you need to be charged and with what crime."

"Now, just you hold on a minute, O'Malley. What's all this nonsense about evidence and a crime? I demand you tell what is going on here," Braddock said as his gaze moved back and forth between his wife and O'Malley.

"No, I think I will leave it to your wife to explain why she may well be charged with people trafficking." As O'Malley and Taylor left the room, herding Rosie ahead of them, they heard a strangled squawk by Mr Braddock. "People trafficking? What the hell…"

"…And that's when the row began," O'Malley chuckled as they waited for Alfred to bring the wagon to the front of the house. "Okay, Rosie; we're going to put you on this wagon with this young bloke who is on his way back to town. He will take you to your mother. I think she might be in for something of a surprise, don't you agree – maybe even a shock?"

"In the interest of maintaining some appearance of propriety, I think it best if I ride back on the wagon. A young girl arriving on her own with a young bloke might raise a few eyebrows around town," Taylor suggested. What he didn't say was that he was more comfortable riding around in his carriage than on horseback. It was a long ride out to Braddock's property, and he had more than enough time on horseback for one day as far as Taylor was concerned. "If you wouldn't mind leading my horse back, I'll join them on the wagon."

Alfred brought the wagon to a stop in front of the trio and jumped down. "Marion!" he yelled as he wrapped her up in a hug.

Two big tears trickled down the girl's cheeks. "You told them; I hoped you would tell someone you had seen me, and that they would come and get me. I didn't think I would ever see you again. Oh, I can't believe I am going to see my mother again…"

"Come on; let's get you up on the wagon so we can start for home." As Alfred helped Marion up, Taylor dismounted and handed O'Malley his horse's reins. He loaded Marion's small bag of possession on to the wagon and then climbed on board himself.

"Right, Alfred, let's head for home. We have a surprise to deliver," Taylor said as he waved goodbye to O'Malley.

Nobody spoke much all the way into town, except for Taylor asking a couple of times if Marion was comfortable. After an exasperated look from Alfred, as they approached the outskirts of town, he fell silent as well. Alfred brought the wagon to a stop behind the store. Marion studied their destination for a moment before asking, "What's this place? I thought you were taking me to my mother. Why are we stopping here?" She started to become agitated.

"It is okay, Marion," Alfred reassured her and, with a meaningful look at Taylor, continued, "If Mr Taylor goes and fetches the owner, you will see why we stopped here." Although not convinced it was safe, Marion allowed Alfred to help her down from the wagon. He directed her to climb up and wait on the loading dock.

There was a rustle of skirts and Ellen came out onto the loading dock as Alfred passed Marion's bag across onto the loading dock. He heard a shriek and almost fell off the wagon as he turned sharply to see what was happening. Then the shriek came again. "Marion! Marion!" and then barely above a whisper, "Is it really you?"

Mother and daughter embraced and tears flowed freely. "I need to collect my horse from O'Malley," Taylor said, anxious to escape the emotional reunion. "I'll leave you to explain," he told Alfred.

"…But I don't know the whole story," Alfred protested, but Taylor was on his way out the front door of the store. He took care of the wagon and returned to the loading dock to find mother and daughter exactly where he left them. Alfred left them to their moment, walked quickly past and disappeared into the store.

Ellen picked up Marion's bag and led her upstairs. "This is your room," she told the girl as she pushed open the door to the small bedroom where William had slept the first night he was back and where Ellen had slept when she returned to live with her parents.

They chatted for a while before Ellen took Marion down and introduced her to Jess and Charlie. Jess took Marion under her wing and, after a familiarisation tour of the store and agency, started the girl's education on dealing with customers. When Ellen emerged from the office some time later, she watched with surprise as Marion cut and wrapped a block of cheese for a customer Jess was serving.

"…Not much I need to teach this one," Jess confided to Ellen later. "She's a quick learner and knows how to deal with people. It will be good to have her here when you go out to Koreelah tomorrow. With less than a week to Christmas, the store is really busy and, when it is as hot as it is at the moment, nobody likes to be kept waiting."

"I was going to take her with me to Koreelah tomorrow," Ellen said, and watched Jess' face fall. "However, I hear what you say. It is much better that she stays to help here this week."

"Thank you; I'll take care of her and they all can eat with me and Alfred tomorrow night while you are at the property."

"Oh, dear, I hadn't even thought about that. That is most kind of you, and I'm sure they will see dining at your table something of a treat."

Ellen left it until as late as possible on Thursday to head out to Koreelah, and left as early as possible on Friday morning to head back to town. As a result, she was back in the store by mid-morning. She walked into the store to find both Jess and Marion serving customers and three others waiting. Donning her apron, she quickly joined the others at the counter. Most of the day continued with customers keeping all three women busy until well after lunch. It wasn't until late in the afternoon that Ellen could retreat to the office to make up the pays for the staff.

As usual, they all gathered in the loading bay area after the store closed and Ellen handed the staff their wages. The two boys watched proceedings from their perch on a stack of bales of hay. "They do this at Koreelah too… first thing every Friday morning," William confided to Reggie, taking the opportunity to air his superior knowledge of all things Koreelah.

"William, Reggie, come on down here. I'm not going to come to you," Ellen told them. The boys exchanged a look, but did as asked. "Here you are Reggie and William, this is yours." Ellen handed each of them their wages.

Both boys stood blinking at the money in their hands, their shock evident on their faces. Neither of them spoke for a few moments.

Reggie recovered the power of speech first. "Is this mine?" Ellen nodded. "All of it?" she nodded again.

"It's a lot of money," William added, finally finding his voice again. "Are you sure we are supposed to get this much each?"

"If you work for me, I expect a fair day's work. In return for a fair day's work, you get a fair and proper wage. That is what you have earned by working in the store this last week. If you would like me to, I could take you to the bank so you can open your own accounts and start saving any money you don't need to spend immediately."

The 'pay parade' ended on high note that continued later when Ellen had her brood seated around her at the dinner table.

Chapter 27

For some reason, conversation at the dinner table that evening centred on Christmas and Christmas Day in particular. Perhaps it shouldn't surprise. After all, regardless of how much they had matured in many ways, they were still children and Christmas was only a few days away on Wednesday of the next week. The children seemed to relish sharing their memories of how they spent Christmas over the last few years. While Ellen joined in with the spirit of the conversation, her heart ached as she heard how much these youngsters missed due to their circumstances.

Late on Saturday afternoon, Frank Woodrow poked his head around the door to the office. "Oh, Mr Woodrow, you startled me. In town for the races today were you?"

"Yes, and I had a couple of things to take care of before Christmas. I see you have a new girl working out front."

"A new girl…? Oh, I see. Yes, she's my eldest daughter, Marion."

"That is great news! How did you manage to find her? I want to hear all about it."

"I will tell you the whole story, if… you agree to come to dinner with us this evening. I assume you are staying at the hotel tonight."

Well, I am now, Woodrow thought as he accepted the dinner invitation and agreed to return at seven o'clock. He left the store and crossed directly to the hotel, hoping against all odds that, on a race day, they would still have a room available. Luck was with him. The race meeting had ended at lunchtime and most of the patrons took advantage of the early conclusion to return home rather than staying in town.

That evening, the aroma of Irish stew mingled with that of freshly baked bread greeted Woodrow as he followed Ellen upstairs. They were sipping sherry in the sitting room when the three youngsters made a rowdy entrance. A chorus of 'good evening' greeted Woodrow. Ellen prevented any further conversation. "Dinner is ready. If you would lay the table please, we can eat. We will be five for dinner this evening."

The children stood by their chairs as Ellen and Woodrow joined them at the table. Woodrow moved behind Ellen to pull out her chair but stopped. "Ahem, I believe I haven't been introduced…" he said to Ellen.

"I do apologise; how remiss of me. Marion this is Mr Woodrow. You might remember him as the manager of the mill where we used to live. Mr Woodrow, this is my eldest daughter, Marion. There, that's the introductions taken care of."

"Not quite, I think," Woodrow said and looked directly at Reggie. Embarrassed, Ellen hastily made the additional introduction, but avoided telling Reggie's story by simply introducing his as William's friend. There was the scraping of chairs followed by bread and butter passed around as Ellen dished up the mutton stew. Once things settled down, William delivered the news he struggled to withhold since they came upstairs.

"Mum, is it okay if we go nextdoor this evening? Jess and Alfred asked us to come over for a game of charades. Charlie will be there as well." Permission was immediate. With the youngsters otherwise occupied for a while, she and Woodrow would have opportunity for the conversation Woodrow awaited: how she found Marion.

The moment the children were gone, Woodrow reminded her that she was going to tell him the story of finding Marion. "Come on; don't keep me waiting any longer. Tell me the story of bringing Marion home again. I didn't know you had any idea where she was."

"I didn't until Sister Justina sent me a couple of clues that she put together from the records of the orphanage. Marion's been here the whole time. This time the situation was a bit different. I didn't have the subterfuge of going to look at a bull, and I didn't have a clue how to go about it without getting into trouble. My solicitor, Mr Taylor, said he would think about the situation and get back to me with a possible plan. That was all I knew until Wednesday when Alfred came back from his deliveries with Mr Taylor and my daughter, Marion, on the wagon with him."

"What sort of approach did they use, and how did they manage to get her away?"

"I'm still piecing the story together. She only arrived here late on Wednesday, and then I was at Koreelah for part of Thursday and Friday. Today is the most time I've spent with her and we've been so busy there really hasn't been a chance for us to talk."

Woodrow's attention then turned to Reggie. He sought details of the lad's story, and asked what his future might be. Ellen outlined how William told her about his mate whose situation was similar to that of young William. She described Reggie's rescue from the Sawyer property. "So, he has become part of the family now. He and William will move out to Koreelah after New Year. Jim will see to their training. Elizabeth, Jim's wife, who was a teacher before her marriage, will spend some time each day with them making sure they catch up on the education they missed out on."

"What does Marion's future hold?" Ellen looked taken aback.

"I'm not sure what you're asking me. Marion will stay here with me, of course. She will help in the store. I will have to find a tutor for her to make sure she catches up on any missed education as well. That reminds me. I must write to thank Sister Justina and tell her of our success in getting Marion back – and send her a sizable donation again, I think."

"…And, what about you now?" He noted her perplexed look. "What will occupy you now that the quest to find your children is ended?"

"I have more than enough to occupy me: the store, the agency, Koreelah. How much more could I possibly need?"

"Yes, you have the businesses to run, but you have nothing else to drive you. You need to have a life as well as the businesses. With Marion working in the store now, there will be extra staff around. You will have more time to yourself. You need to have something worthwhile – some interest – outside the business to occupy your mind and your time."

"I hear what you say – and, maybe I will need and find something else to add to my life – but, for the moment, I don't think it will be quite as you see it. Jess and Alfred have been married almost a year. It is surprising they haven't started a family yet, but I'm sure that will happen soon enough. I just hope we have Marion fully trained by then so that she can take over from Jess when Jess has other things to occupy her."

"I understand your need for forward planning, but I am concerned that you haven't taken a break since your husband's death. You haven't allowed yourself time to live a little. There is more to life than running your businesses."

"When I became a widow and lost my children, I wanted people to pay for what they did. I told myself I wanted revenge, but somehow revenge wasn't enough. I wanted more than revenge. Is there something beyond revenge? I didn't know if anything lay beyond revenge, but if there were a heavier price to extract, that's what I wanted. I told myself I would do whatever it took, and I achieved what I set out to do. McCarthy and my father paid the price for what they did, and I am now able to give my children – what's left of them – a good life and guarantee them a sound future. Perhaps one day, William will run Koreelah and Marion will follow tradition by owning Grimsby's store. For now, all I want is a settled life… one with a comfortable routine and free of upheavals. A bit like yours is I suppose."

"How so like mine?"

"You have managed that mill for some years now and, while situations develop from time to time to break the routine, you have a comfortable ordered life that you can continue to enjoy for years to come if you wish."

"A-a-h, well, you can have too much of a 'good thing', as you see it. I don't want to spend the rest of my life managing that mill. As a matter of fact, I heard that a position might become vacant early in the New Year and I have let the right people know I might be interested." Ellen's face fell, revealing her feelings. "What's the matter, have I upset you in some way?"

"No, it was just so unexpected. I would be sad to see you leave town."

That's encouraging, Woodrow thought. "It's a long way from being a sure thing. I wouldn't expect to know anything until at least the end of January but, if I were successful in getting the position, I wouldn't be leaving town. I'd be moving into town. Let's not talk about it any further for the moment. Nothing might happen."

…But discuss it further – indirectly – they did: why was he looking elsewhere, was the unhappy at the mill, what did Mrs Langton think about it? Although Woodrow believed Mrs Langton would be happy if he moved into town, it was inappropriate to discuss the possibility with her at this stage.

"Speaking of Mrs Langton, would you care to spend Christmas day with us again this year and leave Mrs Langton free to spend the day with her family?" Ellen asked. "There will be more of us this year and I don't doubt it will be rowdier than it was last year with the young ones here now. Jess's mother has gone south to be with her other daughter for Christmas, so Alfred and Jess are having Christmas lunch with Alfred's family before coming back here in the afternoon to join us for dinner. Charlie has no family locally, so he will spend the day with us."

"I was beginning to think I wouldn't receive an invitation this year. I would be delighted to spend Christmas Day with you and your family, and I'm sure Mrs Langton will thank you again this year as well. I can't be sure but, in the hope that you would invite me here for the day again, I suspect she already has a pudding and a Christmas cake for you."

Their laughter mingled with the sound of children pounding up the stairs. Charades was over and the young players were starving, or so they claimed. Marion, ably assisted – or hindered – by the two boys, made supper for everyone. After an hour or so together, the youngsters retired to their rooms and Ellen saw Woodrow out the back door and on his way across the road to the hotel for the night.

Sunday's schedule of chores – housework and cleaning and tidying the store – took less time than usual when the three children insisted in helping. They even made paper chains and hung them up around the store and agency. It was the first time Ellen could remember that the store acknowledged the Festive Season in any way. However, Ellen felt a twinge of concern when she noticed the three youngsters in whispered huddles a couple of times during the day and again just before bed that evening. When finally compelled to ask if something was amiss, her enquiry met with feigned innocence and confusion.

*****

Christmas day arrived hot and sultry. The shower of rain during the night did nothing to alleviate the heat. Nevertheless, above Grimsby's Store, Christmas morning arrived to great excitement. The children were out of bed early. When Ellen emerged from her room to investigate all the noise in the kitchen, she found breakfast almost ready to go on the table. Breakfast disappeared quickly, and the dishes were dealt with in record time. Then the children went bouncing down the stairs laughing and chattering as they went.

Ellen had tasks of her own to attend to in their absence and dealt with them quickly. She was about to call the youngsters back upstairs when she heard them giggling on the stairs. They burst into the kitchen. A chorus of 'Merry Christmas' accompanied their arrival. Then, with sparkling eyes and wide grins, they thrust a large parcel at Ellen. She couldn't speak. The gesture had her so choked up; she could only beckon the children to follow her into the sitting room. Ellen led the way, her present held tightly to her chest.

The children tumbled into the room behind her. The sight of all the parcels laid out on the small table stopped them in their tracks. Finding her voice at last, Ellen simply said, "Merry Christmas everyone. Now, let's get down to the serious business of opening these presents." She gave each of the children a number of small items. The children had pooled their money and bought Ellen a hat and a small drawstring purse. Both items were gorgeous and things she probably would never buy for herself. She complemented them on their exceptional taste. The youngsters felt obliged to admit that, when Elizabeth was in town on Monday, they sought her advice on what to buy. Ellen wondered where she would ever wear the hat. It was beautiful but a frippery. A frothy bit of nothing one would wear to fancy social functions… which Ellen never attended and never received invitations to attend.

Frank Woodrow arrived mid-morning and breathed in the aroma of Christmas lunch baking upstairs. Ellen stood at the stove stirring the custard when Woodrow came into the kitchen. He deposited the pudding and Christmas cake on the kitchen table and passed on Mrs Langton's Christmas wishes. Charlie arrived soon after. The men and the boys set about organising a table in the loading bay area, and then the boys ferried downstairs in relays everything needed to lay the table.

Almost on the stroke of noon, Ellen and Marion carried the food downstairs. Lunch was a long leisurely affair that resulted in everyone so stuffed with food they were reluctant to move. However, after sitting around indulging in idle chatter for quite a while, Charlie suggested a game of cricket. There was unanimous support from the youngsters. A hastily laid out wicket on the rear driveway soon had a raucous game in progress. Woodrow helped Ellen clean up after lunch.

Then he and Ellen retired to the sitting room for a quiet time alone. Jess and Alfred arrived not long after the start of the cricket match and, if anything, the game became rowdier after their arrival. Marion wandered upstairs as evening rolled in and she and Ellen busied themselves with the evening meal. As they gathered up the food to take it downstairs, Marion confided to her mother, "Mum, this is the greatest Christmas I have ever had. Thank you… and I know the boys feel the same way." No reply needed, just a hug instead.

After dinner, everyone except Ellen and Woodrow adjourned to Jess and Alfred's place. As they traipsed off, they debated whether to spend the evening playing cards or charades. Ellen and Woodrow retired to the sitting room with glasses of port and slices of Christmas cake. As the evening crept on, Woodrow felt his resolve stiffen. Whether due to the port or something else, he finally felt able to broach a delicate subject.

"Ellen, I think you know how much I value our friendship and how strong that friendship has become over these past few years. If

I may be so forward, I'd like to ask if there is any chance it might develop a little further."

Ellen looked up at him from under her long lashes. "I think I would like to see where that might lead. However, I do have a proviso. I need to get the children settled and comfortable around me again before introducing anything unexpected into their lives."

"I appreciate that, but I think you might be surprised at how astute those children are and how much wiser than you give them credit for. Nevertheless, I understand what you say. I would not want to upset the children, so my suggestion is that I might come calling a little more often and see how they react. Perhaps you could accompany me to a function or two that I am obliged to attend occasionally."

With the colour rising in her cheeks and not trusting herself to look directly at him, Ellen replied, "I think I might find that an excellent approach."

Soon after, when the children returned, they went straight to the sitting room to say goodnight. They found the two adults looking very pleased with themselves – although a little guilty. "I wonder what they had been up to," William said as the boys climbed into bed.

"Wake up, Will," Reggie said. "Think about it for a minute. My bet is that we will be seeing a lot more of Mr Woodrow around here and a lot more frequently – you mark my words.

"O-o-h, do you really think so? That would be great. I like him a lot… and I think Mum does too. It's about time she had someone to take care of her. I wonder what Marion thinks about it."

"I don't think we should mention it to Marion. Let's wait and see if she makes some comment before we say anything."

The week between Christmas and New Year was uneventful until the heavens opened on New Year's Eve to let the rain come down in a heavy curtain over the town. Ellen's intention was for the boys to relocate to Koreelah straight after New Year's Day. For the boys, the week was one of eager anticipation. However, they suffered another of life's disappointments when the heavy rain flooded creeks, cutting the road to the property. They had to wait until the Thursday of the following week when Ellen made her routine visit to Koreelah before they joined the ranks of the workers there.

The heavy rain and flooded roads also caused the cancellation of the Turf Club's social event. Ellen held mixed feelings about the cancellation of the New Year's ball. Woodrow asked her to accompany him to the ball and the prospect of making their 'friendship' public made her nervous. Cancellation of the ball only delayed that situation, but at least it gave her time to adjust to the idea.

On her first trip out to Koreelah in 1902, and as the store wasn't too rushed, Ellen decided to take Marion with her. As Marion hadn't seen the place, it provided an opportunity for her to see the boys settle into their new lives and to meet the people there. There was only one problem with that plan. The buggy she used would not hold four people. An alternative was to take the store's wagon. It would serve the purpose well as the boys had now accumulated quite a bit of (new) gear to take out with them. Alfred assured Ellen her taking the wagon would not be a problem as he could take care of any required deliveries on Thursday morning before she left and on Friday after she returned.

The trip to Koreelah was an emotional affair. Ellen struggled with leaving the boys behind so soon after bringing them home again, and Marion seemed to relive the trauma of losing William all over again. Another emotion also snuck up on Ellen: jealousy. At one stage, she went looking for Marion and found her in the kitchen with Maggie. The cook was teaching Marion how to make her prize-winning scones. That's my job, Ellen thought. She's my daughter. I'm the one who should be teaching her things, not somebody else.

Besieged by such dark thoughts, Ellen called Marion from the kitchen on the pretext of wanting to show her around the grounds. "You'll have to finish making the scones yourself," was her parting terse comment to Maggie. Their unhurried inspection of the grounds took them around to the rear of the house. Marion stopped and waited for her mother to realise she wasn't walking beside her. Ellen turned and saw her daughter still standing beside the last rose bush they stopped to admire.

She started back towards Marion. "I didn't realise I had left you behind. Why have you stopped? Is something the matter?"

"Yes, I think there is," Marion said quietly. "Why did you speak to Maggie that way? What were you angry about? Surely, it wasn't because she was teaching me to make scones."

"N-o-o, you are right. It was kind of Maggie to do that. I was out of line and I will apologise to her for being so rude to her." Marion nodded her approval but remained somewhat withdrawn for the rest of the tour.

As they neared the end of the tour of the gardens, the boys came back to the homestead. Marion ran to meet them and they all sat together under the house. Ellen went upstairs to speak to Maggie. She apologised for her earlier comment and added, "I don't know what came over me. I value your friendship and appreciate all you do for us… and especially now, for helping to look after the boys."

"That's all right. I can recognise the green-eyed monster when I see it," Maggie replied quietly.

"…Green-eyed monster; what do you mean, Maggie?"

"You were jealous of Marion's time with me – and because I was showing her how to do something. You have only just found her and you're trying to hang on to the girl so tightly in case you lose her again that you run the risk of smothering her. You have nothing to fear. No one is going to take your place in that one's heart. Relax and enjoy your daughter. Now, shall we take these scones downstairs for afternoon tea for the hungry horde down there?" Before leaving for town, Ellen surprised Maggie by hugging her tightly and thanked her for her lesson as well as the one she gave Marion.

*****

Life adopted a steady rhythm. The boys settled in well at Koreelah and both Jim and Elizabeth were pleased with their work. Marion settled in well at the store, and the tutor Ellen engaged for her assured Ellen her daughter's education required little catching-up. On some occasions, Marion accompanied her mother on her trips to Koreelah, giving her the opportunity to keep in touch with the boys. Jim also took to sending the two boys to town whenever supplies needed collecting. The arrangement was for them to overnight at the store before returning to Koreelah.

On one such overnight stay, Marion confided to the boys that she thought something might be going on with Mr Woodrow. "He seems to be around more often, and Mum seems very happy to see him." The boys laughed and shared their thoughts about Ellen and Mr Woodrow. "Wouldn't that be wonderful?" Marion cooed, "Mum and Mr Woodrow together. She needs someone to share life and look after her. She could do a lot worse than Mr Woodrow. …But where would they live – you know – if they got together?"

The boys shrugged in unison. Such mundane matters were not in the scope of their thinking. However, William seemed deep in thought after Marion's comments. A few minutes later Reggie asked, "Where has Will gone? He was here a few moments ago. Did he say where he was going?" Marion shook her head. The three youngsters had retreated to the loading dock area and, perched on hay bales, had swapped yarns about their new lives.

"I didn't see Will leave. He will probably be back shortly," Marion told Reggie.

However, William had decided he had an important mission to undertake and that the time to do something about it was now. Ellen was enjoying the peace and quiet as she worked on the store's accounts. William's arrival startled her. "Hey, Mum, I need to talk to you about something important." Ellen's initial reaction was to chastise him for rudely interrupting her, but she decided against it, motioning him to take a seat instead.

"What's on your mind?" she asked.

"Well, Mum, don't you think it's time you looked at your situation? It's quite a few years since Dad died and you are not getting any younger. Mr Woodrow seems like a rum bloke, steady with a good job. We think you should make a move on him ... before you get too old or he gets away. How to make it happen might take a bit of working out, but we all reckon it's the right thing for you to do."

"You think it's the right ... oh, do you now? ...And who are the 'we' that you are talking about?"

"All of us: Marion, Reggie and me. I reckon Jess and Alfred would be happy to see it happen too."

"Have you been discussing this with them?"

"No, of course not; it will be a good surprise for them when you announce it. I did think about Charlie at one stage, but I decided he's too old for you."

"What makes you think you have the right to discuss my private life in this way... and to make such suggestions?"

"Well, the way I figure it, I'm no longer young William any more. I'm the only William in this family since my father died... and, I suppose that also makes me the man of the house. So, I see it as my duty to give you some advice. We're all in favour of it you know – in case you think it might upset someone." Ellen found herself too stunned to speak. She didn't know whether she was upset or wanted to laugh. "Anyway, Mum, that's all I wanted to say. I'll leave you to think about it now." With that, William was out of the office and gone in a flash, leaving Ellen staring at his empty chair and wondering what had just happened.

With his hands in his pockets and whistling off-key, William joined the others on their hay bales. The smile he couldn't keep off his face was a dead give-away that he had been up to no good — and so Marion told him. "Okay, I can tell you've been up to something. What have you been doing?"

"Nothing much; I just went to give Mum some advice."

"…About what?" Marion persisted.

"…About Mr Woodrow." The only response was two incredulous stares, followed by gales of laughter.

On reflection, Ellen knew that at some time in the future, when she retold William's advice to her, she and Woodrow would laugh. Just when the right time for that would be was something she wasn't sure about.

As Ellen came out of the Post Office one day during the last week in January, she thought she saw Frank Woodrow ride past on horseback. She thought it unusual for him to be in town so early in the day, and almost succeeded in convincing herself it was a case of mistaken identity. However, part of her kept insisting she had seen Woodrow. It shouldn't have been a surprise when he came into the store before lunchtime.

Ellen was serving a customer, so he loitered among the shelves until she was free. As the customer left the store, he rushed up to Ellen and asked, "Could I have a few minutes of your time, please – in private." She led him through to the office and he closed the door behind him. "I know you are busy," he apologised, "But I need to talk to you. I won't take long."

She giggled. "Perhaps it won't take long once you start telling me what's on your mind."

"Okay. Remember, I told you a position might become vacant soon and I made it known I was interested. They asked me to put in a formal application, which I did. I didn't hear anything more until a couple of days ago when I received a request to attend a meeting. I thought it was to attend an interview. I was wrong. It wasn't an interview; they offered me the position. I've got the job!"

Ellen found herself echoing his words. "So, it wasn't an interview. You got the job. The one you were interested in, I presume. Congratulations… I suppose. Now, tell me what that really means." Woodrow, nonplussed by the request, simply shook his head and didn't answer.

"Perhaps you could start by telling me about the job – like where it is and what you will be doing…"

"Didn't I say…? It's with the Shire Council. I will be their new Chief Officer."

"…Sounds interesting; what does a Chief Officer do?"

"The Chief Officer manages all the work the Council does throughout the Shire. He is the Council's manager."

"…And you wanted this job? One that isn't so very different from the one you have. You still will be answerable to a group of elected members, and will be managing a large workforce."

"Yes, again I will be working under the direction of a group of elected people whose re-election depends on the performance of me and my employees, but the challenges are different – more varied and not so seasonal. The intention has always been to retire to my property, but I am not ready yet to give up the challenges – the excitement of the cut and thrust – of running a large organisation. …Maybe only for a few years until my retirement."

"When do you start your new job?"

"In two weeks."

"Two weeks…! You have so much to do, including finding somewhere to live. You won't be able to continue in the manager's house on the mill's estate."

"There are a few places available to rent. I'll talk to an agent after everything is official."

"You mean it isn't official yet?"

"There are steps to take; people to tell. Firstly, I need to accept the position in writing. I'll call on the chairman of the mill directors on my way home and officially resign. He can advise the others at their board meeting tomorrow. After that, I can start to tell staff and employees. However, I will discuss it with Mrs Langton tonight. She's been hinting that she would like to move to town to be closer to her youngest daughter who is the only one of her brood still living here."

"Well, we probably won't see much of you over the next couple of weeks while you get yourself organised for your new life."

"Ah, yes, but then you will see much more of me. I will be living close by in town. May I prevail upon you for some writing materials, please? I need to give the Mayor my formal acceptance of the position and give the chairman of mill directors my written resignation." Ellen laid out the requisite writing materials on the desk and left him to get on with his tasks.

It was the following Saturday evening before Woodrow again visited the store. Ellen enquired how his house hunting had progressed. "Very well and in an unexpected way," he replied. "After the board meeting and the directors knew of my resignation, one of the directors approached me. He bought a house in town some time ago when his wife became ill and needed constant medical treatment. It also was his intention that the house would become their retirement home in a few years when his son took over running the property. However, his son died in the Boer War late last year. His death seemed the final blow for his ailing mother who succumbed to her illness just before Christmas. He will charge me a peppercorn rental to live in and look after the house."

"Things seem to be falling into place for you. What will they do about a replacement manager for the mill?"

"I think they might appoint John Dowling as interim manager to ensure the maintenance programme isn't disrupted, though I doubt he would want the job on a permanent basis."

"This next week will be busy for you. Is there any way we can help?"

"Thank you, but no. I've already started moving my stuff into town. I brought another wagon load in today… and Mrs Langton has cleaned and fussed over the new house ever since I got the keys."

Frank Woodrow's move to town appeared trauma-free, although he did dine with Ellen and Marion most nights during that last week, dropping in for a meal after bringing in a load of his belongings after work. It took little time for news of his appointment to flood the town, and it seemed to receive a favourable reception.

*****

Life took on an added dimension for Ellen. There was the annual weekend-long grudge cricket match with the Ralston team that involved a couple of social events, to which Woodrow asked her to accompany him. There was expectation that Woodrow and partner would attend the debutante ball that occurred around mid-year. Various other Council-sponsored events for which Woodrow required a partner dotted the latter half of the year. Ellen found her social life expanding and her wardrobe needing to match it.

In early-September, for the first time since she started at the store, Jess was too ill to come to work… nothing alarming in that. However, when she remained too ill to work the following day, Ellen began to wonder. She took Alfred aside when he returned from lunch and asked after Jess. "She seems to improve a bit in the afternoon but is struck down again the next morning," he said.

"What do you think it might be? Should she see a doctor do you think?"

"Nah, it's probably just a touch of food poisoning or some bug that's going around. She's a strong lass; she'll beat it."

"You don't think Jess might be pregnant then?"

"Pregnant…? O-o-h, I don't… Do you think it's possible?"

"There's not much point in asking me that question," Ellen laughed. "Is it possible?"

"Well, truth is, she has been a bit down – a bit disappointed, and worried I think – that it hadn't happened before this. A baby…! I don't think either of us would be game to hope that might be the cause of it – not after all the disappointments we've had like." Later that afternoon, Ellen went up to visit Jess, and to suggest dry toast and weak tea for breakfast.

A couple of mornings later, Jess arrived for work along with the rest of the staff. She looked pale and was a bit tentative all morning but improved as the day went on. Ellen found time to ask her the same question she had put to Alfred: was Jess pregnant? "I'm not game to think I might be. I don't want another disappointment. I've almost convinced myself I can't have children, although I haven't said as much to Alfred," she admitted.

After a few weeks, even Jess had no doubts about it. In a few months, the peace above the agency would disappear with the arrival of a baby… and Jess would not be available to help in the store. There was nothing for it, but to make some changes. The population had grown, the town was expanding and the store and agency had never been busier. It was clear to Ellen that, when Jess no longer became available to help in the store, Ellen would not be able to go out to Koreelah every week. She needed to talk to Elizabeth about taking over the office work for her.

Perhaps Jim and Elizabeth should move into the homestead. That would leave their cottage free for another young worker who was about to be married. She was pleased Woodrow was now close by as she found herself asking his opinion on many things these days. Whether to move Jim and Elizabeth into the big house was another matter on which to seek his advice.

"Do you not intend to visit Koreelah at all once Jess has the baby?" Woodrow asked.

"No, I would need to visit occasionally, but not every week. Only time will indicate how often I need to visit. I could stay in the little cottage I lived in when I first moved there, so I would still have somewhere to stay without imposing on Jim and Elizabeth if they were in the homestead… and I could still eat with Maggie and Bert." Woodrow agreed it probably was a sound move and Ellen resolved to initiate the change on her next trip to the property.

Chapter 28

Life was good, although busy both business-wise and socially, but it had a settled and satisfying rhythm to it. It was a long time since Ellen felt so settled and happy. Then, towards the end of October, she faced a new dilemma. Woodrow posed the *big question.*

Late Wednesday evening, after Marion went to bed, Woodrow stunned Ellen by dropping onto one knee in the sitting room and proposing. "Would you do me the honour of becoming my wife?" he asked. Ellen's mouth opened but no words came out. She clapped her hand to her sagging jaw. "Please say yes … or that you will at least consider it," he beseecher her.

The power of speech returned. "Yes, yes, I will marry you," she whispered. "However, you know the fate that befell my previous two husbands," she continued at last feeling stronger. "Are you prepared to risk such a fate? Please say yes … or that you will at least consider it," she mimicked him and giggled.

Suddenly, he wrapped her up in his strong arms and his warm lips eagerly found hers. Is this a proper thing to be happening in my sitting room, she wondered as she felt her heart thumping wildly? Somewhere from the deep recesses of her conscience came the response, 'who cares', and she had no argument with that. When some degree of decorum and composure reigned once more, it was time to make plans. It was also time to tell Woodrow of William's advice to her.

"We need to talk this over with the children first and get them comfortable with the idea before we go any further," Woodrow said gravely. "We have to consider the fact that they might not approve."

Ellen laughed. "Oh, I don't think we have a problem there. Let me tell you about a conversation William had with me." By the time she finished telling the story, they both had dissolved into laughter.

"That is the second best bit of news I've had tonight. Should we wake Marion and tell her?"

"N-o-o," she protested. "I know the boys are coming into town on Friday and staying the weekend before returning to Koreelah. Perhaps we could have a family dinner and break the good news then… and, if it goes well – as I believe it will – we could have Alfred, Jess and Charlie join us for a drink after work on Saturday and we could tell them then."

"I'll wait till after we tell the youngsters before I tell Mrs Langton. She will be beside herself when she hears. She has been dropping none too subtle hints for some time for me to do something about us."

"I just had a worrying thought. What will become of Mrs Langton when we marry?"

"I have a sneaking suspicion there won't be a problem."

Selection of a date for the wedding turned out not to be as difficult as they both expected. Christmas was the obvious choice. That is when the store closed for a couple of days. Woodrow also would have those days off. Where to have the wedding proved more problematic. After looking at various options, Woodrow suggested the Turf Club as a venue for the ceremony followed by a luncheon for a few guests. He thought he could persuade the local magistrate to perform the ceremony there if the wedding was on Boxing Day rather than Christmas Day.

By the time Friday evening arrived, basic plans were in place and the couple felt equipped to answer any questions the children might have. Ellen had even decided on her attendants: Elizabeth and Marion. Woodrow would have William but needed to choose another adult. Even the magistrate had agreed to perform the ceremony – provided he could stay on for the luncheon, he had added tongue in cheek.

With the three youngsters seated and dinner on the table, Woodrow and Ellen stood nervously together at the head of the table. The usual rattle of plates and cutlery stopped as they became aware that the adults had not taken their seats. Woodrow broke the news.

"I know you all are hungry but, if you could just give me a moment, I have something to share with you." There were exchanged glances, but none of the children objected, so Woodrow plunged on. "A couple of days ago, I asked your mother to marry me. She said yes. We wanted to wait until you were all together to tell you and ask for your blessing to go ahead with the wedding." By the time he finished speaking, three beaming faces focused on him. They cheered and clapped. The boys rushed up and shook his hand. Marion hugged her mother.

"Am I safe in assuming there is no opposition to our marrying?" Woodrow asked. A loud chorus of 'YES' rang out, followed by William's assurance to Woodrow that his assumption was correct. "There is one other thing," Woodrow continued. "We would like to tell the rest of Grimsby's staff before anyone else finds out. We were thinking we would ask them to stay back for a drink after the store closes tomorrow so we can tell them. In the meantime, we ask you not to spoil the surprise by talking about it before we tell them." Assurances all round that they wouldn't mention it.

Excited babble accompanied dinner, but Ellen notice that Marion became increasingly quiet as the meal progressed. Later, when she and Marion were alone doing the dishes, Ellen asked the question. "You have gone quiet and I think something has upset you. What is wrong?" Marion needed persuading to open up. She burst into tears.

"I am really happy for you, Mum, truly I am… but what happens to me when you get married? Where will I live… will I have to go somewhere else again?"

Ellen wrapped her daughter in a tight embrace and kissed the top of her head. "You will live here, just as you do now. You will continue to live here with Woodrow and me. Why would you think it would be different?"

"I thought you would go to live with Woodrow at his house… and I knew you wouldn't let me live here alone." Ellen spent some time reassuring the girl before they joined the others.

The 'Three Musketeers' – as Woodrow had taken to calling them – went to see if Jess and Alfred were up for a game of cards. Woodrow and Ellen settled down with a glass of port. After a few moments of enjoying the peace and quiet, Ellen had a disturbing thought. "I think we might be wise to change our plan. Those three are not going to keep a secret all day tomorrow. If you came to the store early tomorrow before we opened, we could gather the staff together then to share our news." Woodrow saw merit in her plan and agreed.

"Before the others come back, I have something for you." Woodrow withdrew a small box from his pocket and opened it. Ellen gasped. "As it is now official – well, official as far as those who matter are concerned – I thought it only proper that we let the rest of the world know that you are now spoken for." With that, he removed a little sapphire ring from the velvet-lined box and slipped it on Ellen's finger. "I hope it fits and, more importantly, that you like it."

Tears streamed down Ellen's cheeks. All she could do was nod. She couldn't speak. After a couple of moments, she found enough voice to whisper, "It's beautiful. I've never had anything like it before. I love you, Frank Woodrow." Somehow, all of a sudden, Boxing Day seemed like an eternity away.

Composure barely returned to the sitting room before the youngsters returned. "Jess was tired, so we only played one hand… and she won that anyway," William announced. As they traipsed off to bed, Woodrow took his leave as well. He hoped to catch Mrs Langton before she turned in for the night.

Woodrow's early arrival at the store that Saturday morning caused a few curious looks from the youngsters. Ellen asked the boys not to go anywhere until after the store opened, but they weren't going anywhere. They told her they had arranged to help Alfred with something first thing, so they probably would spend most of the day at the store.

Ellen gathered the staff in the loading area as they arrived to start their day. Woodrow's presence attracted curious looks. As soon as all had arrived, Woodrow, keen not to delay the opening of the store, took charge of proceedings and delivered the couple's news. Stunned silence prevailed for the length of a couple of heartbeats before rowdy congratulations filled the space.

It seemed like an ideal opportunity for Ellen to ask Jess if she would be her Matron of Honour at the wedding, and if Marion would be a bridesmaid. Woodrow also asked William if he would stand up with him. Excited babble and shaking of hands erupted. Ellen clapped her hands loudly to catch everyone's attention. "Perhaps it might be as well if we opened the store sometime this morning," she said. Everyone laughed and moved off to start their usual morning tasks.

As she saw Woodrow off, Ellen asked if he managed to catch Mrs Langton before she retired the previous night. "I'm surprised you didn't hear her shrieks of joy from here," he said with a grimace. "She was so excited, I doubt she got much sleep last night and she hadn't surfaced when I left this morning."

"Is she aware that she won't have a job after we are married? I am concerned that might impact on her joy."

"She couldn't be happier. Her youngest daughter, who is Mrs Langton's only child still living in town, wants her mother to move in with them. I think the daughter wants her there to help with the children – there are already a few and another on the way. Still, Mrs Langton seems extremely happy to be free to move in with them."

Almost immediately, Mrs Langton and Ellen's two attendants began holding planning sessions. By the end of November, they had decided decorations for the venue and the menu. Mrs Langton announced she would not provide a Christmas cake that year, as she would be making a wedding cake instead. None of the women thought

Ellen should bother herself with any of such details and didn't bother to consult her. At first, all the fuss embarrassed Ellen, but her protests were to no avail. She eventually accepted that the three women were enjoying themselves immensely and left them to it. Her contribution to the planning was to ensure that – although not a white wedding – she and her attendants had outfits that would have them looking stunning on the day. She was amazed that Woodrow seemed to get the males in the wedding party organised with virtually no fuss or bother at all.

In 1902, Christmas Day became something of a lack-lustre event. While there were presents and the usual meal with staff, everyone's attention focused on the Boxing Day big event. Jess sent Woodrow home early as the bride 'needed to get her rest'. William and Reggie would go across to Woodrow's house first thing in the morning and stay there until they all left for the wedding.

William would get dressed along with Woodrow and John Dowling. There was a special outfit for Reggie who would drive the men of the wedding party to the Turf Club in Woodrow's carriage. Woodrow provided Alfred, who would drive the women to the Turf Club, with an outfit similar to Reggie's. He got dressed at home – after spending the early part of the morning cleaning and polishing the store's buggy to a gleaming chariot for the bride and her attendants. Charlie refused Woodrow's offer of a fussy outfit, but settled for an elegant suit, which he considered befitting the dignity of walking the bride into the venue.

The day began hot – no surprises for so late in December – but not as humid as the previous few days. Ellen forced herself to endure the primping and fussing metered out by her attendants. They readied themselves early in the morning and then devoted every minute until they left for the Turf Club fussing over the bride. Almost bursting with pride, Alfred helped each of the ladies onto the buggy before climbing aboard himself and taking up the reins.

"Where are you going?" Ellen asked as Alfred drove off in the wrong direction for the Turf Club.

"Ssshh," whispered Jess. "You have to be late. It's tradition. If we went directly to the venue, we would arrive on time. Alfred knows what he is doing. Enjoy the ride and your last couple of minutes as a single woman." Once again, Ellen felt it wise to let others enjoy themselves organising her and her day. Charlie told her later, she arrived at the Turf Club a couple of minutes late and was about three minutes late by the time he walked her to the table set up for the ceremony.

It seemed the day was so long coming only to be over so quickly. The ceremony was a simple civil affair and took no time at all. After toasting the newly married couple, the fifteen guests took their seats at tables set out in front of the main table. Jim, who sat at the main table with the bridal party, was Master of Ceremony. To everyone's relief, there were only a couple of speeches.

The food and service at the luncheon were excellent. It wasn't until one of the breaks between courses that Ellen found a moment to admire the decorations Mrs Langton and her helpers organised. Coloured streamers artfully hung from the ceiling and around the walls. Fresh flowers – although limited in variety at this time of year – decorated a rudimentary arch behind the bride and groom's places at the top table, and small posies of flowers and fern brightened each of the guests' tables. On a small table off to one side of the room sat a simple wedding cake alongside a long, frightening looking knife that sported a fussy loopy bow.

It was mid-afternoon before the last of the guests left the Turf Club. The two boys left on Koreelah's wagon with Jim and Elizabeth. Marion joined Bert and Maggie in Koreelah's buggy, while Alfred, Jess and Charlie departed in the Store's buggy. Woodrow reclaimed his carriage, and the newlyweds trotted off to Woodrow's house where they would spend the weekend. Over the weekend, they moved Woodrow's belongings into the residence above the store. Other material not moving to the store – such as furniture – would go out to his property sometime during the following week.

With the youngsters at Koreelah for the weekend, the dwelling above the store was vacant. However, Ellen felt more comfortable spending her wedding night and Saturday night somewhere a little more private. Woodrow's place was ideal. With Boxing Day falling on a Friday, the store would open as normal on Saturday. As Marion and Ellen were away, the three other staff members would have to manage on their own.

By Sunday night, Woodrow had moved in above the store and the couple spent their first night together there. The boys would bring Marion back on Monday morning when they brought the wagon in from Koreelah to collect supplies from the agency.

Monday was normal. Woodrow went to work and Ellen went downstairs to greet the staff and open up as usual. Marion returned about nine o'clock to a store full of customers waiting for attention.

She dropped her small bag in the office and began work immediately. It wasn't until after closing and they went upstairs that a degree
of awkwardness crept in. Ellen found herself feeling quite self-con-
scious about going off to bed with Woodrow. That situation continued for a couple of nights until Ellen realised Marion had paid it no
attention and seemed not to give it any thought.

*****

Life was indeed sweet. The years slipped by, each one seemingly
faster than its predecessor. One evening after Jess went off to choral
practice, Ellen wrote up her journal as Woodrow sat reading the paper
and sipping his brandy. There was little to enter for that day and,
instead of writing, she found herself reflecting on the past few years.
The memories brought a smile to her face, a smile that Woodrow
noticed when he happened to glance up from his newspaper.

"What do you find so pleasing in your journal tonight?" he asked.

"It's not what's in the journal; I was remembering. Our fifth
wedding anniversary is almost here, and I was reflecting on all that
has happened over those years. The store and Koreelah have continued to do well – very well – and have made me a wealthy woman. The
building project started three years ago has modernised and expanded
the store and agency floor space. It also provided for an extra bedroom
to the apartment above the agency. Just as well, as Jess and Alfred's
twins are growing fast and will soon need their own rooms. The back
verandah that runs along the length of the rear of the building and over
the rear driveway now provides an undercover loading and unloading
area for wagons. Jim is an excellent manager of Koreelah, and he tells
me the boys are his key workers… and that William has other special
skills that will make him a good manager one day. Marion has many
interests in the town. Tonight she is off practising for the Christmas
concert, and she is now an accomplished pianist."

"When you list it like that, one realises there is much to be thankful
for. …And, for me, those five years have been truly blissful."

Ellen laughed. "I remember someone saying he would only stay
at the Council for a few years until ready to retire. That was almost
six years ago, but I don't see any sign of retirement looming on the
horizon yet."

Woodrow, smiling sheepishly, considered her comment for a
couple of moments. "I do remember that rather rash statement. You're
right though, I still don't feel ready to retire. Maybe in a couple more
years, who knows? Does it bother you that I continue to work? If it

comes down to it, I don't think you are ready either to give up the store and move out to my property with me."

"It is no bother at all, and you are right, I enjoy what I do here. However, these days there are times when I find it exhausting… but not sufficiently so for me to want to give it up yet."

"What will our retirement look like — from your point of view I mean?"

"I'm sure we will be very happy living out on your property, Rangelands. Koreelah is safe with Jim who is unlikely to leave or retire until William is old enough to take over. Marion is wonderful in the store and will be a good manager one day when she is older. I imagine Alfred would manager the store and the agency if needs be until Marion was old enough to take over. The only change I see is the loss of Bert and Maggie. They are retiring and moving to town sometime early in the New Year. They bought Mrs Smith's tearoom to keep Maggie occupied when they move to town. Mrs Smith will continue to run it until Maggie takes over. Jim is still deciding what to do about a replacement gardener/handyman for Bert."

"Well, it seems all is well with the world now and for the future. The next big thing to think about is Christmas and having everyone together for a few days. Mrs Langton, although she no longer works for me, has asked if she may make our pudding and Christmas cake again this year – as she has done for the last five years. I said yes, and invited her to dinner with us on Christmas night. She said she would come: if the grandchildren are okay, and she can get away. It's what she says every year, and every year I collect her and she dines with us here."

"Sometimes we do need to stop and reflect. It is only then that we realise how lucky we are and how good our life is."

*****

Christmas came and went following its usual pattern. The only difference that year was that Alfred's twins were taller and noisier than previously. Everyone doted on them and the adults spent much of the day keeping them amused playing various games. Before the boys left to return to Koreelah, Reggie asked if he could speak to Ellen privately. She took him into the office and closed the door. "It looks like you have something serious on your mind. What's bothering you, Reggie?"

"You know I love being at Koreelah and I appreciate all you have done for me and the opportunities given me, so I don't want you to think me ungrateful."

277

"But…?"

"Well, yes, there is a 'but'. Charlie mentioned in passing that he was thinking of retiring sometime within the next couple of years."

"Yes, he has mentioned a period of one to two years. I don't know how we will ever replace him."

"Uhmm, I was wondering if you might consider training me to replace him. I've always thought it would be interesting to work in a farmers' agency and, since I've spent time here and around Charlie, I know that is exactly what I want to do for the rest of my life. With my time at Koreelah and everything else I've done, I'd bring a good bit of experience to the job. Would you at least consider it, please?"

"It comes as a surprise, but I will give it some thought, and I'll discuss it with Charlie, of course."

"There's just one other thing. If you do agree, could I please work with Charlie for a while before he leaves? There is so much about the agency side of things he could teach me." Ellen assured Reggie she would give his request serious consideration, and the lad went back to Koreelah at least hopeful of a positive outcome. Reggie's long-awaited news didn't come until almost mid-1908.

When the lads were in town early in May, Ellen called Reggie aside to tell him she and Charlie agreed that he was the right person to take over the agency from Charlie. "I still need to talk to Jim about robbing him of one of his workers but, unless he strenuously objects, you can start in the agency under Charlie's direction at the beginning of June." Jim was surprised and disappointed but didn't object.

About twelve months later, in a quiet moment, Ellen confided to Woodrow that she suspected something was developing between Marion and Reggie. "You must be imagining it. They're both kids," Woodrow said.

"No, they are no longer kids. Marion is almost twenty and Reggie is about twenty-two. I'm sure I see romance blossoming between them."

"Does that worry you? Would it worry you if it did develop into something serious?"

"No, of course not, I would be very happy for them – if it works out – but, by the same token, I don't want to see either of them hurt."

"Part of growing up is learning to deal with hurt occasionally. You can't protect them from everything. Your job is to be there to pick up the pieces if things fall apart." Her concerns remained although she knew Woodrow was right.

Chapter 29

Early in 1910, Woodrow confided to Ellen that he was thinking of retiring soon – maybe at the end of the year. "How would that sit with you? Would leaving here and moving to Rangelands disrupt your plans too terribly?"

"No, I don't think it would. Just the other day, I was thinking how I felt ready for a quieter life. I would need to train Alfred up to manage the store. Reggie will be fine to take over from Charlie when he leaves at Easter, and Marion is old enough to live here on her own – and maintain somewhere for us to stay when we come to town."

"I don't know if you have been paying attention, but I don't think Marion is contemplating living on her own for too long." Ellen raised her eyebrows enquiringly. "You must have noticed that Reggie and Marion were 'an item' over recent months. I wouldn't be surprised to hear mention of wedding bells in the not too distant future."

Soon after Easter, Reggie sought out Woodrow and Ellen to ask their permission to marry Marion. Woodrow gave Ellen a smug look. "You only need her mother's permission, lad," Woodrow said.

"I'm delighted for you both. I couldn't be happier than to have you 'officially' become a member of the family. When were you thinking of getting married?"

"We haven't really set a date, but we were thinking a time around the end of the year would work best – maybe even at Christmas."

"That would suit us," Woodrow said. "I was thinking of retiring then and we would be moving to Rangelands. You and your new wife would be able to move in here. What do you think, My Dear, does that suit you?"

"Ellen was brimming with joy. "Perfectly!" was the only response she could manage.

Although planning for the wedding started slowly, it quickly moved into full swing and went on for months. It would be a traditional church wedding and reception, and that meant there was plenty to organise… apart from the bride's wedding gown. Reggie asked William to be his Best Man – no surprises there — and Marion asked Jess to be Matron of Honour. Bella and Ben, Jess and Alfred's twins would be flower girl and pageboy. Maggie took charge of catering for the reception in her newly expanded tearoom.

December proved a busy time for Ellen. Mid-December, Woodrow retired. There were several farewell functions and parties to attend. As well, Ellen found herself embroiled in final wedding preparations and various parties and morning teas arranged by Marion's friends who would not be attending the wedding. Neither Marion nor Ellen felt as though they spent much time in the store during December. Woodrow and a couple of helpers spent the week leading up to Christmas moving belongings out to Rangelands. Anything he and Ellen wouldn't need during the coming two weeks went to the property.

For the week prior to the wedding, Reggie moved in with Bert and Maggie. There was too much wedding-wise happening above the store. He accepted it was inappropriate for him to be living in the same place as the bride right up to the wedding and grudgingly moved out for the week.

Although it was a Saturday, the store and agency closed on Christmas Eve for the wedding. As expected, the day was hot and humid, but it didn't rain, and the wedding went off without drama. Maggie excelled herself with the food for the reception. The newlyweds spent the night in the recently refurbished hotel. Woodrow and Ellen collected them the next morning and saw them safely on board the boat to Brisbane. Woodrow's wedding gift to the couple was a week's holiday in an upmarket hotel in the capital.

Ellen spent the week following the wedding packing their last few belongings, and cleaning and tidying the apartment above the store to have it ready for the return of the young couple. On the Saturday morning a week later, Woodrow and Ellen met Marion and Reggie when they arrive back in town, and delivered them to the store. After a cup of tea, a chat, and a tearful goodbye, Woodrow and Ellen, accompanied by the last of their belongings, headed out to start the next phase of their lives at Rangelands.

While not prepared to admit to it, the transition was not easy for Ellen. The first couple of weeks were easiest as there was much to do. As well as arranging the house as she wanted it, a priority task was to list all the supplies to buy and store in case they became cut-off from town during the wet season. Then came a trip to town – to the store – to obtain and load the wagon with the supplies. There were a number of matters to attend to while in town and, as they expected, they required more than a day there. Ellen and Woodrow overnighted with Marion and Reggie.

On their next trip to town, they again spent the night at the store. Woodrow could see a pattern emerging, one he needed to end before it became too ingrained. Now that they had settled into Rangelands, their trips to town were uncomplicated: pick up supplies, visit the bank and maybe one or two other brief tasks. He decided to take charge of things the next time they went to town. Wet weather and flooded roads delayed their next trip to town for about three weeks.

They planned the trip the previous night: collect supplies for the house and collect a couple of things from the agency for the property, visit the bank and post office. While Ellen took care of those, Woodrow would spend time paying accounts at various businesses around town. No visit to town was complete without the mandatory visit to Maggie's tearoom for tea and a delicate ham sandwich or cream cake. Of course, Ellen needed to spend some time with Alfred discussing the running of the store and agency and with Marion who had taken over the books and accounts for the business.

As they drove into town, Woodrow contemplated their day's schedule. Yes, this was an ideal opportunity to establish future practice. He deposited Ellen and the wagon at the store and went off to pay accounts and meet up with Ellen later for lunch at the tearoom. On her way to the tearoom, Ellen called in at the bank and the post office, and then returned to the store after lunch. After completing his errands, Woodrow returned to the store. Alfred loaded the last of the supplies on the wagon when Woodrow arrived. He chatted to Alfred for a couple of minutes before wandering into the agency to pass the time of day with Reggie. Then it was time for the difficult task.

Woodrow checked his fob watch. It was almost three o'clock. He went in search of his wife, and found her sitting at the desk in the office. "What are you doing in here? It's not your office now. It's Alfred's and Marion's domain."

"I needed to look over the books and accounts."

"You have been here nearly all day, and I know you did that with Marion this morning. If you could take care of anything else you need to do, we will be leaving for Rangelands in about ten minutes."

"No; have you forgotten that we are to spend the night here."

"No we are not. Everything we had to do is done. There is no reason for us to stay in town tonight. We will be home before five o'clock, in plenty of time to unload before dark. You have no need to stay in town, and we would only intrude yet again in Marion and Reggie's life. I wish to hear no more argument. Please be ready to leave by three o'clock."

The atmosphere on the trip home to Rangelands was frosty, with no conversation during the entire journey. This is not the man I thought I married, Ellen told herself as she sat brooding and sullen against her side of the wagon. What has brought on this change… and is this how it will remain? When they arrived home, Ellen quickly climbed down from the wagon and flounced off inside before Woodrow could come around to help her down. He groaned. This was going to be a tense night.

By the time Woodrow and one of his workers unloaded the wagon and stowed the supplies, Ellen had the evening meal on the table. They ate in silence. As he poured himself a port after dinner, Woodrow calmly asked, "Will you join me in a glass of port and come with me to the sitting room so we can talk things over, or were you planning to sulk for the rest of the night?"

"Sulk…! I'm not sulking; I'm angry – very angry."

"Good… and now you are talking again. That's a step in the right direction. So, shall I pour you a port?"

He sat in silence as she unleashed her fiery tirade about his behaviour. Not wanting to interrupt her venting, he waited until she ran out of steam before, with great control, he spoke quietly to her. "Are you unhappy living out here on the property?" he asked. Ellen shook her head.

"No, I love it out here and it is so close to Koreelah, It is easy for me to visit Elizabeth – and William, of course."

"Look, Old Thing, you have to let go. Marion is a grown woman. She is married and she and Reggie have their own lives to live. I know you have to keep in touch with what is happening with your businesses. You should do that, but refrain from intruding in your adult children's lives while you are about it. That applies to William as well as Marion. Elizabeth is your closest friend and it is good you can visit each other often. However, if you insist on spending copious amounts of time with William while you are visiting Elizabeth, it might be construed as his mother checking up on the lad."

"Am I not allowed to overnight at the store in future?"

"That's not what I am saying. There will be occasions when we attend functions in the evening or when our business extends beyond a day, when we would overnight in town. If it suits Marion and Reggie, we would stay with them."

There remained some stiffness between them when they turned in for the night, but the morning saw peaceful cohabitation reinstated. Besides, Ellen was much too busy to worry about spending time in town for the next few weeks. She had to plan and organise a kitchen garden to provide them with fresh herbs and vegetables.

*****

As she sat writing in her journal one evening, Ellen's mind wandered far from the task in hand. Woodrow glanced up from his reading to find her staring off at nothing in particular. "What's on your mind? I am unaware of anything so taxing to record in your journal that would cause such a concerned look on your face."

"I was thinking about William."

"William…? What's he done to cause concern?"

"I hoped that by now he would be settled down with a wife and family. Jim and Elizabeth bought a small farm adjoining one of Koreelah's boundaries. They pulled down the old shack that was there and are building themselves a new home. I know they will be keen to leave Koreelah and move to their own property as soon as the house is finished. Jim assures me William is ready to take over running Koreelah, and that Jim had been stepping back to prepare William for the day when he is running it on his own."

"William's not that old yet. There's plenty of time still for him to meet the right woman."

"So much has happened since we've been living here. Marion now has a daughter and a son, and then the Great War played havoc with everyone's lives. It is easy to forget how much time has elapsed since we moved here. It's a shock to realise William soon will turn thirty… and still with no potential wife on the scene. He needs a son to hand Koreelah onto after him – and I need more grandchildren." Ellen had no need to worry. Fate was about to step in.

*****

Sent by her mother to live with her grandparents when she was sixteen, the intention was for Catherine Ashton to be 'finished' properly in England. From Catherine's point of view, mercifully the War intervened. It curtailed the usual annual rounds of 'coming-out' balls and parties at which young women of suitable age were presented to 'society'. At sixteen, Catherine was too young to rebel against her mother's plans but, by 1919, she was a young woman with a mind of her own. She always eschewed the debutante scene and, despite her grandparents' rigorous objection, spent the War years volunteering at a hospital caring for broken and wounded soldiers repatriated to England.

With the War over, Catherine booked her passage and, by Easter in 1919, was on her way home to Australia. Her father, overjoyed to have his only child back home, ran to meet her and hugged her fiercely as she disembarked from the boat. Unfortunately, her mother did not feel the same way. The failure of her attempt to have her daughter introduced into English society – and perhaps marry into one of the aristocratic families – came as a bitter disappointment. Her mother's dismissive welcome home left Catherine with no doubt about the impact that disappointment would have on her life at home.

The winter racing carnival provided Catherine an opportunity to re-establish something of a social life. She reconnected with a few old friends – most of them now married – and made new young – single – friends. Among the latter was one William Jennings who thought the tall, slim strawberry blonde young woman stunning. She was easy to talk to, and she found the well-spoken tall handsome young man worth investigating further. By the end of the carnival, it was obvious to their other young friends that William and Catherine had more than a friendship developing.

Over the next few months, various friends and acquaintances held a number of social get-togethers that provided opportunities for William and Catherine to be together in a chaperoned environment. By early spring, they each decided they had found their perfect partner. On a Friday night in late August, William asked Catherine's father to dine with him at the hotel before they went on to attend a Farmers' and Graziers' Association meeting. Mr Ashton was aware of the relationship between the young man from Koreelah and his daughter.

Conversation focused on generalities of interest to both men throughout the meal. Once dinner was over and their brandies arrived, William wasted no further time getting to the reason for their meeting. "Sir, I am sure you are aware your daughter, Catherine, and I have gotten to know one another well since her return from England. I wish to formally ask you for her hand in marriage."

"…And, if I withhold my permission for you to marry my daughter?"

"There is a very nice ring, that I think she would like, that won't find a home… just yet."

"Do I take that to mean that a wedding still might occur, even without my permission?"

"If Catherine remains so inclined, that's a possibility, I believe."

Ashton chuckled at William's obvious discomfort at the way the conversation was going. "Catherine is over twenty-one and doesn't need my permission. More importantly, she knows her own mind and is bloody-minded about making her own decisions about her own life. I think she could do a lot worse than you, young Jennings. If you are what she wants, I will not stand in the way of her happiness. Mind you, her mother probably will be less than enthusiastic. Don't be too perturbed about that. Catherine will do what Catherine wants to do – and I will support her."

"Thank you, Sir. I appreciate your honesty and your support."

"Now, Lad, if we are not to be late for that meeting, we had better get a move on."

William had no idea what was decided at the meeting or what even came up for discussion. His excitement and thoughts of Catherine blocked out all else. As they walked back to the hotel after the meeting, Ashton caught up with William. "Perhaps you might like to come to afternoon tea tomorrow. It would be a good opportunity for my good lady wife to look you over… and for that nice ring to find a proper home," he said, and added a knowing wink before going on to speak with another farmer.

Ashton's news of his invited afternoon tea guest did not get a good reception at home. Ashton received carefully worded criticism for the invitation, his wife not daring too strongly to voice her opinion. However, Catherine received no such consideration, and received venomous castigation for attracting the local riff-raff. To her credit, Catherine refrained from comment but, when her mother's tirade ended, she pushed herself away from the table and flounced off to her room.

Catherine felt her stomach tightening as afternoon teatime came round. It became a stilted affair with Mrs Ashton barely uttering a word throughout. Her only contribution was several condescending, highly audible sniffs at various times. In a bid to ease the situation for William, Catherine said, "Before you go, let me show you how we can see Koreelah from here – well, a little bit of it anyway."

She took him out onto the verandah and, pointing to a clump of trees in the distance, explained, "See those trees way over there, that's the stand of paperbark trees on the creek bank on Koreelah." William was surprised, but feigned greater interest than he felt.

"I spoke with your father last evening. He supported my request for permission for us to marry. Will you marry me?"

"I have already said yes once and there has been nothing to change my mind. Yes, of course I will marry you."

"Good, I am pleased about that," William admitted, and slipped the sapphire ring onto her left hand. After a quick check over their shoulders that no one was looking, a kiss sealed their engagement.

After returning inside to take his leave, William was on his way back to Koreelah. With William gone, Catherine joined her parents who remained at the table. Her father made a show of inspecting her left hand and admiring her ring. That only served to release another vitriolic tirade from her mother. Ashton noted his daughter about to unleash on her mother and tried to lighten the situation. He cut across Mrs Ashton's tale of disappointment before she thought she was finished. "How long does it take to organise a wedding?" he asked thoughtfully. "I need to know how much time I have to save up for this big event." He gave his daughter a knowing look, encouraging her to continue the conversation on that line.

"I've heard they recommend about six weeks as the minimum if it's to be a church wedding to allow for any delays in getting all the paperwork approved or whatever. However, a civil ceremony only requires a couple of weeks' notice... and you wouldn't have to save up for it at all. We would organise it – and finance it – ourselves. ... And you know how I hate fuss and ostentation." She ended with her steely gaze fixed firmly on her mother.

After Catherine left her parents still at the table, Mrs Ashton began her protestations again. Her husband silenced her. "My Dear, you really should try to know your daughter better. I have no doubt that, if you persist with your nonsense, Catherine will opt for a civil ceremony, be it in the courthouse, under a tree, at Koreelah, or at some other place of her choosing... and there is no requirement at all for her to have us present. I would strongly recommend you amend your behaviour, because I intend being present to see my daughter marry William Jennings – with or without you by my side."

The couple were married in a low-key church wedding – by Mrs Ashton's standards anyway – at the beginning of November. They spent a few days at a friend's beach cottage before settling into the homestead at Koreelah. Jim and Elizabeth held a farewell to Koreelah party the weekend before the wedding and then spent the few days after the wedding moving to their new home on their farm. William now had full control of what was to be his legacy, Koreelah.

Soon after their first wedding anniversary, the couple welcomed their first child, a son. Over the next eight years, Catherine bore William three daughters.

One evening as they sat watching the sun go down, Ellen shared her thoughts with Woodrow. "Everything has worked out so well. Although I didn't know what that was, I knew revenge wasn't enough, and I got more. I have been so lucky although, when I put it into words, I sound like a hard, scheming, conniving woman – and perhaps I have to accept that's what I am. My revenge on McCarthy was marrying him. Getting Koreelah when he died was a bonus. Revenge on my father for the loss of my children and the way he treated me was sweet. Contrary to his expectations, I inherited the store from my mother, and I can't express the pleasure I felt when I bought the agency after he went bankrupt. All that amounted to more than revenge. Then there was an additional bonus: I got two of my children back – and Reggie. My children are now settled. In keeping with tradition, the store will go down through the female line to Marion and then to her daughter. Koreelah will be William's and, after him, his son will own it. …And in amongst all of that, we were married and have this wonderful retired life out here."

"You forgot to mention that, although you lost your two little daughters, you found their unmarked graves and had them beautifully finished off. That also counts."

"The only shadow I see in all that has happened is that I have not managed to provide for Marion's son."

"Why would that concern you? You have other grandchildren that are not provided for in your will."

"It's different for a son. William's daughters – hopefully – will marry well and have the proper support of their husbands, but a boy, when he becomes a man, needs to be able to provide for his wife. I have not set Marion's son up to be able to do that."

"You shouldn't concern yourself too much. There's plenty of time to see where the boy's interests lie and do something appropriate for him when that becomes clear." Woodrow didn't feel it necessary to enlighten Ellen at that time. With no family of his own to consider, Woodrow already had dealt with the matter that concerned Ellen. On his death, Rangelands would go to Reggie with the intention that it would later pass to Reggie and Marion's son. He knew Ellen's comments about William's daughters were half-truths. Ellen's will contained provision for each of William's daughters to receive a hefty cash bequest.

Chapter 30

Shock engulfed the community. Many, overcome by the shock and horror of the news, wept openly in the street. It took only a couple of hours for the news to spread through the whole community. The local newspaper ensured anyone who somehow miraculously missed hearing about it on the day, could read about it in all its horrific detail the next day. Grimsby's Store and Agency remained closed for a couple of days.

Early on Monday 05 May 1930, on his way into town, the local mail contractor called at Rangelands. It was his practice to call at the property whenever passing as Woodrow often had fruit for him to take to the market. One of the first things Woodrow did on his retirement was to clear a further area of his property and start and orchard. Over the years, he added a small vineyard, and both proved profitable ventures.

After driving a short distance along Rangelands' rough track, something in the long grass off to one side of the track caught the contractor's attention. He detoured over towards it and soon spotted a bloody trail leading up to whatever lay in the grass. His immediate thought was that one of Woodrow's cattle was injured… or worse, that poachers had helped themselves to some prime beef. The horror of what he found sent him reeling. He turned around and, at full speed, headed for town and the Police Station.

The newspaper's report of the grisly discovery slightly embellished the grim reality: *News of the murder of Mr Frank Woodrow, aged 79, and his wife, Ellen Woodrow, aged 70, whose bodies were found yesterday morning concealed in long grass not far from their homestead on Mr Woodrow's Rangelands property has shocked the community.*

Although the paper reported the mutilation of Woodrow's head as his cause of death, this proved incorrect. The Police believed that the attack took place some time on Sunday night as, when attacked, Woodrow already was dressed for bed. It was likely some disturbance near the fruit packing shed, located a short distance from the house, brought Woodrow from the house to investigate. Woodrow probably became somewhat incapacitated from a blow to the head from a stick or pipe by his attacker, before the attacker shot him in the chest several times.

It appears that, hearing the commotion, Ellen ran to assist her husband, the attacker shot her too. Their attacker then dragged their bodies about twenty yards from the scene of the crime in an effort to conceal them in a patch of long grass that stood about three feet tall. Workers on the property, currently engaged in checking and repairing boundary fences, spent the weekend camped by a waterhole adjacent to the section of fence they would work on that week.

That the couple owned two of the most savage dogs in the district was common knowledge. The fact that someone could enter the property and commit the crime without the dogs attacking him baffled Police. When the Police first arrived on the property, they found one dog guarding the bodies. The ferocious dog held Police at bay, preventing them from approaching the bodies. With the animal so distressed and so savage, the Police found it necessary to shoot the dog.

Later, they found the second dog outside the fruit packing shed. That dog, chained up as usual on Sunday night, probably caused a fuss, alerting his master that something was amiss. At some point during the crime, the attacker shot that dog. Police assumed the attacker was not a stranger, but someone who had visited the property previously. That's why the intruder escaped attack by the dog roaming free on the night. A stranger would encounter a very different welcome.

While local Police continued with their investigation, including interviewing people on neighbouring properties, detectives from Brisbane came north to assist with the case. A dry creek bed running through the rear of the property probably provided easy access and allowed the attacker to approach the packing shed unseen. However, no evidence substantiated this assumption.

The coroner established that the blow to Woodrow's skull probably stunned him but was not the cause of death. Police sent the bullets retrieved to Brisbane for forensic examination. They confirmed the bullets as African made and high calibre as used for hunting large animals. Their analysis identified the weapon as old, of an unusual make, and possibly a revolver or rifle – possibly one used in the bush for years before the murder.

Armed with that information, Police searched firearms registration records kept in Brisbane, but with little success. The local Police moved through the district checking all firearms, again without success. They dragged creeks, and pumps brought in drained waterholes in the off chance that the attacker disposed on the weapon somewhere close by.

While the local newspaper and others across the state found plenty to fill column inches over the subsequent weeks, the investigation stalled. The only significant event that occurred was the double funeral held for the couple two days after their deaths. Side by side, their burial in the Watt family plot saw the couple's graves join those of Ellen's grandparents, mother, first husband William Jennings, and Richard, her infant son.

Tributes flooded in for the couple from friends, acquaintances, customers and various organisations such as the Farmers' and Graziers' Association and the Turf Club. No one, including the Police, found any reason or past incident that might have led to their deaths.

The case remained unsolved and the community grew increasingly worried that the murderer remained at large. Women whose husbands worked away from home for extended periods, nervous at being home alone with the attacker still free, locked themselves indoors or went to stay with friends. As Koreelah is not too distant from Rangelands, William sent Catherine and the children into town to stay with friends. Their departure gave him time to grieve alone, although he still spent much of his time assisting with searches of scrubland throughout the district.

Weeks dragged on into months. The Brisbane detectives returned south. On the local front, other cases gradually pushed the Woodrow murders to the bottom of the investigative pile. By July, with all possible avenues exhausted, the case remained open and its investigation left in abeyance. Months later, although family members still held the hope of some breakthrough that would bring the perpetrator to justice, slowly they came to accept the reality: the murderer had escaped justice.

A decade passed and, although the manager of Rangelands did an admirable job, Reggie knew the property had much more to offer. Since inheriting the property on Frank Woodrow's death, Reggie nurtured a desire to move to Rangelands and develop the property to its full potential. However, he knew the difficulties suggesting such a move might cause. Marion point-blank would refuse to consider it. He understood why. Hadn't he found it difficult the first few times he went to check on the place? ...But there were changes afoot.

In a few months' time, his and Marion's daughter would marry her longstanding and patient beau. They were talking marriage a decade ago, but the Woodrows' murders brought life to an abrupt halt. On leaving school, the intended groom worked in a hardware store selling tools and farm implements until about a year ago when he came to help Reggie run the farmers' agency. When they found themselves alone after dinner one night, Reggie decided it was time to broach the subject of Rangelands. "What are your thoughts about when our girl gets married shortly?" he asked Marion as a lead in to the main topic.

"I'm not sure I know what you're asking."

"Well, she and her young man are more than capable of running the store and the agency between them. Perhaps, it would be the right time to do what Frank Woodrow and your mother did for us: move out."

"Move out…?"

"It will be time for us to move on – time to move out and let them take over the business and this home."

"…And go where, pray tell?"

"To Rangelands, of course; it's time I took a hands-on approach to the place. There's so much that can be done out there – clear more land, improve the herd and maybe expand the orchard."

"I can't go out there. You can't possibly expect me to live there, not after what happened at that place."

"It was a long time ago and a lot has changed on the property. I agree, your first visit will be difficult, but you'll see, it quickly will become all right. I know how that happens."

"I will not live at the place where my mother was killed."

"Have it your own way, but where else you plan to live, you will be on your own. I am moving to Rangelands immediately after our daughter's wedding. If you care at all for your daughter and her future life, you will not expect to stay here inflicting yourself on the newly-wed couple." Marion did not take kindly to the final comment and flounced off to bed, leaving Reggie alone to reflect on the outcome of round one of the battle that lay ahead.

A few days later, when William was in town, after closing the store for the day, Reggie joined William at the hotel for a drink. Reggie recounted the discussion he had with Marion about moving to Rangelands. "I genuinely believe it the right thing to do, but I would appreciate your thoughts on the matter. I appreciate that sometimes it is hard to see beyond one's own point of view."

William pondered that matter in silence for a few moments before replying. "I appreciate Marion's reluctance to even visit the place, and I agree the first time would be the hardest. Everywhere she looks will be reminders of what happened there. It certainly would be unsettling to say the least."

"That's just the point, not much remains as it was then. A new packing shed now stands adjacent to the other sheds on the property and quite some distance from the old homestead. A new house is almost complete on that grassy knoll overlooking the stream that cuts across the eastern corner of the place. The new house necessitated a new track in from the road. A new entrance is now further along the fence line than previously and the track now takes a different route to the house. It doesn't go anywhere near the area where the bodies were found. So, you see, she would not have any visual reminders of the past unless she deliberately took herself off to the old homestead site."

"Y-e-s, I see that moving out there under those conditions could work. On thinking on the matter, my advice – and you might not like it – would be to put your foot down firmly, tell my sister she is moving to Rangelands, and that she should start sorting out what to take with her. Exercise your rights as her husband and head of the house, my friend … but be ready to duck, just in case she disputes those rights."

Life became difficult and the relationship strained between Reggie and Marion in the lead up to their daughter's wedding. It worsened immediately after the wedding when Reggie forcefully loaded Marion into the buggy and drove her in frosty silence to Rangelands.

She swung around and stared at him as they drove past the property's original entrance. Reggie pretended not to notice and continued in silence to and through the new entrance with the great sign above the gate announcing their arrival at Rangelands. With sidelong glances at his wife, Reggie watched her change. She now sat upright and alert, taking in everything around her as they made their way along the track. Recent rains had brought the place to life. Ancient poincianas and cassias in full bloom added bright splashes of colour to the lush green surrounds. Close to the new homestead, a jacaranda nearing the end of its flowering period stood amidst its self-made lavender carpet of spent blooms.

"What is this place?" Marion asked quietly.

"Welcome to your new home, My Dear. I would have liked your input to its design, nevertheless, I hope it doesn't disappoint too much."

Marion swept from room to room inspecting every inch of the building, and gradually working her way towards the French doors that led to the verandah. As Reggie held the doors open for her, he noticed a lightening of Marion's countenance... although she still refrained from any comment. Mother Nature was on Reggie's side that day. The gentle murmur of the creek below drifted up to the homestead and, as they stepped out onto the verandah, a chorus of birdsong erupted from a stand of tree a little further along the creek bank.

A couple of chairs rescued by the builders from the old homestead remained on the verandah. Placed there by the builders' for their lunchtime comfort, they now offered Marion a welcome invitation. She plonked herself down in one of the chairs. The light breeze coming up from the creek ruffled her hair as she surveyed the view. A gentle smile slowly lifted the corners of her mouth. "I'm not saying it will be easy living here, but the house and that view are beautiful. I think a vegetable garden over in that corner of the yard will get plenty of sun and be close to the kitchen, and a hedge of my favourite shrubs along that edge of the yard over there will brighten the place no end."

Reggie planted a kiss on the top of her head. The battle was over. They would relocate to Rangelands. There was much to do in the ensuing weeks. Apart from arranging a wedding, there also were the preparations for their move to manage. However, it all went smoothly and Reggie and Marion quickly settled in to their new lives. Although it took them both a while to adapt to not having to open the store and be busy all day every day, it took Marion a little longer. Reggie wasted no time in picking up the reins of running his property, but adjusting to the life of a fulltime housewife took Marion a while.

At first, the memory of what happened here all those years ago became an almost daily visitor. Whenever it arrived, she wrestled it away, fearful lest it linger and take control of her. However, within a couple of months, she found the memory of that dreadful past became a dark shadow hovering in the deep recesses at the back of her mind but no longer haunting her on a daily basis.

With time, even Marion accepted can go on happily in spite of change, and that Frank and Ellen Woodrow's murders would forever remain a perplexing unsolved mystery in the history of the district.

The End

ACKNOWLEDGMENTS

Producing a novel can be hard work, and not just for the writer. It is due to the efforts of a number of people that the release of this book is possible. I thank them all for their contribution. Irene for her continued support, encouragement and comments, and the beta readers and editors for their endurance. My undying gratitude to Tom Marshall for his skill once again in producing the cover design from the vague information I provided.

Lastly, thanks to my husband for his encouragement, patience and forbearance throughout the process.

ABOUT THE AUTHOR

KAYLA DANOLI spent her early years traipsing around Australia and then Europe with her parents, and then completed her tertiary education in England before returning to Australia. There were a variety of jobs in various parts of Queensland before eventually making her way towards the coast. She now lives in a small coastal town on the Queensland coast where she works part-time on a charter vessel.

In the early days after settling in that small town, to fill in her spare time, both when at home and while on cruises, she started scribbling down her ideas for stories. These days, she writes whenever time permits. Her Harbour Plaza series, previously released in 2015 as monthly eBook episodes, was updated and extended and released in 2016 as the Harbour Plaza: built on dreams compilation. Revenge is not Enough, also released in 2016, was her first full-length novel.

Discover more about Kayla and her work by visiting
www.kayladanoli.com
or contact her at
contact@kayladanoli.com .